PENGUIN BOOKS

The Truth About Ruby Valentine

Alison Bond has worked in the film industry for ten years. She started her career at ICM as an assistant to a maniacal boss with a superstar client list and was later an agent at the Casarotto Company representing writers and directors. Her first novel, *How to be Famous*, was published by Penguin in 2005. This is her second novel. Alison lives mostly in London.

The Truth
About Ruby Valentine

ALISON BOND

PENGUIN BOOKS

PENGUIN BOOKS

Published by the Penguin Group
Penguin Books Ltd, 80 Strand, London WC2R ORL, England
Penguin Group (USA) Inc., 375 Hudson Street, New York, New York 10014, USA
Penguin Group (Canada), 90 Eglinton Avenue East, Suite 700, Toronto, Ontario, Canada M4P 2Y3
(a division of Pearson Penguin Canada Inc.)
Penguin Ireland, 25 St Stephen's Green, Dublin 2, Ireland
(a division of Penguin Books Ltd)
Penguin Group (Australia), 250 Camberwell Road,
Camberwell, Victoria 3124, Australia (a division of Pearson Australia Group Pty Ltd)
Penguin Books India Pvt Ltd, 11 Community Centre,
Panchsheel Park, New Delhi – 110 017, India
Penguin Group (NZ), cnr Airborne and Rosedale Roads, Albany,
Auckland 1310, New Zealand (a division of Pearson New Zealand Ltd)
Penguin Books (South Africa) (Pty) Ltd, 24 Sturdee Avenue,
Rosebank, Johannesburg 2196, South Africa

Penguin Books Ltd, Registered Offices: 80 Strand, London WC2R ORL, England

www.penguin.com

First published 2006

1

Set in 12.5/14.75pt Monotype Garamond
by Palimpsest Book Production Limited, Polmont, Stirlingshire
Printed in England by Clays Ltd, St Ives plc

ISBN-13: 978-0-141-01779-1
ISBN-10: 0-141-01779-2

Acknowledgements

Thanks to Judith Murdoch whose insight and enthusiasm help me to be a better storyteller. Thank you to the good people of Penguin, especially Louise Moore, Mari Evans, Clare Pollock, Claire Bord and everyone who made this book look so damn sexy. I consider myself incredibly lucky to have been picked for your team. Rebecca Winfield and Camilla Ferrier, thanks for all your efforts. I'm not sure I would have made it to the last page without a few people – Manny, your suggestions and tea-making skills are invaluable to me; Mum and Dad, my biggest fans (despite the rude bits); Pat and Mike Cowan, who told me inspiring tales of the swinging sixties just when I needed them most. Thanks also to Sarah Valentine, it's all about you.

I

Whenever Kelly Coltrane wanted to feel good, deep down inside, she thought back to the moment when she'd first laid eyes on her boyfriend. Back when he was a stranger to her and full of infinite possibilities. Back before she spoke to him, before she started going out with him, and before reality kicked in.

Kelly and Jez met for the very first time on a deserted beach at sunrise. Kelly was perched on a ragged rock at the high-tideline watching the pale sky slowly take on the colours of the summer day that was to come. She saw him before he saw her. He had his head down like a beachcomber and she was able to study the curious spectacle of his erratic, long-limbed strides as he picked his way through rock pools in the ghostly half-light. He was concentrating hard and she found it endearing, catching her breath if he stumbled or slipped. He held out his hands for balance like a tightrope walker and when he wobbled she willed him not to fall with all the mental powers she possessed. She wondered what he was like.

By the time Jez looked up and saw her he was close enough for Kelly to admire the green flecks in his brown eyes. She was about to say something – hi, good morning, something – when he smiled at her and suddenly Kelly felt as if she didn't have to say a single word. There was a whole conversation in his smile. Hello, lovely morning, I'm a nice guy, is this seat taken?

He sat beside her and together they watched the golden globe chase away the pre-dawn cool. The grey sky gently bloomed into delicate pastel shades that in turn gave way to the blue. She kept expecting him to speak but as the shared minutes went by and he didn't, she got excited. It was romantic, and she was enjoying the mystery. She could feel the warmth of his body inches away from hers. It was as if they were cocooned in a magic spell, one that she didn't want to break with prosaic words.

Then he kissed her and she let him, because moments like that don't come around very often. A perfect first kiss, the early birdsong and the lulling waves the only sounds for miles around. She felt as though they were the last two people alive in the world. Two wandering souls finding each other at daybreak. It was by far the most romantic thing that had ever happened to her. It was as if he was her destiny. She felt like the star of her own private movie.

The truth was far more mundane. Kelly was only out so early because she'd drunk way too much the night before with the girls after work, crawled home and into bed before the ten o'clock news and woken at four in the morning feeling wide awake, bursting for a wee and slightly hungover. Once she'd navigated the bathroom she was even more alert, with an empty fridge and a desperate craving for a bacon cheeseburger. She knew she would not be able to get back to sleep unless she had one. So she'd driven down to the all-night garage and bought one of those microwaveable burgers, which had tasted sublime, and then she'd decided that a bracing walk down to the sea might clear her fusty head and alleviate the nausea in her belly.

Jez was only out unusually early because he'd been rudely awoken by the gruesome sound of someone having an enthusiastic shag in the room next door to his and had been so depressed by his flatmate's success with women compared to his own that he'd slammed out of the flat, hoping to piss off Darren, the flatmate, and hopefully interrupt his stride, so to speak.

These people were the real Kelly and Jez. The pair on the beach didn't yet know that about each other.

The kiss ended and when they pulled apart Jez said, 'I'm Jez.'

'Kelly,' she whispered.

That was almost a year ago. They'd been together ever since. They had some sweet moments, they had some good times, but Kelly had never been able to re-create that feeling on the beach when the world seemed enchanted and her life suddenly overflowed with promise. Sometimes, ridiculously, she resented the fact that they'd had their starry-eyed first encounter, because everything that followed that morning was bound to be a disappointment. Maybe if they'd just met in a club or something she wouldn't feel so heavily invested. It wasn't that he did anything wrong, it was just that when she looked at him her thoughts were not of passion and romance and happy ever after. Mostly when Kelly looked at Jez, she thought: is this it?

*

'Wake up!' said Kelly, kicking Jez in the shin as she hunted under the bed for her missing boot. She had to find it or she'd be going to work in her socks. Even though she spent most nights here with Jez (and Darren and whoever Darren was sleeping with that week), officially she still lived at home and so most of her clothes still lived at home as well. Lately she'd been wondering which would be more tragic, living with Jez and Darren in their eternal student squalor or living at home with her dad at the grand old age of twenty-five.

Under the bed Kelly's fingers dipped into something squishy and unpleasant. She flinched and then withdrew a plate of half-eaten super-noodles. Last week Jez had suggested that she move in officially and they should start splitting the rent. Was it any wonder that she couldn't bring herself to do it?

Beneath the covers he moved. 'Get up,' she said. 'You'll be late for work.'

'Notgoinin.'

'What?'

'I'm not going in,' he said. His dishevelled dark blonde hair appeared above the duvet, shortly followed by his smiling face. Jez still had his utterly disarming smile. She loved it. If only she could move in with a smile. If only she could love the rest of him.

'Since when?' she said.

'Since there was hardly enough work for one person, let alone two. Glynn told me to take the rest of the week off.'

'Paid?'

He looked at her as if she was stupid. 'Well, no, of course not paid. Don't worry, I'll manage.'

Jez worked at a vintage video store. He described it as a niche market. Kelly tried not to think of the money that she'd lent him when he hit zero at the end of last month. She should just kiss it goodbye. Or him. Or something. But not today. She was running late.

Her hand closed around the shiny leather of her elusive boot and she was momentarily elated. 'Got it!' And she still had thirty minutes to get in to work on time. It was practically possible.

'Make us a cup of tea?' said Jez, smiling. And she did.

While she was waiting for the pot to brew Kelly tried to work out what kept them together, but it quickly got depressing so she stopped. He was a nice guy. That should be enough.

Kelly couldn't stand it when people complained endlessly about their jobs. She was a put-up or shut-up kind of girl. As a result she rarely complained about hers, even though she hated it with a venomous passion and felt as though it was slowly and painfully draining away what remained of her soul. She had a recurrent fantasy of walking in and telling her overbearing supervisor, Chartreuse, exactly where she could shove her poxy job. Except the money was pretty good for this part of Wales and inspiring job opportunities for unskilled non-graduates with poor A-level results and a patchy CV were few in Newport.

Kelly worked for a financial management company, a fancy way of saying debt collectors, which was really just another way of saying bailiffs. Every day she fielded phone calls from people all over the country, up to their eyes in debt and up to their necks in sand. They were usually upset or very, very angry and either way they took it out on her. Kelly had been verbally abused, her life had been threatened and she had endured endless tears and tirades from people who got hopelessly carried away on charge cards and then acted put upon when they received a court summons, or worse – men turning up to take away the widescreen television.

Kelly was only three and a half minutes late but Chartreuse raised an eyebrow just the same. An exquisitely shaped eyebrow which Chartreuse had painstakingly plucked around a template supposedly based on the perfectly shaped brows of Elizabeth Hurley. Kelly knew this because Chartreuse had told her. At length.

Chartreuse tapped on the dial of her pink swatch and then went back to lazily flicking through the pages of a gossip magazine, all the while chatting down the phone on what was obviously a personal call.

'Sorry,' said Kelly, except she wasn't.

She plugged in her headset and answered the blinking call. Chartreuse could have answered it but there was a rumour that she hadn't answered an incoming call since 1998 and so, just to add to the fun, this caller would have been on hold listening to a synthetic version of 'Greensleeves'.

'Good morning,' she said. 'First Fiscal, this is Kelly, how can I help?'

'Finally! I need somebody to please tell me what the *hell* is going on,' said an angry, slightly posh voice. 'I miss one bloody payment. It's an outrage . . . daylight robbery . . . making good people feel like criminals . . .'

'I see. And do you have an account number?' Kelly

went through the motions of the call, keeping her voice low and under control, not reacting no matter what he threw at her, just as she'd been taught. 'Every caller is a learning experience,' Chartreuse was overly fond of saying. 'If you feel pressured, refer to the handbook.' The acceptable response to every possible query was written in an exhaustive handbook; Kelly hadn't looked at hers since her first week on the job. 'Remember, there's no such thing as the perfect call,' Chartreuse would say, and Kelly always felt like saying, 'Like you'd know?'

Chartreuse received an extra five grand a year to be their supervisor – correction, team leader – but she didn't actually seem to do anything special other than organizing the rota, which had been the same for as long as Kelly had worked the nine to four shift. Which felt like for ever. Maybe she should ask to switch to the two to nine, just for a change.

Kelly sighed. Was that the most exciting thing she could think of? Switching earlies for lates? Woo-hoo. Wild. But Kelly didn't expect too much out of life. A nice view or a filthy bacon cheeseburger was often enough to raise her spirits. There were, after all, plenty of people in the world who never got the chance to enjoy either. One day she wanted to have adventures, but she was only just getting the hang of being a responsible adult and there never seemed to be enough time in the day to make any serious decisions. So she stayed in a job she didn't much like, and with a boyfriend she wasn't sure about because, really, what was the alternative? Being unemployed and alone? One day maybe, but not today.

*

At twelve noon precisely Chartreuse left the office for a two-hour lunch. Sometimes three hours if she went to the cinema, which she often did. She'd come back into the office having just seen the new Tom Cruise or whatever, and have the gall to tell them about it, usually spoiling the ending in the process. Or she'd go shopping and put on a fashion display when she got back. Sometimes it was all Kelly could do to stop herself from admiring the woman's nerve. Chartreuse was incredibly thick-skinned, whereas Kelly spent far too much time worrying that she'd offended people or embarrassed herself, often for months or years after the fact.

As soon as the door closed behind their leader, the First Fiscal team relaxed palpably.

'Bags I get her magazine,' said Kelly, and dived into Chartreuse's desk drawer before anyone else had the chance. Around her people turned on their mobiles and started texting their mates or surfing the Internet, all the while answering the calls as they came in. If only Chartreuse weren't there, this job would be much more bearable.

Kelly got lost in the lush pages of the celebrity magazine. It was senseless really, she knew, her relentless interest in the lives of strangers, passing judgement on their relationships or outfits or the inside of their houses as if it really mattered in the larger scheme of things. She occasionally used the excuse that her father, Sean Coltrane, had been a celebrity photographer back in his day, though Sean's black and white art was a world away from the latest picture of Christina Aguilera papped without her makeup on. But more often she happily admitted the guilty pleasure she took from paddling in the shallow end. It was fun. Kelly had a healthy appetite for tales of the rich and fabulous and she didn't feel the need to hide it.

And judging by the brief tussle for the magazine when she'd finished it, neither did the rest of the girls.

'How's Jez?' said one of them.

'All right,' said Kelly. 'How's Dave?'

'Pissing me off as usual.'

Kelly didn't really like it when people complained about their boyfriends either but she laughed anyway.

A few desks away a girl was having an argument on the phone with her mother. You could tell it was her mother by the way she spoke to her, impatiently and with more than a touch of teenage histrionics. When the call was over the girl slammed down the phone, sighed deeply and said to anyone who might be listening, 'My mum is a total bitch to me.'

Kelly particularly didn't like it when people complained about their mothers. It was just her and Sean at home. There hadn't been a mother in the picture for as long as she could remember. People who complained about their mothers didn't know how lucky they were. At least they had someone to complain about. Kelly could have said as much, but she didn't. In her experience the tale of a runaway mummy encouraged the worst kind of pity and she didn't need anyone to feel sorry for her. On hearing such a story people invariably think of how it would feel to lose their own mother and how awful that would be, but it wasn't like that for Kelly, and people found it hard to understand. Kelly had no sense of loss because it was impossible for her to miss what she couldn't even remember.

Kelly was totally fine.

Okay, so her job and her boyfriend and her living situation were not what she might have hoped for when she was a little kid. Back then she had imagined a much more interesting life for herself, but wasn't it that way for everyone? As a child you dream of what you are going to be and nobody says, 'When I grow up I want to work in an office,' but thousands of people end up doing exactly that. As the years go by you forget what it was you wanted to be in the first place. She was happy enough. Growing up without a mum only felt as if she was being short-changed once in a while; most of the time she was content. And the gnawing sense of dissatisfaction with her lot was nothing to do with the fact that she thought about her absent mother every single day. Okay?

Just before three o'clock Chartreuse blew back into the office with an armful of Warehouse carrier bags – she must have driven all the way to Cardiff – and she was obviously very excited about something.

Kelly tuned her out. Probably some bloke had called her and for the rest of the afternoon it would all be: '. . . he said and then I said . . .' and Kelly would hate the poor guy even though she'd never met him. Then she noticed that the rest of the office were caught up in Chartreuse's excitement and someone was plugging in the old television in the corner of the room, moving the ailing spider-plant gathering dust on top of it, and trying to get a decent picture. Something was happening and bigger than their team leader's love life, because as much as Chartreuse might have wanted it to, her love life wouldn't make the news. That was the difference between them: Chartreuse read her magazines and felt maliciously jealous; Kelly read them and felt sickened and appalled, but in a good way, the way one might after gorging an entire family bar of Dairy Milk chocolate.

She picked up a blinking call and tried to keep half an ear on the gossip but it was impossible (the woman on the end of the phone swore blind she knew nothing about the debt on their joint credit card, why should she have to pay for a stinking husband's affair?) When the call finished, or rather, when the woman had hung up on Kelly after calling her a bitch, Kelly put her phone on 'Do not disturb' and went over to the television in the corner.

'What's happened?' she said. It must be huge for the television to be dragged into service. She hoped that it wasn't anything too awful.

'It's just so sad,' said Chartreuse.

'My dad was crazy about her,' said someone else.

'I can't believe she's really dead.'

'Who is?' said Kelly. 'Who's dead?'

'Ruby Valentine,' said Chartreuse. 'Yesterday. I heard it on the radio driving back.' Her voice dropped to a dramatic whisper. 'Suspected overdose.'

As she said this the news headlines began on the television and the sombre voice of a BBC newsreader confirmed that screen legend Ruby Valentine had been found dead in Los Angeles.

'Oh, I don't know if I'd say legend,' mused Chartreuse. 'Icon maybe.'

'What's the difference?' someone asked.

'Well,' said Chartreuse. 'I suppose an icon is more like David Bowie, but a legend is, say, Elton John.'

'Can we please listen to this?' said Kelly. 'She was neither. One's a symbol of something and one's a story that may or may not be true, okay?' She shook her head dismissively, earning a sour look from Chartreuse. 'She's an actress.'

'Was,' corrected Chartreuse. 'Sorry, didn't know we were in the presence of such a big *fan*.'

A windswept correspondent on a beach with a pink house behind him reported that although they were waiting for official confirmation there seemed little doubt that Ruby had committed suicide. Then the short news item was over and the weather forecast began.

'Is she Sofia Valentine's mother?' said one of the girls.

'Grandma,' said Chartreuse with authority. 'Can you believe it?'

Kelly wandered back to her desk trying to work out how she could get away with looking at the news on the Internet. Maybe if she angled her screen differently or waited until her team leader went out for one of her marathon fag breaks. She wasn't a huge fan as such but it was an intriguing story, a deliciously macabre piece of gossip. Ruby wasn't exactly Kurt Cobain or Marilyn, she was older than that and her fruitful career had been on the wane, but she was a fallen star nonetheless. Her grand-daughter Sofia Valentine was one of those pointlessly famous people who seemed to get paid an awful lot for not doing very much at all and was always in the tabloids.

Kelly's mobile rang and Chartreuse's head whipped

round, looking for the source of the jaunty ringtone. 'No personal calls!' she snapped.

'It's my dad,' said Kelly. 'It might be important.'

'Keep it short.'

Kelly turned her back before she could see Chartreuse tapping her swatch. Who wore a swatch in this day and age? Did she think it was retro? Was it?

'Dad,' said Kelly, 'what's up?'

'You have to come home,' he said.

'What's wrong? Are you okay?'

'Nothing's wrong but you have to come home.'

She didn't believe him. She could tell by the tone of his voice that something had happened. She tried to ignore her instinctive sense that it was something bad. She promised to be there in a little while and told Chartreuse she had to leave early as there was a family emergency.

'That's impossible.'

'What's the big deal?' said Kelly. 'The late shift will be here in a minute.'

'I wish I could but . . .'

'But what? It's my dad, and he needs me. I'm going. I'll stay on tomorrow and make up the time.'

'Kelly! I said no.'

Kelly was already half-way across the office. 'I'm sorry,' she said, 'but I'm going. I have to.' She was thinking that if Chartreuse gave her one more reason to quit then she would, right here and now. In fact, half of her was begging for an excuse to do it. Unemployment would motivate her to seek out a more interesting life than this. If she was lucky maybe she'd get fired.

She turned and stared defiantly at her team leader, who she noticed was openly reading the entertainment headlines on the Anonova website. Kelly's pale blue eyes were cold and challenging. I dare you.

Chartreuse looked at Kelly in surprise as if she had suddenly seen a new side of her, a side that wouldn't take no for an answer. Not the subservient underling she took for granted. She didn't know how to deal with this rebellious streak.

Kelly held her gaze. She felt strong because she didn't care.

'You look a bit like her, you know,' Chartreuse said eventually.

'Like who?'

'Ruby Valentine.'

That was unexpected. 'Um, thanks. So I'll see you tomorrow.'

Chartreuse backed down and Kelly's thoughts of adventure subsided, which was a relief. She had no idea what she'd do if she lost her job.

'Fine,' said Chartreuse. 'But don't forget what a nice person I am.'

She'd try to remember.

2

It was just starting to get dark by the time Kelly pulled her battered yellow Corsa into the potholed side road which led to her childhood home. The main reason she was still living here was simple. It was a beautiful house. The artist in her father had chosen his backdrop well. It would be hard to imagine a view more perfect than the one which rolled out to greet her as her engine tackled the steep incline of the driveway. Even through the drizzle she could still see the last of the muted winter sunlight somewhere west of here, dropping away into the distant sea beyond the hills. On a summer's day it was magnificent.

She loved growing up here, just the two of them, Kelly and Sean, as tight as the twin shells of a Pembrokeshire clam.

Up close, the ancient farmhouse revealed its flaws like the wrinkles of an ageing screenstar. Bricks were held together with moss and a prayer, the mortar having long since crumbled, victim of the damp Welsh air. Both the attic windows were riddled with cracks, and black holes in the regular pattern of the roof tiles revealed the vulnerable spots like missing teeth in a smile. Kelly knew that indoors there would be the steady rhythm of drips into a bucket or a saucepan. She had long ago stopped nagging Sean to get the house fixed up; it simply wasn't a priority for him and at times she thought that he enjoyed the shabbiness, that it reflected something of himself. She could relate to that.

Besides, now she was all grown up she supposed that bringing their house up to date was her responsibility too and she had neither the means nor the drive to begin. Once that particular realization had hit home, Kelly suddenly found the ailing heating system charming rather than annoying, and thought it was quaint that you could race pennies down the gentle slope of the kitchen floor.

She pushed open the heavy wooden door, which scraped on the stone flooring where the wood had warped and swollen. 'Dad?'

The smell of developing fluid and damp roll-ups tickled her nostrils. The familiar smells of home. There were no buckets, just a puddle collecting behind the back step, following the pitch of the floor. Kelly grabbed a dishtowel from the crowded sink and jammed it into the puddle with her heel. It was instantly sodden.

'Dad?' She looked for a clean saucepan, but there were only two and they were both dirty. She turned on a tap and the pipes rattled like a chesty cough. The house groaned.

'Kelly?'

'It's me!' She wiped the saucepan hastily and placed it under the drip before turning off the tap and running towards the sound of his voice.

Sean was in the most chaotic room in the house. Tucked away at the back, unchanged in two centuries, it had a flagstone floor and no natural light. The room had variously been Sean's darkroom, Kelly's den and a junk room. Now it was reclaimed as an office but Kelly suspected it was still a junk room at heart.

Sean was hunched over his desk, an anglepoise lamp casting a single halo of light in front of him. He was too old for freckles but there they were, scattered over his nose and cheeks, across the pleats of his laughter lines all the way up to his thatch of grey hair. Shy freckles because it was winter, but marks of boyish charm that would never fade away completely.

When he looked up she thought his eyes looked strange. Was it possible he'd been crying?

'Hello, love,' he said. 'Nice day?'

'What's happened?' she said.

A number of scenarios had presented themselves to her on the drive home. They had run out of money and needed to sell the house. He was sick. He had found her diaries from when she was seventeen years old and discovered that she had not, as she'd always insisted was the case, saved herself for marriage. Or maybe, just maybe, it was good news. He'd won the lottery on his first try. One of his old photos was being used in a major advertising campaign. Some of his new photographs were going to be exhibited. He had a girlfriend.

From his expression she could not tell. It was not an expression she'd ever seen before. She walked towards him and as she got closer she could see that he'd been staring at some old photographs. Photographs of Ruby Valentine.

She picked one up. 'This is gorgeous,' she said. And it was. A black and white studio shot of a much younger Ruby, her eyes reaching beyond the camera, maybe to someone out of shot who was responsible for the laughter in her face.

Sean pushed away from the desk to allow Kelly to look at the photographs properly. There were dozens, all of Ruby. Some of them were candid shots taken at parties, some of them were posed, still more featured her on set between scenes. There were photos of Ruby on her own, in company, playing with her children. Intimate shots that captured her over the years. And one of Sean with his arms around her, receiving a kiss on the end of his nose.

'Oh, Dad,' she said, pulling up a chair of her own. 'You knew her? These are incredible. It's awful what happened.'

Kelly had always been aware that her father had had many famous friends in his heyday. To be photographed by Sean Coltrane in the Sixties and Seventies really meant something. She knew this the way other girls know their fathers are doctors or drive trucks for a living, with respectful interest which occasionally drifted into boredom. After all, she could never recognize half the people in his shots. There were only a few survivors, like Ruby, who were still stars. Sean mainly photographed landscapes these days and it was hard to get excited about sand dunes on a greetings card. Landscapes were less rock and roll but he insisted he liked it that way. 'Once upon a time,' he said, 'you were able to catch fame off guard, take a photograph of the person and not the image. Now the image is all they're willing to give. Everyone is "on" if there's a camera nearby.' Sean still occasionally took portraits, as a favour, or for charity. Once, thrillingly, so Kelly had thought at ten years old, for a stamp.

Kelly picked out a stack of photographs to study, her interest grabbed by a more pensive Ruby, heavily pregnant and deep in thought. 'Were you very close?' she said.

Sean raised his eyes to hers and this time there was no mistaking it. Tears threatened to fall. 'I was in love with her,' he replied.

Blimey. 'Did you . . . I mean . . .' How could she ask her dad this question? Did she really want to know? The thought of him having sex was bad enough but the thought of him having sex with one of the sexiest women in the world . . . She wasn't sure if she could handle the mental image that presented. Ugh, too late, so she asked away. 'Did you sleep with her?'

'We were friends for a long time,' he said. 'Then we had an affair.' He took the top photograph out of her hand and traced the curve of Ruby's swollen belly. 'Then we had a baby girl.'

'Huh?' Her train of thought stopped dead and then backed up. What the hell? *A baby?*

'I should have told you,' he said. 'I should have told you years ago.'

'Told me . . . what?' said Kelly, her train of thought thoroughly derailed. 'I have a sister somewhere?'

Ruby's eyes were starting to look hauntingly like her own. Half of her knew the truth before he said it.

'We had you.'

'Me?'

'Kelly, Ruby's your mother. Was your mother.'

The rest of the photographs dropped from Kelly's hand on to the cold stone floor. She fled.

*

When Kelly was at that difficult age, somewhere between eleven and fourteen when thoughts and emotions collide for the first time, creating one big adolescent mess, she used to lock herself away in her room when she was upset and scare her father half to death. She would stay there for a long while, as long as two days, not eating, not answering Sean's anxious knocks on the door. Sometimes Kelly found it hard to believe what a little drama queen she'd been growing up. She would sit on the floor, her back against the closed door, and stare at the wall opposite, wondering if she'd ever feel normal, thinking of who she liked and who she didn't like and what she would say at school the following day and who she would sit with at lunch. The ironic thing was that all the bullies and boyfriends and best friends she had stayed up there worrying about had had no more lasting effect on her life than her passion for shiny boy bands at that time. But the teenage angst was just a cover. She would turn the events of the school day over in her mind and then, when she had calmed down, she would secretly think about her mum.

Just thinking about her mother always made Kelly feel guilty. She felt as if she was being disloyal to Sean. She loved her father intensely and was worried that being curious about the woman who had given birth to her would somehow make him think she loved him less, or that she wasn't satisfied in some way by her childhood. And she was. She had a fleeting memory of asking him why she didn't have a mummy when she was very small, far too young to worry about being insensitive, but could never recall his exact words, no matter how hard she strained for them, only, 'I love you.'

From time to time in later years questions would rise in her throat and she would go to him, determined that this time she wouldn't chicken out, she would just ask him some stuff and it would be fine, absolutely fine. She wanted to know what her mother had been like, that was all, she wanted to know where she came from. Then all the questions would dry up in her throat when she saw her dad, and how his face lit up in eager, loving anticipation of what his treasured daughter had to say. So she let it slide and slide, until it felt far too late to ask, and the gap in their lives where a wife and mother should be was never mentioned.

Kelly only allowed herself to think, Who was she? Where did she go? Will she ever come back? Am I like her?, when she was locked in her room. When Sean was safely under the impression that she was in a bad mood and all she was thinking about was your average teenage trauma.

Kelly thought she had grown out of it but she felt the urge now, as strong as a drug addict needing a fix, to run up the stairs and shut the door.

'Kelly, wait!'

She ignored her dad's shout and only started breathing again when the door was closed and she was sitting on the floor with her back to it.

This was insane. Exciting? No, just insane. She was the long-lost lovechild of a living legend. Not exactly, she corrected herself, not exactly living. Was she supposed to feel sad? Of all the emotions racing through her frazzled head, grief was not the most forceful.

Disbelief? Sure. Shock? You betcha. Anger? Some.

After all this time she'd convinced herself that the truth must be too awful, Sean loved her and so he must be protecting her from something for her own good. But the truth was that her mother was a superstar. Another thought pushed for space in the chaos. God, she must have been *loaded*! All those things that Sean had said they couldn't afford, the horse she'd wanted when she was twelve (okay, so he'd been right, the whole pony thing was a bit of a phase), the holiday to Ibiza that he refused to pay for when she was sixteen (but then, everybody else's parents had vetoed that grand plan too), the second-hand Corsa he'd picked out for her twenty-first birthday instead of the classic MG of her dreams. Ruby Valentine would have had enough money to buy Kelly whatever she wanted, but what Kelly wanted most – a mother – had clearly cost far too much.

Was it really true? She couldn't think of any possible reason why her dad would lie to her. Especially about something like this.

She reached across the cluttered bedroom floor for a cheap compact mirror in her eyeline, a free gift when she'd bought two or more items (one to be skincare). She wiped away a thin layer of dust that had gathered on the glass and studied her reflection. Too many freckles (thanks, Dad), unruly eyebrows, the beginnings of a spot on her chin, a smudge of grey on her forehead that she hadn't even known about. She licked her palm and wiped away the grey smudge. She studied her thick black hair that looked dyed but wasn't, and her pale, wolfish eyes that everybody said were her best feature. These features had come from Ruby Valentine. Kelly realized with a start that she hadn't fully believed it until now, until she saw the eyes of a ghost in the mirror.

'Kelly? Sweetheart?'

Her dad outside her door. It was like being thirteen again. She felt as ill equipped now to deal with unsettling emotions as she had been then. She didn't trust herself to speak.

'I'm sorry,' he said. 'I promised her I'd never tell you.'

What? And now that she was dead it was okay to break that promise? What possible good did it do Kelly to know this now, when it was too late? What on earth was she supposed to do with this revelation? Sell it to the tabloids? And say what? I never knew her, she never knew me, but check me out anyway? It didn't even matter that her mother was famous. She was gone, and for now that was all Kelly could see.

'Leave me alone.' She walked over to her clapped-out stereo and pushed play on the CD, not caring about the song and turning up the volume to drown Sean's repeated pleas for her to come out.

And she sat with her back to the door and tried not to cry.

For as long as she could remember she had thought there was a chance she had a mother out in the world somewhere, but now she knew there was no chance at all. A fantasy she'd had for years – that her mother would turn up and they would become close – disintegrated. And she felt that with it went any hope of ever finding out why she felt so lonely sometimes.

*

Kelly wasn't sure how long she had been sitting there, but the CD had finished long ago and despite her inner turmoil, and the need to process this new information, she was starting to feel a bit peckish. It was slightly annoying to discover that in the middle of an out-and-out drama ordinary things such as hunger could still matter. Idly she wondered if she could sneak down to the kitchen and fix a ham sandwich without running into her dad. She didn't want to see him, not yet. She wouldn't know what to say. Just as she was thinking that she might have pickle on her sandwich there was a gentle knock at her door. She tensed.

'Uh, Kelly? Are you in there?'

Jez. She opened the door.

'What's up?' he said. 'I've been calling your mobile. I thought you were waiting for me after work. You know, so we could go to that place and get that thing?'

She vaguely remembered something about Jez needing a lift into the next town but trying to recall the details was like wading through fog.

She had to talk to someone, it was the only way this would seem real. 'Something's happened,' she said.

'What?' he said. His hands flew to his mouth. 'Oh no, I know what it is. You used the cash card and the machine swallowed it? That's okay, babe. Glynn says there's work coming up next week for sure.'

'No,' she said. 'That's not it.'

She felt hot tears spike the back of her eyelids, and even though she kept them in check Jez must have noticed a change in her expression. He sat down on the bed beside her and laced his fingers through her own and she looked down at their joined hands. They matched.

'There's something I need to tell you.'

She paused to allow him the chance to make an inappropriate joke – if he was going to make jokes then she'd rather give him a chance to do so early on – but he didn't. He just tightened his grip on her hand a tiny bit, tipped his head to one side and bit his bottom lip the way he always did when he was trying to concentrate.

'It's no big deal,' she said, stalling. She didn't know what to tell him first or how – that Ruby Valentine had died or that Ruby Valentine was her mother or that her mother had died? – and in that moment of confusion she lost the will to tell him at all. She pulled her hand away. Forget it. She would carry on with her life as if she'd never known. If she didn't want to confront this then she didn't have to.

'Kel,' he said. 'Tell me. Whatever it is, it doesn't matter.'

'That's classic. Right away you assume it's something bad.'

'If it's good, then why are you so scared of telling me? So scared that you'd rather pick a fight?'

She hated it when Jez was right.

'My mother, she died. Just.'

There, she'd said it. It might be the first time ever that she'd referred to Ruby as her mother but she'd said it. Jez looked concerned and started to embrace her. 'Please don't,' she said, shoving him gently away and crossing her arms across her chest. 'It's no big deal. She left right after I was born. We never met.'

'You never met?'

'Well, maybe we did when I was a baby, we must have I suppose, but I don't remember her.'

'Why did you never tell me that?'

'You never asked.'

'I did once but you got a bit funny about it.'

'I did?'

'It was at that wedding in Manchester, remember? You were a bit tipsy. Don't worry about it.'

'Why should I worry? Funny how? What did I say?'

'You said you hated her more than anyone else in the world including Hitler and then you asked me to get you another sausage roll.'

Kelly remembered that wedding. If she really thought hard about it she could even remember the conversation through the red wine fug. She'd only been trying to be flippant, she hadn't meant it. She just hadn't much fancied having that particular heart-to-heart while competing with the Stevie Wonder from the mobile disco.

'I never knew her.'

'Still, your mum, I'm sorry. That's rough.'

'There's more.'

Jez waited.

Again Kelly hesitated. This was the bit she didn't quite think she could say out loud because it sounded ludicrous. 'She was famous, an actress.'

'Would I have heard of her?'

'Probably.'

Fair play to Jez. She could tell he was struggling to conceal his intrigue. His eyebrow rose almost impercep-tibly but he held his tongue, letting her tell him in her own sweet time. That was one nice thing about Jez, she never felt hassled or judged. He was too relaxed for that and not easily fazed. A bit more reaction would be welcome from time to time.

'Ruby Valentine,' she said. Let's see how unfazed he was by that.

'No way! Ruby Valentine's dead?'

'She died yesterday.'

'Shit.' *See the penny? Watch it drop.* 'Shit!' *There it goes.* 'She's your mother?'

Kelly shrugged. 'Apparently, yes. She was.'

'Apparently?'

'So my dad says.'

'Well, he should know.'

'For some reason he seems to think that now she's dead I might want to be aware of this. Doesn't that seem a bit twisted to you?'

'You didn't know until now?' Jez's voice was becoming more high-pitched with every question and by now he sounded like a nine-year-old girl. He coughed and repeated himself in a more manly way. 'You didn't know?' He was struggling to digest this bit of information. A classic movie buff since his early teens, he had always had a bit of a thing for Ruby. And all this time he'd been unknowingly giving it to her daughter. That thought made him undeniably horny.

He stared at Kelly intently and she had a good idea why. He was looking for the family resemblance. Was this the way it was going to be from now on, would anyone who learned the truth inspect her as if wondering how Ruby Valentine's genes could have produced such an

27

unpretty picture? Kelly thought she scrubbed up okay if she put in the time but she rarely did.

Jez touched her face. 'Wow. You look just like her.'

'Don't lie. I mean, maybe I do a bit, but not really.'

'No, you do. It's incredible.'

Kelly covered her face with her hands. 'Stop it,' she said. 'You're freaking me out.'

'I just can't believe it. If you didn't have the same eyes I'd swear you were winding me up. And she died? How? What happened?'

'She killed herself.'

'*Nooooo!*'

'Allegedly. Pathetic, huh?'

There was an odd little catch in her throat. It made Jez want to comfort her and he tried to put his arms around her again.

'Don't,' she said. 'I'm fine.' She wished that Jez would leave. Talking to him was only confusing her further. Surely, she thought, if you knew me, if you saw me, if you really got me, then you would know exactly what to say to make me feel better. For the second time that day she tried to work out what kept them together.

'So,' he said after what would be regarded by some people as an awkward pause, but Jez never noticed when Kelly was sulking, 'do you think she left you any money?'

She snapped. 'For God's sake, Jez. Why do you care?'

'I was just making conversation.'

'My mother *died* and the first thing you have to say on the subject is did she leave me any money?'

'Wait a sec, Kelly, the first thing I had to say was that I was sorry and that it must be rough, and I tried to give

28

you a hug but you pushed me away and said it was no big deal.'

'Well, it is a big deal, okay? Sometimes, when I say something's all right, it's not. Sometimes I'm just putting on a brave face.'

'Well then, we need to have a signal for when it's one of those times.'

'We shouldn't need to have a signal,' she said. 'You should just *know*.'

They faced each across the narrow bed and Kelly knew this was her opportunity to say so much more, but couldn't organize her tangled thoughts. Meanwhile, Jez was afraid to utter a single word. It was bound to be wrong, whatever it was. This didn't stop his mind racing as he tried to think of what he could say to comfort her, wishing for divine inspiration to put the exact right words on his tongue.

In the end Kelly broke the silence. She had never been able to communicate how she felt to Jez, so what had made her think that they could start now? With this? They should start on something smaller, like dinner plans or what to do on a Saturday night. 'You should leave,' she said. 'I think I need to talk to my dad.'

'Don't do this, Kelly.'

'Do what?'

'Push me away. I want to help you.'

She didn't like Jez to see her like this, vulnerable and unsure. She could hardly bear to look at herself in the mirror when she felt this way, let alone admit to it. And this was a very big deal, not a bad day at work or an argument with a friend. She had just found out the answer to her life's most burning question but it had left a hollow feeling inside and she didn't know how to make it go away. 'This is my thing to deal with,' she said, 'not yours. I'll be fine. Just let me deal with it.'

'I don't think it's supposed to work like that.'

'What's not?'

'You know . . . um. Love.'

'Oh, shut up, Jez, let's not pretend we're in love.'

'Who's pretending?' He grabbed her wrist and put his own next to it. They had matching woven leather bracelets that they'd bought from the market in Penarth. She could remember buying them, she would always remember because it had seemed so utterly simple to be Kelly and Jez that day. She had never felt so chilled out in her life. It was midsummer and they'd taken a massive picnic to a spot overlooking the harbour and had followed the lazy arch of the sun for hours, sharing stories and kisses, with nothing to do but enjoy each other's company. Sitting there, she had thought that maybe she could love him, maybe he was the one.

They'd bought their bracelets just before sunset and solemnly tied the strands of battered brown leather on to each other's wrists. They hadn't tried to express in words what this meant, this small ceremony in the bustling street, but it had meant something to them both. They made a connection that day, the sort of connection that had been lacking these last few months. The romance was dead and gone.

'If we're not in love,' he said, 'then what's going on with us?'

His words reached her slowly, as if she was underwater.

She struggled to fit what he was saying into the whirl-wind that was currently her headspace. 'Not tonight, Jez. Let's not do this tonight. Please.'

She could tell from the look on his face that she was hurting him. She didn't like herself much for doing so, but she couldn't find it in her heart to make him feel better. There was too much going on in there to make room for his bruised ego. Why did everything have to be about him? Couldn't he see that she had more impor-tant things on her mind?

'I'll go,' he said. 'But I do love you, Kel. I thought you knew that.'

'Thank you,' she said, but she couldn't say it back. Lying would only make things worse. Deep down she knew that he was only trying to help, like a good boyfriend should, but every word out of his mouth grated on her tonight like nails screeching down a blackboard. It was better that he left.

Kelly kissed Jez goodbye, feeling like a bitch.

Downstairs Sean's office was empty but the back door was unlocked and his boots and coat were gone from beside it. Kelly grabbed her own coat and started out into the night. She had a good idea of where he'd be.

It had stopped raining and the wind had picked up, driving the clouds out to sea and revealing patches of the starred night between them. It was very dark but she found her way across the rough ground by memory; she could have made it blindfolded as she had walked this way almost every day since the first time she was able to totter about on two legs. Probably before that she'd crawled up here or been pushed. There was a garden bench set at the top of a gentle hill and as soon as she was close enough she could see a burning red dot which was the tip of Sean's cigarette and she knew she'd guessed right.

She paused to try to think what she would say to him. She finally had a chance to ask all those follow-up questions and she didn't know where to start. Perhaps she should have made a list.

Was she being over-dramatic? She knew that her life didn't have to change one iota in light of this bombshell. What bothered her was how much she wanted it to. She had a steady boyfriend, a steady job, the sort of things that would make most people happy. But Kelly was starting to suspect that maybe she hadn't been happy for quite some time. Perhaps that made her ungrateful. Or perhaps that meant that something had to change. She wasn't the biggest fan of change, which was probably why she still lived in this house, in this town, in this mindset.

Her feet scuffed at a stone which rattled down the pitted path. Sean turned and she could just about make out his features. He wasn't crying, she was pleased to note. He wasn't smiling either. If anything, he looked terrified.

She felt a great wave of pity wash away her residual anger. He was probably sitting up here in his favourite spot worried that she would never forgive him. Of course she would. She had never met anyone in life that she trusted fully except for him and if he had made the decision not to tell her this, then he must have had his reasons. She wasn't saying that she was ready to absolve him completely, not right this second obviously – she was more stubborn than that – but eventually she probably would, she had to face it.

Sure enough, his first words were an apology. 'I'm so sorry, sweetheart,' he said. 'I suppose you have every right to hate me.'

She sat down next to him and took the cigarette out of his hand. She put it to her mouth because she wanted to, although she hadn't smoked since she was about nineteen and even then she'd never really started, not properly. She inhaled the prickly smoke, waiting for him to admonish her, but he didn't. The absence of fatherly concern was unsettling and she passed the cigarette back to him.

'I don't hate you,' she said.

'She never wanted you to know.'

'Why not? Was she . . . ashamed of me?' That was one of the questions she'd never asked, one of the big ones.

'Of course not,' he said. 'She loved you.'

'Then why?' The biggest question of them all.

'It wasn't easy,' he said. 'I've been here thinking about what happened. The agonies she put herself through to make that choice. She wanted to stay.'

'But she didn't.'

'No.'

He passed his cigarette back to her. She was oddly pleased. Apparently she'd started smoking. Oh well, if ever there was a good excuse. The shock was wearing off but opening this box of secrets was kind of scary.

'Why now?' she said. 'Why are you telling me today? I mean, I know she died and everything, but why wait all this time and then tell me when it's too late to do anything about it?'

33

Sean ground out his cigarette with his heel, then tucked the stub into an old tobacco tin. He didn't like litter.

'Yesterday,' he said, 'I got this.' He passed her a folded piece of paper, a note. Kelly read it.

Dear Sean
She's my daughter and I will remember her,
*   Love always, Ruby V x*

It was handwritten; flowing penmanship with wide loops that Kelly immediately wanted to send away for handwriting analysis. She knew there were places that did that, she'd seen them advertised in the back pages of some magazine – which one? She couldn't remember – but she'd be able to see what they could tell her about her mother. She was so engrossed in the lettering that she almost failed to take in the words. She was having trouble concentrating. That couldn't be right, surely? This was probably one of the most important conversations she would ever have in her life. It was a picturesque evening and revelations were flying about like the evil contents of Pandora's box. This should be a momentous and memorable occasion but the truth was that she was feeling a bit cold, absent-mindedly wondering if Sean was likely to roll another cigarette, and still trying to remember the name of that bloody magazine.

'It came by FedEx,' said Sean. 'Just that one little note floating around in a thick cardboard envelope. I hadn't heard from Ruby in a long while. I didn't know what it meant.'

Kelly regained her focus and read the note again. She didn't know what it meant either.

'I was thinking all last night,' he said, 'and then today, with the news and everything, I understood. If only I'd worked it out sooner maybe I could have stopped her, called someone, maybe she'd still be alive.'

'You think this is a suicide note?'

He nodded. 'Partly.'

'What else?'

'She's left you something in her will.'

'How do you know that?'

'I just do. I knew her, don't forget. It was something she said, years ago.'

'Are you sure?'

'Completely. So, you see, you would have found out the truth anyway. Better that I tell you than some bloody lawyer should phone you up out of the blue.'

'So what are you saying? There's a good chance you might never have told me?'

He didn't answer. His eyes darted away from hers, and that was enough for Kelly to know that she'd nailed it.

Her throat tightened. 'Never?'

'It was a secret.'

'No,' she said. Blood rushed to her head and anger made an unsolicited return to the front of her mind. 'Stop saying that, calling it a secret. *It* wasn't a secret. *It* was a person. It was me. Didn't either of you think I had a right to know who I am?' She hated to think of other people, even her parents, having such control over her life, making decisions that would affect her for years to come. It made her feel manipulated and powerless.

'You know who you are, Kelly,' said Sean. 'You're my girl. You're clever and confident, you're happy.'

Three words she would never have used to describe herself. What did he know? He was her dad, he was genetically programmed to love and protect her and think good things about her. The gene which evidently went astray in her poor dead superstar mother.

'If that's what you think of me,' she said, 'then you clearly don't know who I am, any more than I do.'

'So go and find out,' he said.

'What?'

'Go to Los Angeles. Find out who she was if you think that'll help.'

'It's too late!' said Kelly. Self-pity was giving anger a run for its money and jostling for position. 'Nothing will help.'

'At least go to her funeral,' said Sean. 'I think she would have liked that.'

Any minute now she would scream. He was being unreasonable. 'If Ruby Valentine ever wanted me to go over and see her then maybe she should have invited me.'

He passed her the note. 'I think she just did.'

'Ha-fucking-ha,' said Kelly. 'Preferably before she went and killed herself.'

Sean winced as though he'd been slapped.

'I'm sorry,' said Kelly, even though a second ago she'd have said she had nothing to be sorry for. She was the victim here, right? The unwelcome result of a fling, the secret. Except she hadn't known Ruby and Sean had; he'd said he'd been in love with her, maybe Kelly should have chosen her words more carefully. She'd read an article in a magazine once about dealing with bereavement. What had it said? Something about listening. People only want to talk.

'What was she like?'

'Happy,' he said, and gave a sad sort of half-laugh. 'Clever, confident. Like you.'

Kelly was sceptical. That didn't sound like the tragic movie actress that Ruby was purported to be – the battles with drink and drugs, the failed relationships, all of which made more headlines than the parts she played. Sean's judgement had been rose-tinted with time, surely? Besides, the woman had committed suicide, wasn't that an undeniable statement of misery?

'So why would she . . . do something like that?'

'I can't say,' said Sean. 'I would never have expected it. That's the thing about Ruby. She was a survivor.'

They sat in the first awkward silence of their lives, so unused to being nervous of each other that they didn't know how to make things right. 'We'll have a wee drink, shall we?' said Sean. He sheepishly produced an almost half-full bottle of whisky from its hiding place in the dark spaces under the bench. 'To Ruby.' He reached across to hold Kelly's hand. 'You can handle this, love, I know you can.'

She didn't want to toast her mother but she felt it was appropriate. The first mouthful tasted as emetic as salt tears yet the next one slipped down easily. Sean and Kelly drank and looked up at the stars. She tried to concentrate on the father/daughter bond but she kept thinking that the stars didn't look as bright as they used to and maybe she needed glasses. And even though she maintained her self-righteous stance and didn't give him an easy time, by the time they finished the bottle Kelly was entertaining the idea of getting on a plane and going to Ruby's funeral.

She could not say she was angry at being kept in the dark if she was too scared to face the light. She couldn't maintain that she had always wanted to know more about her mother if she refused an invitation to find out. Even if it was a posthumous invitation. She could sit here and pretend that the reason she didn't want to go was because she was stubborn, but stubbornness is often just fear wearing a veil of pride.

'If I did go out there, would you come with me?' she said. Kelly had never been to a funeral, something she used to assume was incredibly fortunate, but now she was starting to wish that some distant relative had given her a trial run. This seemed like a very high-pressured way to lose her cherry. 'I don't know if I could do it on my own.'

'Why don't you ask Jez?'

Kelly screwed up her nose. She hadn't even thought about him. 'This is family stuff,' she said. 'It wouldn't feel right.'

'Is everything okay? With you and Jez, I mean.'

'Fine,' she said. It was nice of her dad to act concerned. Kelly sometimes sensed that he didn't like her boyfriend. Or maybe she was just projecting.

'You know how much I hate funerals,' said Sean.

This was true, and probably part of the reason why Kelly had never been to one. Occasionally, more frequently with every passing year it seemed, an old friend of her dad's would pass away and he would stay away from the funeral to spend the day quietly with a view and perhaps a book, paying his respects privately. Kelly thought he was scared of death.

'And you know how much I hate Los Angeles.' This was also true, he hadn't been there for years, but she could still remember the stress lines on his face when he returned the last time. 'That's not to say you will,' he added. 'Los Angeles is a good place to be young in.'

That sounded appealing. More and more these days the town where she lived was feeling like a good place to be old in. A place to settle down into a pattern and count off the living years as they trickled away without incident.

Kelly felt a sharp stab of loss tear through her and with considerable shame she realized that it wasn't her dead mother she was missing, it was the mystery that had always surrounded her parentage. The comforting speculation in her head had been replaced with cold fact. Now the truth was out there she had to face it or forget about it, which she knew would be impossible. Could she really go? Get on a plane and fly away? People did it all the time. Being scared was no excuse.

'I'll go,' she said. 'I'll go on my own.' As the words left her mouth she felt a wash of satisfaction. It was the right thing to do.

She had so many questions. Her mother had been a movie star. She couldn't get her head around that. Did that make her special?

'Dad,' she said. 'Tell me everything you know about Ruby Valentine.'

3. Ruby Norton 1966

Ruby Norton's remarkable beauty went unnoticed for many years but she always fancied she was something special. She waited impatiently through her unattractive childhood, hiding behind a shapeless cloud of dark hair and growing a thick skin as she endured the gentle teasing of her peers. It was frustrating. Then finally puberty bloomed late and long like a fiery Indian summer and her steadfast self-belief was rewarded. Her slightly lopsided smile and unusually pale eyes didn't matter so much any more because the gaze was drawn elsewhere. She had a body that made men grow weak. And firm in other places.

Ruby wore the more conservative fashions of the times, but chose a size too small to flatter her curvy shape. She pulled wide belts tight to emphasize her assets. It was the perfect disguise. Ruby would leave the house wearing cashmere cardigans buttoned right up to her neck, looking thoroughly proper like a younger version of her own mother, but as soon as she was out of her parents' sight she'd open up a few buttons to reveal paradise. Her generous boobs were the best in Wales. Long, luscious legs tapered up to hips that were made all the more voluptuous by an indecently tiny waist. And she didn't mind skipping lunch from time to time to maintain her shape. It seemed a small price to pay for all the attention.

Ruby's perfect boobs were currently receiving lavish consideration from Hugh, the youngest son of the local publican, who had taken his break early so they could have a quick fumble in the beer cellar.

'Bloody hell, Ruby,' said Hugh with his mouth full. 'You're gorgeous.'

'What was that?' said Ruby.

'You're gorgeous.'

'Thanks,' she said. She'd heard him the first time but she liked the powerful sensation that shot through her like pure adrenalin as she heard it again. Hugh was a popular lad in the town and half-promised to a girl from a neighbouring village who was currently sitting upstairs in the back kitchen wondering where her boyfriend was. Right now, however, Ruby had him enchanted and he would have been hard pushed to remember his girlfriend's name, let alone their date. Ruby pulled away slightly just to see the anxious look in his eyes.

'Five more minutes?' he begged. Ruby smiled graciously, flicked her coal-black hair to one side and surrendered.

'I think I love you,' mumbled Hugh. 'Let's run away together.'

'Don't be silly,' said Ruby. Running away didn't bother her, but with Hugh? He might be considered a catch in this town, and he was a surprisingly adept kisser, but Ruby had far grander ideas for her future. Still, it was nice to be loved.

For most of her twenty years Ruby had been a good girl, so it was no wonder that she often felt bored. She had behaved with the propriety expected from the daughter of a prominent local businessman and her parents had slept soundly in their bed every single night. She had done exceptionally well in school and stayed away from bad influences. Consequently she justified her recent fall from grace as simply making up for lost time. With a bit of luck her parents would never find out and, even if they did, they might be grateful that at last she was attracting admirers. For some time now they had secretly worried whether any man would ever be foolhardy enough to take their inquisitive, headstrong daughter off their hands. She was always reading, their clever little girl, and not just novels, which would be bad enough, but newspapers too.

Ruby was expected to settle down with a good local boy, raise a family and be content, but from a very early age she had desired a world outside this small one where she lived. It got on her nerves. She was outgrowing this place. She had untapped ideas and passions that she knew could not be realized without leaving the comforts of home. She didn't know exactly what form her ambitions took; a university education appealed but so did a career. Britain was entering a new age where both things were possible. Women across the country were stepping up and saying 'I can do that' without needing their father's permission.

Did it matter that she wasn't exactly sure what she wanted to do? Surely the important thing was ambition itself? She was confident that her life would be completely fabulous; she'd work out the details later.

But despite all these lofty aspirations Ruby found it

tediously hard to leave. It was easy for the pretty only child of one of the richest men in town to get by. She had been lucky enough to be blessed with both beauty and brains. She sailed through a secretarial course – the undemanding work bored her silly – and was given a perfunctory office job in one of the family's manufacturing plants which provided her with pin money for cocktails and cosmetics. Everybody in town knew Ruby, she had plenty of friends and admirers and she was careful never to compromise her reputation too much, to ensure she remained popular. Ruby wasn't a slut, she was just well liked.

Sometimes, dancing at the Academy or driving with a boyfriend to a quiet spot by the old quarry, she thought that she was happy. She would dismiss her dreams of the wider world as naive fantasy and convince herself, if only for a moment, that this life was more than enough and maybe this man she was dancing with, or driving with, would be the one she would marry. But then inevitably the moment would pass and she would look up at her dancing partner and think about how she would rather grow old alone than marry someone as listless and as narrow as the town itself.

As her twenty-first birthday drew near, Ruby watched yet another friend announce her engagement and realized that if she didn't make a break soon then she too would be picking out wedding china at Howells of Cardiff.

When her father asked her what she would like for her birthday, Ruby replied without hesitation, 'I want to go to London, to live, just for a while, just to see.'

The world was changing. She was reading about it in the newspapers and she could hear arresting new music and impassioned voices on late-night talk shows on the radio. They talked of art and of politics and of revolution. She could sense the change in the anxious eyes of her parents' generation. Post-war Britain was exploding out of its conservative restraints and it made them very nervous. Something was happening out there and Ruby didn't want just to hear about it from the safe shelter of her home town. She wanted to see it. She wanted to be part of it. She wanted change.

Her father protested and her mother wept. To them the city was the source of all sin, where evildoers would tempt their only child into wickedness, but Ruby was resolute. They might be scared of the unknown but she wasn't.

'You're ruining my life,' she said. 'You can't tell me what to do.'

Her relationship with her parents was never the same again. Why should she care? If they didn't understand her then that was their problem. Didn't they know she was destined for great things?

From the moment her train pulled into bustling Paddington Station and she felt the raw energy radiating from the fashionable crowds, Ruby knew that she would not be going back. No matter how hard it was, she would find her place in the world, somewhere near the top.

4

London was brash and unpredictable and Ruby wasn't entirely sure that she liked it. Back in Wales there were two buses – one which went to Cardiff and one which didn't. Here the buses didn't give you a chance to count your fare before hurtling along densely trafficked roads while you hung on to a rail and prayed that you were on the right bus and that you wouldn't bounce right off the back of it into the path of an oncoming car. 'Does this go to Earl's Court?' she asked the conductor, but he either hadn't heard her or chose to ignore her.

It had taken her a few weeks to recognize the creeping sense of apprehension she felt on every corner, to identify why her bravado had gone into hibernation and why she wasn't making any new friends. Then she realized that she felt shy, for possibly the first time in her life. And although she had craved new experiences, the novel sensation of acute insecurity wasn't quite what she had in mind. For all of her life Ruby had relied on her social standing within a small community for company and acceptance. Suddenly to be without any sort of reputation left her unsure of herself. She was lonely, feeling too self-conscious to join in the vibrant scenes she could see in the West End streets as the bus sped past them. That was where she wanted to be. Not stuck in an office with one small window on the world.

As soon as her parents realized that she was determined to do this, references had been despatched and friends in the city were alerted to their daughter's presence. Ruby rented rooms in Earl's Court and had quickly found secretarial work, largely thanks to the glowing references from her father's deputy. It was a modest, traditional firm, the work was hard and the people withdrawn.

Was it ridiculous for her to think that she could just come to a big city like this and find friends, make an impact? She felt small and she hated feeling that way. She wanted to prove, mostly to herself, that her ambitions were more than just pipe dreams and that she was right, not deluded, to believe that she was capable of greatness. This spark she felt inside, it couldn't be the same for everyone. In her heart she thought she was different.

It wasn't fair. In her old life she was considered sophisticated; here she felt unbearably provincial. Ruby hadn't kissed a boy for three whole months, something of a record. She felt frumpy.

Earl's Court had sounded so elegant. But in reality she had a poky little flat with unreliable hot water and too many stairs to climb. But, as ever, she was grateful when she pushed open the door, lifting it slightly to help it across the uneven floorboards. For all its humbleness, this was home now.

She turned up her radio as loud as it would go, even when the old lady upstairs hammered on the ceiling above her, and pretended that she was in a nightclub instead of in her nightdress, about to dine on champagne and oysters, not a cheese and potato pie with a slice of ham.

This life was not the one she had been expecting. Right place, wrong attitude. Starting tomorrow, everything would change. And if it didn't, then maybe she would go home after all.

She slept better than she ever had in Wales. She needed the energy.

Most mornings, before she left the house, Ruby sat at her window in Earl's Court and watched a young woman go into work at the hairdresser's opposite. She was about the same age as Ruby and represented everything Ruby yearned for from a new life. She was the talisman for Ruby's hopes and Ruby was fascinated by her. She wore outlandish clothes with an individual style that attracted stares of admiration or shock depending on which generation was doing the staring. She had fashionably short hair the colour of honey, and when she walked it was as if she was constantly dancing to some unseen beat. She was always smiling.

Today she arrived early. She had several friends in tow, all dressed up and boisterous as if they had just come from a very late party. None of them seemed to care that their celebratory mood was at odds with the slowly stirring London streets, that their laughter was too loud for the quiet of morning. Today she was wearing the shortest skirt that Ruby had ever seen, exposing long legs clad in stripy tights. On top she was wearing a deep pink coat the colour of raspberries, belted tightly around her waist. The finishing touch was a black pork-pie hat, the like of which Ruby was convinced she'd never be able to pull off. Her friends had it too. The look. The look that said, I belong, I'm part of something big. Ruby watched from her window as they all said goodbye with more laughter and hugs, and she couldn't imagine that woman, that *girl* she supposed, ever being shy or unsure.

Things had always come easily to Ruby – she wasn't used to having to fight for what she wanted. If her upbringing had been a little tougher, maybe she would have climbed down from her top deck once in a while to seek out life, instead of expecting it to come looking for her simply because she showed up.

It was all very well to think that she was capable of great things but she needed to be more specific. She would never achieve greatness stuck behind a desk in a nondescript office. She would never experience new things if she kept looking at them through a pane of glass. She had nothing to lose.

That day, after three months of being good, Ruby skipped work. Calling in and feigning a debilitating case of women's problems to the male manager was staggeringly easy. She had been worried that her lie would be transparent, that she would be tripped up and forced to admit that she was being dishonest. But the entire deception took less than a minute and an empty day stretched blissfully in front of her. She made a cup of tea and sat in the window waiting for the hairdresser's opposite to open.

She forced herself to wait for twenty minutes before leaving the house and walking across the road. Ruby was tense. She knew she had as much right as anyone to enter the trendy salon, and she had enough business sense to know that nobody turns away paying customers. Money was money, after all. But as she reached out for the door handle her heart was leaping.

This wasn't like going to Dai Lewis's salon on the High Street for a trim, this was the first symbolic step towards being a new kind of girl altogether. If she couldn't even do this, then what hope did she have? It's just a haircut, she reminded herself, not a revolution.

The bell on the door pealed cheerily as Ruby entered. There was music playing.

The Supremes. I know this song. Ruby was immensely proud to have recognized the tune. All those hours listening to the radio were paying off. She might not look the part but at least she knew the sounds. Maybe she wasn't hopeless after all. Just as her self-congratulations finished so did the song, and it was replaced by something else. Men with guitars and voices like warm sunshine. She didn't know it.

The girl came out from the back of the shop, drying her hands.

'Hello there, come on in, how are you, love?' So the talisman spoke. Her voice was musical and cockney. Ruby imagined that when this girl got excited she would start dropping her aitches.

'I'm fine, thank you,' said Ruby. She was nervous and she despised herself for that. Ruby was supposed to be the one that other girls found intimidating, not the other way around. She cleared her throat and tried to think of something fashionable to say. 'How do you do?' She cringed. Why did she suddenly sound like her mother?

But the girl grinned. 'I do all right, thanks.'

She had lost the raspberry coat and was wearing a simple black polo neck. I could wear that, thought Ruby. Hang on, I *own* that. Immediately she regretted her choice of outfit as she recognized it for what it was: twinset and pearls, without the pearls. Why hadn't she worn the polo neck? How were you supposed to know that such a plain style was in fact hip? Was there some magazine that all the hip girls subscribed to or what?

The salon had a peculiar smell. Underneath the high notes of chemicals and shampoo there was an invasive, sultry scent, like something burning. She looked around for the source and saw a smouldering cone set on a china saucer painted with crude flowers.

'Patchouli,' said the girl. 'You like it?'

'It's unusual,' said Ruby. 'But yes, I think so.'

'You *think* so? What's the matter with you? Don't know what you like?'

'I like it,' said Ruby firmly, warming to this slightly rude but very amusing girl. Her merry smile was infectious.

'That's better. Now, sit down, let's have a look at you.' She sat Ruby down in front of an unframed mirror. Without asking, she snatched the pins out of Ruby's hair so that it tumbled past her shoulders in shapeless hanks. 'Gorgeous colour,' she said. 'Or at least it would be if it had any shine to it.' She picked up a handful of Ruby's raven locks and let them drop listlessly back down. 'It just sort of hangs there, doesn't it?'

Ruby knew she couldn't change her life by having a haircut, but it was a good place to start. She took a deep breath. 'That's why I'm here,' she said.

The music ended and there was silence as the scrutiny continued.

'So what do you want me to do today?'

'I'm not sure.'

The grin grew wider. 'Not sure? Sweetheart, you were here ten minutes after the door opened, and you're not sure?'

Ruby knew she sounded ridiculous but she hadn't really thought any further forward than summoning up the courage to walk in the front door. Now she was here, with unfamiliar sounds and smells and this girl, who she knew was only trying to be friendly but was intimidating all the same. It was a lot to take in.

As if sensing her nerves, the girl moved away. 'My fault,' she said. 'I should have offered you a cup of tea. You have a look at some of these magazines, get a few ideas, and I'll be back in a bit. Name's Ella, by the way. Dad was a jazz freak.'

'It was twenty minutes,' said Ruby.

'You what?'

'I was here twenty minutes after you opened. I sat over the road and counted.'

Ella laughed and went out the back.

Ruby looked through the magazines, blinded by all the images. She thought that some of the people in there looked ridiculous, but maybe ridiculous was big right now. When Ella came back with a steaming cup of tea she was more confused than ever. She spoke without thinking it through. 'I want to look like you,' she said.

'Like me?' said Ella. 'Are you sure?' She fingered her honey crop, two inches short at its longest.

Ruby struggled to explain without sounding like a schoolgirl with a crush. 'You have to help me,' she said. 'I don't know what I like, that's true, and these magazines really aren't much help to me. I mean, could I do that?' She pointed out a picture of a wild afro.

'I don't think so,' said Ella. She giggled.

'I want to look as if . . . as if I could be friends with someone like that, friends with someone like you.'

'That's easy enough,' said Ella. 'Start by telling me your name.'

'Ruby.'

'And you already know mine, Ella, yeah? So that's it, we're friends. Ruby, just relax. I'll make you look the way you've always wanted to.'

'Wait,' said Ruby. 'What are you going to do?'

'Trust me. You want to look modern, right? But not too way out. I'm thinking keep the colour, give it some shape, simple. It's going to look groovy.'

Ruby curled her tongue around the unfamiliar word. 'Groovy.'

'You got it.'

First Ella washed Ruby's hair and then combed it out, marvelling at its texture and colour, and when Ruby could no longer see through a curtain of her own locks Ella began by cutting in a thick fringe. She was intent on her project, pursing her lips in concentration. 'That's better already.'

Ruby gulped as she watched long chunks of her hair fall to the linoleum floor and tangle into the metal feet of the adjustable chair. Her left eye could see a couple of intrigued labourers watching the process on a bench across the street as they ate their greasy bacon butties. As soon as her mouth was clear she took another fortifying sip of tea. Ella was butchering the rest of her hair with long, sweeping strokes; inch upon inch fell to the floor.

'Close your eyes,' she said, and Ruby complied. She could feel the gentle touch of Ella's hand, the occasional cold sensation of the blades and the feather-light clippings stroking her face as they fell. The minutes went by.

Apart from singing along to a tune occasionally, Ella didn't say much. Ruby enquired whether she liked her job. 'I love it,' came the reply. Then Ruby asked her if she lived in London and was told that Ella lived way out east in Essex, 'an hour on the bus, two during rush hour'. It wasn't that Ella was reticent, but that Ruby didn't dare to ask the right questions. Like where does it all happen? And can I come?

'There, now we can see your face. Your eyes . . .' Ella held up a small hand mirror. 'Do you see these little hairs here, and here?' She pointed out the arch of Ruby's eyebrows. 'Will you let me pluck them?'

Ruby shrugged. 'I suppose so.'

Ella set upon her with a pair of tweezers, tugging quickly and cleanly. Ruby's nose twitched as she held back a sneeze.

'Almost done,' said Ella.

Ruby watched with fascination as her new look emerged in the mirror. Her pale eyes looked more wideset, their slight almond shape accentuated, with her brows framing them perfectly in the same way as a new, sleek hairstyle framed her face. She gave her hair an experimental flick and it fell back around her shoulders like raw silk.

The bell above the front door of the shop sang out. Ruby looked up without turning her head and saw a frail old lady with a delicate veil covering her lined face.

'Hello, Mrs Emmerson, I'll be right with you.' Ella raised her voice so that she was practically shouting and then whispered to Ruby, 'Almost deaf, poor love. Not quite her kind of place but she can't walk any further, bless her.'

'I know her,' said Ruby. 'She lives in my building.'

'You live across the street?'

Ruby knew she was running out of time. Ella was nearly finished and Ruby had no idea what to do with the rest of her stolen day. She looked across at Mrs Emmerson and thought of dozens of women back home who looked just like her, trapped in the fashions and the traditionalist attitudes of a bygone era. They were the last Victorians, still ruling over their families, just as her own mother did. Ruby didn't want to end up like that.

'Ella,' she said impetuously. 'I really love your skirt. Where did you get it?'

Ella pulled at the short skirt and looked down at Ruby's legs, bluntly appraising their potential. 'You'd look fab in a mini,' she said. 'Try this place, and this.' She wrote down a couple of names and addresses, both in Soho. Ruby stashed the piece of paper safely in her handbag.

Ella scooped out a small handful of greasy white cream and rubbed it down the length of Ruby's hair. 'If you come back tomorrow I could iron it,' she said and indicated Mrs Emmerson. 'I don't have time now.'

'Iron it? Iron my hair?'

'Yeah,' said Ella and laughed at Ruby's incredulous expression. Ruby tried to conceal it but she wasn't fast enough. Ella, who had two older sisters and had been coming up to London since she was fourteen, couldn't remember a time when she had ever felt lost in this city, but she tried to imagine it and she thought that if she had then her expression would probably be much like the one Ruby was wearing now. Confused, apprehensive and desperate to know more. Ella had a good heart and she opened it. 'What are you doing later?' she asked.

'I'm . . . I don't know. Nothing,' answered Ruby.

'When you're done shopping I could meet you, if you like. Show you around a bit, show off the hairdo.'

'Really?'

'Yeah, why not? I'm meeting some people, more the merrier. Do you know Indica?'

'No.'

'Do you know Southampton Row?'

'Yes.' She didn't, but she could easily find it. She had a street map. She didn't want to give Ella a chance to change her mind.

'There's a theatre there, the Regal. About six?'

'Groovy.'

A few more tweaks and Ella was finished.

'There you go,' she said, and stood back to admire her own work. 'Not quite Vidal but not bad, not bad at all. You're Cleopatra. Don't ever put your hair up again.'

'I look . . .'

'You look like me,' said Ella.

55

The crisp long lines of Ruby's new haircut were nothing like Ella's blonde tufts but Ruby knew what she meant. She'd got exactly what she'd asked for.

The place on Southampton Row seemed more like a smoky jazz club than a theatre. There was no evidence of a play. There was also no evidence of Ella. Unperturbed, Ruby walked straight over to the bar. She now had the clothes to match the haircut to match the people she saw around her. Not that everyone was dressed the same. Not at all. Men in sharp suits stood alongside girls in ragged bits of patchwork; boys who looked as though they'd come straight from work on a building site talked to women in monochrome high fashion. But they all looked distinctive. She was starting to see how it worked – to blend with this crowd one had to stand out. For once, she did. Ruby loved the flare of her new pleated skirt in canary yellow, and she'd played safe with the top, a simple black high-necked number, not unlike the one Ella had been wearing that morning. She'd stashed the rest of her clothes in a locker at the tube station.

Ruby sipped her drink and waited. She exchanged broad smiles with a few people and was amazed that even after twenty-five minutes she still didn't feel nervous at all. The atmosphere was safe and welcoming. Back home where she was well known, she usually felt awkward alone in a pub, aware that she was an unaccompanied woman in a predominantly male environment, and would rarely allow herself to be in that position. But here it was different. So bolstered was she by this continuing surge of confidence that she was about to embark on her first conversation with a stranger when she finally saw Ella walk in and start scanning the crowd with her eyes.

Ruby lifted her hand and waved. 'Over here!'

Ella saw her immediately, waved back and started to walk in her direction, followed by two men and another girl. But then she saw somebody she knew and was held up by an animated discussion.

Ruby felt slightly foolish as she stood on her own and waited, her hand still half-saluting to someone who was no longer looking her way. Ella was half an hour late, she should be over here apologizing. As soon as she'd thought this she reprimanded herself. That was old Ruby, hung up on proper social decorum. New Ruby, the sophisticated city girl with the groovy hair, was above all that provincial nonsense. Manners and suchlike, were they really that important? And could she block out twenty-one years of decent breeding with another lager and lime?

Someone tapped her shoulder. She turned round to see one of the men who had come in with Ella. He had light brown hair and freckles and was wearing a white shirt with a ruffled neckline. When he spoke, his country burr made her think of green space and cloudy skies.

'How are you?' he said. 'I came to rescue you, Ella could be a while. That girl she's talking to? That's Tiffany, she just got back from India. No doubt she has plenty to say.'

'India?' Ruby looked over at the tanned girl with no shoes on. For a second her confidence wavered. Ella had exotic friends who'd seen the world, maybe they were not destined to become the best of pals as she'd secretly hoped. She turned her attention back to the man at her side. If there was one thing she could handle it was men. She'd yet to meet one she couldn't control.

'Thank you,' she said, sticking out her chest and smiling, 'for rescuing me, that's very kind.'

'My pleasure.' He put out his hand. 'I'm Sean Coltrane.'

He asked Ruby where she was from, which led to a brief flurry of mutual admiration for the wild British countryside. 'But London's better,' said Ruby. Sean looked unconvinced.

By the time Ella came over to join them ('Tiff met a real live Swami!') Ruby had been introduced to the rest of her friends, was on her second drink and felt like part of the gang.

Sean knew plenty of people. It was incongruous: he seemed so quiet, almost withdrawn, but he appeared to be the most popular man in the room. Later, Ella explained why.

'Sean's living down near Porton Down,' she said. 'The army base?'

Ruby nodded.

Ella dropped her voice. 'Where they do all those experiments?'

Ruby nodded.

'With *drugs*?'

Ruby nodded again, still not quite getting it. Ella laughed and pointed out Sean huddled in the corner, slipping something into the hand of a sharp-suited stranger.

Ruby's eyes opened wide, she couldn't help it. Drugs.

Okay, there might be a few housewives back home who were a little too fond of their prescribed medication, and there was a rumour that Barnaby Thompson had been chucked out of the lower sixth for smoking marijuana, but Ruby had never seen an illegal pill, much less tried one.

'Is it safe?' she asked.

'Sweetheart,' said Ella, 'they give these things to the army! Her Majesty's finest. Besides, you can trust Sean.'

'So he's a soldier?'

'Hardly. He's a photographer and conceptual artist. He wants to explore an untapped landscape.' She touched her finger to her forehead. 'The one up here.'

Ruby wasn't entirely sure what conceptual art was. She thought it sounded like a good excuse to get high.

There was a commotion towards the back of the room and the numbers suddenly doubled. Ruby was confused.

'The play's finished,' said Ella.

'A play? Where?'

'Upstairs.' Ella pointed out a man at the centre of the new crowd. 'That's Dante Valentine. He's a brilliant director.' She lifted her hand and called out, 'Dante!'

Ruby looked over and she saw a beautiful man. It wasn't a word she would usually connect with masculine good looks but it was the only word that fitted. Dante Valentine had ebony hair which curled over his collar and the noble features of an ancient king. His brooding eyes caught the light when his glance bounced over in their direction at the sound of his name.

Even though it was impossible – he was too far away – Ruby thought she saw herself in the depths of his eyes.

She felt something monumental inside her shift violently as she visualized her life's path crossing with his. The feeling was so intense that she was about to mention it to Ella when she stopped herself, worried that she would sound stupid. Love at first sight was a myth, everyone knew that, something that only soppy teenagers and romance novelists believed in. But that was exactly what it felt like. She was overcome with an almost irresistible desire to throw herself at his feet and promise him anything he wanted.

Dante nodded at them almost imperceptibly and went back to his conversation, thrusting his strong hands deep into the pockets of his long black overcoat. The moment was gone, but she couldn't tear her eyes away. There was the beginning of a beard on his unshaven chin, giving him a look that was at once slightly grubby and undeniably sexy.

'He's from Rome originally,' said Ella. 'Isn't he heavenly?'

'Heavenly,' echoed Ruby. Heat swelled somewhere in the pit of her stomach and scorched a blush on to her cheeks.

'Hands off, he's taken,' said Ella. 'He's mine.' She saw the way that Ruby was looking at him and a sharp warning tone entered her voice.

Ruby continued to sneak glances in Dante's direction. His generous mouth was set in a firm line and his hands twitched in his pockets, as if he was forcing himself not to make gestures to defend some hotly contested point. He could not control his thick eyebrows though and they danced to add emphasis to his every word. Whatever he was discussing over there was obviously not to his liking. As Ruby watched, Dante spat on the ground in disgust, turned on the heel of his shiny black shoes and walked away from his shocked companion. He actually spat on the ground! Ruby was impressed.

'He's your boyfriend?' she asked.

'Well, technically no, but he's so modern. Boyfriend, lover, they're all just labels.' Ella frowned slightly, betraying her true feelings. 'I'm working on it.'

Within seconds Dante was upon them, grabbing Ella at the nape of her neck and kissing her full on the mouth. He was angry, and controlled fury rose off him like steam.

'That dumb shit over there,' he said, 'says they've closed down the Berkeley.'

'Again?' said Ella, closing her arm around his waist like a harness.

Dante nodded. 'Apparently the police raided it last night and some bitch had brought her two-year-old twins because she was fried on heroin. Silly little fuck-up, she didn't know where she was.'

Ruby stood quietly waiting to be introduced, but Dante and Ella were kissing again. His hand was casually caressing her breast through her thin top and Ella gave a groan of pleasure. Ruby was startled and tried to cover this up by turning to the man on her left, but he was watching Dante's hand with lascivious concentration.

Eventually Ella broke away, her red lipstick smudged and her eyes glittering with satisfaction. 'Dante, this is my new friend Ruby. You said we should all be spreading the word.'

Dante's brown eyes locked with Ruby's pale ones. She

felt violated by the depth of his stare. Up close, his eyes looked cruel. She looked down almost immediately and to her great shame the blush returned along with the now burning heat in her belly, spilling south.

'And where did you find her?' he enquired sarcastically. 'The Catholic school?'

Still staring at Ruby, he took a packet of cigarettes from his pocket, tapped out two and lit them both, passing one to her. She shook her head but Dante nodded firmly and Ruby found herself smoking. It tasted disgusting but she supposed that she could get used to it. She coughed a little but not enough to embarrass herself. And all this time Dante was looking at her with the intense scrutiny of an artist appraising his finished canvas.

'Take off your stockings,' he said suddenly.

'What?'

'You heard me, take them off. We have to let you loose.'

She stared at him, incredulous, but he nodded to her and, as she had with the cigarette, she found herself compelled to obey and kicked off her shoes. She passed her cigarette to Ella and wordlessly started to unhook her stockings. A murmur started around them and people turned to see what was happening. Dante smoked, blowing out elegant blue plumes, and watched.

Ruby lifted her left foot on to a chair and slowly started to unroll one stocking down her long slim leg. Her pleated skirt was riding high, almost to her hips, unfurling like the petals of wild daisy. The sexual tension in the room grew palpable as she revealed inch upon inch of creamy Welsh thigh. She switched legs and her audience caught a glimpse in between them as she raised her right foot. She heard Dante's snatched intake of breath and it made her quiver with pleasure and pride.

All eyes were on her now, on this strangely erotic scene orchestrated by their beloved star director. Ruby felt impossibly aroused. Every inch of her body was on fire and the graze of her own hands on her thighs made her breath quicken. When she had finished she stood before him, barefoot. 'There now,' he said. 'Don't you feel liberated?'

Ludicrously, she felt there should be applause. But there was nothing, just an indiscernible pause before conversations continued.

But Dante's eyes remained on her. Even when he was talking to Ella.

Later, Ruby and Ella went to a nightclub on Wardour Street, The Flamingo. Dante stayed behind at the theatre. 'He's so passionate about his work,' Ella said, but Ruby could tell she was disappointed.

The Flamingo was a seedy basement with a flaking black ceiling and it didn't feel like anything special until the band came on stage. Then the place erupted, and it was so hot and Ruby danced so energetically that she was glad she had lost her stockings somewhere along the way.

Ella leaned over to scream in her ear. 'Is it okay for me to stay at yours tonight? You'd be doing me a real favour.'

'Of course,' yelled Ruby. 'It'll be nice to have some company.'

'Thanks,' said Ella. She pressed a small blue pill into Ruby's hand. 'Present for ya.'

And just like that they were friends.

In her dimly lit room, Ella snoring softly on the floor beside her, Ruby sat on her bed and hugged her knees to her chest. She had finally found what she was looking for. The people she had met today possessed enough energy to light up the whole of the West End. She shivered with delight as she remembered the thrill of undressing for Dante. It had felt daring and absurdly empowering. A combination of drugs and adrenalin made her feel more alert than she had in months, perhaps in her whole life. Ella was right, there was absolutely no reason to be afraid of drugs; how could something that made you feel like this, made you feel alive in a world that had abundant possibilities, be bad?

The mirror over her washstand reflected a new smile. The smile of a wiser woman, not an innocent. She dipped her hand into her pocket and pulled out the note that Dante had slipped into her hand before they left. It had his telephone number and a pencil sketch of a woman with raven locks, a thick fringe and wideset almond eyes.

5

It was always a likely possibility that Ruby would fall in love with Dante Valentine. He arrived in her life just as she was searching for excitement and he personified the thrill that she craved. Dante was forbidden.

Ella was crazy about him and talked about him constantly. From the very beginning he was a big part of her and Ruby's friendship so what happened later almost felt inevitable. Because it was indisputably more convenient for the salon, Ella moved most of her possessions into Ruby's small flat, helped out with the rent and stayed there on nights when Dante let her down. Most nights. From Ruby's point of view Dante and Ella looked fragile. They argued constantly, and big evenings out, of which there were many, invariably ended in floods of tears from Ella's side of the bed while she berated his lack of respect for her.

'I used to think,' she said, 'that he flirted with other women to make me jealous. I told him that I didn't like it and do you know what he said?'

'What?' said Ruby, eating up the girl talk with enthusiasm.

'He looked at me like I was crazy, like the idea of making me jealous had never even crossed his mind. He said he'd never thought about it like that. God, Ruby, he doesn't even care enough about me to piss me off.'

Ruby protested weakly but secretly she agreed. Ella harboured unrealistic hopes that she would tame Dante and eventually they would be together properly, maybe even marry. Ella declared herself a radical free thinker, thoroughly anti-establishment, but Ruby could see that Ella wanted a white wedding just as much as the girls back home. And Ruby knew that Dante would never marry Ella as surely as she knew that when Dante brushed his hand against her arse it was never an accident.

'Do you think he loves me?' asked Ella.

'Of course,' said Ruby.

'Honestly? Do you really think so?'

'Yes,' Ruby lied.

Ruby was very fond of Ella. It was her friendship that had opened the door to a new and more exciting life. A life where Friday night could begin at a café sipping bitter coffee and meeting interesting people, and continue with frenetic dancing in the front row of the Roundhouse, scuffing up the dirt floor while listening to a fêted rock-and-roll band, before the wind-down over more coffee at a different café. Without Ella Ruby might be considering accepting the constant offers of dinner from a deathly dull colleague whose conversation skills were second worst only to his dress sense. And, of course, Ella had introduced her to Dante.

Dante treated Ruby like a pet project and she basked in his attention. Under his tutelage she cultivated a favourite play, a favourite poem and an opinion on just about everything. She was for women's rights, against the bomb, she loved Henry Miller and The Who, and when she disagreed with someone she would say so. In this scene it was okay, encouraged even, to say the first thing that came into your head without worrying that it was wrong or stupid. People were not easily offended. She felt loved and that made her feel brave. She started to think that maybe she could lay claim to a man like Dante, not Dante exactly because he was Ella's, but someone like him. Someone exciting. She didn't set out to steal Ella's boyfriend. But then boyfriend was just a label, so it might not count.

Because of her sexy face and her eye-catching figure people sometimes asked her if she was a model. An actress? She would reply that she didn't know yet, and this answer always amused people to the point where they started asking who Dante's new discovery with the sing-song voice was, this alluring Welsh girl with a deadly combination of innocence and glamour. And was she seeing anyone?

But Dante had a thing for her, that much was obvious to all of them, except maybe Ella. His seduction of Ruby was practised. At first it was always the three of them, Dante and his two girls, Ella and Ruby. Then, when he was assured of Ruby's trust, he started to pay her special, individual attention away from Ella's proprietary friendship: a few bottles of wine in a Soho jazz club, a supper or two in the cosy enclave of a basement café in Chelsea, all the while telling Ruby how uniquely beautiful she was, inside and out.

Ruby didn't buy it for a second. She had been chatted up plenty of times in her life and knew that men will say the most flattering things in pursuit of sex. When the compliments came laced with a gentle Italian accent they were easier to swallow, but she didn't get carried away. She didn't want to be *too* easy, as she sensed that Dante was enjoying the chase as much as she was enjoying being hunted. So she relaxed into his compliments as she would into a warm bubble bath. She knew she was pretty, she knew she was spirited, but really – a jewel beyond compare, uncut but dazzling within? He talked about her potential and confirmed what Ruby had always known. There was something different about her, something special.

She never deluded herself. He wasn't in love with her, not yet. She knew that he had used these lines on a hundred women before her. She wasn't stupid, she was just another conquest to him. But over time her loyalty to Ella didn't seem such an obstacle.

One night she left Ella close to tears so that she could be with Dante.

'You seem nervous,' he said over their usual table, tucked away at the back of a restaurant for lovers.

'I lied to Ella tonight,' she said. 'I told her I hadn't heard from you.'

'And you feel bad about that?'

'She's my friend.'

'Then why did you lie to her?'

She had no answer. He was very good at twisting her words, misdirecting her until she had clean forgotten what it was that she felt bad about.

'What are we doing here?' said Ruby. 'You and me?'

'Where I come from they call it romance. You intrigue me. I want to know the real you, the one that you hide so well. I see glimpses of her and she's breathtaking.'

Dante was trying hard. His objective was blatant, and Ruby couldn't pretend any longer. She was quite sure that sooner or later she would allow him to succeed. He had taught her so much already but there was always more to learn.

A few days after that, they went to the cinema to watch an afternoon screening of *La Dolce Vita*. Dante was appalled that Ruby had never seen the film and insisted on rectifying this shocking gap in her education. He didn't let her concentrate though, and whispered dirty thoughts into her ear from time to time. By the end of the film his hand was up inside her skirt, his fingers gently massaging the warm skin at the top of her stockings.

For the last twenty minutes Ruby didn't follow the film at all. She had never felt so wanton and there was a burning sensation between her legs that was turning her to pulp. As the credits rolled Dante took her hand and placed it on his lap so that she would know that he was as excited as she was.

'Come with me,' said Dante. 'Please?'

She nodded, breathless, hoping that her legs would hold up as they stood to leave. This was it. That was the night *La Dolce Vita* became Ruby's favourite film of all time.

From the cinema they went straight to the Regent Palace Hotel. Dante dragged her across the marbled entrance hall so fast that her heels skidded on the shiny surface. She hadn't questioned why they would go to a hotel rather than take a taxi to his flat; the hotel was nearer, she understood.

The old man on the front desk looked bored, as if he'd seen it so many times before. A pair of young lovers, dressed outrageously, full of high spirits and maybe on drugs, unable to keep their hands off each other long enough to take the key to an overpriced room. These kids today . . . things were changing so fast.

Ruby was unbelievably excited. Her insides felt warm and sparkling like the buzz from a gin and tonic, and joy kept a bubble of laughter at the top of her throat. Her pale eyes glistened. There was no going back. For a fraction of a second she thought of Ella and how upset her friend would be to know that they were here. But Dante slept with other women all the time, everybody knew that, Ella railed against it enough, so Ruby was able to cast the sense of betrayal straight out of her mind. It wasn't as if Ella was his girlfriend; Dante didn't believe in labels and neither did she. Ruby was therefore totally innocent of any wrongdoing. She was pleased to be able to rationalize all this, because there was absolutely no way that she was going to change her mind.

Ruby always got what she wanted and she wanted Dante. Right now she wanted him with a senseless abandon that took her breath away.

'Are you ready?' he said as he pushed open the door to their room.

'Are you?' she countered.

'I've been ready since the first time I saw you,' he said.

'It's okay,' said Ruby. 'You don't have to do that any more. The smooth talk. I'm in.'

'Smooth?'

'I've heard it all before.'

He slammed the door behind them, grabbed her by the shoulders and forced her up against the wall, his mouth so close to hers that she could taste him. He searched her face and for once she held his intense gaze, her eyes baring her soul. He ran one hand leisurely down over her body, trailing his fingertips across her throat, past her breast and over the curve of her hip with agonizing slowness. Then in one swift motion he lifted her into his arms. She wrapped her legs around him and pressed herself into him. When he kissed her and she felt those lips and the graze of his rough chin after all those months of waiting, she felt so dizzy that she thought she might pass out. But then she let herself go with the incredible feeling and discovered a whole new level of consciousness.

The first time Ruby slept with Dante Valentine she was convinced that she could exist quite happily in bed with him for the rest of her life. She was quite logical about it and saw it as a genuine possibility. Why not? She couldn't imagine ever needing anything else again. She had no need for food or water when she had Dante's lips on her body and the taste of his skin under her mouth. Her family, her beliefs, her past all drifted into the dark recesses of her mind so that there was more space upfront for this man, for this incredible feeling.

Ruby was not a virgin – she had taken care of that swiftly and unimaginatively a few days after her eighteenth birthday – but the awkward fumbles of a Welsh boy who couldn't believe his luck were a world away from the passionate dedication Dante brought to the bed.

They stayed in the hotel room for two whole days and nights. Ruby learned how to do things that she would never have imagined in her wildest fantasies. As a result her fantasies became wilder still and Dante encouraged her to explore every one of them.

'One day,' he said, 'when you trust me more, you will let me photograph you, perhaps even film you.'

She smiled, not really caring either way. If he got a camera out right now she'd probably be happy to pose, on her knees, upside down, inside out, whichever way he wanted her.

'You have such a singular beauty,' he said. 'On camera you would look even more like a goddess than you do right at this moment. Your body, it's sensational.'

'Dante,' she said. 'I love that you think I'm beautiful. But please shut up and let's do it again.'

The weeks that followed were by far the most exciting of Ruby's life. This is what she'd been seeking, that feeling of living rather than simply being alive. Something to live for.

She existed in a state of permanent anticipation, waiting for the next time they could be together. They stole time whenever they could, sometimes meeting at four in the morning or slipping away from a party for half an hour. Sometimes fifteen minutes in the hostess's bathroom would satisfy them while Ella carried on dancing or talking downstairs. It felt like everything Ruby had expected her first love affair to be. Everything the movies promised it could be. Dangerous, invigorating and sexy as hell.

Sometimes, usually late at night when the reassuring dark gave her courage, Ruby would mention Ella. Dante always said the same thing. That Ella was important to him but that she had nothing to do with his relationship with Ruby.

'You are so conformist in this country. So uptight,' he said. 'You live by these outdated moral standards. The sooner you realize that the world is changing, the less likely you will be to be left behind.'

'But Ella . . .'

'Ella would be happy for us,' he said. 'She understands me.'

Ruby twisted a curl of his hair. Was he implying that she didn't? And she had serious doubts about how Ella would react if she knew the truth. She would feel betrayed and angry, yes. Happy? Not so much.

Dante stretched back on the bed and lazily reached out for Ruby's hand to place it where he wanted it. Obediently, Ruby stroked him. 'London is starting to bore me,' he said.

'But you won't leave?' The thought of life without him made her feel ill.

'I might,' he said. He groaned as Ruby's hand moved faster and he pushed her down on to the bed.

'Dante, I'm so tired,' she said. It was almost morning and he had made love to her three times already. She needed to sleep.

'Here.' He pushed a small black and white capsule into her hand.

She took it, washing it down with the last of a bottle of lukewarm wine. 'Thanks.'

Black and whites were her favourite. She was quite fond of Dex too and would be happy on ephedrine if there was nothing else around. After the first time it had been easy. Drugs weren't evil, they were a doorway into a part of herself she might never have explored; they were a revelation.

Every so often Ruby would take stock. She was living and working in London. Well, actually, her work standards were steadily declining; she'd taken five sick days from the office in the last two weeks and was about ready to quit and see what happened. She wasn't sure what she wanted to do, something in the arts perhaps, or politics, but sitting in an office at the beck and call of dreary superiors was definitely not her heart's true intent. She had hundreds of friends. Well, maybe not hundreds but a few dozen at least. She'd seen some of the best new bands play live, standing so close that if she'd wanted to she could have reached out and touched Keith's guitar amp; she'd met some of the most celebrated faces of the era and one of them, a fashion designer, had said she liked her scarf. She had tried all kinds of drugs, knew how to mix the perfect martini, and was having a passionate affair with one of the most notorious men in town. To Ruby such things measured sophisticated success.

She spoke to her parents once a week and the conversations felt fake, as if for twenty minutes every Sunday afternoon she became the person she had left behind, who talked of work and weather and enquired politely after pets and neighbours. They asked her repeatedly when she would visit and she would make excuses, eventually deciding to say that she was saving up for her own flat.

One weekend her parents came to town, and they had lunch in Highgate, a long way from the places Ruby loved but the sort of traditional restaurant that served proper vegetables and would appeal to her parents.

After lunch Ruby suggested a walk around the nearby cemetery, but her mother thought the ground beneath their feet was too damp and it was too cold to walk among gravestones of long-dead strangers.

'Karl Marx is buried there,' said Ruby.

'Who?' said her mother, and they didn't go.

As soon as she had waved goodbye to them at the train station and they were safely on their way back to Wales, Ruby threw herself into the nearest taxi cab, a rare luxury. She was anxious to reach the Regal and her friends and Dante as soon as possible, to reclaim the person she had become. The person she was destined to be.

It was busy in the bar, hazy with sweet-smelling smoke and the hum of conversation. Ruby inhaled huge mouthfuls of the charged atmosphere, and even though her parents would be only a few miles away on their sluggish train she felt their worlds were light years apart once again.

Dante and Ella were sitting on big cushions around a low table with a few other people, some of whom Ruby recognized. She was welcomed with kisses and smiles and space was found for her to sit between Dante and Sean.

Half a lager and lime miraculously appeared for her to drink and Sean passed her a smouldering joint as soon as she had settled.

This is my family now.

Dante had a new toy, a cine-camera, and was busy discussing its possibilities with a man Ruby knew only vaguely. She listened for a while but they were using lots of technical terms that she didn't understand and for once, she couldn't be bothered to ask for explanations. She caught Ella's eye across the table, similarly lost in the film talk, and they both giggled like schoolgirls. Ella shuffled round so that they were next to each other and took Ruby's hand in both of hers. 'I love you,' she said. Her pupils were dilated so that her grey eyes looked like inkwells; she was so close that Ruby could see her own reflection.

'I love you too,' said Ruby. 'Let's dance.' She knew that when Ella was high she liked to dance. She wondered what Ella was on and if there would be more. The afternoon with her mum and dad had been laborious and she wanted to get smashed and forget all about it.

The music was loud, a beautiful black guy was doing things with a guitar that made her head spin, and the sweaty dance floor was overflowing with high spirits. Ruby closed her eyes and let the guitar riffs fill up her senses, moving her body slowly despite the frenzy alongside her. I'm so lucky to be a part of this, she thought. And then she corrected herself. It wasn't luck that had brought her here, it was her own choice, her own achievement. But being in London at this time in history was special; nobody ever really said it out loud but they all felt it. It was like riding the crest of a wave, a wave that had no shore to reach, a wave that just was.

When Ruby could dance no more she grabbed Ella, who would dance all night unless somebody stopped her, and retraced her steps back to the table.

'How's she doing?' said Sean, nodding his head towards Ella.

Ella had thrown her head back and was fascinated by Dante's cigarette smoke floating towards the yellowing ceiling. She blew gently into the plume of smoke and seemed delighted when it drifted away from her.

'She's fine,' said Ruby.

'Do you want some?' said Sean. 'New stuff from the base, I dropped some last night and it's something else. Clean lines, a sense of the aesthetic, quite beautiful really.'

Ruby loved the way Sean sounded when he talked about his drugs, as though they were paintings in an art gallery. She'd never been offered acid before but she didn't hesitate. Sean explained the drug to her with a reverent respect and suggested all sorts of ways to make the trip enjoyable.

It felt like several hours but in reality was probably only forty minutes later that she turned to Sean and said, 'You're right, it is beautiful.' Her mind was racing so fast that she couldn't keep up with her consciousness; she kept thinking that she was touching the edge of a profound realization then losing her grip on it. It should have been frustrating but it wasn't. The club, and her friends' faces, took on a mystical splendour. She couldn't remember ever feeling this free.

Sean grinned and his smile stretched out to touch his

earlobes. It was weird. She laughed, and Sean smiled again, which only made her laugh more. She was gasping for breath, hearing her own giggles as though they were somebody else's. Then suddenly she was quiet again and Sean's smile resumed its usual proportions. As he reached out and stroked her face, his fingertips felt like downy feathers.

'You're beautiful,' he said, and then he kissed her.

In the middle of the kiss Ruby forgot for one second how soft and warm his lips felt, and how her insides felt as though they were dissolving, and she thought, Sean is kissing me, I'm kissing Sean. She heard a strange noise in her ear and looked up to see Dante with a camera pushed to his eye, filming their kiss and saying 'Don't stop,' so she didn't. The minutes went by. Unseen hands reached out and embraced her waist. She twisted around, vaguely surprised to see Ella. Dante captured it all on a camera. When Ella lifted her face for a kiss it seemed the most natural thing in the world to place her lips on her friend's and for them to lazily explore each other.

Girls kiss nice.

Dante circled them, making Ruby dizzy, and it was easier to close her eyes and allow the feelings to consume her. She didn't know who was kissing her now, Sean, Ella, even Dante or someone else entirely, it could have been anyone. And even when she did open her eyes there was too much heat, too many hands and kisses melting together, and she still didn't know. All she could feel was the welling desire inside her, spiritually intense, the feeling of loving and of being loved that surged in her so violently that a tear slipped down her cheek.

'Are you okay?' A whisper, laced with gentle concern. Sean, she thought, but when she opened her eyes it was Ella. Ella had skin like velvet. Ruby reached out and stroked her back.

'This is amazing.'

'I know.'

There was space on the cushions to lie down and Ruby and Ella lay back together, both discarding some of their layers of winter clothes, continuing to whisper to each other – is this okay? – until their voices didn't sound like real words any more. Ella reached for Ruby's breasts and her nerve endings throbbed like a series of tiny electric shocks under the caress.

What would her mother say?

Dante's camera whirred and Ruby surrendered to pure sensation.

6

Three weeks later, Sean asked Ruby to pose for him. 'I need to work on my portfolio,' he said. 'Right now there's just a whole bunch of trippy abstract stuff. I need to find something more classic. Can I? I'd let you keep copies.'

'Me?'

'Well, yeah.'

'Not Ella?'

'You.'

They arranged to meet the following day and that night Ruby didn't go out. She stayed at home and smothered her hair in olive oil and her face in cold cream. She put two used tea bags on her eyes and tried to relax. Her room felt strangely empty without Ella. She was growing used to her constant chatter. She'd been concerned that she'd find it hard to hear Ella talk about Dante but as their relationship always seemed on the edge of something cataclysmic she was pleased to listen. It gave her hope. She still offered Ella sound advice, or so she thought. Pointing out that Dante didn't like needy women and that she should give him space made perfect sense. The fact that space also gave Ruby and Dante a perfect opportunity to be together was just happy coincidence.

She rinsed the gloop from her hair and smoothed her face clean with a square of muslin. She was excited about being photographed. Everybody said that Sean was good. This could be the start of something.

She toyed with the idea of waiting up for Ella to hear in detail everything that Dante had said that night. But Dante and Ella had been getting on better than usual and there was a good chance that Ella wouldn't come back tonight at all. Ruby might be a fool but she wasn't fool enough to stay awake waiting for someone who was sleeping in the arms of the man she loved.

An early night would guarantee that she looked her best.

Sean had hired a studio and everything. Ruby was impressed. There was a short rack of dresses for her to wear, but only one fitted, and by the time she came out from behind a changing screen in the final dress, spilling out over the ruffled neckline, Sean was mortified.

'You're bigger than I thought you were,' he stuttered.

Ruby took offence.

'I mean . . . up top.'

'Sean,' she said, 'you mean you never noticed?' She was acting coquettish. Getting into character, she hoped. Wasn't this the right attitude for a successful model? From the look on his face she was only scaring him. 'It doesn't matter.' She pulled the best dress from the rack. 'This is lovely.'

It was plain black with a forgiving cut. It wasn't anything special but on Ruby it suddenly looked like a designer outfit.

Sean squeezed off a few shots as she got into position but then stopped himself. He had taken enough candid photographs. They were little more than snapshots when you got right down to it. Fabulous snapshots, but still. He wanted an image that would not look out of place in a magazine. There was just something about Ruby's face, the way she carried her beauty, casually unaware of the impact she had on those around her. She turned to face his lens and smiled, her hands clasped neatly in her lap. She looked so innocent.

After forty minutes or so they were both bored and pretending not to be. Ruby had thought that modelling would be glamorous and stimulating but the truth was that she felt as if she was only half of a person, the physical half. Trying to convey emotion and thought without words was frustrating. Sean had thought that photographing a beautiful woman like Ruby would be inspiring, but in fact he found it too easy. It was impossible to take a bad shot of her, so where was the challenge? It occurred to him then that she would do well on screen. She was a gift to any cinematographer and he had no doubt that the photographs would be sensational. When you looked in those eyes it was almost as if you could tell what she was thinking, whether that was 'Come to bed' or 'Go to hell'. But the truth was he was dissatisfied.

Just then Ruby looked up at the clock on the wall behind him and started to laugh. His finger danced over the trigger. Magic.

'I thought we'd been here *hours*!' said Ruby. 'But it's not even three o'clock.'

'I'm sorry,' said Sean.

'What for?'

'You must be tired.'

'Modelling isn't tiring,' she said. 'Speak to a waitress at the end of her twelve-hour shift, she's tired. Me, I'm just sitting here having my picture taken.'

'I think we're almost done. You should keep some of these, get your own portfolio together. I think you'd do well.'

'At what?'

'Modelling maybe. But I think you're an actress.'

'That's crazy,' said Ruby. 'I don't know the first thing about acting.'

'Really? What about when you first got here and you were scared of everything but pretended not to be? That was acting.'

'I wasn't scared.'

'It's a compliment. Nobody would have known.'

So acting was just telling lies in costume? There had to be more to it than that. People went to drama school for years, they talked about craft and motivation. Were they just practising telling really good fibs?

'What about when you act like it doesn't bother you that Dante's with Ella?'

Ruby looked up sharply. Sean's hand went to the trigger once more. Ruby made such a habit of keeping her guard up that its immediate loss could always be seen in an instant on her face All that vulnerability was enough to break your heart. 'Why should it bother me?' she said.

'Don't worry.' Sean replaced the lens cap on his camera and started packing up. 'Like I said, you're very good at it.'

She didn't feel like lying any more. 'Tell me honestly,' she said. 'Do you think he'll ever leave her?'

'For you?'

She nodded.

'I know that if I had even the slightest chance of being with you I'd do anything you asked.'

Was it her imagination or was that Sean's attempt at a pick-up line? By the way he was dodging her eyes she thought he was nervous. Sean liked her, how sweet. But no, obviously, she was with Dante. Sweet was not her style.

He snapped down the lid of his camera. 'Thanks,' he said. 'You did great.'

'Will you be at the UFO next week?' said Ruby, as she slipped back into her street clothes behind the screen. Then she hesitated, hoping that didn't sound like more than friendly interest.

'Front row,' he said. 'With this.' He tapped the case.

'So I'll see you then if not before.'

'Seeya.'

He kissed her cheek and Ruby tried to shake off the feeling that something subtle had changed between them. As if she'd given something away along with her image. Her brave face, perhaps.

Several hours later, when Sean had developed his film, he studied the contact sheets with the help of a magnifying glass. He'd been right. Every single frame was sensational.

On the night of the big concert at the UFO, Ruby left work early faking a migraine (she'd never had a migraine

84

in her life) and spent over an hour preparing for the evening ahead. By five in the afternoon it was dark like midnight. Earl's Court glistened with lights strung across the crowded streets and festive spirits were reaching new heights.

Ruby ran across the street to hammer on Ella's window.

When Ella came out her cheeks flared in the crisp air. 'Cold, innit?' she said, hugging her green mackintosh close around her.

They went to an Italian restaurant near the tube station, and for a half a crown each they feasted on spaghetti and meatballs, insulation against the night ahead.

They hadn't seen each other properly for a while, although most of Ella's possessions were still in Ruby's flat. Ella had decided to apply to art school and was trying desperately to infiltrate that crowd, wearing a ridiculous beret most of the time and namedropping artists, mispronouncing Monet and Chagall. All this just meant more stolen time for Ruby and Dante, and so Ruby vigorously encouraged her friend's new-found love of art.

'It'll be a wild night,' said Ella. There was a group playing at the club, a homecoming of sorts for one of their favourite bands, and for weeks people had been talking about it. Simply everybody would be there.

'I hope so,' said Ruby, thinking that if Ella drank enough beer she would be able to sneak off with Dante for a couple of hours and they wouldn't even be missed. It was a perfect opportunity. A crowded venue, an attention-grabbing band. They could slip away and be at the Palace within minutes. Underneath her new Biba wrap dress she was wearing the white silk underwear that Dante liked best.

'Do you want to know a secret?' asked Ella.

'Of course,' said Ruby. *Do you?* Lately she had been tempted to let slip that she'd been sleeping with Dante, just to see what would happen. What was the point of an affair if nobody found out? It was the logical dramatic progression. If Ella knew, then they could stop stealing moments and be a proper couple.

'Dante's going to Rome,' said Ella. 'He's bored, he said. How could anyone be bored of all this?' She threw her arms out wide to indicate she didn't just mean the white tabletops and the perpetual smell of onions in their immediate vicinity, she meant the bigger picture. 'But I think I might go with him.'

'Really?'

'He doesn't know that yet. I have to figure out the best way to tell him.' She looked wistful. 'He didn't ask me.'

Ruby was hiding her shock with a mouthful of spaghetti. Rome? He couldn't possibly be serious. What about her?

'Do you think he means it?' she asked.

'Dante doesn't say things that he doesn't mean.'

Not strictly true, he tells you that he loves you.

'Do you think I'd like it in Rome?' mused Ella. 'Dante says it's dead romantic.'

Ruby realized with a start that she would miss Ella almost as much as Dante. That was unexpected. She would miss nights like this. Without both of them she was scared that she might be bored too. Perhaps she could go with them, if she was invited. Perhaps in the spirit of the times she should invite herself. She needed to talk to Dante. Maybe he already had a plan. Surely he wouldn't just leave her?

The pair of them boarded a red bus to take them into the West End. At the back of the bus was a drab-looking girl, around Ruby's age, sneaking covetous looks at them with their bright clothes and volleys of laughter. That was me, thought Ruby. She didn't want to have to go back to that again.

The nightclub was a seething mass of exuberance. Tonight, sooner or later, everyone who was out on the town would end up at this legendary venue. The fevered crowd laced the air with an intoxicating sense of antici-pation. There were hundreds of people and Ruby had to shout to make herself heard. Ella grabbed her hand and they walked slowly through the club, getting distracted every few steps by friends or by strangers who wanted to become friends. Their progress was slow and Ella looked reasonably content, but Ruby was itching to find Dante, to hear him say out loud that he was leaving so that she might believe it. With hand gestures she managed to convey to Ella over the music that they should look upstairs.

From the balcony Ruby was able to look down on the throng as a whole. She scanned the faces for Dante's but she was certain that he would be hidden in some dark corner up here, that was more his style. He was crafting a reputation as an artist in this crowd and so it suited him to be enigmatic. But she was caught up in the tableau of a thousand people all having the time of their life. Two green spotlights carved lines of colour into the grey, smoky darkness. Faces turned upward towards her and Ruby looked down on so many smiles that she felt her heart sing with joy that she was one of them. And she hadn't even taken any drugs yet.

'There!' Ella nudged her and pointed. Dante was hidden in a dark corner, having an impassioned conversation with plenty of gesticulation. For a moment Ruby was annoyed that she hadn't spotted him first but then, thinking of Rome, she softened. She would miss those hands too much.

He kissed them both. When he kissed Ruby he said, 'I have a surprise for you.'

He's leaving her. He's going to ask me to go with him.

When they got to Rome they could be together constantly, no more sneaking around, and Ruby was certain that if she had Dante all to herself then she would be enough for him. This was real, this was love, it had to be. If it wasn't real then why did her body burn for him just looking across the table, why was sex on her mind every second of every day? Only when they were together did Ruby feel complete.

They didn't get a chance to be alone for hours. Ruby tried to use her eyes to communicate with him, but Dante's mind seemed to be elsewhere. Once, he leaped up from his seat and disappeared for almost twenty minutes. Ruby didn't react quickly enough to follow him. When he came back she searched his face for a sign that he had been waiting for her, but his eyes were dancing with drugs and laughter, not any kind of frustration. She asked him to dance but he said no.

People gradually shuffled round the table, so that Ruby

eventually found herself next to him. She relaxed for the first time that night as she felt his strong hand clasp hers under the table.

'What's my surprise?' she said.

'Patience,' was all he would say.

There was a lull in the music before the headline band came on. Someone somewhere was singing a Christmas carol, but it was as if every patron of the nightclub were collectively holding their breath waiting for the main attraction. Then, when the opening guitar chords resonated around the space, the crowd went absolutely wild.

'Come on, beautiful,' said Dante. 'It's time.'

He pulled Ruby to her feet in front of everyone, and just as Ruby was thinking that this was a very public risk, he stretched his other hand out towards Ella. 'You too,' he said.

Ruby was confused as he walked them both to the balcony. She looked down at the band. Was she supposed to recognize one of them?

Ella said, 'I don't get it. Where's my surprise?' and Ruby's spirits dipped. A surprise for them both wasn't the same as an invitation to Italy.

Dante pointed past the band, to the large white screen high up on the wall behind them. The screens were always there and Ruby didn't usually pay much attention to them. They usually featured random images or short films that could entrance some of the heavy trippers for hours. Rumour had it that Andy Warhol always screened there first.

Ruby thought she'd guessed it. Dante was going to

screen his film debut – his big surprise was not really about her at all. It was entirely about him.

Then she saw her own face on the screen. Her own body. And Ella. The pair of them entwined, fifty times larger than life.

Her skin looked awful.

And she was kissing a girl.

She felt ill and for a moment she thought she was going to throw up. She grabbed Dante's shoulder to stop her vision from swimming, so that she could focus on this violating film. It was pornographic. If it was some-one else up there maybe she could be okay with it, but it was *her*. That was her half-naked body up on screen. Her mouth, her breasts, her large thighs.

The camera zoomed in on her closed eyes, and Ruby didn't notice how striking her bone structure appeared on screen; all she saw was that her eyebrows badly needed shaping and her mascara had smudged beneath one eye. She didn't think that it was undeniably exciting to be famous for five minutes; she only thought how shame-ful this was and tried to swallow down a sickening wave of fear. Everyone could *see* her up there.

Once she got over the initial shock she felt worse. It went on and on. Soft-focus images of every touch. Her thighs spilling out where they weren't firm enough, her haircut looking like a cheap wig.

She had been high that night, she hadn't really been aware of what she was doing. These moments were private. She'd thought they even had a quiet beauty of their own and now Dante had ruined her memory of that evening for ever, exposing it to all the people she cared about, as well as hundreds more who were nameless, and reducing the experience to something tawdry and inelegant. She felt wounded.

She whirled blindly towards Dante. What was he thinking? Beyond him Ella was dumbstruck, but didn't look particularly displeased. Dante was enraptured.

'How could you?' she said.

'What? Wait, the best bit is coming up, there's this certain light that bathes you . . .'

Ruby backed away from him, her eyes filling with tears. 'Get them to stop the film, please. Please stop it, I can't bear it.'

'You don't like it?' He scratched his chin, perplexed. 'But it's gorgeous.'

'I hate it,' she said. 'I really hate it. Please.'

'What's wrong?' said Ella. She was smiling, keeping half an eye on the screen.

'What's *wrong*?' Ruby couldn't believe she had to explain herself. 'It's awful,' she said. 'Everybody's looking at me. It's bloody degrading, I look like a whore.'

For that moment she wasn't Ruby, sexy friend of Ella and Dante, the newest face on their little part of the London scene, she was Ruby Norton, only daughter of a small-town businessman, and she hated herself. Her confidence evaporated along with any feelings of sophistication she'd ever felt she had. She wasn't ready for this. When it came right down to the sharp end, the new Ruby was only skin-deep. She was fake.

'I think you look beautiful,' said Dante.

Ruby put her hands to the sides of her face and covered her eyes with her fingers. She couldn't hold on any more and she started to cry.

A stranger's voice broke through the sound of her own sobs. 'I agree.' Dante placed a restraining hand on the stocky newcomer as he approached Ruby, who shrank back, afraid and paranoid.

The young man was wearing a crisp dark suit and a little shoestring tie and he spoke with an American accent. 'I say he's dead right. You sure do look beautiful up there, young lady,' he said.

'Leave her alone,' said Dante. 'She doesn't want to talk to you.'

'You directed this film?'

'I did.'

'My name is Max Parker,' he said. 'You should call me.' He drew a business card out of his pocket and pressed it into Dante's palm, and then he turned his attention back to Ruby. 'And you,' he said, 'you should leave this place and come to dinner with me right now. We have a lot to discuss, you and I.'

'Excuse me?' Ruby had no idea what was going on.

'What's your name?' he said.

Dante glanced at his card and stepped between them. 'Didn't you hear me? She doesn't want to talk to you. Can't you see the lady's upset?'

Ella chose this moment to speak for the first time. 'I'm Ella,' she said, sticking out her hand by way of introduction.

Max glanced at her dismissively. The blonde didn't interest him, it was the brunette who had captured his attention, as she'd so obviously captured the camera's attention, dominating every frame. The film was well made. Max didn't think it was pornographic at all; he thought it was artistic and sensual – back home they'd call it 'European' – and he thought that this woman was the most exciting prospect he'd seen since he arrived in London.

'Forgive me,' said Max. 'I'm a lawyer, I work in Hollywood.'

Dante scowled and looked as if he was going to spit on the floor. Max hurried to reassure him. 'Not that kind of Hollywood, not what you're thinking. There's people out there now who think like you and me.'

'How do you know what I think?'

'You like Fellini, right? And Truffaut, all those guys?'

Dante shrugged. Of course he did, every European film-maker did. 'Naturally.'

Max grinned. 'People who think like that,' he said, 'I can't promise you anything but your work has style, no question.'

'And Ruby?'

Both men focused on Ruby. It was the first time Max had heard her name. It was simply perfect: the most precious and rare of all the jewels, said to open the heart to passion. He felt a sharp buzz of certainty about this girl. Was that how Huston had felt when he'd first seen Marilyn?

'With Ruby it's different,' said Max. 'I can pretty much promise her anything she wants.'

That was easy. 'I want this film to stop, right now,' said Ruby.

'As you wish.' Max twisted around and leaned right out over the balcony. He put two fingers in his mouth and whistled. The piercing sound drove another stake of fear into Ruby's nerves. Max mimed cutting his own throat.

And then the film stopped. There was a palpable sense of disappointment from the crowds below as the erotic images on screen were replaced with a dramatic light show. Max turned back to Ruby to see if she was impressed.

She was. How the hell did he do that? Who *was* this man making promises, promises that he could obviously deliver?

Ruby grabbed his business card from Dante. 'You're a lawyer?' she said.

'Moving into personal management. I'm a Hollywood agent. And you, gorgeous, you're an actress.' It wasn't a question.

Ruby shook her head fiercely. 'No, I'm not. That was supposed to be a private film, we were just having some fun.'

'You're an actress,' he said again. Max Parker was new at this agent game, but he was keen. One day he wanted to have his own company, a powerhouse to rival William Morris and ICM, he wanted to be a player.

'No, I'm telling you, I'm not an actress,' she said. 'And I don't want to be.' She pushed backwards, without looking where she was going. She needed some air, she needed to escape. She stumbled against strangers behind her. 'Excuse me.'

'Ruby! Wait!' Max couldn't bear to lose her. He wanted to take her back to Los Angeles, get her work on a few commercials, maybe a television part for some experience in front of the camera, and then finally a big movie role, a lead, a star-making role. He had it planned out from the moment he saw her on screen. 'Please?'

Ruby took in his beseeching smile, the look of longing in his face. Here was another man who wanted her. Big fucking deal.

She turned on her heel and vanished into the crowd.

7

Ruby didn't venture out of her flat for the rest of the week. As a result she was fired from her job. Sort of. She couldn't be bothered to lie when they called and so she offered two weeks' notice and they told her not to bother coming back. It wasn't surprising. She almost felt sorry for them, remembering how she'd arrived with glowing references and her nice tweed suit. She hadn't turned out to be the good little secretary she'd presented herself as.

Dante didn't call and neither did Ella.

Ruby had calmed down a bit. It had just been such a shock. She couldn't help comparing her reaction to Ella's. Ella didn't care about the film. She was cool. She'd looked proud of herself, while Ruby stood beside her cringing so hard that it hurt inside. It was clear which girl was more suited to a man like Dante. Ruby couldn't shake off the part of her that would always be the girl she was trying so hard to leave behind.

Would Dante ever speak to her again? She knew that he didn't react well to criticism. This was his work, his debut, and she had made a big fuss which detracted the attention away from him. She'd seen the look on his face when she walked away. He'd been furious. She had embarrassed him in front of that man, that Hollywood man, whose business card was buried at the bottom of her wastebasket. And even though Dante had hurt her feelings (betrayed now seemed too strong a word, in bed she had misrepresented herself as someone completely uninhibited), even though she might need to change herself more than she could imagine, she missed him. She badly wanted to see him but she fretted that she had ruined her chances for ever.

Ruby was wakened in the middle of a night by a strange sound. It took her a minute to realize that someone was throwing stones up at her open window and they were landing with soft thuds on the linoleum floor. *Dante. At last.*

She got out of bed as fast as she could, checking the mirror over her dresser and then pinching her cheeks out of habit, forgetting that Dante said she looked better pale – it was more modern, he said, and pale skin complemented her dark hair. 'Blushing is for virgins,' he'd said.

This was so beautifully typical of Dante, surprising her in the middle of the night. She looked for something slinky to wear but everything was either dirty or creased, so she settled for pulling the white sheet around her, hoping that she looked more like a Roman goddess than a Halloween ghost.

She leaned out of the window, an expectant and welcoming smile on her face. Whatever he said, she would make him forgive her.

It wasn't Dante; it was Ella. 'Ruby?' she yelled. 'Is that you?'

'What are you doing here?' Bitter disappointment was tempered with relief. At least she would be able to ask Ella about him, find out how he felt.

'Let me in,' said Ella. 'I have to talk to you.'

Ruby felt a shiver of apprehension. 'It's so late.'

'It's important, please.'

In the dim streetlights Ruby couldn't see her expression. She couldn't tell if Ella was angry or upset or both. She sounded panicked, that much was certain, and she was in danger of waking the neighbours.

'Stay there,' she said.

Ruby ran down the stairs and opened the front door. She could see now that Ella was not happy. A thin stress line was rigid between her eyebrows on a face that was usually so eager and open that she made everyone around her feel cherished. She didn't smile or say hello. Ruby looked at her friend and was afraid of what was to come.

'What is it?' she said. 'What's wrong?'

'Can I come in?'

'Of course.'

When they got to her room the walls seemed to have crawled inward, making the space smaller and more crowded. Ruby stood by the open window. Ella sat on the bed and played with the ruffled edges of Ruby's pillowcase.

'What is it, El?'

'Where did you run to the other night?'

'Home.'

'Dante was very disappointed. He thought you'd like it.'

'I didn't.'

There was an icy atmosphere in the increasingly cramped space. Ella stood up and walked across to the window, looking out at the hair salon. She took Ruby's hand in hers. 'I've asked him not to see you any more.'

Ruby froze and her hand felt clammy. 'What?'

'You and Dante.'

'What are you talking about?'

'I know about *La Dolce Vita*, I know about the Palace, I know about that time at the Roundhouse and that time at Abby's party. Please don't try and deny it. I know everything, okay? But it's over now. I've forgiven him.'

Ruby didn't know how to respond. And judging from the look on Ella's face she had lost them both.

'I've never liked it,' continued Ella, 'but what can I do? I love him.'

'So do I,' said Ruby. She would fight for him if that's what it took. She was new to this sophistication game, she could learn, he could teach her. Dante would like that, a woman to shape in his own image. She couldn't go home, she just couldn't.

'Ruby, you don't even know him, not really, not like me.'

Ruby had a sudden flash of the last time she was in bed with him, as close as it was ever possible for two people to be.

'Oh, bless,' said Ella, and her mocking tone brought tears to Ruby's eyes. 'Do you honestly think that Dante could find happiness with a girl from – where? – from the bleeding valleys like you? Your face at the UFO, it was priceless. I mean, a guy from *Hollywood* offers you the world and you run away. Dante doesn't need a baby girl, he needs a woman. Surely you understand that?'

'I can change,' said Ruby under her breath.

'What?'

'I can change. For him.'

'Nobody can change that much.'

Ella looked directly at Ruby and smiled. 'I'm pregnant,' she said. Later Ruby remembered a hint of smugness in that smile.

'Is it Dante's?'

'Of course. *I* don't sleep around.'

'Will you . . . I mean, have you thought about . . . it's just that I heard,' said Ruby, 'that there's a few places you can go.' She dropped her voice to a whisper.

'You think I don't know that? I know that I don't have to have this baby, our baby. But I will.'

'Okay, I'm sorry.'

'Dante and me,' said Ella, 'we're going to get married.'

Married? She couldn't have heard that right! Was Dante's jack-the-lad attitude all an act? He was stepping up to do the honourable thing.

'He's Catholic,' said Ella, by way of explanation. 'We're going to Rome and we're going to get married. So you see, your silly fling with him, it really is over.'

'You got pregnant on purpose.' It wasn't a question.

Ella answered anyway. 'So what?' She turned her back on Ruby and started collecting her belongings from around the flat. She'd obviously finished her piece.

'And Dante?' dared Ruby. 'What does he say?' She knew in her heart that she was grasping at straws. Things would never be the same again.

'You showed him up in front of everyone at the club. You cried like a girl when someone offered you the chance to make something of yourself. You wouldn't dare. Dante could never love anyone who hadn't any guts or ambition. It was pathetic.'

'I have ambition,' said Ruby.

'Where? Where is it? Show me. You came to London – big deal. Ever since you arrived you've been talking big about all these things you want to do, but have you actually *done* anything? Anything except hang around after me and Dante like a bloody puppy?'

Ouch.

'No.' Ella stuffed a few pairs of tights into her bag. 'It's all just words with you, Ruby.'

'And what have *you* done that's so special?'

Ella pointed across the road. 'I have a job I really like, my art classes, and I'm leaving it all behind to go to Rome with him. I take my chances in life, that's why he loves me. He'll change.' She tied up her bag, slung it across her shoulder and headed for the door.

Ruby couldn't bear to see the best friend she'd ever had walk away in anger. 'Ella, wait!'

Wearily, Ella turned round. 'Yes?'

'What will I do without you?' Ruby knew she sounded feeble but she couldn't pretend not to care.

'Go home, Ruby. Go home and marry someone like your daddy, who'll always think you're perfect no matter what you do.'

'I never said I was perfect,' cried Ruby. 'I wasn't trying to be.'

'No,' said Ella, 'you were trying to be me. You were jealous. Well, it's my life, Ruby, and you can't have it.'

Ruby saw that Ella had missed one of her beaded necklaces hanging from a picture frame. Beads not jewels, Ella didn't have everything. The way she spoke, once so appealing to Ruby, now sounded cheap and nasty. She picked up the necklace and hurled it violently at Ella, an expression of the frustration that was building tears in her eyes. She wanted to hurt Ella.

'It suited you, didn't it?' said Ruby. 'Having me around to make you look good. It must have been wonderful for you to be the sophisticated one for once.'

'Don't be ridiculous.'

'Really? Poor little Ella, lives at home with her mum and dad while she waits for a husband. How very modern.'

'Shut up.' Ella picked up the necklace and shoved it into her bag. 'Goodbye, Ruby, good luck,' she said with scornful insincerity, and left.

Ruby ran to the door and shouted down the stairs. 'Dante will never change! And if you think he will then you're a fool. Why would I be jealous of you? I pity you.'

After she was sure that Ella had gone Ruby raced to the telephone box across the street and phoned Dante. She knew she had time before Ella reached him, she knew he would be alone. She was struck with remorse that she had not called him before now, had not called him immediately, shown courage. She knew that this could be her last chance.

When he answered, the sound of his voice made her light-headed. If he was surprised by her sudden call his voice didn't show it. If he'd missed her he didn't say so. Maybe he hadn't noticed that it had been six days since they were last together. 'You told Ella,' she said.

'I told her ages ago,' said Dante.

'What? Why?'

'We were in bed. We were telling dirty stories. Sometimes she likes to hear about the women I make love to.'

A wave of nausea threatened to consume Ruby. She was a dirty story, one of many. Something that she thought was precious had turned out to be a cheap replica.

'Do I mean anything to you?' she asked. 'Really mean anything?'

'What is this? Ruby, it's late.'

Silent tears ran down her cold cheeks. 'I know,' she said. 'It's just that when we're together I feel like we could be everything to each other. And you don't ever think that, do you? Not about me.'

There was a pause, and Ruby heard the sound of a match being struck and Dante's deep breath. 'Not about anyone,' he said.

'And Ella? She told me you've agreed to stop seeing me.'

'To stop seeing you, yes. But not the others.'

'The others? Dante, how many are there?'

'A few, nothing regular. You're different, Ella sees that and it threatens her.'

A glimmer of hope then, pathetic as it was, and Ruby clung to it in despair. Now that her grasp was faltering she was frantic to hold on to her life here. Dante was a pig, and in some dark corner of her heart she already knew that he would only be bad for her, but she was in love with him. Desire had completely engulfed her senses and burnt away her logic.

'But won't you miss me?' she said.

'Obviously. You are different, Ella's right. But I've made my choice. So, a baby, Italy, it might be fun, don't you think?'

Was this how love ended? A few words and that was that. It wasn't enough.

'Please don't go. It doesn't have to be over,' she said eagerly. 'I would never tell Ella, she won't know.'

'Don't beg, Ruby. It doesn't suit you.'

If she couldn't beg then how was she supposed to get him back? Every word she thought of was a desperate plea. Dante liked guts and ambition. He liked his women to be strong.

She tried to summon the fighter inside her. She must have one, surely? Didn't everyone? Or perhaps hers had seized up years ago, underused because life had never felt this hard before. She always got what she wanted, always. 'You'll regret letting me go,' she said. She concentrated on keeping her voice low and steady. Sexy, even. These could be the last words she ever spoke to him. 'One day, you'll hear my name and you'll be sorry.'

'Maybe I will,' he said. 'That depends on you. You need to find yourself.'

She wiped away her tears and held back the next onslaught until she returned to her room. She threw herself down on the bed and pounded her pillows with her fists, venting some of the pain. She thrashed around like a toddler having a tantrum until she was exhausted.

It kind of worked. She lay back on the bed and caught her breath. Each new mouthful of air was steadier than the last. The chaos in her head began to subside.

She would run away. She had to get out of London. It would be too depressing to see Dante's ghost on every corner. She felt high on the emotions coursing through her, like a bad trip, and acted on impulse. She fished in the wastebasket for Max Parker's business card and made the call.

It was Hollywood or home. Which one would Dante want her to choose? The fight was only just beginning.

If he was to hear her name one day and be sorry, then she must make that name for herself, for him.

8

Kelly had been in Los Angeles for an hour and forty-five minutes and she realized that her mental image of the place might need some adjusting. She hadn't seen a single movie star. It wasn't that she rationally expected a welcoming committee of famous faces but she'd hoped she might see one or two celebrities or at least some designer luggage on the carousel. So far she was not impressed. Her first five minutes of American life were spent irritated by the way that everything was automated: the voices telling her where to go and what to do, the toilet which had flushed surprisingly beneath her when she lifted herself up a tiny fraction to scratch her thigh, even the paper towel dispenser in the ladies. For hygiene reasons, she supposed, but didn't reaching for a paper towel establish that you'd just washed your hands?

The next hour and forty minutes were spent in the biggest immigration queue she had ever seen (admittedly she hadn't seen very many). It was worse than Sainsbury's on the Saturday before Christmas, and there wasn't even a magazine rack to browse through. She was tired and irritable. By the time she spoke to her first honest-to-God American (she presumed they wouldn't let anybody illegal work the passport desk) she had already decided this wasn't going to be her kind of place.

This was supposed to be Hollywood. She wanted

Passport Control to be some kind of red-carpet, bulbs-flashing fashion display, and so far it wasn't living up to her expectations. But when she looked out at the tall palm trees beyond the glass, perfectly at home against the pale blue sky, she couldn't wait to get outside. She was hopeful that sunny California might live up to at least part of the hype.

It had been easy to book a last-minute flight on the Internet. It wasn't even that expensive and it took ten minutes. Just ten minutes to commit herself to an adventure that she was scared to undertake. But what scared her more was telling Jez that she was going without him. So she didn't.

She knew that Jez wouldn't understand why she needed a break from him. She needed to know that being with him was a choice, not a habit. Little things that he did were starting to annoy her, stupid things, like putting empty milk cartons back in the fridge or cracking blue jokes with Darren over breakfast. The way he styled his hair. The way he refused to wear anything on his feet except his scruffy trainers with holes in them and still complained when it was wet. Even the gentle touch of his hand when he held hers could irritate her. And he called it love.

She wasn't brave enough to end it, she didn't even know if she wanted to, but she wasn't sure that she was happy either. Jez was good to her and made her laugh, she still fancied him, but their relationship had stalled. It was the sort of limbo that can only be broken by decisive action. It wasn't running away, she told herself, it was moving towards answers. Maybe by finding out more about Ruby she would understand things about herself, like why she was risking potential happiness with a perfectly decent guy who loved her.

Kelly reached for the two notes in her pocket: the one from Ruby which made her uncomfortable, and one that Sean had given her with Max Parker's contact details. The address and phone number had been sitting in his address book under P for Parker all this time and Kelly had asked him if he ever used it.

'Not for almost twenty-five years,' Sean had said. 'Not since Dante died. But Max is the only other person who knows about you.'

Kelly had taken a crash course in Ruby Valentine. She got what she could from the Internet and Sean filled in some of the blanks. So she knew about Dante. She also knew the names of Ruby's other children – Octavia and Vincent – and her granddaughter, Sofia. But then everyone knew Sofia Valentine, she was in the public eye. Kelly was incredibly nervous about meeting the family but fascinated at the same time. It was the same way she felt when she read Ruby's handwriting.

She walked through Arrivals trying her best to look as though she knew what she was doing. At the gates, dozens of people glanced at her and then past her, looking for the people they were waiting for. There were a few expectant uniformed men holding up cards with names on them. One of the cards said 'Valentine'.

Kelly stopped in her tracks, causing the people behind her to bash their trolley into the back of her thighs. She hesitated partly out of surprise at seeing a name that had been floating at the top of her head for the last forty-eight hours, and partly because she genuinely wondered if someone had sent a car for her. Maybe Sean had called ahead, to Max Parker perhaps, maybe she would be welcomed here.

The middle-aged driver was wearing a smart dark suit and a peaked cap. Was this the sort of luxury she should expect now that she was the daughter of a movie star? Kelly couldn't remember the last time she had been driven by someone other than herself. This was going to be incredible. She walked over and tapped him on the shoulder.

He turned around and looked at her like a piece of shit on his shoe. 'Yes?'

'I . . . uh . . .' Suddenly she was feeling rather foolish. 'I'm Kelly Coltrane.'

'And?'

'Nothing.'

Well, that was stupid. Not the most auspicious beginning.

As she walked away she lost her bearings and turned around in time to see the driver greet a tall, good-looking older man wearing a charcoal suit so sharp that it seemed impossible that it, or rather he, had travelled. His face was clean-shaven and he didn't talk to the driver as they walked away together. He tapped on a flash mobile phone instead. A cousin perhaps? Her heart raced. And not in an entirely familial way. Maybe it was just a coincidence.

She stocked up on essentials – water, gum and *US Weekly* (she'd long been curious about *US Weekly*) – and pulled the smaller of the two notes out of her pocket, covered in Sean's bizarre handwriting. It looked as though a spider had dropped its eight feet in ink and then taken a valium and walked drowsily across the page. Luckily she was used to it. It said: Max Parker, agent, and there was his home address and his office telephone number.

She knew that she should find a hotel and check in. She knew that she should call her dad and tell him that she'd arrived safely.

She located a payphone, dialled a number and a nasal receptionist said 'CMG.'

'Hi,' said Kelly, 'can I speak to Max Par—'

There was a click and half a ring.

'Max Parker's office.'

'Hi, can I speak to Max Parker?'

'He's on a call right now, who's calling?'

'My name's Kelly Coltrane.'

'Can I help at all, Kelly?'

'No, that's okay, I'll call back.'

'If you could tell me what this is regarding?'

'Really, it's fine, I'll call back'

'Max is in meetings for the rest of the day. Perhaps I can take a message?'

'No message.'

'Is this regarding a particular client?'

'What?'

'I'm just trying to be helpful, ma'am.'

Ma'am? 'Actually, maybe there is something you can help me with. Do you happen to know the details for Ruby Valentine's funeral?' There was a click, followed by intermittent beeping. 'Uh, hello?'

She was on hold. A new voice came on the line

'Press.'

'Sorry?'

'You're through to the press office, ma'am.'

Again with the ma'am. 'Well, hello. Someone put me through to you. I was trying to find out about Ruby Valentine's funeral.'

'There is a private family service later this week and then a tribute is being planned in Beverly Hills.'

'A tribute?'

'Yes, ma'am. There will be several photo opportunities.'

'Okay.'

The money in the phone was going down fast and she didn't have any more change.

'Could you tell me where the private family service will be held?'

'No, ma'am, it's private.'

Was this the moment she was supposed to tell him that she was family? She had a feeling that he wouldn't believe her even if she tried.

'Thanks,' she said, 'you've been really helpful.'

Kelly put the phone down and stared at the receiver for a while. What just happened? She realized that this might not be easy.

9

Kelly was soon in the back of a taxi heading for the CMG building on Wilshire Boulevard. After her lack of success on the phone she thought that she'd stand a better chance of a quick result if she just turned up. She hadn't come all this way to be put through to the press office, nor was this a pleasure trip; she was here on business, family business, so while other people might have taken a day or two to acclimatize, Kelly didn't give herself that luxury. She wriggled into some clean clothes in the back seat and hoped that that taxi driver didn't think she was too strange.

Now she was here, in the motherland, she couldn't stop looking at everything around her and wondering how often Ruby had seen the same sights. Kelly found the views eerily familiar. The chaotic freeway gave way to serene luxury, the traffic suddenly becoming lighter and the vehicles more impressive. Sparkling sidewalks fringed elegant parks and gated communities. A woman was power-walking with a mobile phone in one hand and a dog lead in the other, her spaniel trotting after her in matching pink sweats. Kelly did a double take. She'd seen this in the movies but hadn't known if it really happened. She knew they were approaching Beverly Hills even though she'd never been there.

The taxi dropped her off outside an imposing building

of white marble and curved glass. The lobby was intimidating and the elevator spoke to her.

Once she got up to CMG (managing to stop herself
saying thank you when the elevator told her to have a
nice day), she wasn't one hundred per cent sure that the
receptionist on the front desk was the same one who
had answered the phone but they shared the same icy
characteristics and lack of understanding.

'And what is it you want?' Kelly was asked.

'I've already said, I want to see Max Parker.'

'And you are?'

'Kelly Coltrane.' She sighed, why was this such a
struggle? 'Look, is there a problem? I mean, he does work
here, right? Mr Parker?'

'He does. He's the co-chairman of this company. But
I'm afraid it's quite impossible to see him without an
appointment.'

'I'll only take five minutes.'

'You still need an appointment.' The Ice Queen receptionist's smile grew still thinner.

'Then can I make an appointment?' Kelly felt as though
she was talking to a foreigner who didn't speak the
language.

'You'd need to speak to his office.'

There was a pause.

'So can I?' said Kelly. 'Speak to his office?'

'Certainly.'

Another pause.

'Now?'

'Oh, not possible,' said Ice Queen. 'You'll have to call.
Do you have our number?'

Kelly was bewildered at being right back where she'd started. She was beginning to feel as though she must be the dumb one in this exchange. Ice Queen's tone had grown more condescending with every obtuse response. Was this karma for all the callers she hadn't taken seriously at work?

'I do, but when I called earlier . . .' She stopped abruptly. Ice Queen had blanked her. She'd turned the full force of her attention to the smartly dressed blonde in sunglasses who had just walked into the lobby, finishing her conversation with Kelly without so much as a nod.

Huge toothy grins for the newcomer, not a thin smile in sight. 'Hi, how *are* you? He'll be right out.'

The blonde nodded coldly and took a seat in the plush waiting area. Kelly glanced in her direction but kept her attention focused on her goal. She loaded her voice with indignation and pretended to be more confident than she really was. 'Excuse me, but we weren't done.'

'I think we were,' said the receptionist, clearly tiring of this nuisance.

'I want to see Max Parker, right now. He'll know who I am.' *Please let him know who I am.*

The receptionist took a long look at Kelly's determined face and figured that this girl could be somebody else's problem from now on. Turning her back on Kelly, she called down to Max's office. 'There's this girl,' she said to one of his assistants, 'and she's insisting on seeing Max. Says she knows him.'

Kelly waited, half-hearing the whispered conversation. She glanced over at the blonde again, her face inscrutable

114

behind her black shades. Gucci, noted Kelly, unless the massive gold Gs stood for garish.

'Someone will be right up,' said the receptionist, replacing the handset and feeling satisfied, the buck passed.

A few minutes later a stern brunette who looked about nineteen trotted up the corridor towards her.

'Kelly? Hi, I'm Sheridan, Max's assistant.'

Yeah, and? But there was nothing more. Wearily Kelly explained once more that she would like to see or speak to Max. The same old lines. Sheridan maintained eye contact and nodded, but Kelly knew what was coming and pre-empted the unhelpful response. 'He doesn't know who I am, does he?' she said.

'I'm sorry,' said Sheridan, with practised sincerity. 'He doesn't. No.'

Kelly winced. She really had been forgotten then. Sean had been wrong, her name meant nothing. She was so cross that she forgot to be polite.

'I'm Kelly Coltrane,' she said. 'My mother was Ruby Valentine. And I'd like to see Max Parker. Right now.'

An oppressive silence descended over the lobby. Even the phones stopped ringing. A flicker of shock passed across Sheridan's composed expression. Behind her, Ice Queen caught her breath.

Oooh, thought Kelly, a reaction.

Nobody noticed the Gucci blonde stand up and walk over until she spoke.

'Who are you and what are you talking about?' She had a nasal voice that didn't quite match her composed veneer.

Kelly stood her ground. 'I'm just explaining who I am.'

'Are you mad? I'm Octavia Valentine-Jarvis.'

Octavia didn't look anything like the only picture that Kelly had found of her on the Internet. Her dark hair was now blonde, her thick eyebrows were whispers of what they had once been, and her figure was considerably fuller up top. She had the dark eyes of her Italian father, but they were totally void of expression lines.

Kelly was floored. 'I . . .' Her tongue stumbled over simple words, any words. *Come on, Kel. Anything.* 'Nice to meet you,' she said.

Meanwhile, down the corridor in Max Parker's office, Kelly was simply a minor irritation in a jam-packed schedule. Ruby's mid-season suicide was hell on the shooting schedule. Max was shattered by Ruby's death. She was his first client, his oldest friend. He still got through his call sheet and none of the clients had any cause to complain, but he was soulless with it. The jovial, indulgent agent spiel was no longer there, as if her death had broken him. Perhaps he'd lost it. Behind his back people discussed a temporary leave of absence.

Sheridan had yelled out Kelly's name to Max when she got the call from reception, but Max had drawn a blank. Sheridan had cross-referenced the name on every database they had – nothing.

Now, five minutes later, Max Parker froze in the middle of a sentence.

'What?' said one of his other assistants, nervously hoping that Sheridan would get back soon if there was a problem. 'What is it?'

Max stared dead ahead with glassy eyes like a fish. 'Shit.'

'What?'

'Kelly Coltrane. It's the other daughter.'

The assistant hadn't a clue what Max was saying.

'Shit!' said Max again and slammed his fist forcefully down on the table, causing papers to scatter. Then he quickly picked up the phone and dialled the front desk. 'Kendra, honey, it's Max. Look, tell Sheridan to put Miss Coltrane in the boardroom and I'll be there right now. Whatever you do – this is important – make sure that she doesn't meet Octavia.'

His face fell. 'Shit.'

Octavia Valentine-Jarvis had never been especially bright. Nevertheless she was always confident of her opinions.

'Don't you see what's happened here?' she said to Sheridan. 'This girl has obviously stolen Max's schedule somehow and is trying to take my place.'

'That makes absolutely no sense!' said Kelly. 'Why would I give my own name? How could I possibly pass as you?'

Octavia regarded this creased, angry-looking girl as she might a rogue pubic hair on a restaurant plate. 'Quite.'

Kelly could tell when she was being insulted. She was intimidated by Octavia's assumed superiority and deeply regretted not having spent some time under a hot shower before thrusting herself into Hollywood society. She was tired as well. Why had she rushed into this? It was her first mistake. Briefly, she imagined the poise she would have had if she was refreshed and fragrant, but then dismissed the notion, knowing that in truth she would still have been dazed by this strange, designer-clad creature. Her sister.

'Ladies! Octavia, darling, hello.' Max Parker descended on the two women like a bird on to seed, flapping around them, pecking Octavia on both cheeks. The tension dissolved somewhat under his kisses. 'And you must be Kelly.'

'Max, what is this?' said Octavia. She had come here today for a nice lunch with Max, her mother's agent and close family friend, hoping to get a hint as to the size of inheritance she might expect, and the entire episode was turning farcical.

'I was going to talk to you,' said Max. 'Today, at lunch. And Kelly, we've been trying to reach you.'

'Where?' said Kelly. 'Where have you been trying to reach me?'

Max hesitated, caught out in the lie and thinking on his feet. 'I'll have to check with my office.'

'Max!' Octavia was all out of patience (she didn't have much to begin with) and she shrieked his name. 'Why is this person here?'

Max plucked at his eyebrows. 'Octavia, this is Kelly Coltrane, your half-sister. Kelly, Octavia.'

Kelly appreciated that meeting the family you never knew you had took concentration but she couldn't help looking around the restaurant to see if she could spot anyone famous. Adrenalin was taking the edge off her nerves and she wanted to try to enjoy the experience as much as she could. The huge restaurant contained plenty of people who acted as if they were famous, wearing dark glasses indoors and stopping to say hello at almost every table, but none that she actually recognized. For one heart-stopping moment she thought she saw Mel Gibson but then the man turned his face to the left and she realized it wasn't him.

As it was customary for Hollywood lunch companions to overlook one another in favour of who might be coming in through the door, Kelly's behaviour made her look like an old hand. Octavia was threatened, though Kelly would never have believed that. But when you've spent your whole life being Ruby Valentine's pretty young daughter it's a bit of a shock when somebody younger and prettier suddenly appears on the scene. There was also the inheritance to consider.

Max sat across from Octavia and prayed that she wouldn't be overly dramatic in public. He had purposely switched the lunch reservation to a less public venue: his table for two at the Four Seasons had gone to someone else and here they were sitting at Winston's, where they didn't do the Béarnaise sauce the way he liked. But he had a feeling he still wasn't safe, and that if Octavia took it upon herself to make a big old fuss, then there would be photographers at this place no matter how far out it was. Those guys could sniff out trouble at twenty blocks.

'Kelly,' he said, 'perhaps you'd like to tell Octavia your side of the story?'

'I'd love to,' she said. 'Except I only just found out. Why don't you tell me what you know?'

'Yes, Max,' said Octavia. 'Why don't you?'

So Max told them both about Ruby's lost years. And how Kelly was a result of that time, and how Ruby had sworn him to secrecy.

'She was going to give it all up,' said Max. 'Her career,

Los Angeles, everything. Leave it behind and start again.'

'But then she changed her mind,' said Kelly. 'Only one thing got left behind, two if you counted Sean. Right?'

'Oh, didn't you know?' said Octavia, cattily. 'My mother was always very good at that. Inconsistency was her thing.'

'I never knew her,' said Kelly. 'I thought maybe if I came out here, found people who'd be kind enough to tell me about her, I could come to terms with that.' She sipped her water. Why did she feel like crying? It must be the jetlag.

'And so here you are,' said Octavia. There was a barb in her voice like the sharp sting of a golden ant. So brief that it hurts for just a second before you forget about it. Kelly looked up, but Max took the conversation in another direction.

'You'll come to the service on Wednesday?'

'If I'm welcome,' said Kelly.

'Of course you are,' said Octavia. 'We'd adore having you there. In fact, do you have plans for dinner afterwards?'

'I . . .' Kelly didn't. She felt bombarded. The vibe she felt from Octavia had been nothing like sisterly, and suddenly she was adored?

'Then you must come to our house, a small supper, intimate.' Octavia laughed slightly. 'Just family.'

'I . . . That would be lovely.'

She couldn't work out whether Octavia's frequent smatterings of laughter were nerves, mockery or an affectation. She was a bit stiff, like a heavily lacquered haircut that would crunch if you handled it too roughly. But maybe she meant well.

Across the table Max relaxed visibly. Kelly hadn't been aware that he was so tense until he exhaled enough to flutter the small display of rye grasses set in the middle of their table.

'And then there's the reading,' continued Octavia. 'The reading of the will. I'm sure you wouldn't want to miss that, would you, dear?'

Kelly spluttered on her water, screwing up her nose against the sudden burning sensation. 'I'm sorry?'

'Don't be, please. We all know that's exactly why you're here.'

'Hey!' Kelly started to protest but the words caught in her throat. What was she supposed to say? That the money had nothing to do with it? That she would turn down any money that was offered to her? That she'd give it to one of her favourite charities?

'To think,' said Octavia. 'All this time and she never wanted you. Why do you think that was?'

'I don't have any idea.'

Octavia had been trading on her mother's name for many years. It had opened doors to her. She couldn't conceive of her life without that Hollywood heritage. Mother and daughter might not have been especially close but Octavia knew she was lucky to have her. For one thing, it would be impossible to get a decent lunch table without the Valentine name.

'Are you angry?' said Octavia.

'A bit,' admitted Kelly. 'She left me, remember?'

'Ah, but a few days ago she left us all,' said Octavia, trying to inject a little grief into her voice but really thinking about exactly how much Ruby might have been worth, how rich she would be in a few more days and what share of her mother's fortune, if any, would go to this long-lost little sister.

Octavia had spent the last few days mentally dividing Ruby's estate into two, half for her and half for her twin brother Vincent. It pained her to have to revise these sums to include this scruffy young woman whose clothes were obviously off the discount rack and whose hair looked as if it hadn't ever seen the inside of a salon. Kelly stood between Octavia and a chunk of inheritance that was rightfully hers. The fact that Vincent would likely get an equal share was galling enough, but now Kelly had crawled out from the swamp like a little bloodsucking leech.

Octavia and Ruby had had a fractious relationship but Octavia had never badmouthed her to the press or disowned her, no matter what Ruby had put her and Vincent through as children. In the last few years Octavia had even, on occasion, felt close to her. It was more than Kelly could claim.

Octavia couldn't keep the gracious smile on her face a moment longer; the strain was making her cheekbones ache. 'I have to go,' she said. 'I have an appointment.' She had no such appointment but they weren't to know that. The rest of the afternoon would probably consist of a little light shopping followed by a long phone conversation with one of her girlfriends, bitching about this new sister. Mother had kept a big secret from them all, a secret which needed a manicure and a decent outfit. Octavia didn't like feeling out of the loop. She needed to regain control of the situation. She'd have to instruct the chef to prepare something suitably intimidating for dinner on Wednesday and make sure that Sofia stayed in to be as annoying as possible.

She kissed the air on either side of Max's face, then turned to Kelly, clasping her hand in both of hers. 'I'll see you at the funeral,' she said. 'Then afterwards? Max has the address. I'm so looking forward to it. Dinner, I mean.' That laugh again. 'Sofia isn't that much younger than you are, I'm sure she'll be terrific company for you.'

Octavia was banking on her mother being of sound mind when she died, which was plenty to bank on given the nature of death. Surely she wouldn't have given this stray an equal share? Maybe just a token. But that didn't preclude Kelly from challenging the will. When it came to money Octavia was surprisingly knowledgeable. Kelly was the enemy and Octavia knew to keep her enemies close. She walked out of the restaurant leaving behind a waft of Armani perfume.

Max signed for the bill. 'I'm so sorry,' he said. 'You running into Octavia like that. It was clumsy, Ruby would have hated it.'

'That's okay,' said Kelly.

'No, it's not. I mean, I'm not going to beat myself up about it but jeez, if Ruby were around she'd have heard the story by tonight and she'd be tearing a strip off me before morning.'

'What do you mean?'

'Well, even if word didn't get out from CMG, Octavia would tell her: "It was awful, you should fire him" – that kind of thing.'

His sudden familiar tone was a surprise. Was it possible he had been putting on an act for Octavia? He sounded almost as if he was afraid of her, and Kelly felt compelled to reassure him.

'It really wasn't that bad,' she said. 'Honestly, it was sure to happen eventually and at least now it's out the way. Quick and painless, don't worry about it, I know I won't. You have to see the funny side.'

For a few seconds Max said nothing, merely held her gaze and contemplated. 'That sounds like something Ruby would say. She always had a soft spot for the funny side. Couldn't always find it, but when she did it usually worked out.'

He toyed with his bread plate and for one heart-stopping moment Kelly thought he was about to cry. 'You're very like her, you know,' he said eventually.

'So I hear.'

He seemed to snap out of his reverie and was all business again. She wondered if she had imagined the distress in his eyes. 'Where are you staying?' he said.

'I don't know yet.'

'Leave it to me.' He took a cellphone from his pocket and rapidly dialled a number. 'Sheridan?' he said, 'It's me. Is there something free at the Peninsula? Great. Book the patio room for Kelly Coltrane until further notice.'

He snapped the phone shut and turned back to Kelly. 'We keep a couple of permanent rooms at a hotel nearby,' he said. 'You're welcome to stay there while you're in town. As our guest.'

Did that mean for free?

'Whenever you want to check out, call Sheridan and she'll settle the bill.'

Apparently it did. Outside he hailed her a cab and

slipped the driver twenty bucks before he waved her off. Max sure was a useful guy to have around. He organized people as if it was second nature to him. She liked him. He had warmth that belied his considerable power.

Kelly couldn't imagine ever working in an office as lavish as his. She thought of her own cubicle at First Fiscal, so temporary that a gust of wind could knock it down, the pockmarks from a hundred past drawing-pins covering every inch of her moveable walls. Max had more space than her entire department. How hard did you have to work to attain that kind of luxury? You'd have to feel passionate about something to devote your life to being the best at doing it, and Kelly had yet to find her particular calling. And if Max was only Ruby's agent, imagine how Ruby herself had lived. If Kelly had grown up with that kind of lifestyle she might have been a totally different person, someone more like Octavia. This would not have been a good thing.

It was hard to believe they shared blood; they couldn't have been more different. At the very back of her mind Kelly had been half-hoping that a reunion with her long-lost sister would fill some of the gaps she felt inside her, but that was before she met her. Octavia was a disappointment. That might sound nasty but it was true. What had she expected? An afternoon of soul-searching, sisterly bonding, making up for lost time? Yes, maybe. Wasn't Octavia curious to know who she was and what made her tick, or could she tell just by looking at her that she had nothing important to give? Kelly felt naive for expecting too much.

*

The Peninsula was just off Wilshire. Wasn't that where Julia Roberts had stayed with Richard Gere in *Pretty Woman*?

When Kelly arrived at the hotel she was awestruck. Excitement mounted inside her as she realized that this palace was to be her temporary home. It was the sort of place that she would normally be too intimidated to walk into, but she was feeling some of the confidence that comes with travelling in a new place where nobody knows who you are. Tucked away into an alcove behind the busy streets, the hotel was an oasis of calm that looked as if it had no right to be there. Lush tropical plants cascaded everywhere Kelly looked and the cool lobby was elegant and tranquil with spotless cream couches and rich mahogany coffee tables. It had a colonial grace about it and she could immediately imagine sinking into one of those couches for a sundowner.

The hotel receptionist was one of the best-looking guys she'd ever spoken to outside of her Richard Gere fantasies. He had soft green eyes like pale jade and impossibly brilliant teeth. 'Welcome to the Peninsula,' he said, and she filled out a couple of forms without really focusing on anything but his soft golden skin. How could a man that beautiful be stuck behind a hotel reception desk? Surely he should be feeding women grapes somewhere?

She rode five storeys up in the mirrored elevator. It had been a while since she'd seen her reflection and she regarded her tired complexion and ragtag appearance with dismay. The straps on her black vest top had stretched and she was revealing quite a bit of pink bra.

It was a wonder that Richard Gere down there hadn't turned her away, or at least encouraged her to dress a little more conservatively.

No wonder Octavia had looked as shocked as she did. There was absolutely nothing Hollywood about Kelly. She realized that Octavia must have felt as disparate as she did when they first saw each other.

Kelly had landed on her feet. Her massive hotel room was sumptuously decorated in pistachio-green and delicate greys. A stylish rug covered most of the hardwood floor. A single orchid stood in a vase on top of the walnut writing desk. The bathroom was like something from a James Bond movie with a big sunken tub and a stellar view of the Los Angeles skyline.

This was too much. She'd been thinking more along the lines of a Holiday Inn, but this? She dreaded to think what kind of price was normally put on this level of comfort and what it would cost if she broke something. It was enough luxury to make her feel nervous. Too much change all at once was inducing mild panic. She didn't have to be here, she could just go home and forget all about Ruby Valentine. But that was a false reassurance. Now she had met Max and Octavia she knew that she was unlikely to abort this journey. She thought she understood Ruby a little bit better already.

Kelly firmly reassured herself that she was good enough for this hotel. She was here as the guest of a major Hollywood agency, and what's more she was the daughter of a real-life movie star. It was just a hotel room at the end of the day, a bed and a bath, but it was the extras that made it. Like the big bottles of lotions and potions in the bathroom, not fiddly tiny sizes, and the way she could alter the temperature or the curtains or the sound system at the touch of a switch. The way it felt like somebody's home, with personal touches everywhere, a piece of sculpture perfectly placed, or the small scented bags in the drawers.

As a celebrity brat shouldn't she be ripping out the television round about now and throwing it out of the window? Or at least partying so loud that the other guests complained? Instead she was perched pathetically on the edge of a white ottoman and worrying that she might stain it with her grubby hands. This was Ruby's world, not hers. A shower first then, she decided.

The shower revived her spirits. She rinsed away the long flight under the powerful spray and stopped being so negative. Only Kelly could have found anything negative in a stroke of massive good fortune like this. By the time she had liberally daubed her hair in a rich conditioning treatment and wrapped herself up in a plump bathrobe she saw her fantastic surroundings more appreciatively.

She fell on to the bed and laughed at her own luck. If this was what it meant to be the daughter of Ruby Valentine, then she supposed she could get used to it. The bed was thick with soft, buttery fabric and it was enormous. Really too big for one. She thought of Jez and then for a split second pictured the good-looking guy from the airport.

No, she told herself sternly, *Jez*. She had a call to make.

'Hi, babe,' he said. 'How's it going?'

'Pretty well,' she said, which wasn't a lie. 'There's something I want to tell you,' which definitely was. She didn't want to tell him at all.

'Do you want to come over?' he said. 'We don't have to do anything, just watch some TV, maybe get the PlayStation out. I'll cook.'

'I'm in Los Angeles.'

There was silence at the other end of the phone. It wasn't very nice, crossing an ocean without telling your long-term boyfriend that you were going, but she knew that if she had told him he would have wanted to come too. For support or something, he'd have said.

'I have to be here,' she said. 'I'm sorry I didn't tell you. I hardly had time to think. There's so much going on in my head right now . . .' She stopped abruptly, aware that she was over-explaining and sounding trite. There was nothing she could say that would make him feel less hurt.

Momentarily she wished that Jez was next to her. No doubt he'd have cracked open the mini-bar by now and he'd be trying to launch five-dollar macadamia nuts into his mouth by throwing them in the air first, trying to make Kelly laugh and pissing her off in the process because she knew who'd get stuck clearing them up. Then he'd want to order burgers from room service and eat it in bed watching crap American television and getting his greasy fingermarks all over the pillowcases. The desire passed. She needed some space from Jez and she'd get plenty in the kingsize.

'Okay,' he said. 'That's cool.' He was trying so hard to sound as though he didn't care. 'Where are you staying?'

She told him the name of the hotel she was in even though she didn't like the idea of him calling her all the time. But wait! Wasn't the beauty of being in a hotel that you could hang a do-not-disturb sign on your door and tell the staff to do the same with the phone? To Kelly a silent phone and a closed door were the ultimate luxuries. And maybe the fact that Jez didn't know that about her summed up part of the problem. Sometimes she felt as if he didn't know any part of her at all.

'How long are you staying?' he said.

'I'm not sure. I think there are two funerals.'

'Two? Why?'

'No idea. And it could be a couple of weeks before they read the will, maybe more.'

'How much more?'

'I don't know.'

'Like a month?'

'I don't know.'

'Longer?'

'Jez!' said Kelly. 'I don't know, okay?'

'Gotcha. Well, have a good time. Hope you get squillions.'

It was a line which really needed to be a parting shot in order to give his sarcasm maximum effect, but he went and spoilt it by asking the one question she was hoping he wouldn't. 'Do you want me to be there?'

'I don't think so.'

'Right. Bye then. You take care now.'

And this time he really did hang up.

Afterwards she called her dad and left a message saying that she'd arrived safely and making a joke about her luxurious accommodation. He rarely picked up the phone when he was working, she knew that, but she was disappointed not to speak to him. She wasn't feeling good about herself after that conversation with Jez and would have liked someone to tell her that they loved her. To tell her that she wasn't a bitch and that taking a break from Jez was an acceptable thing to do.

She crawled into the big bed all by herself and fell asleep wondering what it would have been like to grow up with Octavia as a sister.

10

Kelly slept off her jetlag for most of the next day and woke up with a plan. If there was such a special purpose to this trip then she should not hit the usual tourist trail. She was going to embark on a very specialized tour: the Ruby Valentine experience. After all, wasn't that why she was here? To find out about this woman, her mother, and hope that by doing so she might discover more about herself and start to feel comfortable in her own skin. She didn't understand what was wrong with her. Jez was kind, funny and good-looking, and she knew she didn't treat him as well as she should. When people got close to her she tended to put up walls, but Jez was fighting harder than most to break them down. Perhaps if she understood her past a little better she might be less defensive. She pulled on some comfortable shoes and left her room.

She was surprised to see Richard Gere still on the front desk. Didn't the guy ever get a break? 'I'm looking for a video store,' she said. 'A big one.'

He was not only beautiful but helpful too. After considering many options and giving her a rundown on all of them he decided that she would be best served by the Virgin Megastore on Sunset, marked it up on a street map with a big red cross, folded the map and tucked it into her hand. 'Now,' he said. 'Shall I have someone bring around your car?'

She briefly imagined a world where everyone was as open and obliging. 'Oh, I don't have a car,' she said. 'Could you call me a cab?'

'No problem,' he said. 'We have a variety of Lexus cars at your disposal. We can charge it to the room. It will be right outside and the drive should take around twenty minutes.'

It took her twenty minutes to drive into work on a good traffic day. Twenty minutes was nothing.

Kelly was quite disappointed that she was going to a Virgin Megastore, they had those in England. Oh well, it was still a trip to Sunset Boulevard, which was exciting, or was it Sunset Strip? Or were they both the same thing? Didn't Johnny Depp own a club down there or something? Maybe he'd be working there this afternoon, and she could stop in and get a drink. In the back of a flash car crawling along Hollywood streets she had felt like the kind of girl who could stroll into a hot club on her own and order a glass of white wine. But as soon as the car dropped her off and she walked into the gigantic store she was right back to being the sort of girl who had trouble with too many strangers in crowded places. It was vast.

The thumping beat of aggressive rap music was loud enough to make her jaw shudder. There were coloured lights everywhere, set into the floor she was walking over, lining each step of the stack of escalators that stretched on for ever, and enough steel, glass and mirrors to make the entire ground floor look like a nightclub.

Fashionable young people stood in small groups,

talking and sometimes dancing – dancing! In a shop! – and ignoring the merchandise towering over them, endless racks of CDs like a giant mosaic of multi-coloured plastic. Even from here she could see that territorial gap between the rockers and the pop fans, which existed in every record store she'd been in. The rockers were over in Metal with uniform black on their bodies and around their eyes; the pop fans were spread across the Charts section with clean faces and less clothing all round. There were a few new categories here though, the boys in baggy jeans over in Hip-hop, the wannabe divas with impossibly short skirts in R&B, and some sensible-looking women at the back who were actually buying things. She couldn't see which area those women were in. Country? Show tunes? Los Angeles might be a cultural melting pot but the flavours would remain distinct. She wasn't sure where she would belong. She feared that her natural home would be with the sensible women at the back.

Kelly picked her way through the crowds to Visual Entertainment. She was here because it was time to see what Ruby looked like on screen. She wanted to see all her movies in one go, back to back, the visual appendix to all her Internet research and Sean's stories. Just get it over with in a single gluttonous marathon. She didn't know why she felt scared, it wasn't real, it was just acting. If Ruby was a half-decent actress, then Kelly should be able to forget that it was her mother up there on screen and simply enjoy some classic films. It would be fine.

At first the Home Cinema department looked promising, a whole floor devoted to DVDs. On closer inspection it seemed that over half the store was all about *Lord of the Rings, Star Wars* and the latest blockbuster releases.

She found her way to Classics but there wasn't a single Ruby Valentine movie to be found. Was that a sign? Nope, she didn't believe in signs. Maybe Ruby just wasn't that popular. Maybe they were only especially aware of her back home because of her British roots. Maybe in the wider playing field of stardom she didn't register that high on the scale. Kelly knew that she was looking for a good excuse not to have to watch the films; to be honest, she was relieved. Unfortunately, an employee chose that particular time to make his pitch for Employee of the Month.

'Can I help you?'

'I'm just checking things out.'

'Are you looking for something in particular?'

'No,' she said. 'Well, actually, yeah.'

He waited patiently.

'Do you have any of Ruby Valentine's films?'

'We're like totally sold out,' he said. 'We have stacks more on order. We're thinking of doing a whole Ruby Valentine display, that's if we get them before she's old news. You never know.'

'Can you think of anywhere else I could try?'

He mused for a moment. 'Not really,' he said. 'Everyone's mad about her right now.'

'Really?'

'Oh, totally. Nothing says glamour like a Hollywood suicide.'

'That's sick.'

'That's Hollywood. Honey, right now she's never been hotter.'

She felt like telling him the truth, just to wipe the tight little grin off his face. But she was concerned that he might make a massive fuss over her, introduce her to all his colleagues and offer to display her too. She wasn't ready for that.

On her way back through the store she stopped to look at plenty of CDs but her heart wasn't in it. She tried listening to some old favourites at the listening stations but nothing could shift her melancholy. Her feet started to ache and she rested them for a while, sitting on a brown leather chair she found hidden in the tiny Classical section and pretending to read the sleeve notes on a recording of *Swan Lake*. She didn't know what was going on inside her. One minute she was looking forward to seeing the films, the next she was relieved when they didn't have them, and now all she felt was a deep sadness that dying had made Ruby more popular than ever.

She suddenly felt very tired and miserable. It must be that damn jetlag again.

Kelly had no idea where to begin looking for a cab. It was beginning to get dark and the area was becoming less exciting and more unsafe, though that was probably her imagination. Just because a car had neon under-lighting and a massive speaker fixed to the outside didn't necessarily mean there were gang members driving it, but she'd played a bit of *Grand Theft Auto*, which was one of Jez's favourites. She knew about drive-bys.

What was she doing here? Not here on the street but

here in this strange city? She was starting to get anxious. She hated the feeling she got when she was stressed, the familiar tight band that constricted her chest, the surge of acid in her stomach and a mind that threatened to seize up under the weight of dread and couldn't grasp simple thoughts. It wasn't worth feeling this way. Strong emotions always confused her; she didn't like the way they could grab you and wrench you from a sure foundation of good sense.

She could find out about any inheritance by making some phone calls; she could hire a lawyer and get them to do it for her. She was being dramatic. Caught up in the tragic romance of an estranged mother's funeral. What did she think she was going to do? Kneel next to the coffin and offer forgiveness? Perhaps throw in a single white rose along with a handful of earth? This wasn't a made-for-TV movie and she wasn't Tori Spelling. She would never meet Ruby, and nobody would ever see her again. Ever.

As she was thinking this, Kelly looked across the street and there she was. A poster, advertising Ruby's TV series *Next of Kin,* with Ruby's face the size of a monster truck.

Kelly may not have believed in signs, but the image was so timely that she laughed. Then an LAPD police car came by, shortly followed by a yellow taxi cab.

Back at the hotel the receptionist had changed. Richard Gere must have finished his shift because now Queen Latifah had taken over. Kelly had been out for several hours.

'Miss Coltrane, you have a package,' she said, when

Kelly asked for her key. 'Would you like me to have someone bring it up to your room?'

'I can take it myself,' said Kelly, triggering a look of astonishment from the receptionist and denying a bell boy his tip.

A package? From whom? The large cardboard box gave no clues. It was heavy, but not hugely so. She didn't want to rattle it in case it was breakable, or Queen Latifah thought she was nuts. She rode up in the plush elevator and looked at her name written in an unfamiliar script. There was no address on the package, which must have been delivered by hand.

She was excited. Who didn't like mystery packages? Maybe this would be the start of something good. As soon as she was in her room she grabbed the silver envelope opener she'd thought she'd never use and slashed her way into the box.

It was exactly what she wanted but the last thing she expected. Every single film that Ruby Valentine had ever made, on a pristine collection of DVDs. She was accosted by different versions of the same face, Ruby's face, on the cover of each one.

There was a piece of shiny fax paper tucked in between *Viva Romance* and *Until Heaven*. She opened it.

> *Kel,*
> *Ordered these from our LA supplier and asked him to drop them off with you.*
>   *Go on, don't be scared, I know you want to.*
>   *Love, Jez xxx*

And he'd drawn a smiley face (which sort of irritated her). There was an invoice enclosed stating that the cost had been paid in full by Jez and Glynn's video shop. She didn't think about how thoughtful he was to organize this, how his Los Angeles connections could have saved her time today, how much trouble he'd gone to. All she felt was that the private wall she had built around this experience had been breached.

What gave Jez the right to assume that she'd want to see these films? There was no way he could have known for sure. He didn't know how she'd be feeling. For all he knew she could be caught in a spiral of grief that might only be compounded by a dozen different versions of Ruby's face. If you looked at the situation that way, then Jez was taking a big chance and risked upsetting her. He didn't know her well enough to take that risk. He wasn't taking her feelings into consideration. Why would he want to hurt her? Why didn't he ever *think*?

At the back of her mind she knew she was being irrational, picking a fight with Jez although he wasn't even here so that she could avoid doing something she was unsure about. But she couldn't help it. It was too easy. After all, it was what she had done every time Jez sounded as if he was about to ask her to move in with him. She'd had plenty of practice.

She pushed the box into the corner of the room. It was too late; she didn't want to watch them any more. But lying alone in her kingsize that night, she freaked herself out by imagining little voices inside the box speaking to one another. All the voices belonged to one woman. Her mother. She'd waited all her life to get to know her and now she was nervous of what she might find out. And she scared herself by thinking that perhaps Jez really did know her after all.

Kelly was determined not to be the last person to arrive at Ruby Valentine's funeral – *Who's this? Oh, it's the after-thought* – so she left her hotel way too early and arrived with almost an hour to spare. There were a few members of the press gathered outside the wrought-iron gates of the cemetery but she slipped past them without attracting a second glance.

An area had been sectioned off with thick coils of red velvet rope and it looked deserted. The perimeter was being stalked by a couple of tall young men who had the ubiquitous look of out-of-work actors. Great teeth, shiny hair and bodies that obviously went to the gym at least three times a week. She swerved away from them. She didn't want to be the first person to turn up for this particular party. She checked that she had her passport. Max's office had called that morning expressly to remind her that without photo ID nobody would get into the inner sanctum.

The cemetery was a picturesque place, but far removed from the quietly crumbling graveyards Kelly had grown up with. Instead of moss-covered stone the headstones tended towards highly polished granite and marble of every colour. Cherubs of glass and metal perched on top here and there, dotting the ordered rows and catching the late sun like flashing tiaras. She wandered through the headstones, killing time by trying to spot famous dead people, and told herself not to feel nervous. She tugged at the hem of her suitably cheerless grey dress and hoped that it was neither too short nor too casual. Suddenly it seemed very important to make a good impression.

Her stomach flip-flopped. She was nervous. Ruby's secret daughter was out of the bag and she had a lot to live up to. She couldn't help thinking that people would judge her by impossible standards. She wasn't beautiful or glamorous like her mother had been, she was just Kelly Coltrane, and this was all frightening and new.

Her thoughts kept drifting to Ruby, imagining things that had never happened, moments that they might have shared if her mother had stayed. A memory of her first white Christmas was altered in her mind like a digitally manipulated photograph, to insert Ruby there, throwing snowballs at an excited five-year-old girl. It was disturbingly easy to create false memories.

She stopped walking and impatiently wiped a tear from her eye. It didn't mean anything. It was only understandable that she should be affected by this place where her mother would be buried. It was a beautiful setting but everything was coated in sorrow, the personal inscriptions on each headstone making it harder to be cynical about the sometimes ostentatious taste. She couldn't possibly be crying over Ruby. How can you miss something you have never had? But she'd felt that hole inside for so long that it had become a part of her memories. Kelly grew up wishing that her dad would find a wife, one whom she loved as much as he did, and who would fill that shadowy gap in their lives. A woman to make up for the one who had left them.

She remembered that once her junior school had held a summer fête. Kelly's class had all been told to bring something for the cake stall. It was not a big class, so it was impossible for Kelly's sorry packet of Jaffa cakes, cut into shapes that were supposed to be flowers but were actually just shapes, to go unnoticed. It wasn't as if her dad hadn't tried. First they had burnt a tray of flapjacks and then they had obscured the bottom of the oven with oozing sponge cake mixture that swelled alarmingly before deflating into mush. They'd had fun baking badly, and when her dad raced off to the general store on his pushbike, his coat flapping like a cape, she'd still thought he was Superman.

It was only when she felt the sorry stares of all the mothers and stepmothers and older sisters, stares that were keener and more painful than the scorching sun overhead, that it occurred to her to be ashamed. Her plated offering was moved to the back of the stall and the delicate butterfly cakes and rich chocolate brownies took centre stage. They whispered about her and her dad, and the single women among their number threw themselves at Sean for the rest of the afternoon. But he wasn't interested.

'I have you,' he'd said. 'I don't need anyone else.'

But she did. Not just someone to save face at school events but to balance her, to complement her dad's best efforts. Someone to turn to as she grew older and tried to work out what it meant to be a girl, with all the complications that brings. Kelly was twenty-five years old and she was still trying to figure it out.

The clock was easing round to a more respectable hour and Kelly reluctantly started to retrace her steps. The butterflies inside her had taken on the energy of angry wasps. She forced herself to take deep breaths and listen to an internal monologue running through her head that said, *You'll be fine, you'll be fine.*

She could see the front gates in the distance, where the press presence had swelled. She thought about what it must have been like for Ruby to live her life under constant scrutiny. Death hadn't changed that, she would continue to be written about and photographs of her would still appear, until every last drop of her had been plumbed. How must it feel to have to share the events and drama of your life with the whole world? To exchange privacy for fame?

She was almost back where she started, where she should have been, when she heard voices close to her, and instinctively ducked off the path. She half-crouched by a chunk of glossy black granite that said 'Sonny Cesare – The Greatest'. *The greatest what? Father? Lover? Mechanic?* Then she recognized one of the men. It was Max Parker.

The pair had stopped a few yards away from her. The other man looked vaguely familiar, but she didn't know whether this was because she would know him, or because he too had that actor manner about him, only this time it was fading as fast as his hairline. At first she thought that if she kept them within her line of vision she could be sure to arrive at the funeral neither too late nor too early, but then she stopped kidding herself, admitted that she was eavesdropping and concentrated.

Max looked tired and edgy. He didn't want to be there. The other man's eyes kept shooting past him back towards the gates where the cameras still lay idle. 'Who are they waiting for?' he asked. 'I thought it was just family.'

'I'm not family. Maybe Octavia was using the broader definition of the term. I don't think Sofia's here yet. Maybe she's not coming.'

The other guy snorted. He obviously didn't think much of Sofia. 'Are you sure they'll cover it?'

'The funeral? Of course they'll cover it,' said Max. 'Ruby was a legend.'

'Once maybe.'

'Trust me.'

'Do you think I look okay?'

Max nodded. 'Yes.'

'If Sofia's a no-show I might get the main picture, what do you think?'

Max pulled at his necktie. This conversation was making him uncomfortable. 'Maybe,' he said.

'Although I guess there's a chance they might lead with a shot of the coffin.'

Max shuddered. The other man didn't seem to notice.

'Did you give any thought to what we talked about?'

'Vincent, I don't think this is the time.'

Kelly froze. Vincent. Of course. That was her half-brother. He was an actor, not a very good one by the look of his credits on imdb.com, an eighteen-month stint on a lesser soap opera and a few substandard movies starring nobody she'd ever heard of. She studied him with increased interest, waiting for an explanation. This wasn't the time for what?

'Max,' Vincent said. 'We need to capitalize on this exposure. The press are all over the Valentine brand right now. Can't you at least sell my exclusive somewhere?'

'I'll try.'

Vincent had the dark hair that Octavia had bleached away, and the thick eyebrows she had plucked into submission. It was only in the eyes that you could see the twins reflected in each other. Dark brown eyes that gave nothing away. He did not look like a man attending the funeral of his mother. His smile was effortless and it was easy to tell that he wasn't thinking about her today, he was thinking about himself.

'It's not that I need the money,' said Vincent. 'But I've been feeling almost like my career was drying up, you know? This happened at just the right time.'

Max's voice was cold. 'I'm sure Ruby would be pleased to hear that.'

Vincent slapped his forehead, then put his hand out to touch Max's arm. 'Hey, I didn't mean . . .' He realized that he had spoken inappropriately and an awkward silence descended. Vincent took on the look of a scolded child and shuffled his feet on the path.

'That's okay,' said Max, and Vincent relaxed, picking up his smile without further remorse.

'You're my agent, man,' he said. 'I can talk to you about this stuff.'

Kelly looked at her half-brother and tried to imagine ever getting to know him, or letting him know her. They would have nothing in common. She would have to get used to the idea that neither of the Valentine children would be a kindred spirit.

A woman with auburn hair was striding towards them and Kelly was glad of the distraction. As both men turned towards the newcomer, Kelly slipped slightly further away so that she could emerge casually as if she hadn't been hanging on their every world. She could still hear them.

'Who's the redhead?' asked Vincent.

'Dolores Murillo, the funeral planner.'

'Seriously?'

'Yes, seriously,' said Max. 'There's the tribute as well of course.'

'The what?'

'The tribute. Sort of like a memorial service but bigger.'

'Okay,' said Vincent. 'Bigger is cool, man.' He had the vocabulary of a skateboarder and the look of a salesman.

'Gentlemen!' The redhead managed to shout and be respectfully classy at the same time. She was dressed in a sharp charcoal suit and a jet-black shirt. Her stiletto heels mashed into the pebbled pathways, making crunching noises with every step. 'We're about to begin.'

They followed her and Kelly followed them.

She overheard Vincent try his luck as she walked a few paces behind.

'So you're a funeral planner?' he said to Dolores.

'Why? Dying?'

Kelly smirked. She found Vincent distasteful – wasn't he married?

After a brief scramble for her ID at the roped entrance,

during which she was certain that she'd lost her passport, she found an empty seat and looked around. There were only a handful of people. Octavia had a prime seat in the front row, a lace handkerchief clutched in one hand and a rather dour-looking man clutched in the other. Her husband, Kelly guessed, although he was several years her senior and didn't look very pleased to be by her side.

Max was there, of course, and next to him sat Vincent, holding hands with a vacant-looking brunette next to three restless children.

And behind them, right at the back, was the good-looking guy she'd seen at the airport, wearing the same charcoal suit and tapping into the same mobile phone. She'd only seen him for a second but since then she'd thought about him more than once. She was positive it was the same man.

This tall handsome stranger was a Valentine of the Ruby Valentines. How? Was it possible that she had another half-brother she didn't know about? He caught her staring at him and gave her an almost-smile. She thought that he was trying to work out if he was already supposed to know her. Reluctantly, she turned her back on him and faced forward. She imagined she could still feel his eyes burning into the back of her head. All her other senses were focused in his direction and she heard the snap of his phone being closed and the shuffle of his body against the chair as he got comfortable.

She saw Octavia look at her watch, scowl, and then nod at the planner, who motioned for the service to begin. Kelly took a massive gulp of air and let it out as slowly as she could. *Here we go.*

At the precise moment that the minister opened his mouth to speak there was a commotion at the main gates of the cemetery. The quiet calm which had fallen over their party was interrupted by a constant barrage of shouting and the sound of running feet and tyres on the gravel. After a few seconds it was possible to hear what they were shouting. Above the chaos one word rang out louder than all the others: 'Sofia!'

Kelly saw a midnight-blue limo escape from the surrounding press pack and drive a short distance towards them, cutting up the perfect grass with its tyres. The limo stopped and Sofia Valentine climbed out of the back seat, all long legs and silver-blonde highlights.

Kelly knew everything about Sofia Valentine even though they'd never met. The outrageous young model was always in the magazines, going to this party or that premiere. She was inoffensively sexy and had outrageous dress sense. Kelly had always wondered if the dumb blonde act was something Sofia put on to avoid answering difficult questions, to lower people's expectations. Nobody who worked the media as shamelessly as she did could possibly be as clueless as she seemed. Maybe Kelly would get a chance to find out. A one-to-one conversation with Sofia Valentine, how would that go? Sofia fitted the role of Hollywood princess perfectly: her grandmother was Hollywood royalty and she was blonde and skinny, with big breasts that she always insisted were natural. It was as if the family glamour gene had skipped the twins and landed on Sofia with the force of an asteroid, obliterating anything that stood in its way.

Sofia was wearing black fishnet tights and five-inch

platforms; her tiny black skirt only just covered her bum, and her platinum hair, which *must* have been extensions, hung half-way down the back of her tight-fitting box jacket, topped by a jaunty pillbox hat with a cobweb veil covering the top half of her face. The veil had a tiny spider subtly embroidered on the hem. *Funeral chic*, Kelly thought, and was briefly envious.

Sofia posed for the press like a professional. She didn't smile. Wouldn't look too good, you know, Grandma's funeral and all that. She tried to make eye contact with as many lenses as she could. She spotted one of her favourite photographers and gave him a special little wave and a wink; she'd let him choose which photo to print, they would both be cute. Then she turned round and saw her mother in the distance. Even from this far away Kelly could see Octavia's face was thunderous.

'Fellas,' Sofia said with a baby pout, 'I have to go now. Would it be okay if you guys waited back over there by the big gate if I promise I'll stop by on the way out?'

Respectfully the cameras retreated. Sofia swung her blonde hair over one shoulder and prepared to mourn.

The ceremony was swift. A press helicopter hovering overhead swooped down lower and the roar of the blades almost drowned out the service.

A brief recap of Ruby's achievements started with *Viva Romance* and ended with *Next of Kin*, not covering much in between. A prayer was said for her, and another for her family.

My family, kind of, Kelly supposed. Would they send one another birthday cards from now on? She couldn't see it. She would go back to her average life and they would go on with their extraordinary ones. That was the way it worked.

She couldn't help staring at Sofia, though she tried not to make it obvious. She'd never been so close to a real-live famous person. It was odd to see the three-dimensional version of the face she'd seen in a hundred magazines; it reminded Kelly of seeing yourself on video instead of in the mirror, something so familiar suddenly looking so novel. When Kelly saw herself on video she usually became aware of a whole new set of flaws.

Sofia was constantly fussing in the large handbag tucked under her arm and Kelly let out a little shriek of surprise when a peculiar-looking creature poked a rat-like head out. What the hell was that? A cat? Some kind of hairless dog? Whatever it was, it was an ugly-looking thing. The subdued congregation all turned in Kelly's direction and she managed, she hoped, to mask her shriek with a hasty sob. She watched Sofia stroke the pink-grey skin and her flesh crawled. Was she supposed to introduce herself later? Nobody seemed to know who Kelly was, or maybe they did but just didn't care.

By the end it was obvious that the minister was rushing, so Dolores discreetly suggested to Vincent that he save the poem he was planning to read until the tribute. Vincent scrunched the piece of paper in his hand into a tight ball, clenching his fist until Max placed a soothing hand on his shoulder and whispered something unheard in his ear.

The process of burial seemed almost clinical and lacked the atmosphere that Kelly had been expecting. She thought she would feel something spiritual as they put Ruby in the ground, maybe she would finally cry, but it went by so quickly that before she had time to collect her thoughts it was all over. She felt as if she had let herself down. She'd come all this way, and for what?

Octavia started wailing as the coffin was lowered but Kelly noticed that her lace handkerchief wasn't even damp at the edges despite being patted to her eyes throughout. Hadn't anybody truly loved Ruby? That wasn't a nice thing to know. In fact it was the saddest moment of all. Kelly knew what it was like to be lonely. Perhaps they could have helped each other.

Afterwards cars started to back noisily up to the very edge of the grave, one by one, so that they could whisk everyone past the press. There was an awkward pause as they waited for their transport. Dolores Murillo looked pained by this unexpected and graceless delay. The ceremony was clearly over and the small crowd mingled like at any other party, albeit one with a graveside venue.

Kelly took the chance to speak to the mystery man. After all, she might never see him again. He was deep in thought, staring out at the open land beyond the cemetery, facing away from everyone else there. All she said was 'Hi.'

He looked confused, which was weird. Had she said something stupid?

'Tomas Valentine.'

'Kelly Coltrane.'

It wasn't quite the kind of introduction she needed and she tried to find the words to ask him 'Who are you?' without sounding like an idiot. Luckily he must have been thinking the same thing because he tipped his head to one side and said, 'Ruby was your grandmother?'

'My mother, actually,' she said, and Tomas looked at her with searching eyes that seemed to reach inside her and set off flares. 'What?' she said impetuously. 'Don't you believe me?'

'It's just that you're so young.'

'Practically a baby.'

They were flirting at a funeral. Not cool. But she very much hoped that they weren't blood relatives. There was something hypnotic about his lively eyes and Kelly pulled her own away from them because she felt as though she might get lost, just in time to see Octavia heading towards her.

'Kelly,' she said. 'Darling.' As if they were close. Then her plump lips curled into the worst grimace they could manage. 'And Tomas. You two know each other?'

'We're old friends,' said Tomas.

Kelly had a moment to wonder why he would bother to lie, and then she saw the sour expression on Octavia's face and guessed that he was just trying, successfully, to aggravate her. It should have made her wary but it didn't.

Octavia turned her back on him, blocking him out of the conversation. 'Kelly, do you have your own car or would you like to come with us?'

'I can probably get a cab,' said Kelly.

Octavia said, 'Don't be ridiculous.'

Sofia called over from beside her purring limousine. 'Mother, hello?' she shouted. 'I'm waiting.'

'One moment please, Sofia,' said Octavia with an edge to her voice that could have sliced meat.

Sofia was standing with one hand on the open car door and the other on her hip, tapping the heel of her shiny black shoe and rolling her eyes towards the sky. Her Siamese rat was moving around inside her shoulder bag, making it bulge alarmingly. Then Sofia screamed so loudly that Kelly physically jumped.

'*Ohmigod, Tomas!*' Sofia ran over with trotting high-heeled steps, grinning like a loon, and embraced him. 'I didn't see you,' she said. 'I can't believe you didn't say hello.' She swatted him playfully and immediately her sullen face was transformed with a coquettish smile.

Octavia flinched. 'Let's go,' she said. Kelly could tell she was struggling.

'Tomas, you're coming for dinner, right?' said Sofia. 'Tell me you're coming for dinner.' She looked from Tomas to Octavia and back and forth. Kelly found herself largely ignored and was grateful.

Tomas shrugged. 'I'd love to.'

Octavia drew her breath quickly and glared at Sofia. 'Of course,' she said. 'Of course.' She pushed out a mechanical laugh even though a laugh was hardly appropriate. 'Perhaps the best thing,' she said, her mind working as quickly as it could within its limitations, 'would be if Tomas were to give Kelly a ride back to the house.'

Sofia looked slightly put out, but recognized that dinner was a small victory and didn't try to build on it. 'Fantastic,' she said. 'Can't wait.'

Kelly looked at the dynamic between mother and daughter. Did they have anything in common? Her crash course in Ruby had uncovered the fact that Octavia had been scandalously young when she'd given birth. Did that make them closer? Did they fight all the time? Or did they share their deepest secrets under their loving seal?

'Sofia,' said Octavia, 'this is Kelly Coltrane. I told you about her last night.'

'Yeah, hi.' Sofia wasn't bothering to make eye contact. Tomas was obviously much more fascinating. 'So, Tomas, I'll see you there?'

Tomas nodded and Octavia dragged her daughter away. Sofia left a trail of drool behind her as she went.

'Kelly Coltrane?' said Tomas, as if he wanted to be sure to commit the name to memory.

'The afterthought,' said Kelly, by way of introduction.

Max was the last to leave the graveside. Before he got into his car he took a white rosebud from his pocket and threw it down on to the fresh earth. It was a sentimental gesture that he knew Ruby would appreciate.

'I hope you're happy, baby,' he said. 'I hope I didn't let you down.'

Tomas had a car waiting nearby and Kelly's story didn't even take them as far as the cemetery gates. The press concentrated on getting a shot of Sofia in the back of her car. Kelly wondered if they were pissed off that Sofia hadn't given them the second photo opportunity she had promised.

'Did you know,' said Tomas, 'that there was actually a tiny rumour at the time, some people who said Ruby had a lovechild. A dresser saw some stretch marks or something. But nobody thought it was true. There was always so much bullshit around Ruby Valentine.'

'And you? I mean, I don't mean to be rude, but who are you?'

'I'm so sorry. I assumed that Octavia would have mentioned me.'

Kelly shook her head and wondered if Tomas was one of those guys who didn't realize how good-looking he was. Maybe that's how he wore it so well. There wasn't a trace of smugness on his perfect features.

'Octavia's my half-sister. Dante was our father. After he divorced my mother, Ella, Dante and Ruby had a . . . thing.'

'A marriage, wasn't it?'

'I guess you could call it that.' He shook his head slightly.

Kelly mentally added a new branch to her family tree and was glad to calculate that fancying Tomas was not theoretically incestuous. Not that she would ever do anything, obviously, he was more Sofia's league. Even on a good day Kelly thought she was a seven, maximum. She could never get a man like Tomas, he was a nine and a half, easy, with his dark good looks and that sexy Italian charm. Oh, and because of Jez of course, technically they were still very much together. She felt a pang of shame that she could think about Jez and consider flirting with a stranger at the same time.

'What happened to Ella?' she asked. 'She isn't here today?'

'She got sick,' said Tomas. 'And then shortly after that, in the summer of 'ninety-seven, she passed away.'

'I'm so sorry,' said Kelly.

'She hadn't spoken to Ruby for years, they fell out. She

remarried, I've got a couple of half-brothers back in England now. They miss her. I miss her too.'

It was shockingly bad taste that the first thing Kelly thought was that they had something in common. No mum. Maybe later they could cry on each other's shoulders.

Tomas and Kelly reached his car. Was it her imagination or was it the same driver from the airport? In fact, didn't his eyebrows jump up in recognition as he opened the door for her?

They settled into the back seat where there was an expanse of space between them. No chance of accidental thigh contact, thought Kelly, with a modicum of regret. Bit better than a cab though. Was that a TV screen set into the dividing panel? She half-expected Tomas to open a concealed bar and offer her a drink. Instead he checked his messages on his phone. It took a while. Kelly watched the world through tinted windows and wondered if after this journey she'd ever be satisfied travelling any other way. It was sheer luxury.

Tomas snapped his phone shut. 'Sorry about that. Where were we?'

Nowhere really. She didn't want to share her deeply offensive thought about their shared bereavement. Kelly's mind raced to find some of the sparkling discourse that a man like Tomas must be used to. 'What do you do?' she said. *Great, Kel, very original.*

'I raise private equity out of New York for independent film finance.'

'Oh. Like a movie studio?'

'Nothing like a studio. The studio system pays for

predictable product. I'm the alternative for film-makers who actually have something new to say.'

'I see,' she said, though she didn't really.

'Films can do one of two things: they can confirm the status quo or they can challenge it. Wouldn't you rather be challenged?'

She couldn't agree that she would, hand on heart. Sometimes all you wanted was for someone to reassure you that the world was a good place, full of good people. Maybe it made her naive but Kelly liked a happy ending. Or at least, she still hoped for one.

'And you?' he said. 'What keeps you busy?'

She toyed briefly with the idea of making up a whole new identity to impress him – a sophisticated aristo maybe; didn't most Americans think that all Brits were related to the Queen of England? – but she didn't think she would be able to maintain such a complicated deceit. 'Nothing as interesting as that, I'm afraid. I have a very boring job.'

'Then perhaps you are in the wrong job.'

Don't remind me.

'Do you see much of Octavia?' she asked, thinking of the only other person they had in common apart from Ruby.

'Octavia and I don't get on.' His face suddenly darkened, but far from being apprehensive Kelly was fabulously excited. When he got passionate about something his eyes flashed like disco lights. 'Let me ask you something,' he said. 'You didn't know Ruby at all? You never met?'

Kelly shook her head. It was kind of embarrassing.

'Your mother was a survivor.'

'That's exactly what my dad said.'

'Then he must have known her pretty well. Ruby wouldn't have killed herself, no way. Not after everything she'd been through.'

They pulled into Octavia's road. A wide avenue of architecturally mismatched mansions.

'So what then?' said Kelly. 'Are you saying it was accidental?' The idea of Ruby making a terrible mistake was confusing. Imagine if she had simply lost track of how many pills she had taken, with disastrous results. Maybe she wasn't even depressed, maybe she was just stupid. So where did that leave Kelly's new-found sympathy for her?

'That's one alternative, yes.' He said this in a way that made it clear he could think of others, but before she could ask him they had arrived at their destination.

Kelly thought the post-funeral dinner was embarrassingly awful for their hostess. It was a terribly mismatched party of people and even Octavia's much-practised routine was unable to conjure up a shred of atmosphere. Eventually Octavia gave up and drank heavily from the full-bodied red that accompanied their frugal meal.

It was a funeral, so maybe it was supposed to be bleak. But despite the ambiance Kelly still wished she could take a photograph so that she could prove to the girls back at First Fiscal that she was actually there, having dinner in Beverly Hills with a bunch of rich people and Sofia, a genuine celebrity. If only Vincent Valentine had been a more successful actor, her celeb count might have gone up to two. Judging from the conversation she'd overheard, he hoped his mother's sudden death might give his career the boost it badly needed and didn't mind how that sounded. Which was sick. Perhaps he had a lot of repressed anger towards his mother that was just coming out wrong.

Given the choice, Kelly would have seated herself next to Tomas and continued her conversation with him, but Sofia latched on to him like a limpet the minute they arrived. Vincent monopolized Max, who looked increasingly drained as each course progressed. Vincent's wife and children kept themselves to themselves and she kept sneaking glances at her watch. Kelly was stuck talking to Octavia's husband, James Jarvis, and had no idea how to escape. She heard more about the California real estate market than she would have ever wished to.

'Everyone keeps saying it's depressed, it's depressed, it's depressed,' said James.

Kelly knew how they felt.

'But when a sliver of Newport Beach is selling for upward of ten mill, does that sound like a slump to you?'

Kelly thought that if he kept using words like depression and slump she might pass out over her minuscule portion of glazed lamb with coriander relish. Who would ever have imagined that the wealthy Beverly Hills set could be so dull?

James Jarvis had obviously spent a lot of money on his teeth and maybe had had a surgical procedure here and there to neaten his uneven features, but despite all his best efforts, he still had the look of a man who had been dragged from the farm and dressed in a designer suit for a cruel fashion magazine photo spread. As he continued to talk and talk, Kelly's mind wandered. This was her new sister's husband? Had he hidden depths, or had his massive fortune been the chief attraction?

'You obviously like what you do?' she said.

'Jarvis Realty: Established 1993.'

Something about the way he said it made her exclaim, 'Wow!' Like she was impressed. She caught sight of Tomas. He was listening intently to Sofia, but when he tried to get a word in edgeways she didn't pause. He saw Kelly watching them and smiled at her. He scraped his fork across his empty plate with an expression of exaggerated hunger, like a starving orphan. A private joke for Kelly alone. She smiled, and it was her first genuine smile for over an hour.

James checked to see what she was looking at. 'That man,' he said, 'should not be at this table.'

'Why do you say that?' said Kelly.

'He's caused a minor scandal.'

That was fine by Kelly. She liked scandal. She had been wondering what it was all about, the bad blood which was flowing around this table, as rich as the red wine.

'What did he do?'

'When his father died, he made a lot of noise about the will. Obviously wasn't content with his share. Which, I might add, was perfectly fair. It made the tabloids, and it embarrassed all of us.'

If this was the family scene, then she was glad she had missed it. Old grudges and public arguments about money. Octavia sloshed at one end of the table, oblivious to her guests, Max morose next to her, with Vincent bending his ear. She could hear Vincent saying, 'And will the whole tribute be televised or just the highlights? Will my poem get air time, do you think?'

James Jarvis turned away from her and awkwardly tried to talk to Vincent's children, treating the twelve-year-old as though he was six and the six-year-old as though she was twelve. On the other side of the table Sofia and Tomas were deep in their own private conversation, though was it just her or did Tomas look ever-so-slightly bored?

These were Ruby's nearest and dearest? It didn't make sense. A star like Ruby should have had a hundred sparkling friends.

James was talking to her again. 'Personally I've always known that she is – was – a bit . . . you know, ill. Mentally.'

Kelly was shocked. A surge of protectiveness rose within her. 'I beg your pardon?'

'Ruby. Crazy. Loco.' He put his finger to his head and made a sound like a cuckoo. 'Well, come on, honey, the little lady just went and swallowed half of Abbott Laboratories, you're going to try and tell me that was the act of a sound mind?'

She found his flippant tone oddly insulting. 'I don't know, but I don't think we should be talking about her that way. Not today, okay?'

James shrugged and gestured for someone to come and fill his wine glass.

There was a general lull in the conversation and Kelly was glad of a few minutes' silence. Then Sofia's cellphone started vibrating on the table, rattling the silverware and skipping towards the crystal. She plucked it up and checked the caller ID. 'It's my agent,' she said to the table at large, and ignoring her mother's disapproving look she took the call.

Small talk resumed as everyone tried to take no notice of Sofia on the phone. She was growing increasingly agitated. 'There must be something you can do,' she said. Eventually she snapped the phone shut and her face was clouded with distress.

'Are you okay?' asked Kelly, as nobody else seemed to care.

Sofia looked shocked by the question, as if expressions of concern were not common around this particular dining table. 'Some stupid old photographs,' she said. 'Which I *thought* had disappeared.' This last was directed at Max, who looked up sharply. 'That's right, Max,' she said. 'The ones from the Mondrian.'

'Is this a joke?' said Octavia.

'I wish,' said Sofia blackly. She turned back to Kelly. 'A while ago – Jesus, almost a year – I was seeing this guy and we couldn't wait for our car to come around, so we, you know, took care of each other in the Mondrian cloakroom.'

Kelly didn't know how to respond. The closest she and Jez ever got to sex in public places was the occasional snog in the park.

Sofia continued, 'How was I supposed to know they'd have security cameras? I mean, when you're living in the moment, who thinks about shit like that?' She looked up at Tomas seductively and licked her finger. Kelly took a moment to review her family tree in her mind. Weren't those two related? Ugh.

'Max?' said Octavia. 'I thought this had been taken care of?'

'It was,' he said. 'But Ruby was my bargaining position. I told them if they ran the story I'd restrict their access to her.'

'So?' said Sofia.

Max looked across wearily. 'Ruby's dead.'

'Well, that's just fucking brilliant. Her timing sucks. Now what am I supposed to do?'

Nobody offered her any answers. 'Max?' prompted Octavia.

'You may be able to negotiate with them.'

'Can't you do that for her?' said Octavia. 'I'd consider it a personal favour if you did.'

Max was good and trapped. 'Sure.'

'I wouldn't mind,' said Sofia. 'But that relationship is so over. The guy's like a total loser.'

So if you were in love with him, thought Kelly, you'd be fine with it?

The evening, which wasn't exactly sparkling to begin with, went as flat as stale champagne. For a while Octavia tried once more to save it but it was finished, everyone could tell.

Kelly didn't want to be the first to say goodbye, it seemed so rude, but she was desperate to escape. Her first sophisticated dinner party and all she wanted to do was get away. She'd thought it would be a night of fine wine and cultured conversation, a chance to get to know her new family in plush surroundings and get a taste of what Hollywood life was really like behind closed doors. If this was the reality of Beverly Hills society then she really hadn't missed out on much. She thought of nights back home when friends came round and ate with her and Sean around their solid kitchen table, lending a hand with the preparation and then lingering around the table for hours afterwards, replete and reluctant to move. Maybe Ruby had done her a favour by leaving her there.

She tried talking to Vincent. She started by saying that she was sorry for his loss and she was certain she saw brief confusion float across his perpetually smiling face. She didn't think Vincent was callous, just, well, *dumb* was the word that sprang to mind, and she realized that his smile was less an expression of happiness, more a stupor of indifference. She asked how he was, again meaning under the circumstances, and Vincent said that he was down to the final three for the co-lead in a network pilot.

'That's nice,' said Kelly and turned away. She had no idea how to talk to him. It was possible he hadn't even grasped that they were related, either that or he didn't care. Kelly said a mental goodbye to her fantasy older brother, who would teach her to fish and beat up boys who made unwelcome advances.

A voice at her shoulder saved her. 'Kelly?' It was Tomas. He was leaving, much to Sofia's distress. 'I hope I see you again,' he said.

Kelly looked around the table at these strangers. 'Could you give me a ride home?' she said. It wasn't like her to be so pushy, but an escape route was an opportunity not to be missed.

As she removed herself from the table, James Jarvis stopped her by grabbing her arm. 'Don't trust Tomas,' he said. 'He's using you to get at Octavia.'

Kelly refused to take such a melodramatic statement seriously, particularly from a man who had spent the last two hours saying nothing of consequence. Why should she start listening now?

Octavia was loud and overly affectionate when she said goodbye. Kelly guessed it was the drink. 'Where are you staying?' Octavia asked.

'The Peninsula,' Kelly said, and Octavia's eyebrows shot up – she was clearly impressed and a little put out.

'You should stay here, we can always find space for family.' Considering the size of this house for just three people, that was stating the obvious.

'That's very generous of you,' said Kelly. 'I'll think about it.'

'Do,' said Octavia and clasped both Kelly's hands in hers. Kelly could feel the sharp stone of Octavia's engagement ring pressing into her flesh.

There were photographers gathered at the gates of Octavia's house. Tomas's car sped past them in a blur.

'Why do they bother?' said Kelly. 'Surely all they ever see is car windows?'

'You can get a pretty good shot through a car window,' he said. 'And sometimes the gate doesn't work and you have to get out.'

'But that must hardly ever happen.'

'You'd be surprised. Funny how often the gateman chooses that exact moment to take a break. You'd almost be tempted to think that the press had tipped him a fifty to make himself scarce.'

'Is that what they do?'

'Either that or block you in somewhere down the road, harass you until you get out of the car because you're pissed. Then not only do they get the picture they want, they also get you with a face like your ugly mood.'

'That's so calculated.'

'That's nothing,' he said. 'Wait until they're camped outside your house for two weeks, keeping you prisoner, trailing your family through the worst days of their life.'

Kelly said nothing. Tomas was talking about his father. The press had gone into overdrive when Dante Valentine died.

'You'll find out,' he said.

'What do you mean?'

'You can't stay a secret for ever. Ruby Valentine's beautiful lovechild? I give it forty-eight hours and then the press will be all over you. I hope you're prepared.'

She couldn't care less; had Tomas just called her beautiful?

'Do you want to get a coffee?' he said. 'I know a place that does the perfect espresso.'

The first time Kelly had slept with Jez it was because he'd offered her 'coffee'. Now coffee had become their euphemism for sex, as it was all over the world, 'Do you fancy a coffee?' becoming a proposition so blatant that it was practically considered consent. How many hearts had been broken or babies born because of an innocent coffee? Was there really any such thing?

'A coffee sounds great,' she said. She tried not to think how Jez would feel if he found out she was having coffee with another man.

He took her to an unimposing brick building tucked into North Beverly Drive. Inside it smelt of wood-fired pizza and fresh basil. 'Just coffee,' said Tomas to the waiter who greeted them. 'And maybe a dessert menu?' He looked at Kelly, as if it was a question, so she nodded.

'Good to see you again, sir.'

They slipped into a booth at the back, next to a loud birthday party drinking shots of grappa. Kelly wondered how often Tomas came here, and who he brought. He was based in New York, she knew that, but either the waiter had a good memory for faces or Tomas made a habit of coming here. Did he seduce women over the single candle stuck into an empty Chianti bottle? She tried to imagine being wined and dined by a man like this, but the fantasy wouldn't come. It was too far removed from the pub/pictures/occasional party cycle that made up her usual social life. Kelly and Jez ate out rarely: local choice was limited and most of the time neither of them could be bothered to make the effort necessary to leave the house – like, for example, wearing shoes. At weekends they had breakfast in a café at the end of Jez's road but she could go down there with a parka over her trackies and still feel comfortable.

Tomas had taken off his necktie and opened the top button of his pale grey shirt, but kept his suit jacket on. Jez only wore suits to weddings and funerals. Tomas looked as if he'd never wear anything else. He couldn't wear a business suit all the time, though. She tried to imagine him lounging around his New York apartment in jeans and a hoodie, but the picture refused to come. She stopped this train of thought as soon as she realized that imagining Tomas in various stages of undress had only one likely conclusion.

She was glad to get away from the torturous dinner party. She guessed that Tomas stopping off on the way back to wherever he was staying meant that he didn't have anywhere he needed to be, he had just wanted to get away from there too. This shared aversion made her feel connected to him.

Was this just a coffee or was it more than that? She tried to picture herself as he must see her, a reserved twenty-five-year-old British girl with a nice figure. She mustn't assume that Tomas was out of her league just because he was handsome and successful. She was something of a catch. Only in town for a short while, unlikely to make too many demands. On the other hand, practically related and currently going through an existential crisis. She might be a little much to take on.

They ordered espressos and two portions of cheesecake. Not one to share, which might have given her a romantic clue, though she couldn't imagine Tomas making lovey-dovey eyes over a shared dessert.

When the espresso came it had a kick like fresh chillies; the first taste scared you but within seconds you were craving more. It sharpened Kelly's senses. She needed to stop deliberating over whether Tomas liked her – how teenage – and start concentrating on whether she liked him. Too often in the past she'd been so flattered by attention that it had clouded her judgement. Maybe that was why she was still with Jez. Technically. But she had never felt this way with Jez, not even during that first kiss on the beach, a sense of excitement as sharp and delicate as broken glass when she looked at him. It was more than attraction, it was something chemical, like chillies, that whetted her appetite.

She looked down at the leather bracelet still tied to her wrist. She thought of Jez and his matching bracelet. If she'd never understood what it meant, did it have to mean anything at all? She wished that she could just press a switch that would make Jez freeze for a few months while she tried to figure out what it was that she wanted from her future, but she knew that was unfair. Jez had his own story to live, he wasn't just put on earth as a potential life partner for her. And that's what he could be, a partner for life.

When Kelly thought that way she didn't picture white wedding dresses and a lifetime of happiness, she pictured life as a sentence. She'd only had two boyfriends before Jez, and had pulled the plug on both of them when they got too serious. But Jez was a serious relationship from the word go and now he was asking penetrating questions about their future, marriage, children, the lot. Sometimes she felt as though she was the perennial bachelor being sweet-talked into settling down. Jez would say, 'What would be so different if you moved in?' She would think, *I'd live here*, and she'd feel as though a net was closing around her and she was about to be dragged to a place where she would no longer be able to breathe. Surely these were not the normal thoughts of a woman in love? Surely a woman in love wouldn't be thinking of having coffee with an attractive other man?

Tomas kept up a steady stream of conversation, talking mainly about things Kelly should do in town while she was here, speculating that she would love New York and asking about Wales. He asked what her dad was like, said that he had a vague memory of an 'Uncle Sean' somewhere in the past, but that his mother and Sean had lost touch years ago.

'You have to remember,' he said, 'that back then they were a group of free-thinking liberals, practically a commune. Then suddenly the Eighties kicked in and they all scattered. Ruby was the only one to come back.'

'What was she like?'

Tomas sipped his espresso. 'I was fifteen the last time I saw her. The day before I moved to New York. Back then she still carried her grief around like a mask she could hide behind. Everyone loved her but nobody ever got close. Maybe over time she changed.'

Or maybe, thought Kelly, she stayed that way for the rest of her life, never remarried and died alone. The bitterness of the espresso matched the thought.

'How do you feel about her?' asked Tomas so directly that she had to take a moment to consider her answer.

'I'm trying not to judge her,' said Kelly. 'But Ruby didn't want to know me, and that hurts. I know I'm nothing extraordinary, but I'm not a bad person. She might have liked me. We might have been friends.'

'She didn't have any friends,' said Tomas. 'Not in the end.'

'What about Max?'

'He was working for her, that's different. He was paid to be nice.'

She couldn't finish her cheesecake. It looked delicious but she wasn't as hungry as she thought she was. Similarly, she was glad that coffee with Tomas turned out to be just coffee and nothing more.

Back in her hotel room Kelly pulled out the box of DVDs from Jez that she'd pushed into the corner and tried to forget about. Which was the real Ruby? The one whose closest family and friends hadn't cried at her funeral? The one who must have been so lonely? Or the gorgeous Oscar-winning actress who had made all these celebrated films?

She cracked open the mini-bar, a temptation she had so far managed to avoid because no matter how thirsty she was the thought of a five-dollar Coke always terrified her, and she sipped Jim Bean straight from the bottle. Maybe it was time to see the other side of Ruby Valentine. Jez would have known that she couldn't resist. It was sweet of him to have gone to all that trouble. She hadn't even said thank you. She was the world's worst girlfriend. In the last few days she had crossed an ocean without telling him, ignored his incredibly thoughtful gift and entertained the occasional fantasy about another man, Tomas, whose knees had touched hers under the table and whose lips had lingered on her cheek when he kissed her goodbye. He had smelt of lemon soap, and while she inhaled the fragrance Jez could have been sitting by the phone waiting for her to call.

She checked the time difference. It was too late to phone him, or rather, too early in his morning. She missed him tonight. She needed another outsider to work through this with, someone who could see how disappointed she was that the family were not what she might have hoped for or imagined and someone who could tell her that she was doing just fine. She would have to watch the films without a pep-talk and thank him later.

Time to see what all the fuss was about. She selected *Viva Romance*, Ruby's very first movie. Her hands trembled as she ripped the cellophane off the pristine DVD and slotted it into the player.

The soundtrack swelled, a panoramic paradise beach filled the screen, and framed by a setting sun, there she was.

13. Ruby Fairbrother 1968

A light breeze floated across the Pacific coast and ruffled Ruby's immaculate hairdo. She turned her face away from the sea and squinted into the bright sunlight. A short distance away she could make out someone running down the beach towards her across the impossibly pale sand. Ruby knew that she was about to be told off. But it wouldn't be harsh, it would only be the kind of deferential reprimand that a minor crew member could give an actress in a movie. Spineless and ineffective. She could take it.

'Miss Fairbrother!'

Her mother's maiden name, chosen by Max because Norton wasn't glamorous enough. She liked it a lot.

Max Parker had made good on his promises. It turned out that Ruby was an actress after all, just like he'd said. She was shooting an honest-to-God movie, a ditzy comedy set in Puerto Vallarta, playing a rich socialite resisting the advances of a dashing but dangerous suitor, played by movie star Andrew Steele. When Ruby was first introduced to Andrew she noticed two things: one, he was much older than she expected, and two, despite the suggestion of a gut and lines on his face, he was still sexy.

'I'm sorry,' she said to the harassed makeup assistant who had been sent down to the beach to fetch her. 'My hair's getting messed up, I know.'

The girl looked confused, as if nobody had ever apologized to her before and she wasn't sure how to respond. 'They need you back on set.'

'It's so beautiful here,' said Ruby.

The assistant glanced out at the infinite blue ocean, shrugged and said, 'I guess' before immediately setting to work on Ruby's hairpiece.

Two people for her hair, two more for her makeup. What would happen, she wondered, if she ever became a big star like Andrew?

From the moment that her plane landed on the Los Angeles tarmac Max had completely taken over Ruby's life.

'Leave everything to me,' he said. 'All I ask is that you do what I tell you. If you do, this should be reasonably straightforward.'

She threw herself into her new career with relentless dedication. This was what she wanted, to succeed far beyond everybody's expectations. To be extraordinary.

For some people burning ambition came from deep inside, but Ruby was never like that. She wasn't chasing a sense of personal satisfaction; she badly wanted to impress others, Dante in particular, and anyone who had ever thought she wouldn't amount to much. She wanted to prove a point. She was fabulous, okay?

Max set her up in a small one-bedroom apartment. At first his plan for her had seemed outrageously ambitious but day by day she realized that it wasn't as ambitious as all that. With a decent strategy and plenty of hard work most things are possible.

The first thing Max did was arrange to have two days'

worth of photographs taken in two different locations –
'to see how the light affects that face'. When the contact
sheets were ready and it was time to pick out the ones
she liked, Ruby struggled.

'Stop right there,' said Max. 'False modesty will slow
us down. Ruby, I know you know you're gorgeous. You've
got to stop thinking that people won't like you if you
admit it.'

'I don't want to seem arrogant.'

'You don't have to worry about that any more.
Arrogance is a currency here. If you don't think you're
hot, then why should anyone give you a job? When there's
a thousand other actresses who'd swear they're God's gift
to this earth?'

'Okay.'

'Who's the most beautiful woman in the world?'

'I don't know,' she said. 'Who?'

Max scowled. 'One more time. Who's the most beautiful woman in the world?'

'Um, me?'

'You got that right.'

So why had Dante left her? Ruby spent too much time
thinking about him. She replayed their relationship
endlessly in her head, hoping to find a mistake that she'd
made somewhere, something she could torture herself
with further. What if she had played harder to get? What
if she'd refused to share him? What if she'd been more
adventurous from the start, not only in bed but in her
life too? It was only when she was facing a camera,
pretending to be something she was not, that she was
able to forget about him at all.

Max signed Ruby up for acting classes and paid the bill. 'I'll take it out of your first paycheck,' he said, and he did.

She lost what remained of her puppy fat by running up and down the stairs in her apartment building and surviving on apples and black coffee. Two months after that Max pronounced her ready.

At the audition for her first job she knew she would get the part as soon as she saw the senior producer shuffle in his seat to hide his growing excitement.

'We need to talk about the casting couch,' said Max afterwards.

Ruby had heard about actresses who traded sex for breaks. She was wondering if it was a job requirement.

'If I ever hear you slept your way into a part I will fire you,' said Max. 'A good actress shouldn't have to do that.'

Ruby was relieved.

'But if you genuinely find the guy attractive, then what the hell, it can only help.'

She thought back to the producer she had just seen. The thought of sleeping with him made her shudder.

'Just be careful,' said Max. 'Try not to break any hearts before they've signed a contract, preferably after you've been paid.'

'And then?'

'Then you can break as many hearts as you like.'

Despite what the tabloid papers said later in her life, Ruby got that first job on her feet, not her back. A couple more commercials followed, then a small part on a TV show, and then, in less than a year, a contract with Celestial Studios to play a badly written part in this honest-to-God movie. Her career was shaping up exactly the way that Max had predicted.

Everything was different in Los Angeles. London had been a carnival of music and fashion and film and art all partying in the same decade. Here, the movie business prevailed and, from what Ruby could fathom, appeared to be in the hands of several men who were old enough to be her grandfather, while beneath these upper echelons of power the next generation was making small earthquakes. Max was watching carefully. He knew that these cheesy studio movies couldn't last much longer, they were failing to pull in the crowds. Some people blamed television but Max saw the lines for the Hoffman kid in *The Graduate* and that downbeat gangster tale with Warren Beatty which was surprising everyone. He knew that there was always serious money to be made in the movie game. This was the transition period, things that failed were simply making space for the next generation. He spent a lot of time infiltrating the directors studying at UCLA, making friends for the future. He saw Ruby as the new Elizabeth Taylor, a less threatening Faye Dunaway, Katherine Ross with more sex appeal. She had star quality, everybody agreed on that.

When Ruby first read the script for this picture, *Viva Romance*, she had wrinkled her nose and said she hated it. She was required to wear scanty clothes and flirt, and that was about it. But Max had persuaded her to take the job for the decent-sized fee so that she could relax a little bit and be more discerning in her future choices. Ruby did whatever Max said. Why shouldn't she? He hadn't let her down yet.

Who wouldn't want to go to work on a paradise beach, with colleagues who catered to her every whim? If she wanted a margarita right this second she could have one instantly, just by waving to one of the crew. And she was nobody. This was an Andrew Steele picture, everyone knew that. He pursued a number of women in the film. He had a bigger trailer, a massive entourage, and if he asked for that margarita at the same time as she did, she'd have to admit that he'd get his first, probably in a diamond-studded goblet. She couldn't wait until she was as powerful as that.

She liked her job. It was permission to put on an act all day long and, what's more, get paid to do so. Faking it for money. It would take her months back home to earn as much as she would for these few short weeks on the beach. Today she would be standing in a red bikini reciting witty, uncomplicated lines that had taken her a few minutes to learn. The hardest thing she'd had to do so far was ride a horse into the sunset.

'Can any of you ladies handle a mount?' they'd been asked on day one, the horse in question standing right in front of them, foaming at the mouth in the hot Mexican sun, bucking like a wild stallion.

'I can,' said Ruby, before anyone else had the chance. Many of the actresses looked relieved that someone else had stepped forward.

Given some of the nags she'd ridden over damp Welsh hills in her time, the scene had been an absolute pleasure. When they had finished that day she'd been swaddled in a warm coat — as if one really needed a warm coat in the tropics.

Everyone was lovely. And everyone genuinely seemed to like her. Not just the casting directors and studio executives on whom her career now depended but Andrew and the rest of the cast, and everyone on the crew of *Viva Romance*. Mainly because Ruby never did ask for a margarita in the middle of the day. She turned up when they told her to, read her lines, and was no trouble at all. Disappearing for a walk during lunch was her first small act of rebellion.

Back on set they were ready for her. A significant portion of the paradise beach had been cordoned off. Dump trucks full of silver sand were unloading, covering the clumps of ground vegetation which somebody had decided spoilt the perspective of this particular shot. Two lesser crew members were brushing away the truck's tyre marks with their heels, shuffling around like enthusiastic cripples.

The star, Andrew Steele, waited. He was deep in consultation with the director, and (if she strained her ears in that direction) their conversation was loud enough for Ruby to overhear.

The two men had antagonized each other from day one. They'd both been in the business too long to consider themselves in need of any advice. Ruby was pleased that the director was distracted and didn't notice her fractionally late arrival on set.

'But what's my motivation?' said Andrew.

The director pointed at Ruby as she took off her robe and the makeup artist retouched her crimson pout. 'That is,' he said.

Andrew Steele looked at Ruby, really looked at her, for

the first time. She gave him a sassy wink that he wouldn't forget in a hurry. The scene between them was electric.

Ruby would spend a lifetime refining her talent but she would always be remembered for that scene, the girl in the red bikini.

It was the last shot of the day. Andrew and Ruby sparked off each other and both felt good when they thought it was over. But the director, Albert, had other ideas. He insisted that they tried it another way, less humour, more sex. Four more takes followed and the crew started to murmur. This was unnecessary; they had some great stuff in the can. At the beginning of the sixth take Albert covered Ruby's bikinied body with an unflattering sundress and told her to tone it down.

Andrew whispered in her ear as they set up the shot, 'So tell me, can you be less sexy?'

'I can try,' said Ruby. 'But it might be hard.'

'I'll tell you something else that might be hard.' He pressed himself up against her side and Ruby gasped. 'Oh,' she said. 'I see.'

The weary voice of the assistant director interrupted their flirtation. 'And action.'

The scene was stale and everyone knew it. Andrew was furious. He stormed off set and Ruby heard him mutter something ominous about quitting.

When she got back to her room she placed a call to Max. 'I'm worried,' she said. 'If Andrew quits then the whole thing could fall apart.'

'I'll be right there,' said Max, and he was.

*

He arrived the very next day, hiding seriously tired eyes behind aviator shades. Ruby was shaping up to be one of his top clients so he didn't want her to be nervous about anything. He had a feeling that a little hand-holding on her first movie would be a good investment for the future.

'Hey, star!' he greeted her. 'I spoke to Celestial and they're pleased with you. Asking if maybe you want to do a bit-part in the new Elvis movie.' Ruby screwed up her nose. 'You have to stop doing that,' said Max. 'You'll get wrinkles.'

Ruby was pleased to see him. He was the closest thing she had to a friend. They went for dinner in the restaurant of Ruby's hotel. The tables were set up on a thatched veranda overlooking the sea.

'I'm trying to arrange a viewing tomorrow for some rushes,' said Max. 'You should come with me. You can learn a lot from the rough footage. See what you're doing right, what you're doing wrong.'

'They won't let you,' said Ruby. 'Something's up, they're being very protective about this film.'

It was true. Each day the director, Albert, was growing increasingly isolated and refused to let anyone, not even his editor, take a look at the footage. His paranoid approach was becoming untenable and there was a buzz floating around that the studio bosses were ready to fly down for crisis talks, possibly firing Albert mid-shoot and replacing him with a younger, more malleable director. Ruby asked Max what he thought about these rumours.

'It's the same on every picture,' said Max. 'Nobody

knows nothing right now. Just keep your head down and don't do anything they could pull you up on later. I sewed up your contract real tight, they might fire Albert but you're safe, they can't fire you.'

'What if the film stops production?'

'They're not about to shut the whole thing down, they've spent too much money already.'

Ruby picked listlessly at her food.

'Are you having fun?' said Max.

Fun? It wasn't the right word. She was coasting through the experience and focusing on the fee she would receive at the end of it. 'I suppose,' she said.

'Maybe these will cheer you up.' He pushed a small bundle of envelopes tied with brown string across the table.

'What are they?'

'Fan mail.'

Ruby laughed. 'I have fans?'

'Yep,' said Max, with considerable pride. 'From the TV show, I guess.'

Ruby flicked through the pile, thinking that it was vaguely ridiculous to have these strangers contact her just because they'd seen her on television. She opened one at random: You are beautiful, it said, what are you doing next? Can you send me a signed photograph? She pushed the letter back inside the envelope. 'This feels strange.'

'But good, right?'

She mumbled non-committally. It was unsettling. It reminded her of the feeling at UFO, a sense of herself as public property. But this time it would be different, this time it was on her terms. She shook her head from side to side, as if trying to physically shake off the insecurity that always gnawed at her insides. She was an actress now, on her way to becoming a star, that's what Dante wanted her to be, she would have to get used to it.

She continued looking through the letters until she came across one with a London postmark. She looked at the familiar British stamps with a twinge of homesickness. There was something familiar about the scrawling penmanship too. She ripped it open and instantly felt happier than she had in weeks. 'It's from a friend,' she said with delight. 'Sean!'

Max watched her devour the contents, her eyes flicking rapidly over the words, smiling occasionally. Then suddenly she stopped.

'What is it?' said Max.

'Nothing,' she replied. 'Just some people I used to know, friends, they had a baby.'

'Happy news.'

'Yes,' she said. 'I suppose.'

It was very sweet of Sean to write to her and she could tell by his careful choice of words that he knew mentioning Dante and Ella might upset her, but to have omitted them entirely from his update would have been equally painful. Her imagination would have conjured up horrible pictures of all the people she had left behind getting together every night to laugh about her and that the whole Rome thing was just a ruse to chase her away. But they had gone to Rome as planned and were married there, returning for a brief visit to show off their new baby boy, just before Dante started making his Italian language debut for a respectable film company back in Rome. They looked well, said Sean – not happy, Ruby noted, just well – though they were both very tired and their visit was a bit of a fucking rush. She smiled at his colourful language but searched between the lines for something more she could take from his words.

Was that it? What had she expected? That the moment she left, Dante would miss her frantically, un-impregnate his girlfriend and chase after her? That Ella would have to apologize and say that she'd been wrong? Maybe. Was that too much to ask? Life moved on. She still loved him. She felt a burn at the back of her throat, her throat swelled and to her absolute horror a big fat tear dropped from her left eye.

'What's wrong?' said Max.

'Nothing,' replied Ruby, but the teardrops multiplied and fell. She pulled her mouth into a smile yet the tears continued. 'I'm sorry.'

She didn't want Max to think she was pathetic. Since arriving in Los Angeles she had presented herself just as she would to any potential employer. She wanted him to think that she was capable and professional and the best girl for the job. She was still ashamed to think of the fuss she had made in front of him at the UFO club in London, and since then she had refused to let him see her vulnerable. She had shown Dante and Ella her secret self and they had both rejected her. But she missed Dante so much.

She looked down at the tablecloth, concentrating hard on the weave of the ivory fabric and trying not to think of wedding dresses. She drew in the deepest breath she could and tasted the sea salt in the air. She used the napkin on her lap to pat her face and was thankful that she had shown restraint with her eye makeup. She willed herself to calm down and the awkward seconds ticked by until eventually it worked.

Ruby was sure that Max wouldn't mind if she checked her face in her compact mirror; he knew where the money was. Not too much damage.

'Are you okay?' He reached for her hand across the table.

She nodded. She still didn't trust her voice, or trust herself to look Max in the eye. He was the only person that cared about her and his concern might trigger her tears again. He was stroking her hand gently, caressing her index finger with his.

'How would it be if I stayed over tonight?' he asked. 'I could visit the set tomorrow, catch a late flight. What would you think of that?'

Finally she had to meet his gaze. Was this the long-awaited pass? Apart from his hefty 20 per cent Max had asked for nothing. She didn't find him attractive but it had been a long time since she'd met a man who hadn't at least tried it on with her. Maybe this was Max's style and he pounced when women were vulnerable. She owed him big. The temptation to let him deeper into her life was intense. She was lonely. Since London she hadn't let anyone close.

'I'm not sure,' she said. 'It's not that I wouldn't want to, because I do, I just don't want any more regrets.'

Max's expression changed in an instant from one of concern to one of exaggerated alarm. 'No, sweetheart, I only meant . . . I meant separate rooms.'

Ruby's insides cringed in shame. Of course he meant separate rooms. Men like Max didn't wait around. If something was going to happen it would have happened way before now. If he found her attractive, which he obviously didn't. How could she have been so naive? Just because Max was the only person in her life didn't mean that she was any more to him than a client. She was so humiliated that she couldn't even blush. Desperately, she tried to backtrack.

'Darling!' she laughed. 'I know, I know. What I meant was that the most important thing . . .' She reached for the next words but they didn't come. What was the most important thing? Why had she started her sentence that way?

'Ruby,' he said as she struggled, 'it's okay. Honestly. I'm flattered that you'd even consider it.'

She wanted to believe him, she really did, but she still wasn't sophisticated enough to be fashionably cool about such things. This entire night was becoming unbearable and she began to wish that Max had never crossed the border.

'I'm seeing someone,' he said. 'In LA.' He glanced around the restaurant. 'Ruby, the truth is I'm seeing a man.'

Ruby stopped thinking about herself with a jolt. She looked at Max who was sheepishly stroking his chin and looking at her with the innocent eyes of friendship. 'I thought you knew,' he said. 'I thought everyone knew.'

Ruby longed for a deep chasm to open up and swallow her whole. So much about Max snapped into place when he said that. His style. His generosity. His sensitivity. His bitchy streak. The men who always stopped to say hello when he took Ruby out to a nightclub. The nightclubs that he wouldn't let her go to and the reason why she'd never seen him with a woman who wasn't a client. She'd just assumed that he was sleeping with all of them except her. Of course he was gay, of course, and everyone probably *did* know. Everyone except her. Idiot.

'Forget it,' she said. 'I have.' Her gates slammed shut on the closest thing she had to a friend. 'Sometimes I think you forget I'm just a girl from the valleys,' she said. 'I make silly mistakes.'

She convinced him with her performance over dinner, all smiles and lightness, that the incident had been forgotten. She ended up persuading him to stay over anyway, separate rooms. With all the rumours flying around about the future of this movie she might need his support.

As soon as she was alone again she read Sean's letter one more time and tried to picture Dante with a baby boy that wasn't hers. But her own face always popped up in these mental images, sharing a child with him, sharing a life with him. She couldn't accept that it would never be that way. She firmly believed that there was another chapter to be written between them, but maybe that was just another unsophisticated assumption of a small-town girl. It wasn't a fairytale, so it might not necessarily have a happy ending. Shortly before dawn she cried herself in to a fitful sleep.

At some point during the night the director, Albert, was fired and the star, Andrew Steele, was asked to replace him. The rumour mill had been generating plenty of heat but the lights were dim; nobody had seen this coming.

Max heard the story first. He was always an early riser and liked to swim. After a dip in the ocean he dried off and ordered breakfast next to the hotel pool. The hotel was accommodating the entire cast and crew and everybody knew each other, except Max. He hid behind his sunglasses and strived to blend in. It didn't take long for news of the incident to break and it was easy for Max to overhear several loudly voiced opinions.

'Steele's been hassling Celestial from the start . . .'

'Albert *cried* apparently!'

'It's the best news . . .'

'. . . the worst decision I ever heard.'

Max returned to his room and started making calls. By the time Ruby surfaced he had managed to reach one of the executives at Celestial who verified that Andrew Steele was now directing *Viva Romance*, effective immediately. Unofficially he also confirmed that Andrew Steele had given them an ultimatum. Either he replaced the director, or he walked.

Max called his office a few minutes after it opened and his assistant filled him in on some phone calls she had already taken. An appointment had been scheduled between Ruby and Andrew. Why arrangements were being made over the phone lines of LA for a meeting that was to take place a few yards away from where he was sitting Max had no idea. This business was starting to overcomplicate itself.

He called Ruby's room. 'Get up, look fabulous. I'll pick you up for breakfast in twenty minutes.'

His instincts told him this was a positive development. Andrew had scheduled a personal meeting with Ruby within hours of being appointed as director, and that boded well. If Ruby was going to be fired, then Andrew would have had somebody else do it for him a little later in the day.

It was convenient for Ruby that a minor crisis had emerged for Max to deal with so that attention was diverted from the events of last night. With a little luck she would soon be able to forget that she had totally embarrassed herself. Max didn't mention it and neither did she. Her restless night had been blended away with a heavy layer of base foundation and although Dante's face and his voice and the memory of his sexy touch were drifting constantly through her mind, she was trying to blend them away too.

'Are you listening to this?' asked Max.

'Yes,' she said. *Focus*.

'If Andrew asks if you've seen the movie he directed before, don't lie, nobody saw it, but say you heard about it, it was about the little Dutch girl.'

'The little Dutch girl?'

'That's why nobody saw it. Don't worry. He'll like that you've heard of it.'

What did it matter now? If it was no longer about getting Dante back, then what was it all for? *Don't give up*. So he was married, so what? That didn't mean it was over.

*

As it turned out Andrew did indeed ask if she was aware of his previous film and she said that she was.

They met in his suite. There were six other people coming in and out of the room and a second phone line was being installed. It seemed that even the spoilt star could think of a few extra perks if his deal was suddenly changed.

He had classic movie idol looks, so perfect that he was sometimes in danger of seeming bland. His floppy blond hair was too polished, his teeth too straight and white. Andrew Steele hadn't changed his image for two decades and still played roles meant for heroes in their twenties.

'What I always hated about this picture,' he said, 'was that my guy, my character, just kinda sleeps around. It's irresponsible and I'm not happy with putting that out there to influence my teenagers.'

'You have children?'

'I don't, no. I mean other people's children.' He was unembarrassed. He paused as if searching for the perfect profound expression. Ruby waited politely. 'The children of America,' he said. He looked pleased with himself for thinking of this phrase and repeated it. 'One love. That's the story this picture should tell to *all* our teenagers.'

Ruby didn't know quite what to say. She wasn't sure that the children of America came to see pictures like *Viva Romance*, particularly if there was no sex. She knew the children of London wouldn't.

'One love, one man, one woman.' He was getting into his theme, his eyes gazing into the middle distance. Then he focused sharply on Ruby and lifted his hands up to frame an imaginary shot, a gesture so theatrical that she could hardly believe he was serious. 'The question is, do you want to be that woman?'

Were they still talking about the film? She was flustered, saying that his ideas sounded interesting.

'Here's the thing,' he continued. 'There's a lot of you girls on this movie. I need to make a choice. Some people are going home.'

Home was easier to find for some people, she supposed. If hers was not with Dante then where was it?

She listened as Andrew explained the new direction that he wanted this movie to take. He was forcing it back to old-fashioned values, but he persuaded her that this would make it charming rather than dated – 'with heaps of laughs' – and the main female role would be drastically increased, which would probably mean more money and certainly more exposure. He told her about his plans for an uplifting ending which would have them weeping in the aisles with pure joy.

'I've been watching you,' said Andrew. 'It's hard not to.'

She didn't want to go home. This was her chance. She knew she could convince Andrew that she was the only woman for him. She'd always had a flair for persuading men to do what she wanted. Dante might have been able to resist but he was a one-off. She had to exercise that feminine guile and prove she still had the knack.

'I want it,' she said, fixing her icy blue eyes on his and giving him the full force of her most seductive stare. She watched his pupils dilate. 'You'll never find anyone as good as me.'

The balance of power shifted. 'Can we have dinner later?' asked Andrew.

Max pronounced this a major career opportunity for Ruby. 'By the end of your dinner he'll be in love with you, if he isn't already.'

'I'll see what I can do,' said Ruby, and she was only half-kidding.

Max left for Los Angeles thinking that this girl was a lucky charm and he'd better not do anything to piss her off. Ever.

Andrew had sectioned off a dozen tables on the veranda so that their waterside table for two was completely private. There was a candelabra blazing at the centre, the flames wavering in the sea breeze. When she walked towards Andrew he leaped up to hold out her chair.

If there was one thing that Ruby knew how to do well it was flirting. She gave an inspired performance. She had steered away from romantic attachments in Los Angeles so she enjoyed turning it on once more. She still had it.

'Everybody's saying how unbelievably brave you were to stand up to the studio like that,' she cooed. 'What happened? Were you scared?'

'Of course not,' said Andrew. 'Albert was destroying this picture, anyone with the most basic film knowledge could see that. I think the studio were grateful someone stopped it going too far.'

'You saved them,' said Ruby.

'I did.'

'Wow. You're a hero.'

Andrew ordered champagne and shellfish for both of them. Ruby asked him questions and listened with rapt attention as he talked about himself.

His eyes really were the crazy shade of blue they appeared to be on screen. She'd always suspected that they were tinted somehow. So inky dark that they flashed black in the shadows that danced across his face in the candlelight.

After the first glass of champagne she started to relax. She was glad she had taken a pill before she left her hotel room. Another one before bed and she would sleep like a baby.

She had constantly to remind herself that this was business because the more she stared at Andrew, the more she wondered what it would be like to sleep with a movie star. She couldn't help it.

Eventually Andrew turned the conversation back to her. What did she like? What did she think? Andrew was a busy man and the Sixties had almost passed him by. She'd listened to bands he'd never heard of and read books he'd never seen.

Before too long Ruby could tell that Andrew was a little bit in love with her. She recognized the signs. This should be the moment when she pulled back, retired to her room with dignity and left him wanting more. But the second bottle of champagne seemed to be even crisper than the first and slipped down as easily as the compliments that Andrew kept throwing her way.

If they could see me now. Her parents, her old schoolfriends, Ella. What would they say? She had Andrew Steele hanging on her every word. What would Dante say?

'You're smart for an actress,' said Andrew. 'Is that a British thing?'

Ruby drained her glass, felt the warm buzz cloud her head, looked at his brilliant smile and felt the urge to sweep his floppy blond hair from his forehead. She decided she was done with intellectuals; they were far too much hard work. Dante had never appreciated her. What she needed was a man with whom she could feel confident, not tested. Andrew wasn't the sharpest tool in the box but he was a movie star so he didn't have to be.

'Are you married?' she asked.

'Divorced,' he said. 'Well, almost.'

Ruby rebounded on to Andrew Steele with the force of a ricocheted bullet.

She got the part.

It was so easy to have an affair on location. All that time waiting around, all those trailers with double beds. The real world is on hold while you work to create a common fantasy. You spend all your time together, flirting with each other and making coy glances for the camera, kissing for the fourteenth time that day but not being allowed to take it any further. The line between fiction and reality blurs and when the cameras finally stop it feels like the most natural thing in the world to fall in love. You must be well matched; the script says that you're the perfect couple.

Ruby tried to play it cool. She tried to remember that this thing with Andrew had only started a few weeks ago, and how the last time she was in love it had turned out to be one-sided and she'd ended up hurt. And this was different: Andrew was not some self-celebrating director that nobody had ever heard of outside of a small pocket of London. This was a movie star, they were on location. It should be painless to define this relationship as a fabulous fling, destined to be one of her life's great stories, and she told herself over and over again that she must not pin her romantic hopes on a household name. But Andrew made it difficult.

He appeared to adore her.

As an only child, and a pretty one at that, Ruby was used to adoration. But Andrew Steele's particular brand of affection was entirely new to her. He seemed fascinated by every thought she had, and nothing was ever too much trouble for him. True, it was easier for a man in his position to do certain things – redesign her entire wardrobe, extend one of her key scenes, kiss her from the right side so that she looked better on camera – but he was devoted to making her happy. When a couple of other actresses on the film had been nasty about her, this total newcomer pinching a lead role out of nowhere, Andrew had instructed someone to fire them both immediately.

He was powerful. That was a massive turn-on.

She could tell that their relationship was making the scenes between them sizzle. When Max found out about them he had said something about it being the other way around – a couple who are making it in real life lack sexual tension on screen – but he was wrong.

She hadn't realized how lonely she was, or that the emptiness inside her was caused by solitude as much as a broken heart. The desolate space had been so easily filled with the discovery that comes with new romance. She'd thought that her life was lacking Dante and lacking a sense of purpose, but really all it seemed to take to make her happy was the constant attention of an adoring man. Wasn't that a bit superficial? Surely she had more to give than this? They talked very little and had sex all the time.

Neither of them mentioned what would happen when the film ended and everyone packed up and moved back to Los Angeles. Even as the final day drew near Ruby still didn't want to force a conversation about that. She didn't want to break the spell that the romantic location had cast on them both, she didn't want real life to intrude. She was content. On screen, as a young girl in love, she was radiant.

The night before the last day of shooting, Andrew hired a fifty-foot sailboat to take them on a starlit tour of the coastline. That was the kind of thing Andrew did, that was why it was hard to keep any sense of perspective.

This wasn't love. It was an affair, pure and simple. Perhaps it was the way that she could have stayed with Dante, instead of being a fool and falling in love. Andrew was miles out of her reach, a movie star who could and probably would have any woman that he wanted. For a few brief weeks at the beach he had wanted her. That was enough. It was about keeping your heart close, not giving it away. If you were sensible and contained those silly daydreams of love ever after, while enjoying every moment, then even the goodbye could be sweet.

Ruby was so busy thinking that she must not fall in love with him that when Andrew bent down on one knee beneath the stars she thought that he must have dropped something, and when he produced a white velvet ring box containing a princess-cut ruby on a narrow gold band she had looked down at him in confusion. Then he said, 'Ruby, my divorce came through last night. Will you marry me?'

Her mind went blank. Then she remembered what a lady was supposed to say in these circumstances and she said, 'Yes, Andrew, I will.'

Two days later the newspapers reported that Andrew Steele and Ruby Fairbrother were madly in love and had married on the beach. There was a grainy black and white picture of the bride and groom. Everyone agreed that it would help the movie.

Ruby's parents only knew of their daughter's wedding because they read about it in the Sunday tabloids. They realized that they might never see her again.

14

Ruby was the flavour of the month for exactly three weeks. The newly-weds returned to Los Angeles via a short honeymoon in Acapulco. For most of the honeymoon, when not doing what honeymooners do, Ruby had lazed around looking at the third finger on her left hand and marvelling at how quickly life could change. She was married! Just like that. It hadn't taken months of indecision or planning, there'd been no heartache, no picking out china for wedding lists, and there were serene moments during the pretty sunset ceremony when she'd felt immaculately happy.

She thought of all the friends back home whose weddings she'd scorned and wondered briefly if all brides felt this way – secure, radiant and above all loved. She had surmised that probably they did and belated good wishes went out from her heart to theirs. Maybe it was easy to be content. All you had to do was take up every offer even if it wasn't your first choice.

When they flew home first-class, she realized her life was being upgraded, not just her seat. Within a few hours of arriving back in LA she'd left her little apartment and moved straight into Andrew's formidable pile in the hills.

There were photographers at the airport and they had followed her around all day long. 'Ignore them,' Andrew said. 'One smile, hello, that's it. If you indulge them they'll get too close.'

So she'd smiled once, and then pulled on a pair of dark glasses and tried to pretend that the photographers weren't there. It was hard. At first their presence felt like validation of her rising star. She imagined the pictures of the happy couple making it all the way to Rome. After a few hours the novelty wore off and eventually she found the photographers irritating.

The newly-weds stayed in for a cosy dinner that first night, ignoring the raft of invitations that were awaiting them from people curious to meet the woman who had persuaded Andrew to remarry so quickly. When they met her they understood. She was sophisticated enough for any room, but simple enough to please. The public warmed instantly to the beautiful new face. For three weeks the press trailed her through a social whirl of dinner dates and dancing, meeting everyone that was already in her new husband's life. For three weeks Andrew Steele's bride was a source of fascination.

Then a Beatle arrived in town with his new American wife and Ruby found herself forgotten.

Dante was never too far from Ruby's mind but in those early days it was good fun being married to Andrew. They shared a beautiful house with all the trimmings one might expect: a swimming pool, a tennis court, a live-in staff of three. Ruby threw herself into her new position with zeal, casting out all her old clothes and spending long afternoons on Rodeo Drive shopping to replace them. She was Hollywood royalty now, invited to every event in town, and should dress the part. Out went the Biba mini-skirts and dark kohl eyes; in came Pucci, diamonds and false eyelashes.

By the time she caught up with Max, Ruby had formed an extremely high opinion of herself. She had never been particularly modest but Max could see her confidence was riding sky-high. High enough to be offputting.

'Congratulations,' he said, and kissed both her cheeks.

'Isn't it fabulous? I knew you'd be pleased.'

Max wasn't pleased exactly. Apprehensive would be a better word. 'Do you love him?' he asked.

'I'm crazy about him.'

It wasn't the same thing as love but Max let it slide. He was convinced that Ruby hadn't thought this through.

'You've labelled yourself, you know that?'

'I don't like labels,' Ruby said automatically, and then regretted it because she knew that wasn't her voice, it was Dante's. If a label came with a house in the hills and the promise of a glittering career then she'd display it proudly. She didn't see that there was any problem with that. 'What do you mean?'

'You're Mrs Andrew Steele now.'

'I know, and everyone's talking about me. Isn't it fabulous?'

'No, they're not. They're talking about Andrew, you're the new addition.'

'Who cares? I'm in all the photographs.'

'But not the headlines. I have to tell you, Ruby, if you thought this was going to lead to a whole lot of offers for you then you're wrong. We had a plan. I wish you'd asked me before being so impulsive.'

'Asked you what? For your blessing?' She bristled. She had hoped that one of the benefits of being a married woman was that she would no longer be treated like a little girl. 'I don't have to ask your permission.'

'No, but you could have asked my advice. Date him, sure, why not? But why did you have to get married?'

'Because he asked me. He's a huge star, Max. I thought you'd be pleased. Don't you want me to be famous?'

Max could sense her increasing irritation. He pulled back. 'Listen, you're happy, I'm happy. Let's open some champagne.'

'Do you think I should change my name?' she asked.

'No,' he said. Privately he didn't think the marriage would last, but that's not the sort of thing you say to your client.

Much to her annoyance, as the months went by Ruby began to see what Max was getting at. She was auditioning for plenty of parts but nothing was happening for her. She was Mrs Andrew Steele and so people were nice to her, nicer than they had ever been before, but she sensed that they were indulging the wife of a movie star rather than auditioning a serious contender. They respected her position but not her talent.

Andrew was locked away editing *Viva Romance*, arriving home late at the end of long days, and Ruby filled her time with shopping and snacking, learning lines for parts she wouldn't get and trying to stay awake until her new husband came home. She got into the habit of having a cocktail by the pool at six, and then brought it forward to five, alleging a better quality of light. By the time

Andrew pulled into the driveway she was usually a bit unsteady on her feet and needed a pill to sharpen up for a few hours.

Andrew promised her that when the film was finally finished to his satisfaction they would go away for a proper honeymoon. He would leave her notes around the house saying things like '*Jamaica?*' and would whisper in her ear as they fell asleep of the fantastic journeys they would take together. For months she waited.

Until one day Ruby woke up to find that she had become the quiet little housewife she had never wanted to be.

Ruby's husband did not notice her growing unhappiness. As far as Andrew was concerned he had married the prettiest girl in town before she was spoilt by the town itself. She was young enough and new enough not to have picked up any of her own habits and so should be amenable to all of his. Andrew was old school. Husbands and wives led one life – his. He didn't stop to analyse why his first wife had left him and realize that women these days needed more than his own servile mother did. Oblivious, he continued to think that Ruby had done well for herself and was content. She was Mrs Andrew Steele; of course she was happy.

Ruby called Max in for crisis talks. 'You were right,' she said. 'Nobody's interested in me.'

'Interested? Sure they are. But wanting to give you a decent part? Not so much. There is one bit of good news.'

'Tell me.'

'The studio want to pencil you and Andrew in for another comedy. Next spring sometime.'

'Not until then?'

'Hey, you're lucky. Nobody's seen *Viva Romance* yet but this proves they must be confident.'

'In Andrew,' she said. 'Not in me.'

'Keep busy,' he said. 'Are you still going to class?'

'Acting class? Well, no, I'm not. I mean, I've been in a movie and everything, on television. That class is for amateurs.'

'No,' said Max. 'It's for actors. You think you're finished learning? We're never finished, Ruby. We're always a work in progress.'

'Until we die.'

'Maybe.'

'Do you think I made a mistake?' she asked.

'As long as you love him, then no.'

She hesitated a fraction too long. 'And if I don't?'

'Then you probably shouldn't have married him.'

She tried to build a life for herself. Private acting classes twice a week, an afternoon in the beauty parlour, the occasional lunch with the wife of a friend of Andrew's, or with Max. She couldn't think of where to start looking for her own friends.

'Shall we have a party?' she asked Andrew one night.

'Great idea. Too busy right now, obviously, but when the film's finished, sure, why not?'

Ruby remembered all those parties in London that started out of nothing. Nobody had to check their diaries and book a caterer weeks in advance, they'd just end up at someone's house and stay all night, sometimes all weekend. It had been so easy to make friends. Was it the same back there now as it had been then? She thought of Dante Valentine every day without fail. She would give anything for one night where she might feel the kind of happiness she had felt back then.

Andrew started to irritate her. She went from wishing they could spend more time together to being glad when she didn't have to see him at all. Now he'd directed a big budget picture he was anxious for more. He became a sycophantic embarrassment on the rare occasions they were out with studio big shots. He started choosing her outfits for her on nights like these, sending an assistant out to shop for cocktail dresses, each one lower cut than the one before. He was happy.

Then the studio executives saw a rough cut of *Viva Romance* and his mood took a downward turn.

Andrew had done his best, it wasn't a mess as such, but it was tired. So the guy got his girl at the end – who cares? There were more important things going on in the world and this shiny, happy playground of beautiful people didn't have any relevance.

'I wasn't trying to be relevant,' Andrew protested. 'I was trying to entertain. Jeez, can't a guy just be funny any more?'

But you were never funny.

Marrying Andrew on the beach at sunset had felt like a fairytale, and the perfect way to prove that she was over Dante. Back home the fairytale ended.

The more she got to know him, the more Ruby grew to realize that Andrew was a man motivated by greed. He had to have the biggest house, the fastest car and, she finally understood, the prettiest wife. It was sometimes flattering to think that he had picked her out for this role. She tried to be a good wife. But she was lonelier than ever.

Some time into their marriage she began to think that maybe if they started afresh, in a new house, she would be happier. If she could have a hand in shaping their life together instead of slotting painlessly into his, she would feel more fulfilled. Already her irritation was developing into resentment but she didn't want to leave Andrew, not yet. Their marriage hadn't lasted long enough to mean anything – either in the eyes of the law or in Hollywood – and she would be left without alimony and out of work, divorced from one of the most power-ful men in town, nothing more than a footnote in Andrew Steele's biography.

She wanted more than that. She wanted to be happy. He was a good-looking, very wealthy man. How hard could it be?

Andrew liked the idea of a new house. Something bigger and better, moving on, moving up. He should have thought of it himself but he'd been so busy. Ruby was such a useful asset.

As soon as she saw it Ruby knew there was something special about the pink house on the beach. To begin with it was just a page from a real-estate agent, a flat picture of an unadorned house, but Ruby felt something in her heart give way and tasted salty air, heard the lul-laby of crashing waves, and saw herself living there, being happy.

It was early morning and they were drinking coffee in bed, served on a silver tray.

'What about this one?' she said.

Andrew glanced over her shoulder. 'Three bedrooms? Are you kidding?'

'There's only two of us,' she pointed out.

'Ruby, it's practically in Ventura,' he said. 'Don't be stupid. Why the hell are you looking through all of these houses yourself? You can just tell someone what you want and they'll find it for you. Then you won't waste your time going in the wrong direction.' He reached over and took the page from her hand. 'Ventura. Honey, what were you thinking? There isn't a pool even!'

So Andrew might have thought it odd then that Ruby made an appointment to view the house the following day.

She didn't tell him. She knew that she was being foolish. Andrew would never agree to live there and so she was wasting everyone's time, but she had to see it. She had all this time on her hands every day and she felt that for once she could do something she really wanted to do. She would take a secret excursion to satisfy her curiosity. Go and visit the most darling house she'd ever seen. Perhaps it wouldn't live up to her fantasy and that would help to dispel the daydreams she had about waking up every morning and stepping straight on to the sand. Andrew's house was beautiful but it was hollow and unloved. She knew that even if she lived there for fifty years she would never feel at home. But this place, she was half in love with it already.

It wasn't that far out of town. Andrew had exaggerated as usual. In less than an hour they were in the right neighbourhood, with pretty avenues and clapboard houses, tatty at the edges but real, some with children playing on the front lawn, some with empty porches where the only movement was the lazy sway of a swing in the breeze. Wild bougainvillea roamed around fences with impunity and tiny finches scrapped over unseen treasure. Ruby clutched a map in her right hand and tried to quell sudden butterflies. It was just a house, why was she nervous? As they neared the location she caught sight of the ocean through a gap in the houses and asked the driver to pull over. 'I'll walk from here,' she said.

She went down to the beach and started to walk west. She wanted her first glimpse to be the same as the photograph she had seen. The heels of her shoes slipped into the sand and she pulled them off, continuing to walk barefoot.

She followed the slight curve of the beach until she saw the boxy two-storey house, perched on a tuft of dunes, the terracotta walls blazing a lusty pink in the sun.

I want it.

She knew that Andrew would think she had lost her mind. What use was a beach house that they would never spend any time in? But if he tried to stop her then Ruby would buy it with her own money – she had enough for a down-payment. He wouldn't have to be involved. If only they'd never been married. If they'd never been married then she could live here all alone with her thoughts.

It had been a mistake to marry him. She thought it

would be beneficial to her career, she thought it would be fun. It was neither.

What was it about this place? It was as if it was summoning her. She was pulled to it like the tides are pulled by the moon.

She was getting closer now and she could see the rough-hewn steps leading up to the terrace, she could appreciate the way the afternoon sun warmed the terracotta tones there. The glass doors of the house were open, allowing a tantalizing peek inside. Her eyes went up towards the big picture window on the second floor: that would be her room, and the tiny space with the skylight in the roof an office.

A movement dragged her eye back to the terrace. A figure stepped out, a man. She put her hand up to shield her eyes, like a sailor, trying to see.

A few more steps and she was close enough to make out a curl of cigarette smoke from his right hand. He had his broad back to her and was sharply silhouetted against the sun.

In the far recesses of her mind she knew who it was. Her steps quickened, like her heartbeat.

Then he turned. And even though a part of her had known, it was still a shock to see him, like seawater on hot bare toes. *Dante*. She must be dreaming.

Dante saw her and their eyes locked. In a moment she was close enough to speak but she didn't want to. If this was an apparition then she didn't want it to dissolve.

She took the stone steps slowly, one at a time, until she was only a few feet away from him. She could hear her own blood pounding through her veins, so loud that surely he could hear it too.

He threw his cigarette down to the floor and ground it with his heel, never taking his eyes away from hers. 'Now I know,' he said.

'Now you know what?'

'Now I know why this house called me here.'

'Me too,' she said.

She wanted to throw herself at him and kiss him wildly. For months she had dreamt of the day when she would see him again. He hadn't changed, the features of his face were still those that she had traced with a fingertip while he slept, his arms were still the ones that had held her close in dark corners, and the smile that now curled across his lips was still the smile that made her weak. Had he come for her at last? She had to stay strong.

'What are you doing here?' she said.

'Same thing as you, I suppose. Househunting.'

'Here? In LA?'

'It's hardly LA.'

'Near enough,' she said. 'You sound like my husband.'

She searched his face for some trace of reaction. *We're both married now, how does that make you feel? Does it make you feel sad, like I do?* But his expression stayed the same, the lazy smile never faltering.

'I hear you made a little movie,' he said. 'Is it any good?'

She shrugged and wondered how he managed to make a big budget studio picture, starring one of the world's leading actors, sound like a thirty-second commercial. 'Better than the cheap skin-flick you made without my consent.'

'That cheap skin-flick got you noticed,' he said. 'Maybe you should be thanking me.'

He was right. And she hated that he was right. He held her gaze with a self-satisfied smile. He was confident that she could not challenge him or prove him wrong.

He could whistle for his thank-you, she was a different woman now. In London she'd been a child. 'You haven't changed,' she said.

'Does that mean you're still in love with me?'

It took all her self-control to maintain the cool, composed image she was trying to project. 'Don't be silly,' she said. 'I'm married.'

'So am I.'

'How *is* Ella?'

Dante glowered. 'You haven't heard?'

'Dante, believe it or not, I do not choose to spend my time hunting down gossip about you. I don't care.' *Heard what? What? What is it? Tell me?*

'She's gone back to England, moved in with her mother. We're getting a divorce.'

Ruby's heart, which had been twisting like a sapling in the wind, sang out. He was here alone. The Catholic was getting divorced, the marriage must have been an utter disaster. He was practically single. She struggled to control her voice. It would not do to let him see how this news affected her emotions; she needed to stay calm. So even though she had a thousand other questions on her lips she adopted a breezy tone. 'I thought you said you'd never live in Los Angeles?'

There was a moment of surprise on his face that he quickly suppressed. Ruby felt a sharp thrill of triumph.

He had expected more reaction. 'It would just be for a while. I intend to make a film.'

'Good for you.' She hoped she'd laced her voice with the right amount of condescending syrup. Enough to unsettle him but not enough to enrage him. 'But don't pin your hopes on this house,' she said. 'Where's the estate agent?'

'Inside,' said Dante. 'I wanted a moment alone with this view.'

'Beautiful, isn't it? It'll be mine,' she said.

He was staring at her curiously. He was seeing the results of her marriage to Andrew. Everything about her glowed from a combination of expensive beauty treatments and Hollywood power, albeit spousal privilege. The change in her went far deeper than the exquisite lines of her raven hair, styled every two weeks by a French wizard, or the custom-blended shade of smoky grey that made her eyes look like snowflakes on the sea. She had a resilient edge that said, don't waste my time. She was more confident, and it didn't matter that she had to fake her poise to hide her nerves; she could reach within herself to find some strength and that was good enough, it was more than she'd been able to do the last time they'd seen each other. A lonely marriage had made her stronger.

She returned his stare full on and waited for him to speak first. She spelt his name backwards in her head to calm her mind and stop her from blurting out any of the thoughts that were swimming there.

'Good to see you, Ruby.'

'You too.'

'Don't be too sure about this house,' he said. 'I love it.'

I love you too. A rush of sexual desire hit Ruby right between the thighs. As she walked away from him she concentrated on counting her footsteps so that she wouldn't look back. It was all about power.

'Ruby?'

She turned slowly, adopting a look of casual nonchalance. What more could there be to say?

'It was meant to happen, this, today. Here. I was meant to find you.'

Ruby laughed, a carefree waterfall of a laugh that mocked his utter sincerity. 'It's a coincidence,' she said. 'Don't read too much into it.'

She threw a final 'See you around' over her shoulder as she walked inside. It was torture but she knew that this was the only way.

The house had a ramshackle charm that she thought Andrew would hate. Ruby walked from room to room in a dream, hardly listening to the eager estate agent who was somewhat overcome by showing the house to such a famous film star's wife. From the top window Ruby looked down on to the beach, searching for a last glimpse of Dante, but he was gone. No matter, Ruby knew she would see him again.

'I'll take it,' she said, interrupting the agent's boring explanation of the ageing heating system.

She made an inflated offer, to be sure to best any others on the table, though she wasn't sure she needed to bother; she could tell that the agent was almost giddy with the prospect of selling a property to big Hollywood names. Ruby would pay for it out of her own money even if it took every last penny she had. Andrew wouldn't even need to know that she had this bolthole by the sea. This was her place, her sanctuary. The idea of having something that she did not have to share with him excited her. Not for the first time she thought about divorce. Then she remembered the look on Dante's face and was glad she had a wedding band as armour against the effect he had on her.

She stepped out on to the terrace where he had stood and tried to trace the pattern of his feet with hers. Was it too much to hope that one day they might live here together? Seeing him again was all the proof she needed that he was the man she was supposed to share her life with. She loved him. All she needed to do was find the patience to let him come to her, to let him dominate. The connection between them was so intense that she could still feel his energy enveloping her. She could never let this house go to anyone else. It was everything to her. It had brought Dante back into her life. Ruby believed in destiny. She often looked to the world to provide her with signs and preferred to base her feelings on instinct, not reason. It was comforting to believe in a predestined path and so blame life's disappointments on fate and not circumstance. And when something good happened, Ruby did not congratulate herself but felt favoured by the powers that be. The world had sent Dante into her orbit once more and their two courses had collided.

The next couple of weeks were agonizing. She wouldn't allow herself to start thinking of finding him. He must find her or it would come to nothing. Dante liked to be in control. He was the hunter. Andrew, when he was around, was of no more distraction than a fly. She was even able to enjoy making love to him by closing her eyes and thinking of Dante.

The day she woke up and felt that she would crack, maybe contact Sean and try to discover where Dante was staying, was the day he made contact.

Max invited Ruby to lunch.

'It's the lead part,' he said. 'The script's interesting, risky . . . but there's something you should know.'

'It's Dante's film,' she said.

'But how did you . . . ?' Max was flabbergasted. He'd been thinking that he was going to have to do a whole song-and-dance routine to get her to consider it. Hadn't Dante Valentine once broken her heart? It was just the kind of film he'd been looking for. Something powerful and edgy with a serious director. For 'serious' read 'European'; he hated to admit it but they were the most interesting guys to hit town for years, directors whose inspiration was not entrenched in Americana. Polanski, Vadim, Coppola: these men knew how to tell a story. Dante Valentine's call had come at just the right time. If they started quickly Ruby could do his film back-to-back with the new comedy and have a year in the spotlight in fabulously diverse roles.

Ruby smiled enigmatically. 'I'll do it,' she said. 'You can kill him on the deal. I'm the only one he wants.'

*

Andrew hated the idea. Mainly because in a number of scenes Ruby had to show a lot of skin.

'People will find out you used to date him,' he whined. 'How is that gonna make me look?'

'It's not about you,' she said, forgetting that in the world of Andrew Steele it was always about him.

'I forbid you,' he said. 'You're my wife and I forbid you.'

She laughed in his face.

Ruby left Max with instructions to oversee the purchase of the beach house. She didn't tell Andrew.

By the time she got on a plane to go and star in Dante Valentine's English language debut, Andrew and Ruby were no longer on speaking terms.

15

After the success of his debut film in Italy Dante could have asked for any actress in the world, yet he had asked for Ruby. He wanted her. And if he had to play out some crazy power pantomime in order to humiliate her before he took her back into his arms, well then, she would let him. It was the way it was meant to be.

The job was difficult from the moment she stepped off the plane. It was a small airport in the middle of nowhere, though it claimed to be upstate New York. The nearest thing of note was the Appalachian Trail, and the town it served was only big enough to sustain two flights a week, three when the local college breaks began and students fled like freed prisoners to the delights of the city.

There was no one at the airport to meet her. Confused, and after so long with Andrew's army of assistants at her side, Ruby was unsure how she should proceed. Her ignorance made her feel vulnerable. Ruby wasn't stupid and she didn't like the uncertainty that overwhelmed her when she felt as though she was.

She called Max in Los Angeles but it was too early for him to be in the office and she didn't know his home number. She would have to ask him for it the next time they spoke. Eventually she caught a cab into town and asked to be taken to the best hotel there was. After a light breakfast in her room she called Max again, reached him this time, and asked for his assistance. By lunch a car had been sent to take her to where she was supposed to be, a much shabbier hotel on the outskirts of town with trucks roaring by and the strong smell of rubber drifting over from a nearby factory. By dinnertime she still hadn't seen Dante.

Something must have happened, she thought. Have they recast my part without telling me? Have they postponed the shoot and forgotten to let me know? She was so excited about this script and about working with Dante that if it was suddenly taken away from her she didn't know if she could cope. Could the world really be that unkind? She would have to return home to Andrew and to Max who would each have their own version of the I-told-you-so speech.

It was thirty-six mystifying hours later that Dante finally put in an appearance. Hassled and erratic, he raced in as she was eating her second dinner alone.

'They told me you checked yourself into the Washington Hotel?'

'What was I supposed to do? There was nobody there.'

'Let me tell you one thing, try and get this into your head. This is not a luxury hotel kind of film. This isn't some beach party with cameras; this is drama, passion and pain. If you don't think you can handle it, you should say so now. It's not going to be easy.'

All the crew hated her, he said, and the rest of the cast. To them she was a studio starlet and nothing more, a piece of fluff twenty years too late for her time. He'd shouldered all their criticism of his choice, he said, because he thought Ruby could do better. In time maybe they'd be proved right and Ruby would, as they predicted, turn this precious film into a dog, but he was willing to take that chance. It was up to her, he said, to prove that she was a good actress, not just a pretty face.

He was actually being kind of mean. His tone was cruel. Was it awful that it sent a shiver of excitement down her spine?

The film was set in a cabin deep in the woods. The story started simply enough: Ruby played a woman on a weekend break with her husband and his two male friends. What happened later, the psychological torture of the woman, her escape into the woods and her subsequent descent into madness, was a powerful interpretation of rape. The dialogue was visceral; the actors she would work with were highly respected. It was the sort of opportunity Ruby had been waiting for and nothing like the work she had done in the past.

'If you can't cut it, you're out,' Dante said. 'I won't find it hard to fire you.'

She had been supremely confident, but he was making her feel as though she might fail. 'You won't have to,' she said.

'A car will collect you tomorrow and take you to set. Be ready.'

Ruby slept poorly that night, concerned that he might have turned dead against her, but when the car arrived she was ready.

Nobody had ever talked to her like that before. From her parents, to Max, to Andrew, Ruby had always been spoilt. It was unsettling but it wasn't impossible . . . she could handle it. Dante obviously needed to work through whatever grudge he had against her. Besides, she used to like it when he was rough with her.

When her car reached the remote location Ruby noticed immediately that she was the only woman. There wasn't a single female makeup artist, or caterer, or anything. Just dozens of men. The atmosphere was coarse without the softening touch of a female presence. Crude language flew over her head, raucous laughter at a joke she did not hear, a makeshift shooting alley set up in the back-yard with a rusty rifle and live ammo, voices shouting when there was no need to shout. Nobody paid her any attention. Dante was right. They did hate her.

'You made it then,' he said, checking the silver watch on his wrist. 'No time to introduce you to the guys, we've got to start right now or we'll miss the morning light. Scene forty-eight. Get into costume. Let's go.'

She didn't seem to have a dressing room; there was a tent with a rack of costumes and she had to find it herself. A pair of jeans, that was all. Scene forty-eight required her to be topless. She met her co-stars with her tits on display.

The scene was short – her character was seen half-naked by a friend of her husband's – but Dante laboured over it. She stood around between takes, her arms folded across her nudity. Nobody offered her a blanket. This wasn't Mexico. The men chatted among themselves and Ruby felt snubbed.

After they had finished she was desperate for a pee. She looked in vain for a proper dressing room or trailer but there was only one large Winnebago to service the entire cast and crew.

'Where do I go to the bathroom?' she asked.

The assistant director pointed. 'In there, with everyone else. Do you think you can handle that, honey?' he sneered.

She didn't have to take this. If people wanted to be rude to her that was up to them, if they had decided that they didn't like her then she couldn't stop them, but she didn't have to react like a victim.

'So this is what they call low budget? I've always wondered.' She cast her eyes around, taking in the dilapidated trailer and the whooping round of high-fives over at the slapdash rifle range. She finished by looking the AD up and down with her most withering glance. 'Classy.'

She swept past him into the tiny bathroom and locked the door behind her. She took her time, spending almost an hour making sure that her eyebrows were identically shaped and free from rogue hairs, smoothing down her hair, massaging her face, trying out facial exercises she'd read that Liz Taylor swore by, and when she ran out of things to do, she just stared at herself in the mirror. A few people knocked but she ignored them. She would share. But she didn't have to be considerate.

The following day there was a bathroom just for Ruby.

Making *Disturbance* was the most harrowing experience of Ruby's life. Invariably each degrading day of shooting ended for her in quiet despair. She would sit in some half-hidden corner of the tiny set, powerless against the tides of sobs that washed her face clean. She felt as if her spirit was being wrenched from safe moorings and cast out to a violent sea. For an hour or more she would shiver there and, on Dante's instruction, nobody would comfort her. She didn't know if she was good enough.

She grew to resent Dante, adding hatred to the myriad of emotions that he inspired in her. As a director he was worthless, giving her little or no help with her character. As a man he was worse. He obviously harboured a deep resentment towards women and his misogyny was wearing her down. But something always stopped her. There was no denying that *Disturbance* would be a frighteningly powerful film, and in spite of herself she respected his total refusal to compromise his vision. At night, after the tears had dried, she found the resilience to face each new day.

Was this his way of punishing her for leaving him? Did he expect to break her? She wouldn't give him that satisfaction. In a perverse way she was excited by the challenge. Ruby's upbringing had held no place for emotional excess and for the first time she discovered a seemingly limitless potential for feeling, as long as she was faking it. She explored the darkest parts of her psyche to identify with her character and relished it. The despair she found and nurtured could only be matched in its intensity by the passion she had once felt for Dante. And so the two things became inextricably linked. Coupled with the recreational drugs that floated around the set like bowls of candy, the whole experience was genuinely mind-expanding. She might even have enjoyed it if she had had someone to share it with.

At last acting felt like real hard work. Everything else

ceased to matter: her home, her husband, even her relationship with Dante. There was no time in her schedule and no space in her head to think about the future. She could no longer see Dante in a romantic light; he became the enemy, someone to wage war against each day. But her fight did not displace her desire. She wanted him still, but in a different way. She grew obsessed with trying to please him. She seized upon any words he threw her way on set as if she was a hungry dog and once, when he almost praised her, she felt so happy and swollen with pride that it was hard to concentrate on her bleak character at all.

No matter how awful he was to her, or how much pain he put her through, she trusted him and would do anything for him. She thought she understood him more every day.

Dante's total perfectionism meant that filming inevitably started to fall behind. The film was weeks over schedule. The financiers were firing off memos every day demanding instant solutions, threatening to withdraw what little support Dante and the film had left.

After a particularly gruelling day Ruby returned to her hotel to find two urgent messages: one from her agent and one from her husband. She called Max first.

'You sound awful,' he said.

'I'm fine.' Her throat was on fire from an afternoon shooting a scene the sound guys liked to refer to as 'when the bitch screams' and her head was stuffy following the customary session of sobs to release the tension.

'We have an issue,' said Max. 'We're starting to come up on the prep dates for *Viva Romance 2*.'

'Tell me that's not what they're calling it,' she said.

'Until they come up with something better,' said Max. 'How's it going out there? The end in sight?'

'I can't see it. What's the problem? Can't the studio just delay?'

'It doesn't work like that. If they bump *Romance* they'd have to bump everything that came after it. They'd sooner shelve it.'

'So let them shelve it.'

'It's not that simple. Ruby, you signed a contract.'

'I don't care.'

'You don't understand. This is your out.'

'My what?'

'Your out. For weeks now you've been telling me how hard it is there. We'll lean on Dante to get it wrapped up quick and get you out. Get you home.'

Ruby felt something constrict in her throat, instinctively clutching on to this experience from inside herself. 'I don't want to come home,' she said. 'I want to finish this. Just because I said it was hard, did you think that meant I wanted to quit?'

Max paused for thought. He'd never come across an actress who liked hard work. He'd hoped that he'd be rescuing her, giving her one more reason to love him and stay loyal. If it came to it, which would he prefer? That Ruby stayed with an untested production or came home to star in a sure-fire hit? Or at least the closest thing anyone could guarantee to a hit these days. Audiences were unpredictable. One minute the audience wanted Julie Andrews on a mountain, the next they wanted to see some easy-riding cowboy get shot dead off his motorbike. Where would taste take them next?

'Ruby, come home,' said Max.

Her husband said the same thing. Andrew was incensed. 'Everybody's talking about Dante's movie,' he said. 'You're embarrassing yourself.'

'Since when was people talking a bad thing for any film?'

'I'm asking you to come back.'

'And I'm telling you no.'

She continued with the film even as the start date for the next project came dangerously close.

The following week things came to a head. It started normally. Nobody on set said good morning to her and she fetched her own cup of coffee, blind now to the coldness of the crew. She sat with a copy of the script in her hand, committing to memory lines that would likely change by lunchtime.

'You're late,' said Dante.

She wasn't.

They rehearsed a scene. It was towards the end of the film. Having escaped, Ruby's character had been brought back to the house and locked in the bathroom while the men discussed how best to punish her. After they'd run through it a couple of times Dante called for the cameras to start filming.

'I haven't been to makeup,' protested Ruby. She was ignored.

'Go with your feelings,' Dante said to the three male actors in the scene. 'Do what you want to her, don't think about the words.'

At first it wasn't too bad. They insulted her, lashing her hands together when she tried to put her hands to her ears. The bindings cut into her wrists. She tried to fight them off but they overpowered her. She kept waiting for Dante to say cut but he didn't. Later she forgot she was being filmed. When one of the actors, Earl, got close to her, he attempted to kiss her and she screwed up her mouth as tight as she could and tried to turn her head. But someone else, she didn't know who, held her head still and his tongue penetrated her mouth. When he pulled back she noticed his glassy wide eyes. What was he on? They'd all smoked something over lunch, and Ruby had popped a couple of speedy pills to keep her senses alert, but Earl looked out of it. He was aggressive and clumsy. He stood on her ankle as he repositioned himself, causing her to scream out in pain, but nobody stopped to ask if she was okay and the men switched places, someone else kissing her now, someone else holding her head. She felt a rip in her clothes, already tattered from her escape attempt, but it sounded distant somehow, unconnected to what she was going through. She concentrated on blocking out their vile language and fighting them off.

'Please stop,' she murmured over and over again. 'You're hurting me.'

Her ordeal seemed to last for hours and she was exhausted, scratched and bruised and genuinely afraid. In the middle of it all she forgot that she was an actress, it didn't seem important. But slowly, as the men started to tire, she came back to herself again.

This wasn't right. She was sure that all three men were

high on some kind of hallucinogen, which meant that Dante probably was too, which meant that nobody was in control. Well, somebody had to be. She kicked out at Earl, hard, and he went flying across the tiny bathroom and slammed his head against the edge of the bath.

'Cut!' Dante raced over. 'Earl, are you okay?'

Ruby hauled herself to her feet and tried to loosen her bound wrists. When she pulled at them they dug further into her flesh. She started to cry.

'Jesus,' Earl was saying, 'that kinda hurt.'

'*Kinda hurt? Kinda?*' Ruby ran across to where he stood and started pounding him with her clasped fists. 'Does this fucking hurt?' She was livid. What had they been doing to her back then? And if she hadn't found the strength to fight back, how far would they have gone? How far would Dante have let them go? Nothing was worth this kind of treatment. Max was right, Andrew too, she should go home.

'That's it, Dante. I'm done.'

He turned his back on her. Pointedly and without embarrassment he turned towards the set so that she was no longer in his eyeline.

'Hey! Don't do that. Look at me, Dante, or I swear to God I'll walk right now.'

He looked back at her. 'What is it?'

'You gave them drugs?'

'An experiment. It worked.'

'I can't do this any more. I thought I could, but it's too hard.'

'Is the princess finding it all a bit too much? Maybe we should have booked a real actress.'

She willed the tears in her eyes not to fall. 'Why don't you do that? I'm finished.'

'Such drama,' said Dante. 'It's a shame you can't bring that kind of emotion to the table when you're working. Finished? I don't think so. You're so desperate for approval. Where does that come from? You'd never walk.'

'Watch me.'

And just like that, with everybody watching and half her dress ripped from her shoulders, Ruby walked off the set.

She didn't leave town straight away. She needed a night to come to terms with what she had done. She had ruined Dante's film and possibly her career. Nobody likes an actress who causes trouble. Her side of the story wouldn't matter. All anyone would remember was that Ruby walked off in the middle of a picture, that she was difficult.

She'd never thought of herself as the type of person who makes a fuss and in the past she had scorned that certain kind of actress who ruins it for everyone else with unreasonable behaviour. But was it really unreasonable to expect respect? It wasn't as if she was asking for a better wardrobe or a different co-star. All she wanted was to be treated like an equal.

Maybe Dante was right. Perhaps she didn't have the dedication required to be a serious actress. She should stick to what she did well, looking pretty and being the backdrop for somebody else's story. Being the supporting character in films and in life. She shuddered when she thought of how much she had been ready to risk for an uncertain future. Her marriage to money and power, steady work from the major studios, and for what? For a film that might turn out to be nothing more than the extended drug trip of a questionable talent.

And though she wouldn't admit it to anyone in the world, she waited so that Dante would have a chance to apologize and beg her to stay. The way that she had once begged him.

She didn't have to wait very long. A message was sent up to her room from production asking politely if she could make a breakfast meeting with Dante the following morning.

Ruby's first emotion was overwhelming relief. There had always been the chance that Dante would let her go without a word, and at some point she would have had to give up waiting in her room and slink out of town. Her second emotion was curiosity. The meeting was in some obscure part of town, in the opposite direction to the set. Was he embarrassed?

And then she was afraid. Today might be the last time she ever saw him. It could be what they called closure, it could be goodbye.

When she arrived, dressed in a conservative wrap-around dress and projecting what she hoped was a professional and determined front, a quiet, elderly man led her to the top of a staircase leading down into a dark basement and left her there. It reminded her of that part in the crime novel when somebody gets killed. Her heart pounded in her chest. He wouldn't, would he? He was supposed to be in love with her. It was meant to be.

As she descended the steps she tried to conquer her growing sense of dread. The dim light from the hallway above faded away behind her. She felt her way with her hands. This wasn't right. She could hear her breath coming in short, panicked bursts. Tears stabbed her eyes. She was sick of being scared. At that moment all she wanted to do was go home. Not to Los Angeles, but to Wales. Home. She felt a pang of longing for an uncomplicated life.

There were no more stairs. She stood still in total blackness.

Suddenly, with a brightness that stung her eyes, a white screen lit up a few feet away from her. The room was illuminated and she could see a row of empty chairs. Confused, she sat down. As she did so she saw herself appear on screen. And Earl, and her other co-stars. It was a very rough assembly of the film she had just quit. She was mesmerized.

For an hour she watched in silence. She forgot that she was watching herself, she didn't even recognize the insecure, quavering woman in front of her. She'd had absolutely no idea that she was that talented.

She was crying by the time it finished. Quiet sobs that she didn't understand. She was certain of one thing: she had just seen a powerful film that was going to be an enormous hit and one that would stir enough debate to become legendary.

'So what do you think?'

She span around in her seat. He stood at the back of the room, more nervous than she had ever seen him before. His hands were clasped tightly in front of his stomach, twisting into each other as if he was trying to stop himself reaching out. 'Oh, Dante,' was all she could find to say.

'I hurt you,' he said. 'I know I hurt you, but it works.'

He was rushing his words, scratching the side of his face in a gesture of self-comfort that made her heart long for him. 'Everything I put you through, it was all for this. Of course they don't hate you, the crew, the others, of course *I* don't hate you, but it works, can't you see that?'

He came closer to her and let his hands rest on either side of her face. When she didn't pull away he kept them there and looked fixedly into her pale eyes. 'You're too confident, too beautiful. I had to put you in a place where you were uneasy. You can see it, can't you?'

He was begging her. At last, he was begging her.

'People will be involved with your weakness,' said Dante. 'God, Ruby. Please, you have to forgive me, you just have to. We must finish this film. It will be incredible.'

'I can't take it,' she said. 'I know what you're trying to do, but I'm not strong enough. I can't.'

'You can,' he said. 'You already have.'

Her face appeared on the screen again, huge, all watery eyes and pain. A slow smile crept on to Ruby's face. She was indisputably gorgeous, the backlight sharpening the angles of her face so that her cheekbones were like polished marble, the tears reflecting the colour of her eyes in hypnotic patterns, her scarlet lips a flash of life in the endless pale space of her skin.

'A few more weeks,' said Dante. 'Six, maybe eight. I know you can finish this. Being the best means competing, and competing means accepting a certain level of discomfort.'

'Do you think I'm a good actress?' she said.

'Ruby, this film will change everything for you.'

'Why?'

'What do you mean, why? Because you'll win an Academy Award for this performance.'

'Are you serious?'

'Completely.'

It was hard to take in the implications of everything he was saying. Dante's taunts were all part of his unique style of direction? His aim had never been to ridicule her but to empower her? What did that mean? Did it mean he cared? And an Academy Award would cement her position in Hollywood for always, regardless of whose wife she happened to be. Everything would be available to her. But it was impossible.

'Eight weeks? Dante, really I can't. We're months behind already. Everyone is waiting for me, Max, the studio . . . my husband. I would let too many people down.'

He moved away from her slowly, dipping his head and looking, just for a moment, so sad that she wanted to gather him into her arms and promise to stay by his side for ever.

'I understand,' he said. 'Of course I do. That's more important. If you've done all that you can then you must go.'

It was a moment that could change her life for ever. In the years that followed she would often wonder what might have happened if she had gone the other way. If she had remained loyal to her responsibilities and carved out a different kind of life, then what kind of life might that have been? The other path would surely have held its own triumphs and challenges. Would she have been happier? Or would her demons have tracked her down all the same?

It only lasted for a few seconds, Dante looking at her while her mind lurched between her choices, trying to cling to the anchors of logic and reason but seeing only the face of this man she loved beyond sense, this man who wasn't her husband.

'So you don't hate me?' she asked.

'No,' he said. 'I never did. You intrigue me, Ruby. I *see* you. One day, believe me, you will be extraordinary.'

'Do you love me?'

'No.'

'But you could? I'm right, aren't I? You might?'

'I might.'

'I'll stay,' she said. 'Of course I'll stay.'

His smile was genuine, suffused with gratitude, but she couldn't ignore the fragment of triumph that she saw in his eyes. He had known. To him she was weak and incomplete. Even though she took pains to disguise her insecurity, weak and incomplete was exactly how she often saw herself. Instead of being concerned by his perception of her she took it as another sign that he was her soulmate.

He covered the short distance between them in a single step and dragged her close into him. He kissed her roughly on the lips, grabbing the hair at the nape of her neck with one hand. He whispered in her ear, 'Thank you.'

Fireworks sizzled inside her. His lips had scorched hers. Even the smell of him was the same, warm and erotic.

'I'll stay on one condition.'

This surprised him. Somewhere along the way Ruby had learnt to negotiate. He admired her for it.

'What's that?'

'Marry me,' said Ruby. 'You said maybe you could love me, I think you already do. I'll make you happy, Dante, you know I will. Marry me.'

'You're married to someone else.'

'If I stay here and do this film then I don't think we need to worry about that.'

'I can't make this film with my wife.'

'When we've finished, then will you marry me?'

Dante was prepared to do anything to complete *Disturbance*. He was prepared to marry for his art. But marrying a woman like Ruby wouldn't be much of a sacrifice. 'Is that really what you want?' he said.

'It is,' she said. 'It's what I've always wanted.' Her breath was shallow, and adrenalin was rushing through her veins like heroin. She knew that she had him. She could tell by the look in his eyes that he was lost to her. She wasn't just a girl any more, as she'd been in London. She had lived. She was a movie star now. And she knew that he wanted her. It was a moment of triumph, a moment of intense desire.

Without breaking eye contact she unfastened her dress, pulled it off and let it fall to the floor. Underneath she was naked except for the white silk knickers that he'd always liked. She walked towards him on her high heels and pressed her body against him, letting him feel her fabulous tits up close, to remind him what he had been missing, to show him what he was getting by saying yes.

She placed a long, sexy kiss on his lips, working at his belt with her hands. Her tongue danced in and out of his mouth, over his throat, his neck. He groped all the bare skin she had on offer. She teased him, only lightly touching him no matter how much he tried to press harder against her hand. When she could sense that he was on the edge, she broke away, turned around, and bent herself forward over one of the chairs, waving her ass at him. He grabbed her hips. She looked over her shoulder. 'When we're married, you can screw me all the time.'

'Yes,' he said.

'Yes what?'

'Yes, I'll marry you.'

She could have made him wait until the wedding night, or at least until she was divorced, but as she felt his fingers around her and in her all she wanted, with a desire that was out of control, was the feeling of him inside her again, filling her up. And she was so happy that he'd said yes. So she let him. And it was ecstasy.

Six weeks later an envelope was hand-delivered to Ruby on set. The envelope contained a petition of divorce from Andrew Steele. Despite his repeated requests she had failed to return to Los Angeles in time for *Viva Romance 2*, the picture had collapsed, and all of Hollywood knew that she had defied him. Most of Hollywood knew that she was cheating on him too. He was humiliated.

Ruby didn't care. She was part of a new power couple now. She didn't need Andrew any more.

16

Kelly Coltrane awoke from uneasy dreams and found herself transformed into a celebrity. The word was out. Everybody knew about Ruby Valentine's long-lost daughter and they thought it was sensational.

Kelly had stayed up very late the night before in her hotel room, watching old movies starring her dead mother. She had slept deeply, her mind still turning over the images she had seen. When the telephone rang she was more than a little confused. Since when had she had a phone in her bedroom? She managed to remember where she was and picked up the telephone.

'Miss Coltrane? This is Richard on the front desk.' *Gere?* She looked at the clock on her television; it was only nine, she'd been up until gone four – she needed to hold her calls and get some more sleep. 'Sorry to disturb you,' he said, 'but there's a growing situation down in the lobby.'

'What kind of situation?'

'A large number of press have gathered. Here at the Peninsula we like to try and contain such incidents. We have the privacy of our other guests to consider.'

'Huh?'

'Would it be possible for you to see them, or organize someone to give a statement on your behalf?'

'I should come down?'

'That would be ideal.'

If Kelly had been a little more awake she might have reconsidered. Or at least reached for something other than the pair of jeans screwed up on the floor and the t-shirt she'd been watching movies in all night, covered in mini-bar peanut crumbs.

The lobby of the hotel was totally mobbed. She wondered what was going on. She walked curiously towards the front desk.

'There she is!' All at once people surged forward, each brandishing their weapon of choice – photo lens, television camera or microphone. 'Kelly? Kelly Coltrane? How did you feel when you found out your mom had killed herself?'

There was a sharp elbow in her back and she stumbled forward.

'Kelly! When was the last time you saw Ruby?'

'Is it true you're a test-tube baby?'

Someone had a camera a few inches away from her face, another had a microphone up her nose, still another bashed her over the head with his Dictaphone. 'Kelly? Where were you when you heard the news?'

She was pushed from all directions as if she was in the mosh pit at a rock concert. At one point she was quite sure that both her feet were off the ground and she was been carried along by the crush. It was confusing and scary, too much was happening at once. Just fifteen minutes earlier she had been sound asleep.

'Kelly!' A broad English accent stood out in the drawl. 'Chrissie Merton, *Daily Mirror*. What do you think of Los

Angeles and is it true that Ruby wanted to have an abortion?'

Kelly tucked her arms around herself and put her head down. She ignored all the questions and concentrated on edging back towards the elevator, one slow step at a time. Her heart was racing and she had no idea what she was supposed to say. All she wanted to do was escape.

The pack sensed they were losing their quarry and changed tactics.

'Guys, guys, give her some space, yeah?'

'You okay, Kelly?'

'Any message you'd like to send back home?'

She continued to ignore them. A small man in a grey suit slid up close to her. 'There'll be plenty of offers for your story,' he said. 'But bear in mind we're the only ones that'll let you keep the clothes.' He waved his business card at her but she refused to take it.

'One picture, Kelly, just one picture,' said a photographer who had been flashing constantly since she arrived and must have taken a hundred.

A couple more steps and she reached the elevator. She slammed the button with the heel of her hand and the doors opened. She stepped inside and backed as far away as she could, still looking down. The brief seconds it took for the doors to close again dragged by agonizingly as the camera flashes continued but eventually they did close and the abrupt silence inside the elevator was deafening. What the hell?

Upstairs, the corridor was deserted and she slipped into her room wondering if they would stay there all day. Would she ever be able to leave the hotel again? She'd have to order room service. Now that she was safely away from all of them she stopped being frightened and with a shock realized that the wobble inside her was no longer fear but a sensation bordering on excitement.

She was being hounded by the press. Crazy. Was she really that important? She'd had a famous mother she'd never met, that was all. Surely it wasn't enough to send the world's press to her door? All those strangers thinking that other strangers, the public, had a vested interest in who she was and how she felt inside. Was she supposed to talk to them, to sell her story? What did they want from her?

And how had they known where she was?

There was only a handful of people who knew she was in Los Angeles and she tried to think why any of them would have tipped off the press. Tomas – doubtful. Dad, Jez? – no way. Octavia? Max Parker?

She caught sight of herself in the mirror and groaned. Had she really just gone downstairs looking like this? A smear of yesterday's mascara was on her cheek. She hadn't even brushed her hair. She went to the bathroom and splashed cold water on her face.

This was ridiculous. The phone was ringing again. She answered it. 'No more calls,' she said.

'Kelly?'

'Dad!'

Sean sounded worried. 'Are you okay? What's going on?' he asked. 'I've got a lady from the *Sun* newspaper outside the house.'

The *Sun*? She was going to be in the *Sun*? But . . . she was just Kelly, it was hard to get her head around. 'I've

239

got the rest of them over here,' said Kelly. 'Downstairs. Dad, they know about Ruby. What do I do?'

'You've got nothing to be ashamed of,' said Sean. 'Go down there with your head held high.'

'I can't.'

''Course you can,' said Sean. 'Come on, Kelly. Isn't this what you wanted? A bit of adventure?'

There was a loud banging at the door and she jumped. They'd found her.

'What was that?' said Sean.

'The door.'

'Who is it?'

'Dad, I can't see through doors.'

'Go and have a look.'

Through the peephole she saw Sheridan, Max's assistant.

'It's a girl from Max's office,' she said. She heard Sheridan shouting, 'Kelly? Hi, it's Sheridan, from CMG? Max sent me.'

'Go with her,' said Sean. 'Max will look after you.'

'I'm scared,' said Kelly. 'I'm not what they're expecting. Ruby's daughter shouldn't be someone like me.'

'Why not? You'll be fine,' he said. 'Try to enjoy yourself. Call me later.'

'Hello? Kelly?' Sheridan again.

Kelly said goodbye and hung up. She thought of Sofia and how gracefully she courted the press, and winced when she looked in the mirror again. There was no comparison. Sofia was so obviously the rightful heir to Ruby's dazzling reputation. Her dad was blinded by his fatherly affections. Couldn't he see that Kelly would be a disappointment to Ruby's fans? She didn't fit in.

She opened the door.

'Great, you're here,' said Sheridan. She walked into the room uninvited and Kelly could see her inspecting the detritus of her marathon movie session.

'I would have cleaned up,' said Kelly sarcastically, 'but I wasn't expecting company.'

'And now you have more than you need, right?' Sheridan grinned. 'What a nightmare for you. Don't worry, I have a car parked at the service entrance. Why don't you take a shower and get yourself together? Time to check out. Take as long as you need.'

Kelly spent ten minutes under the hot spray and when she came out Sheridan had packed up all her belongings except a pair of clean jeans, a plain white shirt and a change of underwear. Kelly was mortified to think of this freshly pressed young woman seeing all her dirty laundry.

'Put those on,' said Sheridan. 'I'll give you some privacy.' She went into the bathroom and Kelly could hear her collecting all the personal stuff in there. Should she ask her to nick the complimentary toiletries or would she do that anyway?

Mechanically she dressed. It was soothing to relinquish all control to another person for a while. Sometimes the best way to deal with the unexpected was to let someone else do it for you. Was it like this for Ruby? She had Max to hold her hand through everything, all the scandals and the bad publicity. Kelly thought that maybe that would give you the courage to take risks. Ruby could make a mess and know that she didn't have to clear it up. How many times had Max come to her rescue? Thinking about it gave Kelly a shot of courage. Ruby had had to deal with this attention for most of her life. What would her mother say if she could see her now, panicked by a few photographers? She could either crumble under pressure or try to savour it. She had a feeling that Ruby would tell her to savour it.

'Are you decent?' Sheridan came out of the bathroom and looked her up and down. 'Lipgloss?'

Kelly looked blank. Sheridan dipped into her designer purse and produced a Juicy Tube. 'Here.' Kelly applied the sticky gloss and rubbed her lips together. 'Ready?'

'I suppose.' Ready for what? Kelly had absolutely no idea what to expect.

'Then let's go.'

In the elevator Sheridan took the sunglasses perched on top of her head and gave them to Kelly. 'Wear these. Just in case.'

'Seriously?'

'Don't take them off even when they ask you to. Air of mystery, get it?'

'Okay.'

They took the elevator all the way down to the base-ment and then emerged in what looked like a laundry and walked through the piles of linen to an elevator on the other side. By this point Kelly was wide awake, excited and more than a little amused. *The funny side*, she kept reminding herself, *see the funny side*. It helped. She was pretending that she was in a witness protection programme or something, a television show about covert FBI agents and underground passages. Her adrenalin was pumping and in her head she heard the high-tempo soundtrack that would accompany this part of her life story if it was made into a movie.

The elevator opened on to an empty stairwell. 'Come on,' said Sheridan and kicked the fire door open.

The sudden sunlight would have been blinding without the expensive shades. A small group of photographers was running towards them shouting her name. They clicked and flashed as Kelly caught a glimpse of herself reflected in the tinted windows of a black car that pulled up on to the sidewalk. Sheridan bundled her into the back of it. 'Go!' she said to the driver.

Kelly sank into the car seat and exhaled. She thought the shades made her look quite glamorous.

The car accelerated and the press pack scattered, still snapping pictures as they fell back. In a moment they were out of sight.

Sheridan kept checking the rear window for a minute or two, then turned around. 'It's okay. We lost them.'

Kelly laughed out loud. 'That was fun,' she said. 'Can we do that again?'

'You might have to,' said Sheridan. 'Last month I had to move an actress four times before we lost them.'

'Oh.' Kelly had been kidding. 'Where are we going?'

'That's up to you. There are a bunch of hotels we could try but, well, they're quite expensive. Max thought you might be happier at Octavia's.'

Goodbye, free hotel room, she thought. *Hello, happy families.*

Max called Octavia and explained the situation. What could she possibly say? She had a vague, wine-soaked recollection of inviting the girl to stay with them after the funeral. Besides, the closer she drew Kelly into the bosom of the family, the less likely Kelly was to turn on them if she didn't like the size of her inheritance. She'd told Max that of course Kelly must come here, they'd look after her, he shouldn't worry about a thing.

Octavia greeted Kelly standing in the front doorway as cool and crisp as an iceberg lettuce in a pale blue shirt and beige chinos, a white sweater tied around her shoulders. The perfect at home outfit.

'Welcome,' she said.

The driver deposited her bag on the doorstep and Kelly went to pick it up.

'Is that all your luggage?' asked Octavia. 'Leave it, the maid will get it.' She called out over her shoulder, 'Carmen?'

She ushered Kelly into the house, ignoring Sheridan. Kelly had time to throw a quick 'Thank you' at her and then Octavia closed the door.

'Max called,' she said. 'Said you needed a safe haven. Carmen made up a bed in the guesthouse.' She led Kelly out into the extensive back garden, with a swimming pool clad in plastic rocks complete with tropical waterfall. She saw Kelly looking at it. 'Do you love it?' she said. 'We just had it remodelled.'

'It's impressive.'

'Please feel free to use it. There are plenty of clean towels in the changing room.'

Why would you need a changing room when the pool was in your back garden?

The guesthouse was a simple wooden structure

dwarfed by the main house but with ample room for a family of four.

'Carmen will bring you anything you need. You can use the intercom.' She indicated a complicated panel of buttons by the door. 'Make yourself at home.' With that Octavia left.

Kelly sat down on the edge of the bed, noticing the firmness of the mattress and the immaculate white sheets. An hour ago she had been asleep, an anonymous girl in a swanky hotel room that was really too good for her. Now she was hunted and hiding. This was not what she had expected from her trip. Or was it? Nobody had made her come out here. Did she want to acknowledge her mother so that the world would find out? As if in some way the world knowing about her would compensate for Ruby not wanting to know her at all? It still burned. Why hadn't Ruby wanted her to know the truth about who she was? She couldn't help but compare Octavia's modern mansion with Sean's decrepit old house in the valley.

Watching those films last night, Kelly had expected to feel sad or angry but instead she had felt proud, which was unsettling. Whatever she had done, whatever mistakes she had made, her mother had been a truly great actress and many people would mourn her loss. The more Kelly found out about Ruby, the more she missed her. She'd grown up with a dull sense of loss for an indefinite mother figure, but what she felt now was sharper and more painful. She was talented, brilliant even, and Kelly wished she'd had the chance to tell her so.

She unpacked her bag, which took all of three minutes, and lay down hoping to catch up on some sleep. As she drifted away she noticed that the view of the gardens, with jacaranda blossoms gently fluttering against the sliding-glass doors, the distant sound of cascading water and a butterfly dancing just outside, was pretty. Almost as pretty as home.

Kelly awoke to an abrupt cackle. She jumped up and for the second time that day she had forgotten where she was.

The intercom was flashing and a tinny, distorted voice was saying, 'Hello?' Kelly stumbled towards it.

'Are you there? Press the red button on the side,' said the voice, which Kelly now recognized as Sofia's.

'Hello?'

'Great,' said Sofia, 'You're there. I wanna talk to you, come up.'

The house was so enormous that Kelly had to ask Carmen for directions to Sofia's bedroom, and the maid insisted on escorting her, which made Kelly feel both stupid and demanding. They climbed the ornate stair-case, turned left at the landing and walked along a wide hallway. At the end of the hallway was a door painted pale pink like the inside of a seashell.

'Sofia,' said Carmen, and left her to it.

'Thank you,' Kelly called after her. She knocked on the door and pushed it open.

Sofia's open-plan living space stretched endlessly before her. A bedroom with an en-suite bathroom and separate dressing room led through to a sitting room which looked like a stylist's vision of rich bitch heaven.

An L-shaped purple leather couch stood in the middle of the room, littered with black lace cushions and fake fur throws. There was a drinks area with a canary-yellow fridge, a couple of Boba stools and a mirrored bar. A plasma screen was set up so it could be viewed from any part of the room, with a games console plugged into it, trailing wires across the mosaic coffee table, threading through obstacles of remote controls and magazines. There was a haphazard pile of DVDs on the floor. The sophisticated stereo system was humming gently and the display flashed on pause.

On one wall was a collage of blown-up snapshots featuring Sofia with her weird cat, Sofia with a bunch of girlfriends, Sofia on a beach, Sofia at a concert with her arms wrapped around a man with a tattooed face. Hanging on the other wall were some framed magazine covers with Sofia on the cover and a blue neon light that said 'blue'. There was a prevailing smell of perfume in the air.

Sofia was sitting at a flounced dressing table holding up two different earrings to her lobes. 'What do you think?' she said. 'The bling or the gypsy?'

'Bling,' said Kelly, thinking that Sofia couldn't pull off gypsy no matter how hard she tried and that her dressing room was bigger than Kelly's bedroom back home.

Sofia stood up and walked to the bar. 'Drink?'

It was eleven-thirty in the morning. But then it had been one hell of a morning. 'Sure.'

Sofia opened the yellow fridge and pulled out a bottle of Cristal. She squeezed out the cork with practised ease and poured two glasses of the champagne.

'So here's the deal,' she said. 'I had to give that magazine something to stop them printing photos of my tits, so I gave them you. I couldn't wait for Max; ever since Ruby died he couldn't give a shit about the rest of us.'

Kelly wasn't sure that she understood. 'You told the papers about me?'

'A magazine, yeah. But I guess word got out. It's not a problem as long as they have the exclusive.'

Kelly was stunned. 'Why would you do that?'

'Listen, topless shots in St-Tropez? No problem. Photos of me getting felt up by an out-of-work record producer after a long night of cocktails? No, thank you.'

'So you just told them where I was?'

'No, I just told them you were in town. You checked in under your real name? It isn't hard for them to find you. You gotta use an alias.'

'I didn't expect to be running from the press.'

'Hey, don't worry about it,' said Sofia. 'Totally not your fault.'

No. It's yours. She was waiting for an apology from the girl she'd read so much about in the tabloids.

'So we're cool?' said Sofia.

Kelly had two choices. She could insist that no, they definitely were not 'cool', and tell Sofia exactly what she thought of the little media bargain she'd made entirely at Kelly's expense. Or, option two, she could say yes, they were cool, and perhaps get a little bit closer to the one member of the Valentine clan she thought she already knew.

'We're cool,' she said.

'Fantastic! Top up?'

*

Sofia's life was as colourful as a rainbow. Anybody who thought spoilt Hollywood princesses led vacuous and empty lives would be sorely disappointed with the reality of being Sofia Valentine.

'I call myself a model but only because I've got to say something. Nobody has a word for what I do.'

'I still don't get it,' said Kelly. 'What do you do?' She giggled. The second glass of champagne had gone right to her head.

'I do a tiny bit of product endorsement and then the rest of the time I party. I'm under contract to three different venues and I pick up plenty of one-offs.'

'Under contract?'

'Yeah,' said Sofia. 'Like a new club opens up, they want to make sure they get in the right columns and stuff, I show up twice a week, bring a few girlfriends.'

'And they pay you?'

'Usually we cut an investment deal on ownership of the club. The one-offs pay cash.'

'You part-own three nightclubs?'

'Two nightclubs and a restaurant. I'm thinking of opening a bar in Santa Cruz.'

'But why . . . ?' Kelly couldn't think of a way to phrase her question. Sofia was a gorgeous-looking girl but there must be thousands of them. She had a Hollywood heritage but no discernible talent.

'Why me, right?' Sofia laughed. 'I couldn't tell you. I try not to get too deep into that. Life comes in waves, yeah? You can either surf them or drown.'

'This is your wave?'

'And I'm riding it. I don't know, maybe it's because I'm

fun. My friends are a really great bunch of people. We grew up together, you know? We all get it.'

'Get what?'

'This place, a city like Los Angeles, everything is fast – the traffic, the fashion, the food. You have to have the energy to keep up. Los Angeles is a terrible place to be miserable.'

There was something inherently likeable about Sofia. When she talked about her charity work, Kelly didn't feel that she was trying to prove she had a meaningful life, it was just something that she did, another way to have fun.

'Especially when it's kids,' Sofia went on. 'But that's the best part, you get to choose – I mean, leave the obscure diseases and the ballet to someone who gives a shit – I get to take the kids to Disneyland.'

Okay, so Sofia loved the sound of her own voice. But so what? Self-help books talked about the importance of self-esteem, being happy in your own skin, owning yourself; why shouldn't Sofia have her moment in the sun? Kelly had a feeling that plenty of people wished they could like themselves as much as Sofia did. Even her weird cat, which had recently uncurled from a nap on its white fur cushion and was licking its naked bits, had an explanation.

'I love watching people freak out when they see him. He makes me laugh every day, ugly little thing.' She picked the cat up and rubbed her nose into his back. 'Plus I look good next to him. You can borrow him if you like.'

'Now that I'm famous?'

'I guarantee the press would have found out sooner

or later. You might as well enjoy it. You didn't honestly think you could stay a secret for ever?'

'I'm only just getting used to being a secret at all.'

'You only found out like a week ago, right? When she died?'

Kelly nodded.

'That's insane,' said Sofia. 'Did you lose it with your dad? All this time you could have been living the high life.'

'It's not his fault. She's the one that left.'

'So why are you here? Mom says you want a slice of the family fortune but I'm guessing there's more to it than that.'

'It was a shock,' said Kelly. 'I needed some space. I was running, I guess.'

'From what?'

'My dad, my boyfriend. I get this massive surprise dumped in my lap and I'm just expected to deal with it. Like I deal with everything.'

'And how's that?'

'Like it isn't happening.'

'If you wanted to avoid Ruby Valentine's untimely departure then you're in the worst place in the world for that. It's all anyone is talking about right now.'

'I know,' said Kelly. 'I wanted to see her – does that sound twisted? Just be a part of her life, even though she's not here. This is her funeral, you're her family – this is still her life.'

'I totally get what you mean,' said Sofia. 'Plus, knowing Grandma, I bet there's more drama to come.' She went to refill her glass but the bottle was empty. 'Damn.'

She wandered over to an intercom identical to the one in Kelly's guesthouse and pressed a button. 'You hungry?'

Kelly was ravenous. She'd had no breakfast. 'A little.'

The intercom buzzed, Sofia pressed the red button. 'Carmen, hey, hi. Can you bring up some of that salmon stuff with the water chestnuts? And a salad. Great. And some water. Thanks.' She came back to where Kelly was sitting on the purple couch. 'You gotta try this Asian salmon thing I've been eating. Totally Atkins, high GI, everything. We'll eat, then a quick freshen up and then we'll go, all right?'

'Go where?'

'The photo shoot? For the magazine?'

'Today?'

'Come on, you're in the city now, you've got to keep up, remember?'

Kelly ate her Asian salmon thing, which was delicious, and drank the best part of a litre of water to wash away the champagne. Sofia picked at her food and then at her wardrobe, choosing things to take to the shoot.

'You could borrow some outfits,' she said, 'but you're quite fat around the thighs, aren't you? I'm not sure anything will fit.'

Kelly looked down at the offending thighs. Not her best feature, but she wouldn't call them fat exactly, and there weren't many people who would. Sofia was as direct as a smack in the face but nowhere near as painful. Her blunt statements were like the bluster of a tipsy maiden aunt. She got away with it.

'They'll have a stylist, don't worry, but I like to take a

few of my own pieces. Keeps me popular with the designers. More free stuff, right?'

'Right,' said Kelly, as if that sort of thing happened all the time back home. Why was it only the rich people who got the freebies? She wondered if Sofia even realized how different her life was to a girl like Kelly's. Did she think the rest of the world had Cristal for brunch and a maid service at the end of the intercom? It was Tuesday, and Kelly thought of where she would normally be on a Tuesday, sitting at her desk and trying to decide whether to have egg or tuna for lunch, cloaked in mayonnaise and shoved in a sandwich, before going home and putting her feet up in front of the television and watching programmes about girls like Sofia.

On the way to the photo shoot, Kelly gave herself a brief reality check. *I'm in LA, in the back of yet another chauffeured car, with Sofia Valentine, on my way to a photo shoot.* It was better than working for a living. She felt as if she'd stepped into a special world where people told her what to do, but for once she didn't mind. She had started her day following Sheridan's lead and now the baton had been passed to Sofia.

Sofia was checking her eye makeup in a compact mirror. She snapped it shut and focused on Kelly. 'Okay,' she said, 'this is media training: tell whatever lies you like as long as they're not about other people. Stay away from the hot topics – you know, abortion, war, gay marriage, the president – but they're not going to get into all that stuff today. This is a fluff piece – favourite thing about LA, favourite movie.

'They'll probably want to know about you, your life, your love life, your dad – especially your dad because he slept with her – what you think of Ruby. Do you love her? Hate her? Most of all – how do you *feel*? Do you have answers for all that?'

Kelly was dizzy. 'No,' she said. 'I don't have answers for any of that.' The truth about who she really was inside cascaded down on her like rain and dampened her spirits: up until that moment she had been happily oblivious of what an interview actually entailed. She imagined describing her life to a magazine and was ashamed of its quiet insignificance. Finding out she had a famous mum wouldn't suddenly make her fascinating. Nerves cut through the fragile excitement. 'Sofia, I really don't want to do this, do we have to?'

'Oh, sweetie, of course we don't have to. Just say the word and we'll turn the car around. So my tits are in a magazine? So what? I'll handle it. But . . .' she ticked off points on her perfectly manicured fingers, '. . . one, you'd be doing me a big favour and two, it really is better this way. If the exclusive is a done deal everyone will leave you alone for a while afterwards, they know how it goes.'

'No more photographers?'

'There'll still be photographers, but not hounding you, just when you leave the house.'

'Fantastic.'

'Oh, come on. You can't be jaded already. You must like it a little?'

Kelly thought back to that morning, the sound of dozens of photographers shouting her name, Sheridan whisking her off, racing away in the fast car. 'Maybe a bit.'

'Here,' said Sofia and passed her a sequinned clutch bag, embroidered to look like a peacock feather. 'My friend will give me two Gs if his bag turns up in this particular magazine. You take it; if they use it you can keep the money.'

Two thousand dollars for carrying a handbag? 'He's going to want a picture of you with it, not me,' said Kelly. 'You're the famous one.'

Sofia laughed. 'Not any more. You're it. Didn't you get the memo?'

The venue for the photo shoot was a club in West Hollywood. They were met by Tatiana, the features editor of *Sheep* magazine – 'It's ironic, yeah?' – who introduced them to the photographer and his assistant. 'The concept for this piece,' said Tatiana with a big white smile, 'is that you guys are on a girls' night out, getting to know each other. I thought we'd do a couple of outfits by the bar and then get you dancing in some of the dressier stuff. Any questions?'

'Sounds great,' said Sofia.

'We change our outfits half-way through our girls' night out?'

'Don't knock it till you've tried it,' said Tatiana. 'Sofia, am I right?'

Sofia nodded. 'So many outfits, so little time.'

'Isn't the club a bit . . . empty?'

The smile on Tatiana's perfectly painted lips faltered. She wasn't used to people taking her 'Any questions?' bit seriously. 'No, honey. Don't worry about that. We fill in the crowd later, digitally,' she said. 'I know this is your first time, just relax.'

It was a novelty for Kelly to get her makeup and hair done by a professional, something she'd thought that only brides did on their wedding day. When she looked in the mirror after forty-five minutes she had a pleasant surprise. Her hair, with its tendency towards big, had been encouraged. Some people would say it looked fabulous, some would say it looked as if she'd stuck her finger in an electric socket. She was wearing five times as much makeup as she normally would but her skin looked even and clear, her eyes wide and seductive, she had cheekbones. She looked more like Ruby than ever.

Next Tatiana helped her to pick out the outfits, taking great pains to explain that she wouldn't be able to keep all the clothes. When she was ready Sofia took one look at her and said, 'Wow, my auntie Kelly is *hot*!'

They posed and smiled for the camera. 'Don't look at me!' the photographer said constantly. 'I'm not here, yeah? You're out, you're having a wild time.'

A family member died and here they were having a wild time? It didn't feel right to Kelly, in fact it felt stupid, and as much as she tried to enjoy herself on the dance floor in a two thousand-dollar Prada dress, she felt like a fake. She doubted that a nightclub like this would even let her through the door if she was wearing her usual clothes.

Afterwards Tatiana sat down with them and asked them a series of undemanding questions. 'We're trying to play down the dead mother angle,' she said. 'No offence.' Kelly thought that she could have phrased that more delicately, but as Tatiana raced ahead with her interview she didn't have a chance to complain. And if she had, what then? She could already see who was in charge here: Sofia and Kelly were just subjects for observation, Tatiana was running the show.

Sofia chatted easily and Kelly noticed that she used every opportunity to plug her investments. Particularly the bar in Santa Cruz which was at this point little more than an idea. Sofia made it sound like a going concern.

'We're gonna book the best bands,' she said. 'There's a party every night.'

Kelly started to relax when she sensed that the interview was coming to a close. She could handle this, she could be a media personality, no problem.

'So, Kelly,' said Tatiana, 'do you have a boyfriend?'

'I, uh . . . not exactly. Do I have to answer that? Sorry, I mean, I do, yes. He's called Jez and we're very happy, we have our ups and downs – doesn't everyone? – but basically we're okay. Yes, I do have a boyfriend.' Kelly swallowed and her mouth was dry. 'Can I get a glass of water?'

Tatiana motioned for the assistant without turning around. 'I see, and Sofia, are you seeing anyone special right now?'

'Everyone I see is special.'

In a little under three hours they were done and Kelly was in the car on the way back to her new home.

'That wasn't so bad,' said Sofia. 'I really appreciate you doing this for me.'

'It wasn't as bad as I thought it might be,' said Kelly.

'And you're right. I'd rather do a controlled thing like that than blurt out stupid answers to a reporter on my doorstep.'

'Kinda messed up with that boyfriend question though, huh? What's the deal with you two?'

'He loves me,' said Kelly. 'But I think it could be over.'

'Have you told him that?'

'No. I just got on a plane.'

'Been there, done that,' said Sofia. 'It won't work. They don't understand dramatic gestures, you just gotta tell him straight – it's over, now fuck off.'

'But what if I'm wrong? What if I'm throwing away something real just because I have this fantasy that some sophisticated, exciting guy is going to sweep me off my feet?'

'Prince Charming?'

'Right. Is that stupid?'

'Hopeful, maybe. Not stupid. What about Tomas? You guys looked pretty tight the other night.'

'He'd never go for me. Too complicated. He's family.'

'I know, man. Isn't that a bummer?'

Kelly was disappointed that Sofia didn't correct her.

They were giddy when they got back to Beverly Hills. Unlike Tomas, Sofia had made full use of the car's integrated drinks bar.

Octavia was waiting for them, which somewhat dampened their high spirits. 'You're back,' she said.

'Well, duh!' said Sofia.

'Kelly, Max Parker called. There will be a preliminary reading of the will tomorrow morning at ten.'

'Right, okay.'

'I'd offer you a ride,' said Octavia, 'but I have some errands to run. Will you be able to find your own way there?'

'I'll be fine.'

'I'm sure you will.' Octavia was trying so hard to be nice. 'Sofia darling, could you give us a moment?'

'Sure,' she said. 'Kelly, I'll be in my room if you want me. I'm going to a Weezer gig later, wanna come?'

'I don't think I will,' said Kelly. Where did Sofia get all her energy? The sun had only just set but Kelly was already exhausted. 'Thank you for today.'

'Are you kidding? Thank *you*.'

Sofia disappeared and Octavia suggested that they went outside. 'It's such a beautiful evening.'

'Sit down,' she said. 'I have something for you.'

Kelly perched uncomfortably on the edge of a sun-lounger, tensing her muscles so that she didn't tip the thing over and end up in the pool.

Octavia passed her a white envelope. 'I was going through her things and I found some photos. I thought you might like this one.'

Inside the envelope was a colour photograph of Ruby sitting at the edge of a pond holding a baby, her bare feet dipping into the water. The giant grey sky and green mountains were unmistakably Welsh and Ruby was laughing at the camera as if at a friend. She turned the picture over but there was nothing written on the back.

'Is that me?' said Kelly, recognizing the fat cheeks from some baby photos back home.

'I assume so.'

There was a house in the background of the picture, a white stone cottage with a slate roof and two chimneys. Not Sean's house but a view she knew by heart and could see every time she closed her eyes.

'I know that house,' she said. 'It's in Wales, near us. My dad used to take me to sail homemade boats on that pond all the time. Not for years though. There's a bench at the top of our garden that looks down on that view.'

Ruby looked serene. She was happy and healthy. Had Sean taken this picture? Had Ruby looked at it over the years? She must have kept it for a reason.

'Where was it?' said Kelly. 'I mean, was it in a photograph album or hidden away somewhere?'

'It was in her day-planner,' said Octavia. 'Next to her credit cards.'

'Thank you,' said Kelly. 'This is . . .' She stopped, a bit emotional. 'Thanks. I think I'll, um, turn in now.' She had never been forgotten then, just forgone.

'Of course,' said Octavia. 'You must be tired. Goodnight.'

Octavia watched Kelly walk to the guesthouse, only taking her eyes from the photograph when she needed to find the doorknob. It was a calculated risk to give Kelly the photograph and tell her the truth about where she'd found it. An emotional tie to Ruby might send Kelly running off to a lawyer, but more likely, she hoped, it would satisfy Kelly and send her home.

17

Octavia arrived at CMG at twenty to ten. Max was due to read Ruby's will at ten o'clock.

'I just wondered,' she said to Sheridan, who was despatched to make sure that a hideously early Octavia was comfortable, 'if I might have a few minutes alone with Max first.'

'He's got to make two very urgent calls,' said Sheridan – she suspected that Max would be reluctant to grant Octavia a private audience – 'but let me see what I can do.' Which left her options.

Max waited until five minutes to ten and then told Sheridan to show Octavia in.

'How are you?' he asked, and they air-kissed.

'Fine. You?' Octavia had no intention of wasting any time on pleasantries. Despite her fondness for Max Parker she didn't care for the unnaturally close relationship he'd had with her mother. Max had been in her life for as long as she could remember. Octavia had exploited the relationship to her own end and she'd asked him for plenty of free advice, but he was often hard to reach and she suspected that he dodged her calls. As of today, she intended to retain alternative counsel. James played golf with a lawyer who was much more accessible.

Max was avoiding her eyes. She didn't trust him.

'I'm still a little numb inside, I think,' he said.

Octavia was momentarily confused and then realized that Max must be talking about Ruby's suicide. Didn't the man know how to move on?

'Do you think we'll ever know why she did it?' Max asked.

Octavia kept her thoughts to herself. *Because she was a self-pitying lush.* 'It haunts me, Max, it really does, but I don't think we should try and judge her actions.' She tried for a smile that conveyed benevolence, grief and dignity, but the result was an unflattering grimace. She waited for a beat of three, out of respect, and then continued.

'I'm having cash-flow problems,' she said. 'James is waiting to close an enormous deal but we all know that the real-estate market is not what it once was. The funeral planner sent me a bill for the funeral which I can't pay; I assumed CMG would be picking it up. You know that Ruby used to contribute to the household, and presumably that won't happen any more.'

Max was well aware of the monthly sum that Ruby paid to prop up the Valentine–Jarvis finances. Personally he thought that James Jarvis was the most spectacularly unsuccessful real-estate agent at the high end of the game. He gave the appearance of wealth but he was not a rich man. Someone with limited skills like Jarvis should be dealing in one-bed/one-bath condos and turning them over cheap and quick, not trying to move multi-million-dollar mansions, but his wife's steady income meant that the pressure simply wasn't there. As long as he shifted a handful of properties every year they could maintain the lifestyle of excess and leisure that they loved. Max thought it was shameful, but Ruby used to say that

Octavia had already been unfortunate enough to make a bad marriage and she shouldn't be made to pay for it in more ways than one. Max dutifully saw to it that Octavia's steady drip-feed of cash continued.

'Give me the bill,' he said. 'I'm sure we can take care of it.'

'I hope so.' She pulled the papers out of her bag. Max glanced at them and saw that the fee for the private funeral was tiny, dwarfed by the many thousands CMG had contributed towards the cost of the elaborate tribute still to come.

'How long do you think,' she said, 'before it's all legal? The inheritance, I mean. Believe me, I don't want to sound mercenary but it would allow me to plan.' The prospect of riches glittered in her eyes like sexual excitement. Max needed to curb her expectations.

'Octavia,' he said, searching for the words that he had rehearsed in the car on the way to work, 'Ruby was a fantastic television actress, but she was a television actress all the same. I get the impression that you may be over-estimating her wealth.'

Octavia tried not to react but her heart took a dive. 'She wasn't a television actress, Max. She was a movie star.'

'Sure, a long time ago, way before movie stars made serious money.'

'What are you saying?'

'There's the house of course,' Max continued, 'but it's a considerably modest piece of real estate.'

Octavia had taken the liberty of getting an independent valuation, so she knew that 'considerably modest' was an understatement. The house was a steal for three bedrooms and a sea view. But Octavia also knew that her mother would have been able to afford a house ten times as expensive and only stayed out at the shore for sentimental reasons. 'So, all in, what are we talking?'

Max braced himself. 'Around one point seven.'

Octavia felt like crying. One point seven million wouldn't even pay off the mortgage. They also had considerable store-card debts. James had talked about giving up work, maybe writing a book about the Civil War. That would have to be put on hold. She was so busy revising her calculations and dreams that the sheer absurdity of the figure escaped her for several seconds.

'Hold on,' she said finally. 'That's impossible.'

'I'm afraid not.' Max had been waiting for the explosion.

'Max, my mother was the most tight-fisted woman I know. She'd buy two of anything that was on sale. She had very few excesses and worked at the top of her game for the last four decades. You're telling me that all she has to show for her life is one point seven million dollars and a beach house?'

'No. That's not what I'm saying.'

'Thank you, Max, I was seriously worried there.'

'It's one point seven *including* the house,' said Max. 'Or thereabouts,' he added, woefully aware that the difference would be minimal.

For a moment Max actually thought that Octavia would faint. Her eyes glazed over and she seemed to sway in her chair. She dragged in a lungful of air through clenched teeth and struggled to focus.

'Why, that can't be,' she said, sounding faintly like Scarlett O'Hara.

Max held her hand as if he had just told her of a death in the family. Octavia bit back her tears and used every ounce of grace she had to recover her composure. She gave a gay little laugh that wasn't fooling anyone. 'How is that possible?'

'Just because Ruby worked constantly she gave the impression of being extremely successful, and she was, but she wasn't wealthy. She did movies before they were expensive and television when it was cheap.'

'But her deal for *Next of Kin* was huge. I read about it.'

'That was a three-year deal. Eventually it would have made her rich, but you have to realize *Next of Kin* was always a risky project; everyone involved wanted to make sure they had a hit on their hands before doling out inflated salaries,' said Max.

'Everyone involved meaning you? You're a producer on the show.'

'It was in my interests to make sure that Ruby was paid as much as possible. My first loyalty was always to her.'

Octavia was horrified. She was known as Ruby's daughter, now Ruby's orphaned daughter, and with that came a certain status. Without money to back it up such a reputation was worthless. One point seven million was a paltry fortune by Hollywood standards. A fresh horror dawned on her. An abomination. She might have to get a job.

'My mother had a share in the profits,' she said. 'There must be more money, there simply must be.'

'Her points didn't kick in until season three, I'm afraid.'

Max felt a stab of sympathy for Octavia. It couldn't be easy to suddenly realize that you had to fend for yourself, that the safety net of Ruby's maternal generosity had finally been snatched away. Max had watched Octavia grow up spoilt; she didn't have the means to be self-sufficient and her husband wouldn't be much help. 'I know this is a shock,' he said gently, 'but properly invested one point seven million will bring in a substantial return. I'd be happy to advise you.'

'You honestly think I would take advice from you?' spat Octavia. 'One point seven is a joke. You were solely responsible for Ruby's financial affairs, so if this is the sum of decades of hard work you'll forgive me if I take my business elsewhere. How much did she make you over the years? You have a house in Malibu worth five times as much.' Octavia's voice was rising to an alarming pitch. Max fought the impulse to tell her to hush, knowing that she wouldn't respond well to such a request. 'What's your cut of Ruby Valentine? Twenty per cent? Thirty? Did you make her change her will when you saw she was on the edge?'

Max tried laying a conciliatory hand over hers on the desk top but she pulled away as if she had been burned.

'I'll have you investigated,' said Octavia with a note of triumph in her voice. 'I want to know about every commission that you took and I want you to justify it. This is embezzlement.' Octavia pushed her chair back and stood as tall as her diminutive frame would allow. 'You're a common thief,' she shouted, and in his outer office a bunch of people turned to stare.

'Sit down!' hissed Max, and stood up to put a restraining hand on her shoulder.

'Take your hands off me,' shrieked Octavia, but she sat down all the same. She didn't want to make an exhibition of herself. This was too much information for a brain which was soft from lack of use. The most pressing concern of this week until now had been deciding a colour scheme for the new master bathroom.

A fresh thought came to her. 'What about the rubies, Max?'

'We'll come to that.' Max walked to the door and opened it, grateful for air that wasn't contaminated by Octavia's blatant avarice.

'Sheridan? Are the others here?' he asked. 'Send them in.'

Kelly could sense the tension in the room and she thought that Vincent could feel it too. They looked from Octavia, who was pink-cheeked and breathless, to Max who was fussing unnecessarily with papers on his desk. Vincent gave Kelly a weak smile which she returned, and then Max began speaking in the formal tone he reserved for special occasions.

'The last will and testament of Ruby Valentine has been in place since 1985 and an insubstantial amendment was notarized in 2003,' said Max. Kelly didn't miss the firm eye contact he made with Octavia as he began. 'This is a preliminary reading and it's very straightforward, so if there are no objections I think the best thing for me to do would be to progress directly to the pages that contain her final wishes.'

He paused, presumably waiting for objections. Octavia looked at the floor.

'It states: "My entire estate shall be split equally between my son Vincent and my daughter Octavia."'

Octavia relaxed an infinitesimal amount. At least the little half-sister wouldn't be taking any of her share.

'My estate as herein defined shall consist of all my assets in their entirety excluding the items detailed below.' He turned a page and kept on reading. 'I would like my youngest daughter Kelly Coltrane to have my jewels, which are currently entrusted to a secure insured facility at Western Bank, 1368 Olive Drive. These are to be retained or sold as she sees fit but my intention was to provide for her secure future.'

Cha-ching. Kelly got the impression that these jewels were not costume. A secure future?

Octavia was livid. 'Objection!'

Max almost laughed. 'This isn't a courtroom, Octavia. You're not a lawyer.'

Octavia stood up and turned on Kelly. 'Are you happy now?'

Kelly didn't know how to respond.

'Octavia, give her a break,' said Vincent.

'Shut up,' said Octavia. 'You have no idea. How much do you think our mother was worth? Go on, guess.'

'Sit down,' said Vincent. 'You're making a scene.'

'I don't care! I'll tell you, shall I? One point seven. That's everything, the house, the investments, everything. The rubies are the only asset worth a damn.'

Vincent's eyes widened briefly with surprise. 'Is that right?' he asked Max.

'It's approximate, but yes, about that.'

Kelly found it unpleasant to listen to people scrapping over what was to her an obscene amount of money. She tuned out and considered what it meant to be in Ruby's final thoughts. As she grasped the notion that Ruby had remembered her, a final dam of resistance broke inside and tears welled up in her eyes. She tried anxiously to swallow the lump in her throat but it was too late. The tears that she had failed to shed at the funeral streamed down her face as she considered what she had lost. Someone who was looking out for her future, someone who'd always cared. Something that she had wanted for as long as she could remember. A mother.

'Are you crying?' Octavia looked down on her with contempt, breaking off her rant. 'Stop it! How dare you?'

Kelly was so shocked that her tears dried instantly.

Octavia turned to Vincent and raised her hands in submission. 'Do you have a lawyer? We can sustain it.'

'You mean contest it?'

'You know exactly what I mean.'

'Hey, listen, on what grounds?' said Vincent. 'Okay, so maybe it's a little shy of your ideal figure, but I don't know if I want to get into all that.'

'A *little* shy?' Octavia didn't know what to do next. She needed legal advice and most unfortunately she'd normally go to Max for that kind of thing.

Max passed Kelly a box of tissues from his desk. 'Why doesn't everyone just calm down?' Kelly blew her nose on a man-sized white Kleenex.

Vincent checked his watch and wondered if he'd make the audition he had scheduled for noon. It was starting to look as if he might need the money. Unlike his sister, Vincent wouldn't be lost without his mother's wealth; he wasn't a great actor but it paid the bills. And unlike Octavia, he thought that one point seven million split two ways sounded like a proper windfall. Enough to move into a nice big house and take the whole family on holiday to Aruba. He wouldn't be inviting Octavia. She was spoilt. He blamed their mother. In fact, Vincent blamed their mother for quite a lot.

Octavia sat down, arms crossed, defiant. 'Everything in the house is mine? She only gets whatever's at the bank?'

'That's correct,' said Max.

'She has a safe at the beach house. I know the combination. Vincent? Are you coming with me?'

Vincent shuffled in his seat. Kelly got the impression he was scared of his sister and she didn't blame him – right now she was scared of her sister too. 'I have to do something,' he said.

'Fine, I'll go on my own. Kelly – we'll talk about this later.'

Kelly felt as if she'd just been scolded.

The house was under twenty-four-hour protection: there had been reports of fans gathering for vigils outside and so Max had arranged for armed security staff to stand guard. Octavia called ahead to make sure that she was expected. This was an excellent idea, she should have done it earlier. There were a number of pieces at the house that would look wonderful displayed in her home, including a valuable Orla Mackey vase which would be perfect for the dining room. The uniformed guard on the front gate looked up from his meatball sandwich, checked Octavia's driving licence and waved her through.

Bouquets of slowly decomposing flowers were crowded around the porch and Octavia picked through them with distaste. She supposed something ought to be done about them. She opened the door and her jaw dropped in horror.

The place was a mess. More flowers covered the floor in the hallway and the fetid, sweet stench almost made Octavia retch. Dusty cellophane crunched beneath her feet as she walked into the main living room. By the fireplace burnt-out candles had spilt their hot wax over the flagstones and on to the wool carpet. There were pictures of Ruby everywhere. Trimmed from magazines and scrawled with brief messages of devotion, they covered all the walls like a grotesque art gallery. People had written their condolences wherever there was space and the indelible graffiti crammed into the gaps between the tattered images of Ruby. Octavia pushed aside the rotting floral tributes with the point of her snakeskin court shoe and started to climb the stairs. With a squeal of anguish she realized there was a big empty space on the landing where her coveted vase should be.

In the bedroom she noticed more missing items. Ruby's wardrobe had been totally decimated and only scraps of clothing survived. Everyone had taken some sort of memento. A glance up at the mantel in the master bedroom confirmed that Ruby's Academy Awards had gone too.

Octavia retraced her steps and confronted the guard on the front gate mercilessly. 'What on earth is going on? This place is supposed to be under constant protection. It's a mess in there, things have been taken.'

'Yes, ma'am, that's why it's under protection,' he said. Was he mocking her? Octavia checked for a smirk but his young face was devoid of expression and he looked dead ahead. Ex-military, she could always spot them.

She returned upstairs and slipped open the fake back of the closet. She was fearful of what she might see but the safe was untouched. Her fingers tapped in some familiar digits, the date of her father's death, on the electronic combination. There was an agonizing moment of delay and she was terrified that Ruby had changed the magic number, but then the metal door swung cleanly open.

Inside there was two thousand dollars in cash, Ruby's passport and a plain gold wedding band. That was it.

Octavia could see that the safe didn't contain anything else but she launched a fruitless search regardless. She simply couldn't believe it. The house was trashed and everything of value had gone. What other day-to-day items had they stolen? She realized that the moment Ruby's death was announced somebody should have foreseen this and put a guard on the house immediately. Surely this wasn't all her fault?

Octavia pocketed the cash and called Max from the car. 'It's like the shrine from hell.'

'I know,' he said. 'But everything's insured, it's represented in the estate. Do you want me to arrange for someone to come in and clean up?'

'Yes, of course,' said Octavia, 'I'm very upset that you haven't done it already. That's your responsibility.'

Not really, thought Max, it's yours. But he simply agreed to take care of it. He had a feeling that he had given Octavia enough shit to deal with for one day.

18

When Kelly left CMG after the reading of the will she was confused. Nobody had speculated on the value of these mysterious jewels, and given Octavia's outburst it had hardly seemed the right time to ask. But it was obvious that their value was substantial. Why else would Octavia, with her miserly one point seven million, consider them a prize worth having?

And now they were hers.

Ruby had wanted her to have a secure future. What did that mean exactly? If she meant financial security then – boom – perhaps with one sparkling bequest Ruby had guaranteed that. So why didn't Kelly feel more secure? Was this how people felt when they won the lottery? Buy a big house and a great car, take a holiday and then what?

If only it were that simple. She had a feeling that Octavia wasn't about to let go of these jewels without a fight. Was she about to get tangled up in a complex legal battle? Although the notion was not without its *LA Law* appeal, Kelly had been in town just about long enough to realize that the expectation was often nothing like the reality. She probably wouldn't be turning up to court every day in a Ralph Lauren suit and pleading her case to a wise and humorous judge. It was more likely to be an acrimonious and expensive business. It wouldn't be a commercial TV hour of gripping legal debate, where by the end everyone had a learnt a little something about themselves, but would more likely be an often dull, drawn-out experience. Was that really how she wanted to spend the next year of her life? Waiting to see if she was rich?

And even if she kept the jewels, then what? Would she sell them off and live on the proceeds, never working again? Wouldn't that be boring? Would she move to LA and become Sofia's new party buddy, one of the in-crowd whose family money and stamp of approval meant guaranteed success for the latest nightclub? Somehow she couldn't picture it.

Kelly had tried to enjoy these last few days but she felt she didn't belong here. Surely anyone could see that. If she stayed long enough would she get the hang of it?

She missed her father. On impulse she crossed the street into Rexford Drive and headed for the bank of payphones outside the library. She checked her pockets for change, pumped all of it into the slot and dialled home.

'Hello?' Her voice cracked. She was so pleased to hear his voice. She should have called him every day.

'Kelly? What is it? Where are you? What's wrong?' He was immediately concerned.

She loved the way he knew her so well that the slightest trace of emotion in her voice alerted him to her mood. She hadn't needed two parents. She had one amazing parent and he was a gift.

'Nothing's wrong. Everything's good actually.' She told him what Ruby had left them in her will.

'I had a feeling she wouldn't let you down,' he said. 'So when are you coming home?'

'Not for a while. Everything's different here. I'm somebody. I think I could grow to like being Ruby Valentine's daughter.'

'There was a bit about you in the paper here yesterday. The phone's been ringing so much I took it off the hook last night. And some girl called Chartreuse came round to the house, said she was one of your best friends.'

Chartreuse? 'Hardly,' Kelly said.

'She was most put out when I wouldn't tell her where you were staying.'

'Well done.'

'You have to be careful now,' he said. 'Not everyone will be the same. Tell me what else has been going on.'

'I've moved,' she said. 'I'm staying with Octavia now. Max set it up.'

'I told you he'd look after you. How are you managing?'

'I'm living in a Beverly Hills guesthouse, I've got an appointment later in the week to go and look at my jewels, and yesterday I had my first magazine photo shoot. I'd say things are pretty good.'

She was trying to keep it light. She didn't want him to worry, and if she told him that she was equally paranoid that Octavia hated her, that Sofia was trying to make money out of her and the press were about to portray her as a clueless foreigner, she knew he would fret. It scared her sometimes how much she needed her dad. It was impossible not to think of his mortality occasionally on this trip, surrounded as she was by the ceremony and paperwork of death. She was a grown woman and sooner or later she was going to have to make it on her own. Why not here?

'It's amazing,' she said resolutely.

'Don't get carried away,' said Sean. 'Remember, it isn't for ever.'

She felt the warm California sun on her bare shoulders. 'Maybe it could be,' she said. 'I could stay.'

'But Kelly, what about your job, what about Jez, what about . . . ?' The last was left painfully unspoken: what about me?

'You'll survive,' she said. She knew he would, but could she?

She told him about Octavia's outburst over the contents of the will. He listened quietly as Kelly made it into a funny story.

'Don't you think she has a point?'

'Dad, Ruby left a lot of money. Octavia's just greedy.'

'That's nowhere the amount that she was worth. Trust me.'

'That was a long time ago, maybe she spent it.'

'Maybe she did,' he conceded. 'But Ruby was always very careful with money. Almost cheap. You don't think she bought any of those jewels herself, do you? They were gifts, all of them. She lived in a relatively humble house, she wasn't one for the regular party circuit.'

'She could have changed. People do.'

'You think?'

From the way he said it Kelly could tell that he didn't agree. But if people didn't change, did that mean that Kelly was destined to remain the same way for ever? Would she never get the chance to be more like Sofia?

Not caring what anyone thought, just getting out there and surfing the waves. Would she never be the kind of girl that a man like Tomas would be attracted to, but always end up with someone safe like Jez?

'People change,' said Kelly firmly. 'You said yourself you didn't think Ruby was the kind to kill herself.'

'I still don't,' said Sean.

'What do you mean?'

'I can't stop thinking about it,' said Sean. 'She just wouldn't have done it, not the woman I knew.'

'Somebody else said that too. Tomas.'

'Tomas Valentine? Ella's kid?'

'That's him.'

'You met him?'

'Yeah, we . . . we went out.'

'On a date?'

'Not really.'

'Isn't he a little bit old for you?'

'Da-ad!'

'Okay, I'm sorry, what does Tomas think?'

'Oh, I don't know, I think he was basically just trying to annoy Octavia. He said that's there some conspiracy and that things are never what they seem.' She didn't really like to talk about it. The thought that there might be secrets and lies around her made her uncomfortable. What was supposed to be a simple and private pilgrimage to her mother's home town had already become far more complicated than she'd expected. She had been naive to think it would be otherwise. She didn't expect to meet people like Max and Sofia, whom she liked, people like Tomas whom she could get a crush on. She didn't know if she wanted to delve any deeper than she already had. She was afraid of what she might find out. She was starting to like Ruby too much. Already it would be hard to let go.

'Tomas could be right.'

'Ruby didn't have enemies, she didn't have friends either, but everyone seemed to love her. Why would anyone want to harm her?'

'For money?' said Sean.

'She didn't have any money.'

'But I just told you: she did.'

An automated voice interrupted them to tell Kelly she was running out of time. She didn't have any more coins. 'I love you,' she said.

'I love you too, sweetheart. Pay no attention to me, I'm rambling.'

She tried not to think about what he'd said. She tried to convince herself that he must be wrong. The coroner's report had agreed suicide; there wasn't even going to be an inquest. If anything looked suspicious Max Parker would surely have made sure it was investigated. Except for Sean and Tomas, two men who hadn't seen her in decades, everyone concurred that Ruby was unhappy, lonely and suicidal. Nobody was shocked. Not even Max.

Did she trust Max Parker? Ruby had, implicitly. But Ruby was dead.

Ruby was in heaven. Love ran through her every vein and was the lifeblood of her existence. She had Dante all to herself at last and it was everything that she had hoped it would be.

They were married in a simple ceremony at the pink beach house, presided over by a seventy-year-old judge and witnessed by strangers. Ruby's first wedding to Andrew had been a superficial whim, an undemanding day through which she smiled and looked pretty, a day she would easily forget in time. But this ceremony was different, every word of her vows was branded on to her memory and would stay there for ever because she meant them. He was her heart, her soul. She no longer existed.

On their wedding night Ruby felt as if they had fused together. One spirit united against the world. Dante felt confident he'd made a sound decision. Ruby would be good for his career and she was a knock-out in the sack.

Almost a year later, exactly as Dante had predicted, *Disturbance* garnered Ruby a host of accolades. On the night of the Academy Awards, she sat in terror at the Dorothy Chandler Pavilion, flanked by Dante on one side and Max on the other.

During the whole crazy build-up she had said so many times that being nominated was honour enough that she had started to believe her own modesty. But when the moment actually came she wanted the Oscar so badly that it scared her. She wanted them to say her name so that she could publicly thank Dante. The award would belong to both of them. Her face shared the giant screen with the four other nominated actresses, four wonderful actresses, and she wanted them all to walk away empty-handed and broken-hearted. None of them deserved it and momentarily she hated each and every one of them. It was hers, it had to be. In those brief seconds before they announced the winner she spitefully imagined all of those other actresses putting on good-loser faces and having to congratulate her.

Please, please, please.

They said her name.

She turned to Dante to be certain that she hadn't imagined it. How embarrassing it would be to leap from your chair when only your wish was making it so. But it was real, she had won the Oscar, and Dante was embracing her and Max was standing to applaud her as she took to the stage in a daze and made a speech that helped America to believe in true love again.

Ruby was dry-eyed and dignified as she dedicated the award to her new husband. Her mind felt dislocated and she was able to watch this beautiful actress cloaked in gold Dior accept the highest accolade her profession could bestow. She congratulated her fellow nominees. Was that really her? She'd come so far. She thought of people in her past glued to the television seeing what had become of her. Little Ruby Norton, didn't she do well? Except it wasn't Ruby Norton any longer, nor Steele, she was Ruby Valentine now and since the very first moment she laid eyes on Dante that was who she had always wanted to be. The self-satisfaction was intoxicating.

Afterwards, almost sick on adrenalin and champagne, Dante presented her with a splendiferous Mogok ruby, the size of a silver dollar, which had once belonged to his mother. And for the very first time he told her that he loved her.

'What took you so long?' Ruby asked.

'I had to be sure.'

She had her award clamped firmly in her hand. She was the belle of the Governor's Ball and everybody wanted to spend a couple of magical moments with Ruby and her Oscar. Even on this night of nights Dante could still make her feel insecure.

'I love you too,' she said. 'I always have.'

'I know.'

They set up home out at the beach house and as 1970 drew to a close children followed swiftly, twins. A girl, Octavia and Vincent, a boy. A perfect pair whose little faces unmistakably shared their father's dark good looks. It seemed right to bring children into the world together as a natural extension of their love. The sex was so good that it had to serve a higher purpose.

Ruby wasn't sure if she would ever fully understand Dante. He was a complex man but that was part of his allure. She didn't mind that he sometimes sank into black moods for a day or two, she didn't care when he pointed out flaws in her character. He was always right so she had no cause to be hurt. She endeavoured to change. She loved him and all she wanted was for him to be happy too. Not only did Ruby finally understand the lyrics of the romantic songs on the radio, more often than not she sang along.

He told her that he had never felt so much for anyone, he told her that she was his angel, and she took that to mean he felt exactly the same as she did. That nothing terrified him more in the dead of night than lying awake thinking of what life would be like if they had never met.

It was an exciting time, a run of golden years. Ruby made four more films, was nominated for one performance and acclaimed for all of them. Dante helped her to pick every role and his input was invaluable. She was one of the most successful and recognizable women in Hollywood and the fact that she chose to hide out in the sticks with her weird European love match, entertaining their arty friends, was a source of constant frustration to the press. They painted her as a hedonistic recluse, an image which reinforced her glamorous appeal. Everybody in town secretly longed to be invited to one of the parties at the beach house.

In an effort to preserve her looks Ruby had initially refused Dante's offers of recreational drugs until he pointed out her hypocrisy. He cited the blue and yellow pills she popped with increasing regularity.

'These are pharmaceutical,' she said. 'I get them from a *doctor*.'

'All my stuff starts life at the doctor's surgery,' he said. 'Except the grass, and you don't object to the grass. Take this, baby, and shut up.'

So she did and it was fabulous. She abstained when she was very pregnant but otherwise much of her time was spent in a blissful half-state where nature and friendship made rivers of well-being which burst their banks inside her and she'd never felt so free. When she vocalized thoughts like this friends laughed and said she was the only millionaire hippy they knew.

Max wasn't overly concerned. It was the times. The Sixties were behind them all now but some people refused to let the good times go. Ruby's haven on the beach was the last vestige of an easier age. As long as she kept showing up for work and performing at the peak of her considerable powers, he wasn't about to change a single thing. He also thought that a life left-of-centre suited Ruby's image. It suited her much more than marriage to the establishment. Look at Andrew Steele now, grasping for decent parts the way a dog begs for the crumbs below the table. Meanwhile, Ruby's star had never been brighter.

Despite her devotion to her husband, even Ruby sometimes required space and solitude. She liked to take a morning walk on the beach when she needed to escape the gentle mayhem back at the house. It was almost breakfast-time but a supper party had been underway for the last three days and showed no sign of coming to an end. Dante was enamoured of a new director that Max had uncovered and half a dozen other people were joining in the mutual ego-stroking. Ruby had enjoyed herself. Life was good. The sea breeze sharpened her senses. She was secretly glad that nobody else had joined her when she'd announced her intention to walk along the surf.

Some of her best friends were back at the house, as well as the man she loved, but even though her capacity for approval was vast, there was a point where praise inevitably started to sound insincere, and that was always the perfect time to leave a party. Otherwise paranoia would kick in.

Even though she'd won awards and got her man, she was inclined towards self-doubt and so was always half-waiting for the world to cotton on to her deception. She was just a girl from the valleys and she'd fooled them all. What a performer. The greatest actress of them all. She could see the funny side.

She felt light enough to fly and oddly detached from herself, the remnants of some serious drugs rattling around in her consciousness. She took off her shoes and sank her feet into the damp sand, watching it squeeze up through her toes, enjoying the tickling sensation.

She didn't have long before the twins would be awake. Vincent was never too much trouble but Octavia was a daddy's girl and often wouldn't behave until he had spent some time with her. She knew that Octavia only acted this way because her father's love was so sporadic. He was incapable of anything more. Did that mean Octavia would grow up always craving male attention, just like her mother? Ruby hoped that today Dante would spare more than a minute for his daughter. Vincent would play quietly until called for dinner and then for bed. He was placid, almost detached. She worried that the balance between the twins was uneven. Octavia loudly requested affection and so received it, often at her brother's expense. Just because Vincent wasn't so demanding he might still need the same amount of cuddles and Ruby only had one set of arms. She had suggested getting some live-in help with the children but Dante had objected. 'The house is too small,' he'd said. 'She'd cramp our style.'

'I worry about the children,' she'd said.

'Why?' he'd asked, and whirled Octavia up in his arms to her enormous delight. Vincent was standing nearby and Ruby tried to see if he was jealous but his tight little face gave nothing away. 'They're perfect.'

Ruby had acquiesced, as she often did, and the idea of live-in help was forgotten. Dante had proved time and time again that he knew best. Their life was testament to his good decisions. She had everything she wanted. A flourishing career and the man she was meant to be with. She was slated to make another film within weeks, a street thriller with a denouement as dark as the midnight sky. Dante said she would win the Oscar again with it if she didn't mess up.

If she had thought that her first Oscar win would cement her Hollywood standing she was wrong. It was still hard work, she still struggled with disappointment sometimes. Maybe a second Oscar would help. Surely there had to come a point where life became easier? For all her success Ruby remained anxious about every career move. Without Dante she might make mistakes.

She heard a scream coming from the direction of the house but paid it no attention. It wasn't a scream of pain; it was just one of the bland models who had latched on to the gathering getting excited about something. Maybe a new shade of nail polish, Ruby thought, and then giggled at her own sourness. They were all the same, these scrawny girls. They thought that if they befriended someone with clout, they would eventually be cast in a big film and emerge as fully fledged stars. Ruby hadn't the heart to tell them there was only room in their circle for one star. The truth was that Dante kept a selection of pretty young things around for window-dressing, in case one of his male friends required an undemanding playmate. Privately he would tell Ruby how little respect he had for their type. 'They may have been made beautiful,' he'd say, 'but they expect too much in return for God's grace.'

Ruby expected nothing. She thanked God every morning for making her beautiful and then she went to work.

When Ruby returned to the house things had started to slow down. Dante was lying back on their leather couch watching his new director friend kissing one of the scrawnies on the rug in front of the empty fireplace. Over by the record player three more people were poring over their extensive music collection. She couldn't quite remember how many people there had been before, but if there'd been more then they had disappeared. Dante saw her come in and backoned her to him.

'My love,' he said. She watched his eyes fire in the morning sun before going to sit beside him and nestling deep into his waiting arm. He continued casually to observe the kissing couple.

'How are you feeling?' she asked.

He shrugged.

'Can I get you anything?'

'You should get some rest,' he said. 'You start work in a couple of weeks.'

She was flattered by his concern.

'You need to look your best,' he added.

She thought about the coming months when her movie would keep them apart. She lived for the days when she was next to him; without him she felt lost. Food was more nourishing when Dante was around, music and art more rewarding, thoughts and feelings were worthwhile. Apart, it was just a matter of counting the grey days until she could be with him.

'I'll miss you,' she said. She gazed up at him until he dragged his eyes away from the sex show on the rug. She knew what came next, she wanted it. He took her hand, they stood up and they walked upstairs.

Of all of her treasured beach house Ruby loved the bedroom most of all, with its view of the ocean, cool airy space, crisp white sheets and luxurious en-suite bathroom. But mostly she loved it because the bedroom was where Dante always made her feel like the most powerful woman in the entire world. She pushed him on to the bed and he tore off his clothes impatiently. Quickly now, then they'd rejoin their guests and come back in a few hours' time, then again a few hours after that, and when their guests finally left they'd spend some time together in unhurried exploration.

Sex with Dante was more intoxicating than any drug Ruby had yet to try. In those times with him she felt as though she accessed the perfect version of herself. She was his goddess. It was impossible for her to imagine that anyone on earth could generate the same intense passion as they did. Nobody else could touch them. They were the best. If everybody had sex this good, nobody would ever get any work done and the planet would grind to a halt. It got better and better.

Ruby would give up everything to spend all her time in bed with him but Dante forced them to be strict. Ruby contained herself as best she could and faithfully promised him that she would never masturbate without him. They spent hours in the bedroom shutting out the world, days if they could, yet it was never enough. As long as they made love like they were doing right now Ruby believed they would be together for ever. It was meant to be.

Dante was close to orgasm. She knew from the sound of his breathing and the movement of his enjoyably familiar body. She slowed her pace and pulled away, teasing him, enjoying the thrill of being in control. Dante was the most stubborn and headstrong man she had ever known but at this moment she could have asked for anything she wanted and he would comply. But the only thing she wanted was for him to explode inside her. She adored watching his beloved face as he came, to know that she was responsible for such total euphoria and watch him in that tiny pocket of time when he was aware of nothing except ecstasy. She always felt closest to him then.

She started to rock back and forth more forcibly. She was sitting on his lap, facing him. He grabbed hold of her shoulder and pulled her deeper on to him. She could feel the force of his orgasm building inside her and knew he was beyond the point of no return, lost to her, a moment of total oblivion, a little death.

She pulled her head up to look at him. He was clutching a handful of her hair and pulling it painfully, but she hardly noticed. She squeezed her magic muscles the way he had taught her to. A thousand hours of pelvic exercises to make his pleasure more exquisite. He was almost there. Almost.

'Oh, Jesus,' he cried. 'Carla!'

Who the *fuck* was Carla?

20

If Ruby chose never to challenge Dante about calling out another woman's name did that make her weak? Or did it simply prove that she trusted him beyond doubt? Yes, another wife might be throwing his possessions out of the second-storey window and demanding a lifetime of alimony but she was better than that. She was strong.

It was possible that he had been fantasizing; that was acceptable. As far as she knew, in five years together they had never met anyone called Carla. It was also possible that she had misheard him completely and constructed this threat from her subconscious, a manifestation of her own insecurity. She reassured herself with this theory. It sounded like something Dante himself might say.

Why would he cheat on her? She had done nothing wrong. Or had she? She thought back over her behaviour these last few months. As far as she could tell she hadn't done anything to upset him or drive him away. The one thing Dante always prized above all was freedom. She had given him this. She had also given him two beautiful children he adored. It was an awkward package to wrap correctly but she had achieved it. The children were still small enough to accept life the way it was presented to them: a lot of time with the nurse, plenty of Ruby and just a dash of Daddy to add flavour. If he was in the mood, Dante would happily amuse himself with the children for hours at a time – he came alive in their company – but he was easily distracted and someone was always there to take over from him when he suddenly got bored. Was he worried about what would happen now the children were growing up? Was he starting to feel trapped? It wasn't possible. Dante lived fiercely in the moment and scorned those who spent time worrying about things that hadn't happened yet. And he was happy. She made him happy. She must. She had organized their entire life around his desires. She was attentive but independent and she never refused sex. What was not to love?

'What would you do,' she asked one evening, 'if I slept with another man?'

'I would fight him.'

The thought of being fought over by two men was thrilling. She imagined a bare-knuckle fight that ended in bloodshed. She would look on in feigned horror, clutching a handkerchief and begging them to stop, but secretly loving every second. Dante would win of course, and she would tend to his bruises and treat him like a hero.

'Would you leave me?'

'That would depend.'

'On what?'

'On how you made it up to me.'

'I would never do anything to risk losing you,' she said. She wanted him to echo her sentiment, she needed to hear him say that she was the only woman in his life and that she always would be.

'You could lose me without trying,' he said. 'Nothing is for ever.'

She buried her face in his broad chest to hide the

anguish that his words caused. It was like a stab through the heart.

The only way she could think to protect herself was to strive to be better. A better wife, a better lover, a better movie star. The strain of constantly clamouring to be perfect grew exhausting. She had achieved so much, but her relentless push towards the next goal distracted her from her achievements.

At the pinnacle of her career Ruby slowly started to feel like a failure.

She tried to bring everything to her next role but it wasn't to be. Her portrayal was lacklustre and she spent too much time thinking about what Dante was doing and who he was with instead of giving herself over to her character. The role which could easily have won Ruby a second Oscar was instead one of her most awkward performances. She was a disappointment to the men who had hired her and people started to whisper: maybe she's lost it; maybe she would never be as good again. She didn't listen to them. She got through the shoot by thinking that every day of work was one day closer to Dante.

When the movie finally wrapped she didn't stick around to lift a glass with the crew, a decision which made her even more unpopular. Instead, she was on the very first plane back to Los Angeles and in Dante's arms within hours. When she was with him she felt in control. As long as she could reach out and hold him, he couldn't go far.

Then one night a gorgeous new girl showed up at one of their parties and Ruby felt as if her world might end.

As soon as the girl entered the house Ruby's hackles rose like a hissing cat's and she was disproportionately aware of her fresh face. She was at least six feet tall and walked in with long, loping strides. Her hair was thick and sun-bleached and her skin was the colour of pale caramel, against which her wide, sexy smile stood out. Even in the physically obsessive city of Los Angeles Ruby was used to being the most beautiful woman at any party but this leonine blonde drew everyone's attention and for once Ruby felt overshadowed. *No tits though*, noted Ruby, *I've still got the best breasts in the room.*

Dante made his way over to the new girl and kissed her on the cheek. Ruby watched as she lifted up her hand to conceal a whisper into Dante's ear, a waterfall of silver bracelets cascading down to the crook of her elbow. She was all long limbs and laughter, this girl, more charming than the usual models, and she seemed to know an awful lot of Ruby's friends. Ruby turned away and engaged in light-hearted conversation with another guest. She could feel seeds of jealousy sprouting in her hot belly and she knew that if left unchecked they would destroy her evening and cause an argument before they went to bed.

'Ruby? I want you to meet someone.' They were coming towards her, Dante and this girl who suddenly made Ruby feel like the oldest woman in the room. She was so young, no more than twenty, with a lifetime ahead of her. In the moment right before he introduced her, Ruby already knew who she was. She could tell they were sleeping together simply by the way Dante led her across the floor and the way she let herself be led. So relaxed, so tactile.

'This is Carla,' he said.

Ruby gathered her into a hug to hide the devastation on her face. Carla's hair carried the scent of sun-ripened oranges. By the time Ruby pulled away she was composed. 'Welcome,' she said. 'If you need anything, just ask either of us. What are you drinking?'

'Something cold? A beer if you have one,' said Carla.

'Dante? Would you find a beer for Carla?' *Do you dare to leave me alone with her?*

Apparently he did. He went off in search of Carla's beer. Since when did Dante like a woman who drank a man's drink?

'Have you been here before?' asked Ruby. *Tell me the truth. Have you been here with Dante? Have you walked naked across my landing to use the bathroom while I took the children shopping for clothes? Have you sat at my dressing table and tried on my perfume? Have you had sex in my bed?*

'No,' said Carla. 'I love it.'

'So do we.'

There was a flicker of understanding in Carla's ridiculously wide-set eyes. They looked at each other for a moment and it was all Ruby could do to stop herself from grabbing this whore by her bony shoulders and begging her to leave them alone. Pleading with her not to destroy everything she had ever wanted. But she did not. Later, Carla thought she must have imagined the momentary chill that descended in that moment because Ruby's open smile was back in place and she offered Carla a pull on the joint that was circulating.

It took a superhuman effort for Ruby to remain relaxed for the rest of the evening and she pretended she was playing a part in a film. She could hear an imaginary voice in her head giving her direction – *okay, Ruby, in this scene you are totally unaware, that's right, oblivious, nothing is wrong, you've got it, great work* – and was confident that nobody would see through her witty banter to the nervous wreck inside. It was some of her finest work.

She was extremely tired. The party was winding down and normally she would have made her excuses some time ago but tonight she didn't want to leave Dante alone with Carla. She forced her eyes to stay open, even though fatigue was drawing deep, unflattering lines in her face. This was ridiculous. She couldn't keep watching him for the rest of her life and never sleep again. She must learn to trust him. She must at least try.

'Dante?' With her eyes she told him she was going to bed. With his eyes he replied that he would stay up a little longer.

Carla was still there.

Ruby said goodnight and went upstairs to her room where she lay on the bed and strained to hear the muted mumbles through the floor. She started to imagine that every laugh was a laugh about her. Did everybody know?

What did she do now? Her desire had soared to another level; the fear of losing Dante had snapped her devotion into razor-sharp focus. There was no doubt in her mind, he was sleeping with the girl. The question was, could she live with it?

If she asked him to end his affair it would be as good as asking him to move out. He would not stand for demands. So what then? Continue to act oblivious? The idea of performing for the rest of her life, through a thousand more evenings like tonight, was exhausting. It would feel like a defeat if she was forced to pretend that nothing had happened. Dante admired strength and resilience. Would he respect her more if she threatened to leave him? No, because a threat was merely a veiled demand. He would leave her.

She heard the front door slam and a minute later the sound of a car pulling out of the driveway. Somebody was leaving. Had that left just Dante and Carla? Would they do it here while she was upstairs? She imagined them falling on each other insistently, delighted to be finally alone, Dante's hands curling into all that blonde hair as she ripped off his shirt. She saw him pushing her to her knees as he snapped open his fly. The vile pictures in her head became more and more graphic until to her horror she felt unmistakably aroused. Then the front door slammed again, another car pulled away, and she heard Dante's footsteps on the staircase. She knew what to do.

'All gone?' she said.

She watched him undress and thought about losing that body next to hers, and it strengthened her resolve. 'Darling,' she said. 'Who's Carla? I've never seen her before.'

'Harry found her behind the bar in a strip club in Nevada. Gave her a little part in his next film.'

'She's amazingly beautiful.'

'A modern beauty, I think. Of its time. Won't work on film.'

'I love her body,' said Ruby. She reached out for Dante and began to stroke his chest, slowly letting her trailing fingers drift south. 'Her legs, her little breasts, everything.'

Dante exhaled deeply and gave a murmur of agreement and pleasure.

Ruby continued to caress him, speaking softly as if casting a spell. 'I wonder how a woman that beautiful would be in bed. Do you think she's wild? Do you think she likes it like I do? I think she wants it fast, and a bit dirty. Lots of sweat, lots of panting. I bet she screams like an animal when she comes.'

She climbed on top of Dante and they started to move slowly. He tried to increase the pace but she was in control. She whispered in his ear, 'If you fuck her will you tell me?'

So Dante's affairs became an ingredient in their life. Given the choice between sharing them with him and being closed off from that part of him, she preferred to be involved.

It wasn't difficult to endure his bedtime stories of illicit romance. Within a few months it became obvious that Carla was not the first, nor was she the only one. The affairs were not frequent and none of them seemed to last very long. Ruby swallowed her jealousy, but the dread remained. What would happen if one day he met someone who gave him all the freedom she did but in a prettier package? Already she could see the signs of time on her face: fine lines that were invisible to everyone else, but which she could tell were warnings of what was to come. And even though she knew that alcohol aged the skin, it helped to go through the evening with a bourbon buzz, so her consumption rose steadily until one morning it occurred to her that a bourbon buzz might soothe her days too, days that rarely went by without the choking sensation which overcame her when she thought of a life on her own.

If only she had someone to talk to, but she didn't; all her comfort came in liquid form. Sometimes she thought of Ella, left alone raising a son Dante did not know. She was determined that she would never have to face that kind of loneliness.

She made a lunch date with Max and told him that she didn't want to take any more out-of-town jobs. At least, for the time being. She wanted to be constantly near Dante and provide him with everything he needed.

'It's not a good idea,' said Max. 'You have to go where the work is. Quality should be more important than location.'

'Well, it's not. Not to me.' She picked at her overpriced salad and hoped that Max wouldn't take too much persuading. She didn't have the energy.

'There's nothing decent coming up in the greater LA area.'

'Then I won't work. That's just the way it is.'

Max knew her well enough to sense that she would not move from her position. Personally he thought Dante was poisonous, but there was no denying that her liaison with a director from the edgy set had helped Ruby's profile. It was sometimes hard for an actress as beautiful as Ruby to attain credibility, and an association with Dante had guaranteed that. But since *Disturbance*, Dante had made only one picture, an ill-conceived thriller that had attracted a cult following and got plenty of bad press for being too violent. It didn't exactly storm the box office either. Unless Dante made another film soon his reputation was bound to waver, and Max didn't want Ruby to be dragged down with him. In Hollywood one could only be an artist for so long before people got bored and wanted to be entertained.

'No problem,' said Max. 'Local only, I get it.' He would leave the battle for now but if it became career-threatening he would see that she took the best part available, even if it shot on the damn subcontinent.

'One more thing . . .' he said.

'What?'

'You're getting thin, Ruby. Did you notice?'

She tugged at the waistband of her gypsy skirt. It pulled a couple of inches away from her tiny waist. 'I've lost a little weight maybe.'

'Try not to lose any more, okay? Look after yourself, eat, get some rest.'

'Are you criticizing the way I *look*? Because the way I look paid you plenty of commission last year.'

'Last year you had hips.'

Ruby was insulted. 'I get other offers, you know that, don't you? Every agent in town would be happy to have me.'

'I know they would,' he said. 'I apologize. You always look fabulous. Shall we order dessert? The cheesecake here is unbeatable.' He stared at her over the calorie-laden dessert menu and winked.

She narrowed her eyes suspiciously and then looked away. 'Fine,' she said. 'Cheesecake. Make mine a large one.' She knew that if she met his eyes she would laugh. She would never leave Max. He was too good.

21

Limiting herself to Los Angeles gave Ruby a degree of freedom. She enjoyed taking life a little slower, instead of relentlessly chasing down the few outstanding roles for women. She should have taken a break years ago. Of course Max was bound to tell her that career breaks didn't work in this industry, his percentage depended on it, but she thought he was wrong. Her star couldn't fall that quickly. Meanwhile, Ruby enjoyed the time she spent with Octavia and Vincent, feeling like a normal wife and mother instead of a movie star with an open relationship. Would a movie star be filling empty yogurt pots with water and throwing them into the bath tub as it ran? The twins' amusement far outweighed the sophistication of the game, but they delighted in making the room as wet as possible and themselves as slick as seals. Ruby's bare feet slipped on the damp floor and she was just starting to wonder whether this game was practical, or indeed safe, when the doorbell chimed.

She couldn't very well leave the children with all that water, so she grabbed one with each hand and called out that she was coming. She caught sight of herself in the mirror in the hallway – half of her hair was soaked, and she hoped that it wasn't anybody important.

She looked through the spyhole in the door and exclaimed 'Shit!' in front of the kids.

It was Ella. Ella and a boy who Ruby knew with sickening certainty was Dante's son, Tomas. She took a sharp breath and held it, spinning away from the door and backing up against the wall, her heart pounding.

Why was Ella here? She was supposed to be in Essex, never to be seen again. How had she found them? And what did she want? The beachside bubble in which Ruby existed suddenly popped. She thought she could handle other women, but not this one, not Ella. How was she supposed to compete with the mother of Dante's firstborn son? For a moment she was not Ruby Valentine, Oscar-winning actress and bona fide superstar. She was just Ruby in London, nervous and unsure in the shadow of her vivacious friend. Perhaps if she stayed very, very quiet Ella would go away.

As if on cue, Octavia wailed and wrestled free, bored of her hand being held with a vice-like grip. Her brother revved up to follow suit, Ruby could see it coming. Then Ella's voice surprised all of them.

'Come on, Ruby. I know you're there. You shouted out, remember? I'm not gonna bite your head off. Let me in. Tomas needs a wee.'

With a shaking hand Ruby opened the door. Ella had hardly changed in ten years. A little plumper maybe but she wore it well. Ruby missed a breath when she saw Tomas properly for the first time; he looked like Dante in miniature. A son in his image? Dante would never want them to leave. If she was lucky, they would be gone by the time he got home. She knew from past experience that he would probably be very late.

The two women had not spoken since that fateful night

in London when Ella told Ruby to stay away from Dante. When she told her that it was over, that Ruby had lost him. Scared though she was, Ruby wanted to enjoy this moment of victory. She could clearly remember Ella telling her that she would amount to nothing, and the way that had made her feel. Utterly hopeless. Now she noticed that Ella was wearing cheap shoes and up close you could see the lines around her eyes when she smiled.

Why was she smiling, Ruby wondered. Wasn't this humiliating? Ella had been wrong. Ruby had won. She braced herself for confrontation.

'Where's the bathroom?' asked Ella. 'We're bursting.'

She caught Ruby off-guard. 'Upstairs,' she said. 'Through the master bedroom.' She didn't usually like guests to use her private bathroom but she wanted to make sure that Ella saw the Oscar on the mantelpiece.

'Cheers. Come on, you.' Ella grabbed the little boy by the hand and hurried upstairs. 'You're looking good,' she threw over her shoulder as she disappeared.

Was she? Ruby checked her face in the mirror again and tidied her damp hair. She pulled some toys out of the big cane basket in the corner of the room and sat Octavia and Vincent down in front of them. 'Play nicely,' she whispered.

Perhaps Ella wanted money? Why else would she have turned up on their doorstep after all this time? Ruby waited anxiously and wondered how much she would have to pay her to get them to leave. She walked across the room to the writing desk and took her chequebook out of the drawer there. She had been steadily building up her cash investments over the years. It cost almost nothing to live the way they did. They had friends who lived in mansions five times the size with armies of staff – why? So Ruby had accumulated a sizeable fortune that she was prepared to spend to protect their way of life, to protect her family.

When Ella came back downstairs Tomas noticed the toys straight away and ran over to the twins. 'I'm Octavia and this is Vincent,' said Octavia formally, speaking for her brother as she always did.

'I'm Tomas.'

'Okay.' They looked at him curiously but moved aside and let him share like the innocents they were.

Ella was wiping her hands dry on the side of her flared jeans. 'Nice place,' she said.

'Thanks.'

'Any chance of a cup of tea?'

And so Ruby found herself rattling around in the kitchen, pushing aside the margarita mix to find a box of English tea bags and wondering if Ella would object to soya milk, which seemed to be the only kind they had. She even dragged out a box of cookies that were really meant for the children, going so far as to arrange them on a plate.

When she walked back into the living room she saw Ella sitting cross-legged on the floor with the children, *her children*, laughing and tickling Octavia's tummy. The little girl was in hysterics.

'Please don't do that,' said Ruby. 'It's almost her bedtime and I don't want to get her overexcited.'

'Sorry,' said Ella, and pulled away. 'Tommy will probably want to sleep too, he must be shattered, and you and I can catch up properly. I can't wait to hear what it's like to be you. You're dead famous, Ruby. There's not a week goes by when you aren't in the papers. Nobody believes me when I tell them we're friends.'

'Friends?' said Ruby. She'd had enough. This wasn't a public bathroom. This was her house, her family, not a rest stop. 'Ella, what are you doing here?'

'What do you mean?'

'Do you want money, because if that's it . . .' She pulled her chequebook out from beneath her cushion. 'Dante should provide for his son. That's only fair.'

'Ruby, what are you talking about? Where's Dante?'

'He isn't here.'

'Where is he?'

'I don't know.' She didn't like the way that sounded but the truth, that he was probably with another woman, would sound even worse. Something in Ella's expression made Ruby think that she needn't have bothered to lie. It was hard to remember that Ella would know what Dante was like to love, to live with and have a child with. She knew.

'He did tell you, didn't he? Jesus, Rube, please tell me that he told you.'

'Tell me what?'

'Tomas and I. He invited us to live here, we're moving in.'

The look of horror on Ruby's face said it all.

'He didn't ask you?' said Ella. 'Blimey, how embarrassing. It's just that he knows that things aren't great for us back home, we were still living with my mum, you know?'

Ruby didn't know. For a moment she felt the painful stab of ignorance. There was a sense of betrayal. Why hadn't Dante discussed this with her? They were opening up their home to his ex-wife and child? For how long? Was she supposed to be down with this? Had their open-house policy suddenly been extended to include enemies from the past? Ruby was all for freedom and a *mi casa su casa* mentality, but it was understood that everyone went home eventually. The beach house she adored suddenly felt tiny and crowded. Should she backtrack and pretend that of course she knew? That of course Dante hadn't done this without asking her opinion, considering her feelings? The house was in her name, it was her home. She couldn't pretend to be at ease with the situation, no way, even Ruby wasn't that good an actress.

Ella continued, 'It's been impossible for me to get back to work, what with this little terror.' She ruffled her son's dark hair affectionately. 'Dante's cheques were the only thing keeping us going and then . . .'

'His cheques?'

'Yes,' said Ella hesitantly. She lifted her china cup, stalling for time. She should have expected something like this from him; how Ruby had stayed married to him all this time she had no idea. 'Sod the tea,' she said. 'Have you got anything stronger?'

Once the children had been settled upstairs – three to a bed, new best friends – Ruby and Ella made tentative steps back towards amity. Dante had been sending substantial child support cheques this whole time. He considered himself close enough to them to invite them to stay. They were a part of his life and so they were a part of hers.

Maybe this wouldn't be so bad. Ella could be her ally. 'What are your plans?' asked Ruby.

'Nothing for a while, just relax, regenerate, you know? I need a break.'

Ruby didn't ask if she planned to support herself, that wasn't the way it worked at the beach, but Ella must have read something in her eyes. 'I'll look after the kids, obviously,' said Ella. 'If you have to work or whatever.'

If Ruby had a problem with Ella being mother to one of Dante's children, was she really prepared to let her start mothering all three?

'Do you still love him?' asked Ruby.

'Dante? No! But I love my son, and Dante will always be a part of that.'

'What happened with you two?'

'In Rome? Nothing that hadn't already happened in London. Drugs, other women. I don't know why I thought he would change. Men like Dante don't change.' She paused awkwardly. 'I mean, obviously, unless they meet a woman like you.'

Ruby tried to smile as if she had tamed him, but in the face of her oldest friend she couldn't keep up the charade.

'It's different for me,' she said. 'You don't understand. If he left me I don't think I could go on. I love him so I let him do what he likes.'

'Sweetheart,' said Ella. 'Don't you think that's . . . submissive?'

'No, I think that's what makes me special.'

Ella was shocked. 'You don't think you're special? Ruby, you're a star, a brilliant actress, an Oscar winner. That's not enough?'

'I'm not the only actress in town, not the best or the most beautiful. Every year there's another winner.'

'Dante couldn't survive without you.'

Had he told Ella that? Had he said he couldn't live without her? Did he love her as much as she loved him?

But Ella continued, 'He's never had a penny. He's only done those two films, right? Low budget. The man hasn't got a pot to piss in without you.'

Ruby didn't really think about money. She had that middle-class hang-up about talk of money being vulgar. She knew she had quite a bit. She just had Max send her fees into her account and then paid for everything that they needed. Their laidback lifestyle was not expensive.

'Did you have to marry him?' said Ella.

'Of course.'

'It would be easy for him to get a piece of you. If you divorced.'

'We won't.' She would make sure of it. The thought of divorce was revolting.

'Just protect yourself, Ruby. You'd carry on without him, even if you think you couldn't. And you are unique, okay? It's not about money or Oscars, you just are.'

Ruby could see that the roles had reversed. It had been years since she had last sat and talked this way with Ella, and even now Dante was still the main topic of conversation. One girl consoling the other, reassuring her that she was worthwhile no matter what he said. Only this time it wasn't Ella's heart that was breaking, it was Ruby's.

'I was scared when I saw you,' said Ruby. 'But now I don't care what happened in the past. I'm glad you're here.'

'We were children then,' said Ella nostalgically. 'What did we know of love?'

Ruby started to smile but stopped as she heard the sound of a car pulling up in the driveway. Her eyes darted around the room as if she was nervous. 'You won't tell him about this, will you?'

'About what?' said Ella, genuinely confused.

'I can handle it,' she said. 'The drugs, the women, all of it. I didn't mention divorce, you did.'

'Calm down,' said Ella. She watched Ruby check her face in the mirror and smooth imaginary creases out of her silk dress, thinking that for a woman who'd just found out her husband was moving his ex-wife and child in, she was acting oddly. If it was Ella, she'd be preparing to give him hell. But then Ruby was different, maybe she was right, maybe that's why their love would work. She didn't recognize the twisted mix of apprehension and adoration on Ruby's face as love, however.

'He's coming,' said Ruby, and ran to the door to welcome him. She was clearly besotted. Maybe Dante had changed.

It made the papers. Ruby and Dante Valentine taking in his ex-wife and child. News of this thoroughly modern arrangement was accompanied by editorials berating the declining moral standards of the country. Ruby's popularity faltered. Audiences stayed away from her latest film.

She laughed it off and enjoyed the notoriety. The newspapers made it sound like a drug-fuelled ménage à trois but the truth was that their bizarre little family functioned well.

The children grew up happily together and it was good for the twins to have an older brother, just as it was good for only child Tomas to have them. Ella was as entertaining as ever – time and motherhood did not seem to have subdued her. She threw herself into the Los Angeles arts scene: one month she wanted to be a concert promoter, the next she wanted to open a gallery. After a couple of years it was as if they had always been there.

Ruby considered the situation a personal triumph. Not many women would have had the strength of character to adapt so easily to these circumstances. She had not only accepted it but embraced it.

The only problem now was Dante. He was fearful and restless, taking too many drugs and growing increasingly paranoid. He wanted to get out of Los Angeles, he kept calling it hell.

'It's over,' he said. 'The soul of the place has gone. Listen.'

Dutifully Ruby cocked her ear to listen for something.

'Do you hear it?'

She didn't, but she nodded. He was convinced that if he could only escape the limitations of the West Coast then he would flourish. Ruby knew that it had nothing to do with the city, it was the drugs. He was taking an enormous amount of cocaine, the first line of the day before his morning coffee, and Ruby suspected that he was experimenting with heroin. She didn't push him on the subject. But sometimes, at night when she couldn't sleep and he was out cold beside her, she searched him for needle marks, checking first his arms and then gently between his fingers and toes because she knew he'd try to hide it. She never found anything and was deeply thankful but darkly sure that it was only a matter of time. She didn't know what to do.

She would be in love with an addict, supporting a habit that would eventually kill him. Could she handle that?

But Dante's fragile mental state had a hidden benefit for Ruby. For the first time in their lives he admitted to needing her. 'Don't go,' he said on the morning of a costume fitting for her next movie.

'What?'

'Don't leave me.'

Ruby was about to start shooting her first film in two years, the only good script to shoot locally in all that time. Decent part, big budget. But the moment Dante asked her to stay by his side she couldn't have cared less.

'Don't you want me to work?' she asked gently.

'You love your career more than me.'

'Never,' she said. 'You are the most important thing in my life.'

She thought back to when they had met. She had been so raw then, little more than a teenager. 'I'd be nothing without you.'

'That's right,' he said. 'And I'm asking you to do this one for thing me, to stay with me, and you won't. Fuck it, Ruby, if you don't love me any more just say so.'

'Please don't,' she said. 'I don't want you to be angry.'

'Then don't piss me off!' He stood up and slammed the tumbler he was holding down on the table so hard that the glass shattered. There was blood on his hand.

She begged Max to release her from the contract but he stood firm.

'I can't make you,' he said. 'But it would be career suicide to walk off this film so late in the day.'

Ruby was distraught. She was acutely aware of her slippery grasp on the ladder of success. Her last film disappeared without a trace; her previous film hadn't fared much better. She needed a hit. If she lost her reputation as one of the world's leading ladies then she would have to work relentlessly to get it back. And if she wasn't a star then she was scared that Dante wouldn't love her any more.

She was torn. Dante needed her, but he needed her rich and successful. Without the fame and the money, who was she? Nobody. A man like Dante would never love a nobody. Reluctantly, she decided to uphold her contract and make the film.

Dante sank into a black mood, punctuated by episodes of drug-fuelled belligerence. Ruby was terrified.

It wasn't good. It wasn't even passable. Her heart wasn't in it and that was blatantly obvious to everyone. Max received his first complaint about Ruby just nine hours after they started shooting.

'She's distracted. She's trying to fake it but she's still on the page.'

She hadn't even learnt her lines? Max apologized and concocted a story about how Ruby never got up to speed until day two.

He telephoned her immediately although it was very late. 'How's my favourite client?'

'She's exhausted,' said Ruby. 'This is not an easy gig, Max. Did you know they have me working back to back? I'm on the call sheet every day. Is that right?'

'It's a big production,' he said, 'lots to get done. They treating you okay?'

'I could do with a person, you know, an assistant or whatever. I don't want to miss any calls.'

He gathered she meant calls from Dante. There was nothing in her contract about a dedicated assistant and he doubted very much that they would stretch to it. 'I'll see what I can do.' He didn't like to think how that conversation would go – 'Hey, can I have an extra crew member to wait around by the phone in case the husband calls?'

He had to be careful. Ruby couldn't make too many demands. She didn't have the power she once had. There's a magical stage in a star's career when the film needs you more than you need the film, but the hardest thing to do is make that moment last for ever. After this film it would probably be time for Ruby to enter a second phase of her career, character parts, supporting roles. As she approached her mid-thirties, forty seemed to loom ever closer.

Ruby invited Max to lunch on set later that week and he noticed how she made it sound like a social event, as though she was inviting him to a leisurely meal at her own home. She didn't seem to realize that film sets were becoming more like factory floors, and that time was money to the film-makers in a way that had never been so conspicuous before.

'Do me a favour?' he said, just before he ended the call. 'Get the lines down and the whole thing will seem much easier. You need to be able to focus on the character and not the words. It's a fantastic part and you'll steal the movie.'

'What the hell, Max? Are you trying to tell me how to do my goddam job? I could do this shitty little part in a fortnight if they knew what they were doing.'

'Just learn the lines, sweetheart.'

'I know the lines,' she said. 'I'll see you.'

She put the phone down and contemplated the fact that someone on the film had called Max to complain about her. Max didn't have to tell her that. It was obvious. How dare they? She was an Oscar-winning actress, not some rookie on a learning curve. She poured herself a glass of wine and paced around the kitchen. So she hadn't learnt her lines? So what? The film was all cut, cut, cut –

a hell of a lot of style but not much substance. She had played parts where the camera stayed on her for fifteen minutes. She had *seen* films where shots lingered for twice that, artistic films that didn't try so hard to titillate and entertain. Films that gave you time to think. But now they'd rather cut to the car chase. She could act circles around everybody else in the cast if she applied herself.

She picked up the script with the intention of being word-perfect for the scenes that she was scheduled to shoot the next day. *EXT. VINE STREET. DAY, 'I'm worried about you'* – it was all pretty basic stuff. Then she heard Dante's car in the driveway and stashed the script away. He was home.

The following day it was raining. Ruby was so unused to rain that for the tiniest of moments she thought she had woken up in Wales and was a girl again. It was the smell. But then the dull ache in her head and the persistent buzzing of her alarm reminded her that she was old enough to drink and was expected to go to work.

Dante was not in bed beside her. At some point in the night he had gone. It wasn't the first time. Eventually she had to trust that he would be back.

Ella was downstairs happily feeding all three children. Perhaps it should have been unsettling for the woman of the house to see somebody else in her kitchen but Ruby enjoyed the way Ella's contribution allowed her the freedom to be Dante's wife first and a mother second. She knew some women who said that their children were their number one priority; in Ruby's opinion these women had unhappy marriages. She quickly compared Ella, smeared in butter and pancake batter, with her own reflection – beautiful, award-winning actress on her way to work. Was it any wonder Dante had chosen her?

'There are some messages for you on the machine,' said Ella.

'I'm late,' said Ruby. 'They'll have to wait.'

She only just remembered to take her script with her, which she had not studied last night. After sex with Dante it had been impossible to concentrate. She hoped that she could wing it. She forced herself to read the script in the car on the way to set. The rain was torrential, streaming down sun-baked hills in small rivers and turning everything from sepia to Technicolor. She noticed that they were heading towards the hills, not downtown as the script suggested.

The crew were all in place when she arrived. The set-up surrounded a table in a closed café. One small problem though: the café scene was not what Ruby had been expecting to shoot today.

'It's the weather,' said the irrepressibly perky assistant director. 'We switched scenes. Didn't someone call you?'

Maybe they had. She should have checked. She was tired and finding it hard to concentrate.

The AD was still speaking. Something about new pages. Good, if the scene had been rewritten then she wouldn't be the only one who didn't know the lines.

She climbed the rickety stairs to her trailer, spacious by anyone's standards. That was the great thing about these bigger-budget movies, they took care of the talent. Taking care to lock the door behind her, she unearthed the emergency cocaine that she had stashed in her purse.

As soon as she'd taken a line she felt better. Her head cleared and her senses were alerted. She skipped through the pages for the new scene. There was nothing to worry about, she was fantastic. A quick check in the mirror confirmed that she was still lovely. Gorgeous, in fact. Everything was cool.

Her makeup and hair took longer than usual but she hardly noticed. She was too busy thinking about how she was going to go out there today and remind them why they had hired her. She would fucking blind them with her brilliance! The other actors in the scene would feel humbled. The whole crew would be awestruck by the time she had finished. 'We're so sorry we doubted you,' they would say, and then she would ask for an even bigger trailer just because she could.

She was wearing red shoes with five-inch heels but walked on set with consummate poise. That was star power, right there.

She fluffed the first take. That was fine, the first take is always a kind of practice, everyone knows that. When she messed up on the second she was sure that it wasn't her fault, her co-star's timing had been off, but she thought she saw the sound guy exchange glances with the first assistant, glances that were loaded in her direction. She stopped herself from worrying; maybe she was being paranoid. On the third take she wasn't sure what went wrong but it rattled her because she jumped on her lines too fast on the next one, inadvertently cutting off her co-star. On the next take a plane flew overhead and they cut for a fifth time.

'Okay, break, everyone. Ten minutes.'

The director took Ruby aside. 'What's up?' he said.

Her eyes sparkled unnaturally brightly. 'Nothing. I'm great. A little cold though, I should have a blanket between takes.'

'Are you getting sick?'

'I don't get sick.'

The director shouted for a blanket and a floor runner scurried off to oblige. 'So on this next take,' he said, 'can we try for a straight run? I love what you're doing with it but let's just try and get something in the can, then we'll have time for some proper coverage.'

A question speared her confidence. 'You think I'm slowing things down? Me? There was a bloody plane in case you didn't notice.'

'Whatever, let's just get through this set-up and then we can move on. It's not a big deal.'

The runner produced a blanket and it was wrapped around Ruby's shoulders. The director gave her a final pat on the shoulder before walking away. She was insulted. What the hell was he talking about? She'd been doing fine, more than fine.

When they were ready to go again Ruby waited for her cue and then rattled off the first few lines. The scene danced along and she was certain that everybody would be happy with it; she hoped the camera was catching her good side. She was taking care of her part so the only thing that could mess it up now would be the technical guys. How could they ever have questioned her ability? She was flying up here.

There was a long silence. Was she supposed to say something?

'And cut!'

Everybody was staring at her. She had forgotten her line.

The director was deep in conference with his assistant. When they broke it off the assistant rushed to one of the production trailers immediately. The director then huddled with his cinematographer and the script supervisor.

Ruby smiled at her co-star and shrugged, like 'These things happen.' Her co-star did not return the smile.

'Okay, people!' The idle crew turned to their director. 'Let's move on, we're losing the light. We're gonna take an early lunch and pick up with the Brooks scene after, what? An hour?'

'One hour,' confirmed the second assistant director.

Ruby was not playing the part of Brooks. Did that mean she was done? She looked around for instruction but everybody seemed busy. She waited for the director to scold her for that mistake but he was summoned to the production trailer, so she mentally scolded herself instead. It was a momentary lapse in concentration, that was all. Maybe she needed another line of blow. She walked back to her trailer and waited for someone to come and tell her what to do.

An hour passed and nobody came to fetch her. Finally, just as she was feeling the slightest bit apprehensive, there was a knock on her trailer door.

'Max! What are you doing here?'

Max hated this part of his job most of all. 'I think you'd better sit down,' he said.

'Has something happened?' A shadow fell across her heart. 'Oh God, has something happened to Dante?'

'No, sweetheart. That's not it.'

She looked at him curiously. He was scaring her. Whatever it was she wished he'd just spit it out. 'What then?'

'They've been talking,' he said, waving his hand in the general direction of the partially dismantled set. 'And the thing is, they want to go another way. With this part. They want to try another actress.'

It took a second to register. 'I've been fired?'

'It looks that way, yeah.' Max rubbed at his temple, the way he always did when he was nervous. The producer had done him a huge favour, letting him know first so that he could break the news to her himself. Ruby could have been publicly dumped on set and then it would be impossible to stop the rumours coming out.

'Creative differences,' said Max. 'That's all. Personally I'm sure they'll regret it.'

He was already working on damage control. This was a recasting, nothing more. The best thing would be to get Ruby working on another film right away and maybe try to make it look like she'd walked out on them. Which was better for her reputation, getting fired or being irresponsible? Definitely the latter.

'Can they do that?' said Ruby. 'I signed a contract.'

'You'll still get paid.'

'For nothing?'

Max nodded.

Ruby was deeply ashamed. Everybody would *know*. Why hadn't she taken the time to learn the script? Why had she stayed up so late last night making love to Dante? Why had she taken that line of cocaine before she went on set? She was supposed to be a professional. And now she was unemployed. Some other actress would get to shine and win awards and the film would probably be a massive hit and people would tell the story of how she'd missed out on a second Oscar yet again as an interesting after-dinner anecdote.

'Get them to give me one more chance,' she said. 'I swear to God, I'll straighten out. I'll do it great.'

Max knew that was impossible. 'It won't work. They needed to make a quick decision and they made it.'

Ruby buried her face in her hands. It was over. She wasn't good enough. She'd always suspected that they'd catch up with her in the end. Little Ruby Norton from the valleys trying to make out she was something that she wasn't. She'd coasted on a lucky wave but it was breaking up around her.

'But Max,' she said, 'what will I tell Dante?'

Max Parker was a patient man but he had his limits. 'I don't care. He's so bad for you, Ruby. Are you the only one that can't see it?'

'What? How can you say that? He gave me an Oscar.'

'No,' said Max. 'You won that Academy Award yourself. Dante has given you nothing but grief.'

'You can never understand. Dante completes me. I hate the person I was before he came into my life. I was insignificant. I can't go back.'

'You think all your success is because of him? Because of a second-rate director with a drug problem? You can't be that stupid.'

'Wait a minute, you work for me, remember? How dare you?'

'I have to say it, Ruby. Somebody has to. You need to take a long hard look at your life. He's destroying you. Dante is toxic.'

Ruby raised her right hand and slapped Max hard around the face. The sound of the slap ricocheted around the small space. 'Get out,' she said. Max was stunned. He backed out of the trailer clutching his crimson face.

'And tell them they can all go to hell,' she shouted, and kicked the door of the trailer shut with her red stiletto.

After he went she wanted a drink. It was an urge so strong that for the first time Ruby acknowledged she might have a problem.

Maybe Max was right. Her husband treated her like a fool. He had slept with and continued to sleep with other women. She gave of herself constantly and he did whatever he chose without considering her at all. She was pathetic.

You should leave him. Her heart raced and suddenly she felt as though she was struggling for breath. *You should leave him.*

She pulled at her tight shirt, tugging it away from her neck, and ran to the open window, trying to take in the air, but her breathing came in shallow little gulps that she could hear as if from a distance. There was a flare of pain in her chest that made her scream, but it hurt to scream so she stifled it. Her vision narrowed and she started to panic. What would she be without him?

She grabbed hold of the window frame and desperately pulled in one quavering and painful breath. Gradually, one stuttering breath at a time, she was able to regain control. For a moment there she had thought that she was actually going to die.

Ruby could never leave Dante. Where would she go? She knew that he loved her as much as he was capable of loving anyone, and even though at times like this she knew it was not healthy she loved him back. It was an addiction, pure and simple. They both had their habits and Dante was hers. He fed a hunger within her. She could go to a shrink and tell him all about her childhood and together they could come up with some reason why she was obsessed with a man who would always be emotionally out of reach – was it a hunter instinct? Was it masochism? Was she repressing something? Expressing something? – but all the therapy in the world wouldn't change a thing. Her own self-worth had been tangled up with her feelings for him for so long that she was genuinely afraid of being alone in case she shrivelled to nothing.

You should leave him. It would never happen.

She gathered her things and walked over to her usual car. She could see the crew setting up for the Brooks scene in the distance. They stopped what they were doing and looked over at her. She walked with her head held high. And she would be keeping the shoes. Dante might enjoy them on her.

She never got a chance to show him the red high heels. Ruby never saw Dante again. That night he never came home. At dawn two uniformed policemen came to the door to tell her that her husband had been found in a hotel room in Santa Monica with a blonde in one arm and a needle in the other.

23

Kelly was having trouble adjusting to the Beverly Hills lifestyle but she couldn't deny that it had considerable advantage over her usual routine. In 90210 she woke up without an alarm clock, had a brief shower and then went straight for a swim in the outdoor pool. She liked to stand under the tropical waterfall and pretend she was in Belize or somewhere, trying to ignore the hollow sound the rocks made when she tapped them. She used the changing room to dry off. Then she walked inside for another shower, a proper one this time, using all the yummy toiletries that the cosmetics firm Zyma had sent over in a 'Welcome to LA' basket.

Honestly, people were being so *nice*! She felt like landed gentry, famous by virtue of birth alone. Famous without even trying. She'd received 'Welcome to LA' gifts from people she'd never heard of, and she had been sent so many flowers that she'd exhausted Octavia's considerable supply of vases. Word of this got out somehow and a ceramics café sent over more vases.

People who hadn't even met her wanted to be her friend. She was invited to everything. She couldn't help but feel that people would be disappointed when they saw who she really was, a nice middle-class girl from Wales who had less glamour in her whole body than Ruby had in her smile.

She knew that this was her wave, she should try to enjoy it, see if she could squeeze a lifetime's worth of being a celebrity kid into this one brief moment in the sun. This was everything that Ruby had denied her. She deserved it. But she had never felt more undeserving in her life. All she had done was show up.

She wandered into the main kitchen for breakfast. If Carmen wasn't there, she was happy to make breakfast herself, but today the maid was there, and what's more she was fixing some thick pancakes with ribbons of fried bacon that Kelly would have previously called 'streaky' but now just called 'bacon'. She drowned her plate in real maple syrup, bacon included, and was still surprised how good the salty-sweet combination tasted. 'This is great,' she said. Carmen smiled and indicated that she should wipe her chin.

Kelly wiped a smear of syrup from her face and felt a bit slovenly. It was hard not to in a place like this. Everything was white and spotless and if you left a few crumbs and an empty cup next to your book while you went to the loo you would come back to find the crumbs swept away and the cup removed. It was impossible to say thank you for everything Carmen did. Sofia had noticed Kelly trying and said that she usually found it easier to say one big, all-encompassing thank you at the end of the night when Carmen went home. Unless she was out on the town, obviously, because then she couldn't. But Kelly thanked Carmen for everything and eventually Carmen herself had taken Kelly aside and told her it wasn't necessary. 'It's my job,' she had said. 'And I like to do it.'

Kelly tried to imagine how that would feel.

*

Tonight was Ruby Valentine's Hollywood Tribute (fanfare!) and Kelly had neither a date nor an outfit for the occasion. She had received her personal, non-transferable invitation, which would be valid only if presented with corresponding ID, the day before by special delivery. It was a much sought-after, hugely publicized event and every day the guest list was added to with more luminaries who'd made time for Ruby in their busy schedules. Kelly's invitation was for plus-one and she had failed to provide organizers with a name twenty-four hours in advance. She had toyed with the idea of selling her plus-one on e-bay to the highest bidder. She didn't know anyone in Los Angeles and had planned to go alone. Sofia was scandalized: 'All eyes will be on you,' she'd said. 'We'll go together. And how can you not know what you're wearing?'

Kelly wasn't too bothered. She could easily buy a dress, she had all day. A date wasn't necessary. It wasn't such a big deal. Or so she told herself.

She hadn't called Jez and he hadn't called her. She missed him, but not enough to pick up the phone. Something stopped her. She didn't want to be reminded of her old life while she was getting used to this new one. She wanted to be herself, not one half of a pair, for just a little while longer. The truth was that she wanted to be something better than herself. She wanted to be as special as the people of Los Angeles thought she was.

She liked being somebody. She knew it wouldn't last, so why not enjoy it while she could? After tonight, after the tribute, things would calm down. The spotlight would move from Ruby to the next person, the wave would break, and Kelly might be able to breathe again. Then she would be able to think about going home and picking up the threads of her life, try to weave them into something that she felt good in. She would be able to see things more clearly, she hoped. Right now she needed to concentrate on sharing the only part of her mother's life that she ever would. The big finish.

Octavia came into the kitchen and gave Kelly a cold smile. Since the reading of the will Octavia had been friendly, and hadn't said a word about her moving out, but Kelly sensed her half-sister's envious eyes on her as she went around the house.

'Good morning,' said Kelly pleasantly. 'Have you had breakfast? These pancakes are delicious.'

'I've been up since six-thirty,' said Octavia, 'I ate some time ago.' She went to the fridge and poured a glass of Swedish mineral water from the bottle there.

Kelly munched her breakfast and wondered why a woman like Octavia, with no discernible employment and one fully grown child, needed to get up so early.

'Sofia forgot to set the security alarm,' said Octavia. 'If the pair of you are going to continue coming home in the middle of the night then I'd be grateful if you didn't put the rest of the family at risk.'

'Sorry,' said Kelly.

Since she was reborn as Ruby's long-lost daughter Kelly's social life had been totally transformed. Sofia took her out to some mind-blowing places. At least three different stop-offs per night, no matter how good a time they were having. Los Angeles was fantastic if you knew all the best places to go. And Kelly had to admit there was something very satisfying about bypassing the long queues and slipping straight into the VIP area. And since she'd had her hair done at Art Luna – 'My treat,' said Sofia, 'I absolutely insist. I cannot be seen out with you looking like that' – she was happier having her picture taken. She looked almost fabulous with her new cascades of shiny black tresses.

Last night at least six different guys had tried to get her number. None had succeeded. They didn't want to date Kelly Coltrane, they wanted to date Kelly Valentine and would be disillusioned when they found out that she didn't exist.

There was only one person she knew of who genuinely wanted Kelly Coltrane – Jez, and she had no idea why. She wasn't anything special. It worried her that Jez was so sure he was in love with her, when she felt she didn't even know who she was yet. She was still growing. What if she wanted to change? She poured extra syrup on her last pancake.

Octavia picked up the newspaper from the counter-top and started flicking through. With satisfaction she noted that Ruby's tribute was previewed on the front page of the Life supplement. Despite the facts that CMG were paying for it, Dolores Murillo was planning it and Octavia had merely been invited like 400 other people, she considered herself to be the hostess.

'Excellent coverage for the tribute,' said Octavia. 'Did you see?'

Kelly had only glanced at the newspaper. She'd noted the picture of the President on the front cover, and something about the rising cost of policing in the greater Los

Angeles area. It looked like hard news so she'd given it a miss. Who could know there was a glossy entertainment supplement hiding within?

She looked at the picture of Ruby. It was one of the last pictures taken of her before she died, the caption said. Did she look like a woman on the edge? Not really.

'I've been meaning to ask you something,' said Kelly. 'About Ruby's money.'

'What about it?' Octavia's voice was razor-sharp. Her dark eyes flicked around Kelly's face suspiciously.

'You're right. There should be more. Obviously.'

'I'm often right,' said Octavia. 'People just don't listen to me and they should.'

Kelly wondered what Octavia's life was really like. It couldn't be easy living with Sofia. Kelly had yet to see them fight but Sofia had told her that when they did they were ferocious.

'You said you were going to have Max investigated,' said Kelly. 'Are you?'

'Certainly.'

'Have you spoken to anyone about it?'

'Like who?'

'Well, I don't know, like an investigator?' She had no idea how one would go about something like that; she'd been hoping that Octavia might have it all sorted out and then the nagging voice of her conscience would let her be. It didn't matter how hard Kelly tried to dismiss what her dad had said, she was still obsessing over it. What if somebody was ripping Ruby off, right in front of her family's nose? What if that somebody was Max?

'To be frank, with finances the way they are, it will have to wait.' It pained Octavia to say these words. Especially to the jewel thief. 'Of course, if you wanted to sell a necklace or an earbob or something and contribute . . . ?'

'I could do that,' said Kelly. 'If you'd like me to help.'

Octavia's glass of water stopped half-way to her mouth. She hadn't meant to be serious, just sarcastic. Why should Kelly care that she and Vincent had been left penniless? And if another damn person tried to persuade her that one point seven million dollars was a decent amount of money she would scream. Even Sofia had joined in. It was all very well for Sofia, she had business investments worth nearly that amount and she was only twenty-two.

'Why would you want to be involved?' asked Octavia cautiously. She didn't want to scare Kelly away from the idea.

'I think if somebody – and hey, it might not be Max, remember? – has stolen money from Ruby then they should be punished.'

'And we get the money back?'

'It might not work like that,' said Kelly. 'The money might be gone.'

'Then why bother?'

'As a favour for someone who can't speak for herself.'

'I am perfectly capable of speaking for myself, I'm just having a little cash-flow problem.'

'I meant Ruby.'

'Oh,' said Octavia. 'Right, of course.'

Kelly felt a sense of loyalty towards Ruby. She wished

she didn't; Ruby had left her and forced her father to hide a secret for life, and it would be so much easier to hate her, but the more she found out about her mother the more she admired her. It was getting harder and harder to understand why a survivor like Ruby would give up after everything she had overcome. And almost impossible to believe that she had died without leaving a substantial fortune.

They were interrupted by the sound of synthetic church bells chiming. Kelly was momentarily confused and then remembered she had bought a new cellphone. The essential accessory for the flavour of the month. 'Hello?'

Octavia disappeared, taking her water and the newspaper with her. She wasn't the kind of woman to stand around and wait for people to finish their calls.

It was Sheridan from CMG with a rundown of the latest press enquiries. People had taken to contacting Kelly through Ruby's agency and so almost by accident Kelly found her fledgling media career handled by one of the best outfits in town. There were a couple of requests for magazine interviews, which she turned down, and a seemingly endless amount of charity appeals. An invitation on to a crappy talk show that Sheridan said they should blow off while they waited for one of the big three. Secretly Kelly was longing for Oprah to call. She thought she was perfect for the show: abandoned, resilient and female. At the same time the thought of revealing herself on national television, or even in print, made her feel uncomfortable.

'This could be interesting,' said Sheridan. 'A reality

show. A dating thing, but no, you've got a boyfriend, right?'

Had she? So much had happened in such a short time that Jez felt like part of Kelly's past. Did she want it to be that way?

'Is it a serious relationship?' Sheridan continued. 'Because I think you have to be single for this show. It's called *Desperate to be a Housewife*, ten girls, one guy and a prize of two hundred thousand dollars and a luxury starter home in Glendale. They're looking for ten celebrity singles.'

'I'm not desperate to be a housewife.'

'I don't think that matters. It's for ten weeks in a mocked-up house on one of the studio lots. Network. You get paid, obviously.'

Kelly considered this half-heartedly for a moment and then respectfully declined. She would hate to become one of those people who pop up on some reality show and make the whole audience say, 'Who's that?' She wasn't a celebrity.

'Wanna bet?' said Sheridan. 'You know who I had on the phone this morning? *Vanity Fair.*'

Kelly's heart skipped a beat. She drew in a deep, steadying breath. The mother of all magazines. If *Vanity Fair* thought you were special then you must be special.

'Nothing concrete,' said Sheridan. 'It could take months.'

But surely her moment in the spotlight would pass by then? This wasn't real. Soon she would have to get on with the life that was.

'Think it over and get back to me,' said Sheridan. 'One

last thing. Who will you be wearing tonight and what's your date's name? They need it for the copy on the early editions.'

'Huh?'

'What dress are you wearing? Who's taking you?'

'I don't know yet.'

Sheridan sighed. 'Okay, I'll spin that, make it look cute. You know, homey.'

Kelly had no idea what she was talking about. 'Fine.'

She said goodbye to Sheridan and buzzed Sofia on the intercom. 'Want to go shopping?'

'Always,' said Sofia.

Two hours later Kelly was trussed up in scarlet satin worrying that she looked like a hooker. 'I can't wear red to a funeral.'

'It's not a funeral, it's a tribute,' said Sofia. 'You can wear what the hell you like. Unless . . . hmm, do you think there'll be lots of people wearing red? You know, ruby-red?' She plucked a scary-looking yellow dress from the extensive selection that the Barney's personal shopper had selected for them.

'I'll go with the red,' said Kelly. She looked at the price tag. 'Uh, Sofia? Seven hundred dollars? I can't afford this.'

'Damn it, I keep forgetting you're, like, poor.'

Kelly was certain that any minute now the hole in the wall would stop providing her with ready cash. She had already spent everything that her dad had given her for this trip (a cellphone, sunglasses and other essentials) and was rapidly working her way through her meagre savings. 'I was offered a job today,' she said. 'A reality show.'

'Are you gonna do it?'

'I don't think so. It's called *Desperate and Dateless* or something like that.'

'I wonder why they didn't ask me?' said Sofia.

'They know you're not that desperate.'

'I'm serious,' said Sofia. 'I need to work on my profile otherwise I'll be known as Kelly Valentine's has-been niece.'

'My name's Kelly Coltrane.'

'Sure, on paper maybe but not in people's minds. You should think about changing it. You'll get upgraded at the airport and hotels and stuff if people recognize the name on your credit card.'

Interesting. Okay, so maybe people don't ever truly change but perhaps she could be two people: Kelly Coltrane who lived in Wales and had a nice local boyfriend with whom she could settle down and have a family, and Kelly Valentine who visited Los Angeles and partied with Sofia wearing scarlet satin. That way she wouldn't have to worry that being one was not enough, and being the other was far too much.

'Put the dress on my charge account,' said Sofia. 'Dolce are dressing me for free tonight. Pay me back when you sell some jewellery.'

Everyone seemed to assume that Kelly would be selling off Ruby's jewels as soon as possible. As if they didn't mean anything except money.

'I can't spend that much money on a dress.'

'Why not?' said Sofia.

'Because it's just a dress. That's like two weeks' wages.'

'Wages!' said Sofia. 'How cute!' Sometimes Sofia would

say something that illustrated clearly just how far away from the real world she actually lived. 'Give it to me,' she demanded.

Sofia marched over to the nearest salesperson and asked to speak to the store's PR manager. Within ten minutes the dress had been wrapped, bagged and given to Kelly on loan.

'Nice work,' said Kelly.

'Sweet-talking's what I do best,' said Sofia, giving a little curtsey. 'You really should try it.'

Kelly knew she wouldn't be able to. She didn't have Sofia's gift and was unlikely to develop it. Kelly had been brought up not to expect something for nothing. Those kinds of values didn't just disappear overnight, no matter who you suddenly became.

'What time is it?' said Kelly.

'Almost one. Why? Do you wanna head to the fifth floor and grab a salad?'

'No, I have to meet Max,' Kelly replied. 'We're going to the bank.' And on the way she might head to a sinful fast-food chain and grab a burger.

Her mouth watered as she waited in line at McDonald's, a Pavlovian reaction to the familiar smell of gherkins and fries that reminded her of home. Her forefathers would have been upset to know it wasn't the scent of lava bread or clams that took her thoughts back to her native land but the warm sweetness of a burger chain identical in almost every way to the one in Newport. She was just trying to decide what to order when her cellphone chimed.

'Hello, gorgeous. It's Tomas.'

All thoughts of a quarter-pounder with cheese dissolved. Kelly stepped out of the line and out of the restaurant, as if somehow he might not like her if he knew that she was doing something so unglamorous. She said hello and was surprised when a girlish giggle escaped from her throat. *Be cool.*

Since they last saw each other she felt as if she'd had a lifetime of experience. Kelly Coltrane might not be Tomas's type, but she knew that Kelly Valentine could be.

'How's it going?' she asked casually, as if gorgeous men called her all the time.

'I've been thinking about you,' he said. 'I saw a picture of you and Sofia at *LA Standard*. You look like you're having plenty of fun.'

'I am,' she said. 'Los Angeles is a fun place.'

'Sure,' he said. 'As long as you don't delve too deep. But then that's not what this city's about, is it?'

'Why? What do you find when you delve deep?'

'Zilch,' he said. 'That's the problem. Why do you think it's the New Age capital of the world? Everybody's got a gap to fill where substance should be.'

He had a point. Maybe Kelly could fill her own gaps more easily with a hatha yoga class than with Ruby. Finding out more about her mother was only creating new problems, not fixing anything. Not telling her what she should do with the rest of her life. 'So I take it you'll be leaving town soon?' she said.

'I don't know. There's this new girl around that makes the place a whole lot more interesting.'

He was talking about her, right? She didn't want to embarrass herself by assuming so. Should she say thank you or would she just look like a fool when he went on to tell her about some woman he had met? She thought it was safest to say nothing.

'I mean you,' he added, as if sensing her insecurity. 'So will you let me take you to this jamboree tonight?'

'It's a tribute,' she said. 'I'm going with Sofia.'

'Come on,' he said. 'You'll have a better time with me.'

It was possible, she supposed, that a night with Tomas would be more fun than another night with Sofia, but she didn't want to spend the whole evening on tenter-hooks wondering if he was flirting or just being polite, if there was a spark between them or only in her mind's eye.

'Take both of us,' she suggested impulsively. She didn't trust herself to be alone with him.

'You think I can handle two women?'

'If anyone can,' she said, 'I'll bet it's you. I want to try and have a good time. I feel like we owe it to her, to Ruby.'

'I'll pick you up at seven,' he said. 'Both of you.'

'See you then.'

'And Kelly?'

'Yes?'

'Just so you know, I'll be trying to get you to myself all night.'

She decided to pass on the cheeseburger.

Max was waiting for her in the lobby of Western Bank, a grey concrete stack just north of the Santa Monica

Freeway. He had the key to the safety deposit box in his hand.

'I don't have much time,' he said.

Kelly thought he was acting shifty. But then again, that could have been her imagination. Real life, she kept reminding herself, is not a movie. Even when you feel like you've temporarily switched lives with a star.

They were led to a private room to inspect the contents of the box, a simple metal container with a counter-weighted lid that flipped open easily. Dark velvet boxes were tucked neatly inside, their muted appearance giving no clue as to the treasures that lay within.

Kelly, who had never owned a serious piece of jewellery in her life, opened the first box she came to and gulped. A princess-cut ruby on a thin gold band. The sort of ring that a man gave his sweetheart when they were engaged. The next box contained a long strand of black pearls with a unique lustre which even Kelly's untrained eye could tell meant that they were real.

She worked her way slowly through the rest of the contents. She tried not to think about the cash value of the items, but concentrated on their delicate construction and the sheer beauty of the stones. She could imagine where Ruby might have worn them and pictured her gliding up a stairway to accept some award, the weight of her ruby choker pressing gently into her shoulders as the stones blazed in the spotlight. She tried to picture some of the admirers who might have given her pieces as gifts, and how it would feel for someone to give you something so precious. There were diamonds too and some delicate gold links. But the prizes in Ruby's collection were all of the stone for which she was named. They ranged in colour from the palest baby-pink right through to a deep blood-red. Kelly stared into the largest of these fiery jewels and saw a slice of reflection in the glassy surface. For a split second she thought it was her.

'Impressed?' said Max.

'Overwhelmed.'

'It will be some time before this is all legally yours, but I would be able to recommend some buyers.'

'I'm not selling them, not straight away.' She thought of her offer to Octavia and the money she owed her dad, the repairs that the house in Wales needed. 'Maybe one or two pieces.'

'Meanwhile,' said Max, 'if you ever wanted to wear something, it's all insured.'

'Really?'

'I thought maybe for tonight? The tribute? I think Ruby would have liked that.'

Kelly thought she might be too nervous with thousands of dollars hung around her neck. She was about to say no, but the jewels were seductive. As she searched for the perfect necklace to go with her new dress, Max explained how soon she would be able to take full possession of her inheritance.

'Best-case scenario a few weeks, worst-case . . . longer, maybe a year or more.'

'Why so long?'

'Octavia is not happy. There's a real chance that she might opt to contest the will. That could hold things up for some time.'

'And I can't sell a thing until then?'

'No. It's Octavia's move. We have to wait.'

Octavia was waiting for the funds to make her move. Funds that Kelly would not be able to provide until she could sell some jewellery.

Kelly's eye fell on a ruby pendant the size of a silver dollar. 'I like this,' she said.

'Interesting choice,' said Max. 'That was her favourite.'

She slipped the velvet box into her bag and silently prayed, asking not to get mugged on her way back to Beverly Hills.

Perhaps if she just spoke to Max he could give her some answers. Maybe he would be able to tell her what really happened, why Ruby killed herself and where all her money had gone. Her instincts told her that Max was hiding something, but perhaps she just hadn't asked the right questions.

'Everybody I've spoken to says you knew my mother best of all,' she began. 'Could we talk? There's so much I still don't understand.'

Max guided her out of the room gently with his elbow. Their business here was complete. 'You want me to tell you about Ruby?'

'It would mean a lot to me.'

They entered the elevator and Max pressed the button that would take them back to the lobby. 'She was a complex woman,' he said.

At last, here was the man who had been with Ruby every step of the way. The last person to see her before she died. He was smiling down at her and Kelly felt in her gut that he hadn't done anything wrong. Would anybody with a guilty secret be so willing to share? She was glad. She liked Max, and obviously Ruby had shared a very special relationship with him. She didn't like to think that either of them could be such a bad judge of character. Octavia's suspicious mind had got to her. Tomas and his silly conspiracy theories. Sean, who hadn't seen her for over twenty years. There was nothing sinister here. This was Ruby's closest friend. Finally she would be able to talk to someone who knew everything. He wouldn't let her down.

'I have so many questions,' said Kelly.

'Right. You should call my office,' said Max. 'We'll do lunch sometime.'

And he kissed her on the cheek and left her there without any answers. He could not have got away any faster.

24

Just after seven o'clock Tomas Valentine arrived to escort Sofia and Kelly to the tribute. Sofia wholeheartedly approved of the new arrangement.

'If we turn up without a man,' she said, 'they'll only say we're dykes. Which turns everyone on for about five minutes but is so not worth it. Besides, Tomas looks great in a tux.'

Sofia was right. He looked stunning. Kelly could immediately see that they were going to make a sensational picture. Three high-ranking members of the Valentine clan: a platinum blonde, the new-found curvy brunette and a dark man of mystery. She felt a shiver of excitement.

Was it wrong to be excited about a funeral? No, she corrected herself, not a funeral, a tribute. She decided that it wasn't wrong at all. In fact, being proud of Ruby's career was something that she could feel good about and was therefore one of the healthier reactions she'd had in the last week. Bad mother, bad drunk or bad person – there was no denying that Ruby had left a legacy of celluloid that would endure. Kelly had now seen all of her films. Always alone, always in secret, always feeling guilty. Sort of like having a porn habit.

'Good to see you again,' said Tomas, and kissed her on both cheeks. 'You look sensational.'

She caught his lemony scent, just a trace, and a twinkle of suggestion in his eyes when he took in her appearance. The scarlet dress that she couldn't afford looked striking with her dark hair and blue eyes. Her previously pale skin had succumbed to the Californian sun and taken on a luscious golden hue that made her look a little less like a tourist. She looked, she thought, as though perhaps she could be the daughter of the world's most beautiful woman. She held Tomas's appreciative gaze boldly, longer than she normally would, the way Ruby might.

Sofia seemed to notice the charged atmosphere and positioned herself between them, linking her arm through theirs. 'This is gonna be so much fun,' she said. 'You know, for a wake.'

Tomas's eyes flicked down to Kelly's necklace. 'Was that hers?' he asked.

'Do you recognize it?'

'My father gave it to her just after they were married. It's magnificent.'

Yes, and do you notice the way it accents my boobs? She tried not to fancy him. But it was very hard.

In the car – Sofia in the middle, Kelly half-relieved and half-anguished that she wasn't squeezed up next to Tomas – they passed several billboards for *Next of Kin*, the new series Ruby had been working on when she died. It would premiere the following day.

'That show is getting stacks of free publicity out of this,' Sofia observed innocently.

'Almost as if they planned it,' said Tomas.

344

Kelly looked across Sofia to catch his eye. Was he serious?

He shrugged. 'And the tribute tonight? Perfect timing.'

Sofia was oblivious to the implied accusations, but Kelly knew that Tomas was throwing up some grim possibilities. She was determined to corner Max tonight and accuse him outright. She thought she might be able to learn something from his reaction. In a few days she could be gone. She had nothing to lose.

Soon they were approaching the venue. Despite Ruby's well-known affection for the beach, and her near-disdain for the consumer orgy that was Rodeo Drive, the tribute to her was taking place bang in the middle of Golden Triangle.

'Look.' Tomas pointed up ahead to the back end of a queue of limos and beyond that was a magnificent art deco hotel, with endless white walls and elaborate gold scrolling, growing out of the street. Searchlights sliced through the darkening sky. A gigantic black and white photo of Ruby was projected on to the largest, most visible wall. It was the same shot used on the invitation Kelly held in her hands, no words, just an actress at the peak of her beauty looking as though she hadn't a care in the world.

As they drew closer in the dawdling line of cars Kelly could see the crowds that were gathered outside, some with placards and banners proclaiming their love for Ruby. She was dazzled. 'All the people!'

Sofia grabbed her hand and they shared a moment of anticipation. Sofia didn't have to say anything, it was all in her eyes. It was as close as Kelly had ever felt to her.

She sensed that Sofia was experiencing an intense moment of pride in her grandmother. Something similar fizzed through Kelly's stomach, a feeling of enormous respect for the achievements of a single woman. Ruby made mistakes, but she also made history. For one night only Kelly wasn't going to think of Ruby as the abandoner, but as the legend.

'You look happy,' said Tomas.

'That's bad, isn't it?'

'No, it's sexy.'

Sofia heard him and felt briefly jealous. She liked Kelly. She didn't want Tomas to steal her away.

They deposited the car with the valet and Kelly stepped out into the night feeling like a movie star. The cameras flashed like a fireworks display. Kelly fought her instinct to look at the floor and get away as soon as possible and instead smiled for the cameras in an attempt to make her mother proud. The entire forecourt of the hotel was laid with red carpet and several huge potted palms were lined up like a guard of honour along the main walkway. Sofia dexterously nudged them into line, Tomas in the middle, a girl on either arm, perfect.

Kelly's head was spinning and she felt drunk. Her vision swam as she saw herself reflected in a dozen lenses and countless eyes. The noise of the crowd sounded as if it was coming from far away. For one dizzying moment she thought she might faint but she concentrated on the slight pressure of Tomas's hand on the small of her back and the patch of warm skin underneath it.

The security was massive. Guards stood shoulder to shoulder in front of the wrought-iron gates and were scattered in clusters all the way to the doors. Personal bodyguards shadowed individual guests so that the red carpet was dotted with a large number of antisocial tough guys. Progress was slow along the clogged artery of the hotel forecourt. Towards the main doors a pen of reporters jostled for space and for quotes and coverage. Kelly's ticket was checked not once or twice but five times. Tomas held out his hand for her to take as they waited. Just hers, not Sofia's. His strong hand cradled her small one and she thought how good it felt to have someone as self-assured as Tomas on her side.

The crowd erupted into cheers and Kelly turned to see a genuine superstar get out of a car behind her and wave his hand to acknowledge the response. The hairs on the back of her neck stood up and she wondered how she would ever keep her composure tonight amid all the big names and the megawatt smiles. *I have a right to be here, I'm family.* She tried not to stare like a great big fan as the superstar walked across to please the crowd, shaking their hands and posing for pictures and talking into their mobile phones. Kelly dragged her eyes away. He was shorter than he looked on screen.

A few yards away she saw that Sofia was in her element, enjoying some verbal sparring with the press. She glittered under their slavish attention, she giggled and posed, and Kelly knew that even if she stayed in Los Angeles for the rest of her life she would still never have the easy relationship with the camera that came so artlessly to Sofia.

A second wave of cheers rose from the crowd as the vertically challenged superstar bestowed kisses on some lucky fans. The atmosphere was one of riotous celebration and each successive guest looked surprised and then relieved when they emerged from their limousines to be greeted with such enthusiasm. Who wouldn't rather go to a party than a funeral? Kelly touched the pendant around her neck and thought about her pedigree. An explosion of flashes went off close to her face. She tried to imagine what it would have been like to do this alone, without the support of her new friends. She would have rushed inside, gutlessly failing to speak to anybody or smile, and would have missed the chance to savour this once-in-a-lifetime moment.

She looked around her, taking in the crowds and the famous faces, the searchlights carving into the sky like a beacon. A beacon which summoned the great and the good to gather at this place tonight. What if she had never got on the plane? She would never have known what it was like to be on this side of the fence. Intimidating, a little bit scary, but exhilarating in the very best sense of the word. She felt as if she was glowing from within. A thought struck her: tonight she might have the same radiance as the stars, the sheen of other-worldliness that sets them apart. Maybe fame was best described simply as plenty of attention and a red carpet beneath your feet.

'Kelly!' Somebody thrust a microphone in her face. 'Quite a night.'

Was that a question?

'It's completely overwhelming.'

Bad answer.

'And what would Ruby think?' The microphone was

so close it was tickling her nose; she could almost taste the breath of those who had gone before her.

'She'd think it was the best night of her life,' said Kelly, thinking that was a suitably whimsical reply.

'Kelly Valentine, thank you very much, have a great evening.' The reporter thrust the microphone towards the next person in line. Kelly didn't bother to correct her name, just as she hadn't bothered to explain that as she'd never actually known Ruby it was difficult to theorize about what she would have thought of her own tribute. She was learning fast that the press didn't essentially care what Kelly thought; all they wanted was a neat quote.

'Well done,' said Tomas.

'I'm getting better at it,' she replied.

Sofia found her way back to Kelly's side. 'You do know,' she said, 'that there'll be a bunch of photographs arriving on press desks tomorrow of Tomas holding your hand?'

'So what?'

'The newspapers will get ahead of themselves, pronounce you guys in love, and then deliver a ruling. I'm just saying, be ready.' She shrugged and her attention wandered. 'Ooh, look, is that Paris?' Sofia darted back down the line, her focus lost.

'Don't worry,' said Tomas, and squeezed her hand.

'I'm not worried.'

Kelly wondered what it was like for showbiz journalists to spend their days writing about people they didn't know. For example, passing judgement on a relationship that didn't even exist, not yet. It seemed so ridiculous that it was impossible to be offended. This was the world in which her mother had lived, where you could be condemned or applauded for a single out-of-context sentence or photograph, where the press create a persona which might be only one-tenth accurate. How could you ever truly know a woman who lived in a world like that? And how did Ruby pick the people that she could trust from within it?

There was a commotion some distance away, by the railings that held back the general public. Kelly peeked across to see what was happening. It looked as if some guy had climbed over the railing and was struggling to get past the frontline of security. The excitement had overcome his common sense. She turned away quickly.

Then she heard someone hollering her name: 'Kelly! Kel!' so loud that it soared above the constant rumble of the crowd. She could make out a figure waving at her. At first she thought it was a photographer. She looked closer. No camera.

She took a few steps in that direction, leaving the main flow of the red carpet and dragging Tomas with her. There was something familiar about the movement of the waving arms. She stepped a little closer.

Holy shit on a stick, it was Jez. Kelly dropped Tomas's hand as if it was on fire and felt as if she was struggling for breath. What on earth was Jez doing here? In Los Angeles. Wasn't he supposed to be in Wales? It *was* Jez, right? Wasn't it? Oh-God-yes-it-was.

'Do you know him?' asked Tomas. His eyes were amused and curious.

'I do, yes.' *He just saw me holding your hand.*

'Then you'd better go over and say hi.'

'Yeah, I better had.' She stood motionless until Tomas had to give her a little shove.

Jez was still calling out for her and in an effort to make him stop she waved her hand in acknowledgement. She was embarrassed. Her self-confidence plummeted and she didn't feel like a movie star any more, she felt like plain old Kelly, girlfriend of Jez, miles away from home, an impostor.

Jez had a ridiculous grin on his face. 'Hey, babe!' he said. When she reached him he tried to hug her over the railings, where he had been firmly put back in his place by security, but settled for rubbing her right arm so hard that she thought she was in danger of getting a friction burn. 'What are you doing here?' she said.

'I went to the Peninsula but you'd checked out. Your dad didn't have your new number. How are you?'

'I don't mean here-here, I mean here in Los Angeles.'

'You know, support and stuff. My mum gave me some money for a cheap flight. She knew I was worried about you.'

Kelly wasn't smiling. She didn't need anyone to be worried about her. His delight at finding her was starting to fade as he noticed it was not reciprocated. He carried on talking but his enthusiasm lost colour. 'I thought I'd just fly out and then either keep trying your dad or just find you. Which I guess I did. So here we are.'

Kelly was stunned. He wasn't allowed to chase her across an ocean on the off-chance. It made her feel claustrophobic. He had asked if he could come with her and she had said no, hadn't she? Seeing him here suddenly, a remnant of her normal life in this crazy circus she was visiting was all wrong. She was mortified.

'Who's your friend?' asked Jez, shooting a filthy look in Tomas's direction. He was jealous, and Kelly was ashamed of how much that excited her. Jez was never jealous. She could talk about the new guy at work, or the new barman at the local pub, and his trust in her would never waver.

'He's family, sort of.'

'You've met the family?' he said. 'That's great. And you like some of them well enough to hold hands. Excellent.' Still jealous, now a little bit sarcastic too. A less attractive combination.

She wanted to retreat back into the circus where decisions seemed meaningless because it didn't feel like real life. Jez made her remember that she had a past, that she had made mistakes. She was in shock. Seeing him was a moment of clarity about where she really belonged, and for a second she hesitated about the whole shebang (no, tribute) because what she really wanted to do, more than anything, was go back to whatever cheap motel Jez was staying at, hang out with him, order room service and watch crap television. That would be so much easier. But she wanted more. She had started to feel as though she was getting somewhere on this journey, beginning to understand Ruby, and so herself. She couldn't derail. She had to do this on her own.

'I have to go,' she said.

'It's okay,' said Jez. 'Look.' He pulled off his dark grey hoodie to reveal a perfectly respectable black suit. 'I can come with you.'

'You can't,' she said. She waved her invitation in front of his nose.

'No, wait, I spoke to the people here a few days ago and gave them my name, explained the situation. They said if I managed to track you down I'd be on a list, I should bring ID, you'd vouch for me and it would be cool.' He countered her invitation by waving his passport in her face.

'Explained what situation exactly?'

'You know, that I'm your boyfriend and you'd want me here, but what with the bereavement and us both coming from overseas and everything . . .' He trailed off. 'You don't want me here at all, do you?'

Kelly said nothing. She just stood there in her scarlet satin and wished that he would disappear. He had come all this way. And all she wanted was for him to go so that she could get back to pretending to be more than she was.

'Won't you at least tell me where you're staying?' he said.

He wasn't making a fuss. She was grateful that he gave up so easily. You could always count on Jez not to make a big deal of anything if surrender was an option.

She pulled a pen out of her handbag and scrawled down her cell number on the back of his hand. 'I'm sorry,' she said. 'It's just that you won't know anyone and it'll be intense and . . .'

'Forget it,' he said.

'Call me later,' she said. 'Don't be pissed off.' But who could blame him? She knew that she could bring that gorgeous smile to his face by saying, yes, please, stay with me, hold my hand. But the words refused to come. She felt like a total bitch. Why couldn't she just welcome him, be glad for him? Not many guys would cross an ocean just to be by her side. She was so mistrustful of love that she kept pushing him away no matter what he did.

'It's okay,' he said. 'You're all at sea. I understand.'

It was the perfect description for how she was feeling. He knew her too well. She almost relented, but not quite. He reached out for her hand and as he did so his glance bounced off her bare wrist.

'You cut it off,' he said, looking for the leather bracelet.

'It didn't go with my outfit.' The words sounded callous and she saw the stab of pain in his eyes. 'I'm sorry.'

'Just go,' he said. 'Enjoy yourself if you can.'

It was her last chance to say that she wanted him. This could be the end of Jez and Kelly. What she was doing to him was unforgivable, but she couldn't stop herself. Being mean to him was easier than letting him close enough to hurt her.

'Go,' he said, and this time it sounded like he meant it.

Kelly walked away feeling small and obnoxious. She stole a look back over her shoulder. Jez was watching her and he smiled broadly, but it was a hollow smile.

Sofia met her half-way. 'Who was that?'

'Jez,' said Kelly flatly.

'The boyfriend? Cute. Great smile.'

'You should see it when it's genuine.'

'He just turned up?'

'I didn't even know he was in LA.'

'I don't know whether that's adorable or pathetic.'

'Me neither.'

As soon as the words were out of her mouth she

354

regretted them. She was just being smart, trying to be funny to impress Sofia. Sofia laughed and Kelly's gaze ducked back towards him again, hoping that he hadn't seen. Girlfriend walks away with famous new best friend and they start laughing. She wanted to blow him a kiss, to say sorry, to reassure him that she was still the same girl deep down, except she didn't know if that was true. Anyway, he had gone.

The two of them rejoined Tomas and thankfully he didn't ask Kelly to explain the over-eager fan. She had no idea what she would have said. She pasted a smile on her face and tried to stuff her mixed-up feelings about Jez into a box marked 'Later'. They walked up to the elegant main doors and stepped inside the marble-floored reception room of the lavish hotel.

Even Sofia said, 'Wow!' A harpist was set up at the far end of the cavernous space playing Mendelssohn. The acoustics, it had to be said, weren't great. The high ceiling of the reception room was wreathed in red roses and ivy, twined around trellis, and matching displays of red roses and white baby's breath stood on a dozen plinths throughout the room. It could have been a wedding. Tomas guided her so effortlessly through the chattering throng that she felt as if she was being led on the dance floor by a pro. Her emotions might be all over the place but at least she was sure-footed.

Beyond the reception room was another hall, even more impressive than the first. The red roses continued but here they were scattered over the white Irish linen tablecloths and the guests crushed loose petals beneath their feet as they searched for their seats. The sound of the harp gave way almost seamlessly to the lilting accompaniment of a string quartet, tucked on to the first landing of a sweeping staircase good enough for Tara, playing something melodious that Kelly couldn't place. The walls of the dining room were covered with projected images of Ruby over the years, the beams interrupted by the people walking by and casting jumpy shadows throughout the room. The light split into crazy patterns as it refracted off the crystal smothering each table. Kelly stopped looking where she was going and stared at the pictures instead. A hundred different Rubys flirted with the camera and smiled down at the assembling guests.

'A-list turn out,' said Sofia, as they all scoured the beautifully presented seating plan. Tomas was looking for their places, Kelly was being hit between the eyes by familiar names.

'Were all these people her friends?' she asked.

Tomas laughed. A big, hearty laugh that surprised Kelly. 'No,' he said. 'Not at all. Some of them may have been, she was around for a very long time, but no. They all dipped deep.'

Kelly didn't understand.

'Into their pockets,' he said. 'This is Los Angeles, it's a benefit, people like a black-tie photo opportunity that prints the word "charity" on the same page as their name. They pay for the privilege.'

'How much do you think?'

'Thousands.'

'For a table?'

'For a plate.'

'What's the charity?'

'I don't know and they don't care. Ask anyone here and I bet they couldn't tell you.'

She was tempted to do just that, turn around and ask the first person she saw. She wanted to know which charity had been chosen and how. Who had made that decision? Had Ruby worked with many charities? Had she been a patron of any of them? Had she given them all of her money over the years?

'Who paid for me?'

'I don't know. Max, I guess. Who invited you?'

'Octavia. She said Max would organize it.'

'There you go,' he said. 'Max paid.'

He found their names listed on separate tables. Kelly was on the family table with Sofia. She looked around for Sofia who had wandered off in a flurry of air-kisses with some people Kelly didn't recognize. Eventually she saw her settling at a table right up front next to the stage.

'I'll look for you after dinner,' she said.

Tomas placed his hand on the swell of her bum. 'Shall we both ditch this scene right now and go back to my hotel?'

He had to be joking. 'Maybe later,' she said, trying to sound cool, as if the suggestion didn't fill her with equal parts of excitement and dread.

'I hope so.' He kissed her cheek and turned away. She lost him in a sea of black tuxedos.

A lot of women were wearing black too. Kelly stood out in her ruby-red, which was not necessarily a good thing. She picked her way through the people and took her seat across the table from Sofia, next to Vincent's wife and an empty seat with no place card.

She chatted to Vincent's wife for a while, which was not very interesting. The woman talked about her children incessantly. Sofia had angled her chair away from the family table and was laughing effortlessly with a horde of famous faces behind her. That's the difference between us, thought Kelly, Sofia belongs with that crowd, and I belong on this side bemoaning the lack of a good baby-sitter.

The words floated over her as she thought about Jez and wondered if she could run outside and find him and say, 'Let's go home,' but she knew that it was too late. She had a feeling reminiscent of the morning after, knowing that she'd acted stupidly and trying not to regret it too much, hoping that it wasn't as bad as she remembered. It had been such a surprise to see him standing there; she didn't do well with surprises. Would he call? She wouldn't blame him if he never spoke to her again. If she didn't want him to love her, then why did the thought of a future without Jez in it make her feel sick? What had she done? She had acted like a schoolgirl in the playground – don't come near me, I've got my new friends – saving face by being mean just because she felt uncomfortable. Attacking to defend herself and hurting those close to her in the process. She felt like a bully. He didn't deserve to be treated like that; all he had done was love her. Was that so bad?

The cellist from the string quartet played the opening notes from a piece by Handel, loud enough to silence the hum of the crowd, and Max Parker took the stage. The cellist faded into the background the moment he began to speak.

'Ladies and gentlemen, Ruby Valentine would be honoured that so many of you have taken the time to come here today and celebrate her life and mourn her untimely death.' He paused to be sure he had the attention of every guest. 'I would like it if you would all take a moment to look back with me over some of the best work of a truly gifted actress.'

The lights dimmed. The small pictures of Ruby projected all over the room changed into stark squares of white light that danced across the walls like shooting stars until they all came to rest on the giant screen behind Max. A montage began. The guests were spellbound as Ruby loved and fought and wept over the years.

Kelly felt goose bumps spring up on her bare arms although it wasn't cold. She wondered what Ruby would make of all this fuss and decided that she would think it was absurdly over the top but would secretly love it.

In the near darkness Kelly felt someone slip into the empty seat beside her. Max. He saw Kelly next to him and his eyes widened in shock.

The film drew to a close with Ruby's name and the dates of her life and then the screen faded back up to white. The guests were sniffing noticeably and women were delicately patting their eyes, using their pinky fingers to wipe away any stray mascara. The applause was evangelical. Then dinner was served and attention moved abruptly from the woman of the hour to the contents of a shellfish terrine.

'Good to see you again, Max,' said Kelly. Softly, softly, wouldn't do to scare him away. Although the idea that a mega-agent like Max Parker could be scared of a nobody like Kelly was, frankly, ludicrous.

'Kelly,' he nodded. 'You'll have to excuse me. I just want to say hello to Octavia but then I have to conference with the planner.' He stepped away from the table, sidled over to Octavia, kissed her cheek, said something Kelly didn't catch that made Octavia put on her fake grief face, and then left.

If Max wasn't scared of her, then why did he keep running away?

Kelly ate her meal quietly, listening to Vincent's wife and searching across the room trying to see if she could spot Tomas. She couldn't shake off the image of Jez, standing forlorn behind the railings that separated them. The idea of Jez and Tomas being in the same time zone made her anxious. It wasn't as if they'd even kissed. It seemed like such a trivial thing to be concerned about during a tribute for her dead mother.

After dinner, and after far too many stories about children Kelly didn't know, she saw Max again, untouchable under the spotlight. 'Ladies and gentlemen, if you'd like to follow me through to the roof terrace.' He gestured towards the ornate staircase.

There was immediate confusion as chairs were pulled back and women searched for purses and wraps. Four hundred people then climbed the wide stairway to the shaded terrace. Potted tree ferns intertwined with tumbling bougainvillea and the sweet scent of jasmine filled the air. Golden fairy lights were twinkling among the foliage. Waiters offered liqueurs and a cocktail they called a Ruby Valentine, which people said tasted suspiciously like a strawberry martini, and Kelly thought tasted like drinking a lip balm. There were too many people for such a small space and she felt hemmed in. She lost sight of Sofia and wondered if the girl ever stayed still. But she found Tomas, or rather, he found her.

She was having a brief chat with a waitress who had a British accent. The waitress seemed to have no idea who she was and Kelly liked it that way. Kelly admired her shoes, she complimented Kelly's dress. Tomas appeared and gave them both a look which made the waitress dissolve into the background.

'What's wrong?' he said. 'So bored you've started mixing with the help?'

Kelly was offended on the waitress's behalf. 'Is there a rule against that?'

'Not a rule, more of a principle.' He smiled when he said it so Kelly gave him the benefit of the doubt; he was probably joking. 'Are you enjoying yourself?'

The truth was that Kelly was starting to find the whole thing a little insincere. All this celebration of Ruby's life was ironic, when the lady herself hadn't valued it enough to stick around. 'It's an extraordinary party,' she said.

Tomas nudged her on the hip and pointed towards a stairwell which led up to the roof proper. 'Fancy some air?' He held out his hand for Kelly to take and, curious, she did.

It was dark on the roof, and if she peered over the edge she could see the crowd milling a storey below them, but they had the empty roof all to themselves. Alone at last.

Her heart was beating fast in her chest. She searched for some stars in the sky to rein in her feelings, to remind her of home, but it was a cloudy night. It seemed ridiculous that only a fortnight ago she had been looking for the same stars back in Wales, wondering if she was the kind of girl who would ever have adventures, and now she was here, and the only stars were the ones who were guests at the tribute. She was looking down at the Los Angeles skyline with the hottest man she'd ever met. She spoke in a whisper, even though there was no need.

'I don't think we're supposed to be up here.'

'No,' he said. 'We're not. Don't you like breaking the rules? Taking risks?'

'Not really.' She liked playing it safe. But what was safe about being in a foreign country, among hundreds of strangers, and wearing red to a memorial tribute? It was a risk to admit that her life wasn't turning out to be everything she'd hoped and search for answers. It was a risk to be alone with Tomas. Playing it safe, she decided, was overrated. 'Look,' she said, and pointed.

In the distance, standing out against the black hills, the Hollywood sign kept watch over all of them and suddenly, above it, flaring crimson fireworks lit up the night, explosion after explosion forming chrysanthemums of blazing red until the smoke haze surrounding them seemed to stain the clouds a perpetual pink. It was a gaudy, magnificent display.

Kelly's neck ached from looking upward and she rested her head on Tomas's shoulder, not thinking of anything but how he was broad enough to make her feel deliciously feminine. He started to hum in her ear, a sweet tune she vaguely recognized, and slowly moved his feet so that they were dancing.

The explosions continued and she could hear the applause of the people below, but all she could feel was his warm breath in her ear and a heartbeat that could have belonged to either of them. He cupped her chin in his hand, lifted her face to his and then kissed her. She froze. He pulled back and laughed at the expression on her face.

Kelly couldn't hide her shock and started to babble. 'I wonder how much they cost, the fireworks, it's a lot of money that's basically going to go up in smoke, isn't it? I wonder if they charge per firework or what?'

'About a thousand dollars a minute,' said Tomas, amused. 'They charge by the minute.'

'Oh.' She looked at the weatherproofed surface beneath her feet – who would have thought that a flat roof would be littered with so much crap? Cigarette butts and soda cans, a gym shoe, an empty egg carton . . . anything so that she didn't have to look up at his face.

He bent to kiss her again. 'I have a boyfriend,' she blurted. 'That was him, downstairs. Jez. He's my boyfriend.'

'So what?'

'So I can't.'

'He never has to know.' Tomas pressed his lips down on hers and clamped her arms firmly by her side. She twisted her head away from him. His eyes didn't look twinkly and suggestive any more, but cold and mean.

'But I'd know,' she said. 'I'm sorry.'

'I think I get it,' he said. 'You're not as sophisticated as you like to make out, are you? You think you can keep up with Sofia but really you're a little prick tease, just like all the other Californian girls.'

He pushed himself closer into her and she started to feel nervous. She struggled against him. 'Don't,' she said. 'Please.'

'Come on,' he said. 'I thought you wanted to have a good time tonight?'

She was scared for about three seconds and then she remembered all the people downstairs who would hear her if she were to scream. It would be a race to see who got to her first, security or the press. She strenuously reclaimed a few inches of personal space to have a bit of room to manoeuvre and then she slammed her knee into his groin as hard as she could. He instantly released his grip. 'Bitch!'

Kelly fled.

She took the stairs two at a time. What had she been thinking of? She was so stupid. She could flirt with him, dance under a starless sky and pretend that she was a different kind of woman, but it was all romantic nonsense. She didn't know him at all and after what had just happened she could tell that he was no Prince Charming. And she was no princess. She wasn't red satin and priceless rubies. She was jeans and a t-shirt. She was walks in the countryside and dodgy old films on cable; she was a cup of tea, not the perfect espresso. A pint down the pub, not a first-class air ticket to New York.

She'd been happy that way and she hadn't even known it.

This wasn't real, none of it was. Who was she trying to kid? Maybe what she'd had back home was as happy as it got for a girl like her. She didn't deserve anything more. No wonder her mother had left.

Kelly started to cry. She wiped the tears away impatiently. She didn't even know who she was crying for. Jez? Ruby? Or the lost chance of being a princess?

She ducked past the remnants of the crowd in the dining room and found herself in a dimly lit hallway, the more private part of the hotel. At the end a door was ajar. She slipped inside.

It was a library. A few tables were dotted around the warm space, looking out on to floodlit gardens. She needed a place to get her head together, to think about who she was and what she wanted to be. There was so much she still didn't know about Ruby but she was scared that even knowing everything about her would still not fill the gap she had always felt in her life. Perhaps the gap had less to do with her mother than she thought. Perhaps she was just another twenty-something starting to feel as if life was progressing down a one-way street taken only by chance.

Kelly could only see one other person in the library, sitting alone at a table in an alcove. She could see the back of his head. He had an open bottle of brandy beside him. She knew it was Max.

She sat down opposite him. 'Don't go,' she said.

Max looked up as if he had seen a ghost.

'My dad told me you're the only one who knows what really happened.'

'When?'

'When I was born, when she left.'

Max slowly picked up the brandy and poured himself a glass. A movement of his hand made another glass magically appear from an unseen waiter. He poured some for Kelly. 'Your dad,' he said, 'Sean Coltrane, how's he doing these days?'

'Please tell me,' said Kelly. She was frustrated by Max's evasiveness. 'Tell me where I came from.'

'Your dad saved her life, did you know that?'

'I want to know everything.'

25. Ruby Coltrane 1980

News of Dante's spectacularly unglamorous death spread like wildfire. So quickly that the source was most likely the chambermaid who'd found his body, wrapped around the body of a cheap blonde who turned out not to be a stripper or a hooker or a drug dealer but an under-age girl from Minneapolis whose parents were still hoping she'd be back home soon. The picture that all the newspapers printed of the girl was as wholesome as home-baked bread.

The beach house was surrounded by reporters. Cameramen set up camp with stepladders and huge telephoto lenses. They brought snacks. The tourists came later, hoping for a first-hand glimpse of suffering.

Inside it was possible to hear the crowds. Ella was managing to keep the children distracted. But they all knew their father was dead. They were old enough to understand what that meant, but not old enough to know why all the people had gathered outside and wouldn't go away. Vincent and Octavia kept asking for their mother.

Ruby had barricaded herself in to the bedroom and wouldn't answer Ella's increasingly frantic knocks on the door. 'Please, Ruby, say something. You're scaring me.'

Ruby lay flat on her back on the bed, tears cascading over her cheeks and drenching the cool white sheets beneath her. She wasn't aware of Ella knocking, she couldn't hear her voice. There was a rushing in her head which began when the police officer told her that her husband was dead and had not stopped since. It was like being permanently on the edge of blacking-out, except the release of unconsciousness never came.

Ruby systematically considered the best way to commit suicide. Nothing with blood, she wouldn't do that to Ella. Pills then, except she might not have enough to do the job. If only they lived in a penthouse she would have jumped. Ruby had always struggled to believe in heaven but suddenly she had faith that there was an afterlife and that's where she would see Dante again. She could not comprehend living in a world where he wasn't.

For hours she lay completely still thinking of all the years they had spent together. Trying to recall every single time they had made love, starting in London, ending here, as if meditating on his spirit could bring him back. There was an ache in her belly as though she hadn't eaten for days. Had it been that long? Or was the pain she felt the flight of her soul which surely had left with him?

Good morning, Ma'am, I'm afraid we have some bad news . . . You might want to sit down . . . A hotel room in Santa Monica . . . Dead.

There was a loud crash and the bedroom door flew open. Ella stood there, slightly out of breath, rubbing her shoulder. She'd rammed the door. 'Good,' she said. 'You're alive.' Octavia and Vincent ran into the room. Octavia threw herself into her mother's arms and began to cry. Vincent, too, hurled himself on to the bed.

Ruby looked down and could hardly recognize her own

children. For some abstracted reason she wasn't sure where these little parts of Dante came from and why they were still here when he was gone. She only knew that she couldn't bear to have these arms around her, she didn't want to share the bed, their bed, with anyone but him.

'Get off me!' Their faces crumpled as Ruby pushed them away.

Ella looked on with horror as Ruby shoved Octavia so hard that the little girl fell from the bed. She hustled the children from the room and said to Ruby as she left, 'I was worried about you, that's all. We all were.'

Ruby turned back to stare at the ceiling and said nothing.

After several days the press outside grew restless. In the absence of any hard news or photographs of Ruby they started to delve into Dante's past and dragged out a number of women who were also grieving but were willing to share their feelings with the wider world. A picture was painted of a bad husband and a worse father. The children, when they returned to school, were teased about their junkie dad.

For weeks Ruby couldn't even think of Dante without the searing pull at the back of her throat warning of imminent tears. She felt as though she was rotting from the inside out, collapsing into her own black heart.

Ella forced her to eat and gradually she was able to find a few moments' release from the gut-wrenching pain. She would do this by focusing on a time when she was happy, to remind herself that she was once capable of being so. She would think about her first haircut in London, or her first job in Los Angeles. She would remember winning the Oscar or how she felt at the end of a hard scene well done. Most often she delved further into the past, back when she was a child and everything was simple and happiness could be found in a butterfly skipping past your face on a summer's day. A time before fame, a time before Dante.

This temporary respite only ever lasted for a few moments. No matter how hard she tried not to think about Dante it was impossible. She felt as if she was losing her mind, but the thought of escaping from reality was oddly comforting. It would be better if she had never loved him.

She planned to kill herself as soon as she had the energy to do so.

Ruby was vaguely aware of a ringing sound in the room. Several seconds went by before she realized it was the phone. A few seconds after that she remembered how phones worked and picked it up.

'Ruby Valentine, you're one tricky lady to find.'

'Who is this?' she said, instantly alert to strangers.

'It's Sean. Do you know, I had to speak to three different people before I got this number from Ella?'

Sean? Did she know somebody called Sean? She thought she might have done many years ago, back when she was someone else, someone free.

'Sean Coltrane?' he prompted.

'Sean.'

'That's all the hello I get? Jesus, Ruby, it's been years.'

She knew who he was, she did, but had it really been in this lifetime that she'd known simple pleasures like friendship?

'I'm so sorry about Dante,' he said. 'Ruby, it's awful what happened. He was an amazing person, a great artist and a friend. I'll miss him.'

She didn't know what to say to such a genuine expression of regret.

'I felt bad about missing the funeral,' he continued. 'I was away. My thoughts were with you.'

Ruby had left her bed briefly for the funeral, but she wouldn't be able to tell you the name of a single person who was there or what prayers were said.

'Ella thinks you need a break.'

She started laughing then and the tears that fell down her cheeks were half relief and half hysteria. It felt good to laugh. Out of the ordinary. A release.

Sean waited until her mirth had subsided. 'What's so funny?' he said.

'A holiday will fix me? Is that what Ella thinks?'

'I'm here for you,' he said. 'We were friends once. I've rented a massive house, miles away from anywhere – come and stay for a while. Get some space.'

'I can't.'

'My sweet girl, you can do anything.'

She hung up and yanked the plug from the socket.

When Ella next brought her food Ruby confronted her. 'You spoke to Sean about me?'

'I had to talk to someone, you can't go on like this.'

'Like what?'

371

'You're hurting yourself and you're destroying the children. I hate seeing you this way.'

'Then leave. This is my house, mine and Dante's.' Just saying his name caused a fresh stab of grief.

'I would never leave the children with you while you're in this state.'

'Take them then, I don't care.'

'You don't understand what I'm saying. You need to go. The children can't take much more of this.'

'The children, the children, think of the children,' parroted Ruby. 'What about me? I lost my husband.'

'And they lost their father. For Christ's sake, do you think you're the only person that loved him?'

'Yes.'

'Please, Ruby. I would take them away if I had anywhere to go.'

'You're asking me to leave my own house?'

'Yes, and if you don't I'll talk like this every day until you do.'

'Fine,' she said. 'I'll go.' Let Sean deal with the aftermath of her suicide; he was a man, it would be better that way.

26

Ruby flew to London where she checked into the Dorchester under an assumed name and called Sean Coltrane.

'I'd be glad to have you,' he said. 'But you'll be needing warm clothes.'

He drove all the way through the night to collect her. He didn't ask any questions on the long journey west into the Welsh valleys, like how long she would be staying or how she was feeling. She was glad of this because she wouldn't have been able to give him any honest answers. He simply chatted about his plans for the new house, his latest photographic subjects. Topics that required her only to nod from time to time. And when the scenery outside grew ever more wild and extreme, highlighted by the rising sun, he said nothing at all and allowed her to drink in nature's gifts through the car window and feel peace shyly try to enter her closed heart.

How fitting it was that Sean had rented a house in Wales. Ruby was reminded of the last time she had travelled through this scenery, on the train to London all those years ago, convinced that she was going off to make a better life for herself. Full of disdain for the choices her parents had made, wrapped up in a superiority complex that insisted she could, and would, do better than this. She had been convinced that there was nothing there for her. But the reality was that all she had found in the big bad world were larger failures and greater disappointments which had eventually led her all the way back home.

Life could have been so much easier if she had never left. She felt bitter about how arrogant she had been then. What had she been so afraid of? That she would end up the same as everyone else? That she would be normal, ordinary and dull? She would gladly give up all the highs if she could escape the lows. She would give her Oscar away for a bit of normality. She'd been happy as a girl. What went wrong? When had her ambition turned into self-destruction?

Arriving at Sean's house, she remained silent. It was shabby and in need of attention. Unloved. It made her feel sad. Objectively she could see that it was a lovely old house with a spectacular view but she took no satisfaction from the landscape. It was as if she'd lost the part of her soul that could feel pleasure.

Sean led her upstairs to one of the guest rooms. She didn't notice how beautifully he'd furnished it for her, nor how her room was the only one from which you could see the sea. She just closed the door on him and went to bed.

After a deep, dreamless sleep she awoke at noon and stole into the kitchen where she saw a bottle of whisky on the kitchen table. She picked it up without thinking and supplemented the tea that Sean seemed to think would cure all her ills with generous slugs from the bottle for the rest of the day, going back to bed and snoozing until she passed out.

Maybe it was because Sean had known her before she was famous, or maybe he was simply careless, but he didn't pay her much attention. You'd think if an old friend, a movie star to boot, turned up, out of her mind with grief, you would watch her closely. But apart from asking her once if she had everything she needed he ignored her. He would smile if they passed on the stairs and that was it.

On the third morning she ran out of whisky. She asked Sean for the keys to his car but he insisted on driving her to the nearest supermarket to get whatever she wanted. She looked for her wig and sunglasses.

'You won't need them,' said Sean.

'I don't want attention.'

'This is way out west. Nobody will have a clue who you are, trust me. If you wear sunglasses on a day like today, however, I can't make any promises, they might take a photograph just to laugh at it later.'

Thick grey clouds were lingering outside, making the day perpetually dark. He was right. There were only two other people doing their shopping that day and neither they nor the little granny who took Ruby's money paid her anything beyond the mild interest afforded to a stranger in a small town.

Ruby bought a case of whisky and some Marlboro cigarettes. Dante's brand. She stayed drunk for as long as possible, half-expecting Sean to take the bottle away from her and firmly suggest that she slowed down. But Sean kept on smiling at her if he passed her on the stairs and let her look for salvation at the bottom of every bottle. When the bottles ran dry, replacements miraculously appeared in their place.

She took the occasional walk in the lonely country surrounding the house. Twice she ran into neighbours and both times they called her Mrs Coltrane. She didn't bother to correct them.

Her deadened mind eventually limped back to life and when it did she was angry more than anything. Her thoughts were as dark as the rainclouds overhead and she scared the sheep with her drunken wails. What did it matter if she drank herself to death? Who would miss her? The children had Ella, her fans had new idols; nobody would notice if she left the world. Sod everyone and everything.

She neglected her appearance, chewing her perfect fingernails down to the quick and not washing her hair or her clothes until she began to smell fusty below the top notes of her boozy breath. One night she smashed the mirror in her room by hurling an empty bottle at it. She heard frantic footsteps on the wooden stairs and Sean appeared. But he only glanced at the mess and then went back downstairs for a dustpan and brush and a cardboard box for the shards of glass. 'Accidents happen,' he said.

Eventually there didn't seem to be any point in crying any more. Dante was dead and her tears had not resurrected him. Her career was over.

The following morning while she was pouring herself a cup of tea she didn't lace it with her new favourite tipple. It was no great statement; she just didn't feel like it. She was queasy and exhausted.

It was a relief to stop thinking about it all for a while.

Thinking about what had happened to her life and what she was going to do next. Her head was clear for the first time in months but no easy solutions presented themselves, instead there was a blissful kind of nothingness through which idle thoughts would drift harmlessly. It reminded her of the first time she got stoned, before the paranoia had a chance to get its grips on her permanent high.

On her third day of sobriety Sean suggested a walk. 'I don't have a dog,' he said, 'so you'll have to do.' He bundled her up in two of his coats and pulled an unflattering woollen hat on to her head. Her feet, in four pairs of socks, were encased in Wellington boots several sizes too big.

She followed him dumbly as he set off into the countryside at a fast pace, not waiting to check on her progress. The going was all uphill and she was sweating underneath her clothes by the time they reached a wide plateau and he stopped.

'Look at that,' he said, and she gazed upon the most enchanting view. The low winter sun cast pale gold shadows over the frosted hills and in the distance a small pond sparkled. It was the quietest moment she had known, without so much as the flutter of a bird's wing to break the silence. She inhaled a deep breath of the crisp air, feeling her lungs expand greedily for more. The chill of it numbed some of her sorrow.

'Isn't it beautiful?' said Sean. 'Come on.'

They walked on further, into the view itself, and Sean took her gloved hand to help her over the rough ground. Her calves were starting to burn but she got pleasure from feeling her muscles work, reminding her that she was human, and that she had a great pair of legs.

They reached the immaculate surface of the frozen pond. Next to it there was a sweet white cottage with a stone jetty out over the water. Ruby stumbled down the last few feet to the edge, took off her glove and touched her fingers to the sparkling ice. It burnt. She stepped on to it, wanting to get a closer look at the adorable house.

'Careful,' warned Sean. 'It's been getting warmer, the ice might not hold.'

She looked back at him and just then heard a terrible cracking noise beneath her. Her feet slipped and she was on her backside on the ice, then she dropped through into freezing black water and went under.

All her senses were driven berserk by the sudden sensation overload. It was as if a million white hot needles had pierced her skin. She couldn't breathe, she couldn't scream. The icy water was everywhere, in her ears, up her nose. It soaked through her layers of clothing, making them heavy and dragging her down.

Her body started to shut off the pain. It was quieter under that water than back in the real world. It was peaceful. Her frantic kicks subsided and the muted light from above grew dim until she wasn't sure which direction she was facing any more.

She saw images of herself dancing as a little girl, of her parents' faces, of her children, of Dante, and she thought, well, what do you know? It's true what they say about life flashing before your eyes. Then she felt a primitive desire to survive, gave one final almighty kick and a powerful hand grabbed hold of her hair and hauled her gasping to the surface, dragging her away from the jagged edge.

'I told you to be careful!' said Sean, and collapsed on to the safety of the shore.

Ruby lay flat on her back, shivering and fighting for her first steady breath. The sunset traced pink scars across the mackerel sky above her and she felt happy to be alive.

Sean broke into the white cottage. 'It's empty,' he said. 'It's been on the market for months. This is an emergency.'

He found matches in the kitchen and smashed up a wardrobe from one of the bedrooms, then lit a fire. Within a few minutes the flames were enveloping them in much-needed heat and the flickering light sent their shadows skittering across the bare walls. Sean disappeared again and came back with an armful of curtains. He shook the dust from a thick brown set and wrapped them around her.

Ruby sat as close as she could to the fire without burning and gradually the warmth seeped through to her core. 'I thought I was going to die,' she said.

'Disappointed?'

'Why would you say that?'

'I did think perhaps you were trying to do the job slowly with the whisky. That'd be a good choice, incidentally; what a way to go. But you stopped. I haven't seen you touch a drop since the day before yesterday.'

'I didn't know you were watching me.'

'Somebody has to.' He shuffled over so that he was sitting next to her and rubbed her arms vigorously. 'Do you want to know what I think?' he said, and continued without waiting for an answer. 'I think you've given up. Life must be lived, Ruby.'

'Dante never loved me,' she said. 'He told me that he did but only because that was what I wanted to hear. I wasted my life trying to impress him. I hate him.'

'You have to let him go. People die, Ruby, we all do. That's what happens.'

'You have no idea what I've been through.'

'Pity the poor movie star, her diamond shoes are too tight.'

'How dare you!'

'Listen to me, Ruby.' His voice had a sharpness that was unfamiliar. It changed him from a bumbling artist to somebody to take seriously. 'You know me, you know you won't get special treatment here. I'm happy to let you stay drunk for a month, for a year if that's what you need to do. I've no argument with you, but the flip side is that when you need telling, I'll tell.'

'What exactly is it that you think I need telling?'

He took a deep breath. 'I've no doubt you've got a lot of pain inside you, but nobody can make that go away. It's up to you. Drop the Zelda Fitzgerald bit and I'd bet there's still a real person behind all the histrionics.'

'It's not an act, Sean.'

'I know that. But from what you've told me, you and Dante were never happy. You could start again.'

'We were happy,' she whispered. If she had never been happy with Dante that would mean that she had driven herself to despair trying to maintain something that was never real to begin with.

She couldn't start again. It was impossible. She was Ruby Valentine and everybody knew it. They knew that she had a dead husband, a floundering career, a borderline drink problem, a nefarious past. You couldn't start over when you were well known. You carried your successes and your failures around for life. And what was the point if fame didn't protect you?

'Fame means sharing your mistakes with the whole world,' she said. 'I can't take it any more.'

'Maybe,' he said. 'But the question is: can you live without it?'

27

A quieter life was difficult for Ruby at first. She pottered around the isolated house thinking that perhaps she was losing her mind. What did people do with their down time if they weren't making love? She read every novel that she could lay her hands on and when they ran out she started reading the complete works of Shakespeare a play at a time and, as an exercise, forced herself not to read the better female parts aloud.

She took long walks, often back to the stone cottage to remind herself of that night she'd come close to drowning. She spent several days cleaning the house from top to bottom, wondering what the world would say if they could see Ruby Valentine in her Marigolds, hair tied back with a nylon stocking. And when the shabby paint-work was back to its original white she decided on a whim to strip it all off and start again. Sean came back from the post office to find her knee-deep in paint scrapings.

'Good,' he said. 'You need a project.'

She transformed the tired old house into a bright and airy home, wiping decades of grime from each leaded window pane and taking up the carpets to hang them on the low branches of the oak in the garden and beat them clean with a broken tennis racquet. She nourished it, she restored it, and as she did so, something of herself came

382

back. When there was nothing more for her to do on the rented house, she taught herself to cook.

The whisky bottle on the kitchen counter winked at her when she was bored but she stayed off it. It wasn't so hard. She knew that if she lost herself in the bottom of a bottle she would still have to crawl out eventually.

Gradually her anger was silenced. She no longer despised herself. Then one day she found herself humming as she thinned out the fresh basil she was growing in pots on the windowsill and decided to make pasta for dinner.

So this was how it felt to be organically relaxed. It was a wonderful discovery. These days when a neighbour called out, 'Good morning, Mrs Coltrane,' she smiled and said good morning back. She'd been married twice and nobody had called her Mrs anything before. It made her smile.

She contacted her bank and made an outrageously high offer to the owner of the house. She bought the house and the surrounding land as a thank-you to Sean. She had plenty of money. She was glad of the privacy and the security.

But there was no passion in her life. No drug-fuelled rows to be ended with ferocious sex. No challenge. 'Could I be happy?' she wondered. She supposed that she could try.

Ruby called Max and told him she was taking some time out.

'How long?' he asked.

'A year, maybe.'

He whistled. A year was a long time in Hollywood. 'Are you sure you know what you're doing?'

'No,' she laughed, and Max wondered if that was the first genuine laugh he had ever heard from her. She sounded completely different.

'Okay, stay there, whatever you want, you're the client,' he said. 'But if anything spectacular lands on my desk will you read it?'

'A script, you mean? If I said no, would that stop you from sending it to me?'

'Probably not.'

'Then don't ask.'

There was a pause. The conversation was over but Max could sense there was something Ruby was not telling him.

'What is it?' he said.

'The twins. Are they . . . do you ever . . . ?'

'Ruby,' he said, 'tell me you speak to your kids. Please tell me you call your kids. What is wrong with you?'

She was ashamed. She didn't want Max to think that she was a bad person, even though deep down she suspected that she was. Bad to the core.

'Ella came to see me,' said Max. 'Weeks ago. She was in a mess with money.'

'A mess? What kind of mess?'

'The kind of mess you find yourself in when your friend dumps her children on you and leaves town. She was half a minute away from calling social services.'

'But she didn't?'

'No, I talked her round and set her up with a generous allowance; she's okay. But seriously, Ruby, you can't do that to people. What if she'd gone to the police?'

'The police? Ella *told* me to go, she practically threw me out of the door.'

'Abandonment, desertion. The newspapers would have been all over that and you'd have come home to a warrant.'

'Thank you. Thank you for taking care of it.'

'This is not a broken contract for me to take care of, Ruby, these are your children.'

'I know.'

'Yours and Dante's.'

'I know, okay? Please, just call Ella. Check that she's okay. Tell her to call you if she needs anything, or the twins need anything.'

'They need you.'

'No,' said Ruby, 'I've failed them, I know that. But I'm scared.'

'Scared of what?'

'They're so like him, like Dante. I'm scared that I'll hate them for it for the rest of their lives. I know that sounds impossibly cruel but it's the way I feel.'

'I'll call her,' said Max. 'I'll explain that you need more time.'

His voice was ice-cold and Ruby knew that he was sickened by her apparent lack of human decency. She thought he was overreacting. Surely this was better than boarding school, the only other alternative? She could not be a mother now. She simply couldn't. She could hardly take care of herself. If she'd realized that being a mother meant never having the chance to be selfish ever again, then perhaps she never would have tried.

*

The following month, inspired by giant blue skies, she finally wrote to the twins. She told them that she loved them, and that they should be good for Ella. She wasn't sure if she would ever see them again. In this quiet life with her placid thoughts and a good man for company, she could hardly remember the woman she used to be.

It was a mistake. Nine days later Ella tracked her down. 'What is this shit?' she said. '"*Be good, I love you, you will always be in my heart*"? It's like a bloody suicide note.'

'Just read it to them, please,' said Ruby.

'I already did,' said Ella. 'Vincent stuffed his hands in his ears after the first couple of lines, started to cry and then locked himself in his room for the rest of the night, and Octavia . . .' Ella sighed.

'What?'

'She let me read the whole thing, she sat there and listened like a good girl, and then she asked me to give you a message. What was it again? Oh yeah, that's right, *fuck you.*'

Ruby was shocked. 'She's only ten!'

'No, Ruby, she's eleven. Eleven going on nineteen.'

'Are you trying to force me to come back?'

'You stay there as long as you damn well like. This is a better life for us, for me and Tomas, better than I could have hoped. I'm saying that when you do come back, *if* you come back, your children are going to have some serious issues.'

Max sent her scripts from time to time. At first about one every month, then every six weeks or so, and eventually they slowed to a quarterly trickle. She never got past the first few pages of any of them. The parts were all the same – long-suffering wife/girlfriend/lover/partner (delete where applicable) of the hero. She always said no. After a while she started to wonder to herself, 'Is that really what I once did for a living?' She found it bizarre.

Sean made no demands on her and he never tried to give her advice. Not once did he ask what she thought the future held. It was a revelation to find a man who was emotionally self-sufficient. Living with Sean was like stumbling on an oasis after an arduous trek through the wasteland. She was able to unwind her nerves, which Dante had tangled into a tight ball of despair. At first she missed the crutch of her neuroses, without anything to obsess over she didn't know what she was supposed to do with her vacant thoughts. But as her mind slowed down she realized that there was a whole world of things to think about besides herself. She understood the simple pleasure of a sunset or a fine meal with good conversation, reading a book or listening to music, things she had barely found time for over the years.

Then as Sean and Ruby approached their second winter together there was a subtle shift in their relationship. She blamed the long dark nights. He blamed the red dress she wore on Christmas Eve.

Making love to Sean didn't change the way they felt about each other. The old Ruby would have destroyed the friendship by tormenting herself with what their new sexy pastime meant, what it would do to them, how he felt about her. But she refused to go down that road; she understood that it would lead her nowhere. Instead she chose to enjoy being exactly where she was, wrapped in the arms of a man she trusted, a man who had saved her. Neither of them was embarrassed, it didn't ruin the friendship, and it didn't happen every night. Sometimes she needed to be touched, she wanted to fuse with another human being. She wanted to feel alive, and sex was the best way she knew how. It was cosy to have company beneath the sheets, it was harmless.

She was three months pregnant before she realized why she'd been so tired lately.

It was definitely not part of Ruby's plan to be a mother again at the age of thirty-six. If this had happened in her old life she would have been frantic with anxiety. Would she be able to work again? Would Dante be angry? Would she be able to cope? How soon would she lose the weight? How many pelvic-floor exercises would it take to get back to normal? She wavered for only a day or two, thinking how inappropriate it was for her to start a second family when she had failed so miserably with the first. But here, with Sean, it felt uncomplicated, he made everything seem easy, and his delight was smeared all over his face every time he looked at her.

Kelly Coltrane came into the world silently. It was the most awful silence that Ruby had ever heard. The doctors pulled Kelly from her and immediately she could see the concern in their eyes.

'What's wrong?' Ruby said. 'What is it?' She struggled to pull herself upright, the agony of nineteen hours' labour instantly forgotten. This brief moment of hushed activity was infinitely more painful. Sean held her hand and tried to catch a glimpse of his daughter through the back of white coats. He saw one tiny foot, bluish and covered with Ruby's blood. Ruby and Sean locked eyes and held on to each other in mutual dread. The seconds ticked by at an excruciatingly slow pace. Ruby thought, I was never meant to have this child.

Then the newborn Kelly cried out with fierce indignation and everybody relaxed. She was placed in her mother's arms and Sean thought the baby-pink of her skin was the most beautiful colour he had ever seen.

Kelly changed everything. There were no more languorous days of freedom. The new member of their little family was as demanding as hell. Thank God for Sean. He fell helplessly in love. From the moment he peered into Kelly's pale blue eyes, he was besotted. He looked after her. He protected her.

Ruby had been the centre of attention for so long that she had grown used to it. This tiny baby took part of Sean away and she was jealous. He didn't even want to screw her any more.

Was that it? Was a part of her life over for ever? No more sex? Nothing made Ruby feel older than when Sean suggested that they keep their separate bedrooms. He would often bring Kelly into his bed if she was restless and he didn't want Ruby to be disturbed. Ruby felt excluded, and reacted by trying to forge a relationship with the children she already had. Which did not go as well as she might have hoped.

She made a series of telephone calls over the next few

weeks, speaking first to one uncommunicative child and then the next. Almost teenagers, they had lived most of their lives without her. Because she'd been wrapped up in Dante, because now she was absent. She felt as though she hardly knew them at all. She couldn't even blame them if they hated her. She had left it too long.

If she was no longer part of their lives, then did that mean her place was really here? She found this house grew smaller every day. This world. The same oppressive hills she had looked upon as a child now encroached on who she thought she had become.

And the sad truth was that she hadn't come very far at all.

28

When Ruby picked up the ringing telephone she had no idea that her life was about to change.

'Ruby? It's Max.'

It had been almost a year since they last spoke. A year since she had turned down another insipid script which constituted Max's idea of a good comeback movie. She figured her repeated refusals had eventually worn him down and he might never call again. But he was still looking out for her, still hoping that one day she would come back to what was no doubt by now a formidable client list and he'd collect another 20 per cent.

'How are things?' he asked.

'Fantastic,' she said, and she thought that she meant it. It was a beautiful spring morning and she could see a bank of indigo crocuses from her window seat. She'd planted them in the first frosts of November and now they were perfect. 'You?'

He paused, unused to clients showing concern for his welfare. Nobody ever asked him that. 'Not bad,' he said, then moved directly on to business. 'I'm sending you something.'

Ruby sighed. The very idea of Hollywood seemed abstract now. And a little exhausting. But she admired his persistence. 'What is it?' she said.

'I don't want to spoil it for you. I know you're not wild

about the idea of doing anything, but just read it, okay? For me?'

'Sure,' she said. She had plenty of time and their television was on the blink.

Forty-eight hours later a FedEx package arrived from Max with an ordinary white script inside. It was called *Fell in Love with a Boy*. Each page had Max's name xeroxed lightly over it in pale grey shading: a security measure so that any stray copies could be traced back to the source. It must be a hot property. On the front, in black magic marker, Max had scrawled the name 'Vivienne!!!!!'. A quick flick through showed her that Vivienne was the name of one of the main characters. She threw the script into a magazine rack and went to take a bath.

A week went by before she bothered to read the first few pages. It was dark outside and Kelly was fast asleep. Ruby was curled up in a friendly armchair, half-watching the raindrops chasing down the windows and sipping a hot cup of tea with just a dash of whisky in it, but within fifteen minutes the rain was forgotten, her tea had gone cold and she was transported inside the mind of another woman.

Vivienne. A woman about her age, with a young family and a devoted husband. Nothing special. A woman who risked everything for the wild obsession of a younger man. A woman who let her heart decide her fate, with horrific results. The dialogue crackled, the tension raced across every single page. By the end of the script Ruby was scared half to death and knew deep down inside that this film would be huge.

She couldn't sleep that night. She kept thinking about Vivienne and the awful choices people make when they are blinded by desire. She understood what it meant to be destructively consumed by love. She could see now that Dante had stopped her from growing up; fear of losing him had kept her trapped in the insecure mindset of an adolescent. Love made you crazy. She knew that. She kept thinking about Ruby Valentine, the actress she once was, and believed that finally Max had got it right. This was a comeback movie, a proper chance. Not a polite request to re-enter the game but a brazen demand for the spotlight to be repositioned and fall on her once more.

Could she still turn it on after all this time? Yes. But she was different now, wasn't she? Hadn't she changed? She didn't even want the spotlight any more, much less crave it. But as she tried to talk herself out of this all she could think of were the possibilities.

The following day she called Max.

'Who's the director?' she asked.

'You like it?'

'Who's the director?'

'Patrick Mahon.' Patrick had directed Ruby once before, years ago. She'd been nominated, he'd won the Oscar, and Ruby was the first person he had thanked in his speech.

She drew in a sharp breath. If it had been anyone but him. If only it could have been some kid she'd never heard of, someone she didn't like. If it had been anyone but Patrick she might have been able to forget all about this dynamite character.

'From your silence I'm guessing you're tempted,' said Max. 'It's about time. I thought we'd lost you. I have to say, you're not on the top of any lists these days.' The truth was that the last time he'd suggested Ruby for a gig some twenty-something casting assistant had asked who she was.

'How would this work?' she asked. 'I mean, how long would it be for, what are the dates, where does it shoot?' Max realized she was more than tempted, she was almost sold.

'Four-month shoot, six weeks' time, Los Angeles,' he said. 'Does this mean you're considering it?'

'Of course I am,' she said. 'Max, have you read it?'

'Yep. Great stuff, right? Best Original Screenplay, guaranteed, if they market it right, which they will. I wish I could say I worked the play for you but you're his first choice.'

Ruby didn't know what to do. She felt anxious, as if she was about to dive from the highest cliff into the most treacherous ocean. She was nervous about telling Sean she had even read a script, she was nervous about going back to Hollywood and proving herself again, but most of all she was nervous in case everything fell apart. Ruby remembered how it worked. These people didn't give you a lot of time to make up your mind. Los Angeles had its own pace, which was a great deal faster than in Wales. Maybe once, a long time ago, when Ruby Valentine meant something, she might have been slowly courted, but not now.

'How long do I have?'

'You've already had a week,' said Max.

'Give me one more.'

'Forty-eight hours would be even better.'

She simply had to raise the subject with Sean. It felt wrong to be keeping secrets from him. Everything up until now had been shared.

He tried to pretend that he would keep an open mind but she could tell he was upset. 'So when you said you didn't ever want to go back to that life, you were what?' he said. 'Kidding?'

'No, I meant it. I meant it at the time.'

'And now?' he said.

'I don't know.'

They sat in uneasy silence. The only sound was Kelly's contented gurgle from her nest of blankets in front of the fire. She was just starting to talk. Dadda, juice; not Mummy, not so far.

Ruby looked around this place where she had learnt to be a real person again, where she had mended her broken heart and felt safe. 'It's just . . . is this it?'

'Is what it?'

'This. Our life. I'm a housewife, Sean. If I'd wanted to be a Welsh housewife I could have stayed where I was all those years ago, saved myself a whole lot of grief.'

'You said you loved this place.'

'I do, I really do.' She would definitely miss the serenity of life here but it was this very absence of challenges that would eventually get to her. She could already tell. 'I'll come back.'

But they both knew that it would never be the same. Sean muttered under his breath.

'Don't,' said Ruby. 'If you've got something to say . . .'

'You're right. I'm sorry,' he said. 'But would it be so bad? Here with me? I thought you were happy.'

'You could come with us.'

'Us? You're not thinking of taking Kelly?'

'I thought . . .'

'This is her home, Ruby, she's my daughter.' She knew he was deadly serious. 'I'll fight you on this, I swear I will. If you take her I'll never see either of you again.'

His commanding voice cracked at the final breath. He was close to tears. Ruby couldn't remember ever seeing a man cry. Not her father, not Andrew, not Dante.

'At least this way,' he said, 'there's a chance you might come back. For good.' Sean rubbed the beginnings of a beard on his chin. He wondered why he didn't feel shocked. Was it because he'd always known that it would end this way? That Ruby was only visiting? It didn't matter that he had fallen in love with her.

'You can keep the house,' said Ruby. 'I'll have the deeds transferred into your name.'

'It's not about the house,' he said. 'You think this is about a bloody house? Ruby, I love you. I'm in love with you. I have been for a very long time.' It was the first time he had told her.

'Please,' she said. 'Don't make this harder for me than it already is.'

'You're going, aren't you?' he said. He knew she had already decided. There was nothing he could do to stop her.

'I think,' she said eventually, 'that this could be my last chance.'

'Then you should take it,' said Sean. 'If it's what you want to do. Take it and make it count.'

She looked at him and down at their beautiful little girl and tried to imagine what it would be like if she stayed here for ever. In time she knew that she would grow to resent them both. Wouldn't it be better for Kelly to grow up in a place like this, with a father who was devoted to her, rather than with the erratic life of an actress and all the pressure that comes with growing up fast in a sophisticated city? Ruby had already failed once at being a parent to the twins. She could strive to fix things in the few years of childhood the twins had left. But she didn't know if she could cope with the guilt if she ruined one more child all over again.

Most persuasive of all, though, was the stark, un-wavering fact that she was not in love with Sean. She loved him, sure, only not in a way that would ever be enough. They were friends, and perhaps they would always be, but deep down in her soul she knew that her life was only ever meant to have one grand love. And Dante was gone.

If she could live without him, she could live without anyone.

29

So Ruby went back to Hollywood. She finally won her second Oscar for the lead role in Patrick Mahon's ground-breaking thriller, acclaimed by many as the performance of her life. She stopped being the girl from *Disturbance* and became the woman from *Fell in Love with a Boy*, associated for ever with Vivienne, a new feminine archetype for the Eighties' power revolution, admired by women, feared by men. She was on every talk show and on the cover of every magazine. As comebacks went, it was huge.

In the beginning she thought about Sean and Kelly every day with longing, then after a while her time in Wales started to take on all the substance of a dream. She couldn't relate to the person she'd been there. Had she really gone for weeks without wearing makeup, unrecognizable in a woolly hat and scarf? Had she honestly shopped at the local store and exchanged the odd bit of gossip with people who only knew her as Mrs Coltrane? How had she survived without mass attention? She easily forgot that she had been happy. She was back in the habit of using other people's opinions to bolster her ego and wondered how she had survived out of the public eye. Mrs Coltrane ceased to exist. Max was the only person who knew the whole truth, that there had been a baby. And although she never forgot that she had another daughter, gently she let go. She didn't want to destroy Kelly in the way she had obviously destroyed the twins. Better to allow her the chance of a normal life.

Octavia and Vincent despised her. Of that she was certain. They had been forced to grow up too quickly, to fight for themselves before they were ready. 'What have you done to them?' she asked Ella, desperate to blame someone else for the loss of two happy children who had been replaced by these monsters.

'I didn't do this to them,' she said. 'You did.'

Ruby should have been grateful to Ella, she should have been down on her knees and thanking her. But instead she chose to destroy the closest thing she had to a friendship.

Ella packed up her things shortly after that and arranged for herself and Tomas, by now almost a man and as cynical as Dante had been, to move to New York where she'd been offered a job at a gallery. Before she left she told Ruby something. 'My father died,' she said, 'while you were away, and you know what my mum said? She said she was glad they'd had more good years than bad. And you can't ever say that, can you? Every year was bad for you two. And yet my mum was out and about within weeks, bless her, after forty happy years of marriage. Whereas you, you walk out on your own children. You're selfish, Ruby, and you always were. God help you.'

They never saw Ella again. She cut herself off from the family completely, and when Ruby told the twins they wouldn't see her any more she could see how much they'd loved Ella, and she knew exactly who they blamed for her departure.

Ruby drank an entire bottle of vodka that night. What did Ella know? So what if she was selfish? She was a bloody movie star. She was allowed to be.

It was far too late to build bridges with her children. She hardly bothered to try. In the blink of an eye they would leave home and she would be all by herself. She looked forward to that day. A succession of nannies came and went, driven to despair by the disrespect of their precocious charges.

Vincent was sullen and withdrawn, preferring his own company to that of other boys. He seemed for the most part to be happier this way, but his fascination with complex role-playing games and cheap fantasy novels was a symptom of the disillusionment he felt with the real world. He had no ambition beyond the following week and didn't seem to want to fit in. Ruby gave up hope of ever understanding him and he drifted further away, lost in his imagination.

Octavia was impossible to ignore. Unlike Vincent, she baited her mother, getting twisted pleasure from confrontation and tension. Octavia wanted to punish her for what she had done. Ruby had no choice but to take it and Octavia was a constant cause for concern. She was running with a fast crowd and Ruby noticed a change in her of late, a sudden onset of pseudo-sophistication that she feared could only be the result of one thing. She'd had sex. She was barely fourteen years old.

Ruby sensed that some advice on birth control was expected from her but she had trouble communicating with Octavia about trivial things, never mind something of consequence. The irony of giving a lecture on unplanned pregnancy did not escape her. She did try once to sit her down and talk but Octavia was so spiky and hateful that Ruby ended up in tears.

'Are you trying to be a mother to me?' said Octavia, when Ruby stopped her on her way out of the house. 'Is this some kind of joke?' She was wearing a neon tube dress that screamed jailbait and Ruby thought she had been smoking.

'I'd like to meet some of your friends,' said Ruby.

'Why?'

'Because I think I ought to know the people you're spending so much time with. You're hardly ever home.'

'Yeah? Well, you weren't home for nearly three years and you don't see me giving a shit who you were with.'

There was the sound of a car horn in the driveway and Octavia made to push past her. 'Wait!' said Ruby. She put a restraining hand on her daughter's arm.

'Get off me,' said Octavia. 'I'm warning you.' There was venom in her eyes and Ruby recoiled in shock. Those eyes were Dante's when he was angry. She instantly removed her hand.

'I'm sorry,' she said. She hated herself for sounding so weak. She hated being scared of her own daughter.

Victory gleamed in Octavia's adolescent eyes. She knew she had won a battle.

'Where are you going?' asked Ruby.

'Some kids at school have organized a gang bang,' said Octavia insolently. 'I'm going to take on all comers. Fifty bucks a fuck.'

'Octavia,' Ruby whispered, 'what's wrong with you?'

'I couldn't care less.'

They rarely spoke after that.

Ruby threw herself into her career; it was the only area of her life where she still felt in control. *Fell in Love with a Boy* was a big hit but she couldn't relax, she wanted to capitalize on it. The parts available for a woman of her age were fiercely contested, and Ruby had to ensure that she was the best choice. That meant four sessions a week with her personal trainer, strict adherence to her nutritionist's diet plan, trips to Palm Springs for detoxification and a non-surgical facelift. In order to be the first actress that everyone thought of, she needed to be seen. She could no longer hide out at the beach and wait for the party to come to her. She attended every high-profile function and attached herself to the most fashionable causes. It was a relief to be busy. Memories of Dante haunted her still and she saw him in the faces of her unloving children. She felt as if she had failed in the first half of her life and was desperate to make something of the rest.

'That's ridiculous,' Max said. 'You've had more success than most people dream of in their whole lives.'

So why did she feel as if she was constantly chasing the next wave? It was exhausting to stay on top, but when she thought about the alternative, a quiet slide into obscurity, the fear that shot through her kept her going.

When Octavia announced that she was four months pregnant, the news leaked and the press went wild over the scandal of a gymslip mum with Hollywood heritage. Ruby was devastated, but couldn't help but be a tiny bit grateful to be back on the front pages as a result of the scandal. When Sofia was born – father unknown – Ruby privately enjoyed the flurry of publicity. The beach house was too small for all of them – herself, the twins, the new baby and the three full-time staff – so Ruby bought a pile in Beverly Hills. Octavia and the baby had their own suite of rooms and round-the-clock nurses. She never sold the other house. She couldn't bear to let go of the memories.

She called Sean to let him know her new address. 'In case anything happens,' she said.

'You're never coming back.' It wasn't a question.

Ruby couldn't conceive of it. She was working almost constantly, struggling to find the next hit movie. She went away for months at a time, paying through the nose for an army of housekeeping staff. She had failed to bond with her granddaughter: perhaps little Sofia could sense that the thought of being a grandmother repulsed her, or, more likely, Ruby just wasn't a big enough presence in her life.

She had often heard her contemporaries say that their friends kept them grounded, that their love for their families was what life was all about, real life. She didn't feel that way. Ruby never felt more real than when she was pretending to be somebody else, when she was in front of a camera. The mother, the grandmother, the friend – these were the fantasy figures she could not fully grasp. Ruby Valentine was an actress. That was where real life ended.

'What about Kelly?' asked Sean.

'Haven't you seen the newspapers? I'm a terrible mother.'

'I've spoken to a solicitor,' he said.

'A solicitor? Why?'

'I don't want you to turn up out of the blue one day and take Kelly away from me.'

'I would never do that,' said Ruby.

'Then you won't mind if I write that down and get you to sign it?'

Ruby thought she could hear a child laughing in the background. 'Is that Kelly?' she asked. 'Can I speak to her?'

'I don't think so.'

Her throat burned. She wouldn't even get the chance to say goodbye. 'If something happens to me,' she said, 'she's my daughter, and I will remember her.'

'What do you mean? You think I want money?'

'One day Kelly might want something that she can't afford. Like a secure future.'

'To make up for her insecure mother?'

He was being too hard on her. She couldn't take it. 'Do you hate me?' she said.

There was a long silence, broken only by Sean's disappointed sigh. 'Oh, Ruby,' he said, 'stop judging yourself through the eyes of other people. What does it matter as long as you can look at yourself in the mirror every day?'

But what if you can't look at yourself in the mirror? What if for the next twenty years all you can think about is how you once had happiness in the palm of your hand but let it fly from your grasp because you didn't know what it was?

30

'This is bullshit,' said Kelly.

Max spat out a mouthful of brandy and looked like a slapstick comedian from an old silent movie, struck dumb by Kelly's interruption. For almost an hour she had been listening to his stories of Ruby, lapping them up, asking pertinent questions, sitting there with those big blue eyes that reminded him so much of her mother.

'You're saying my father forced her to leave me behind? No way. That isn't how it happened.'

'That's not what I said. It was mutual. She always meant to go back.' He almost smiled when he said that but tried to hide it.

Kelly noticed, and her face burned. Was it so ridiculous to think that Ruby might have been happy with her and Sean in their leaky old house by the sea? 'What's so funny?' she demanded.

Max pushed his glass aside. 'It's getting late,' he said. 'People are leaving. We paid five thousand dollars a plate and we missed the party. That's what's funny.'

'It's a tribute,' she said automatically.

'And it went great,' said Max. 'You can see how much she meant to people.'

Was that right, exactly? Kelly could see how many people came out for a photo opportunity, how much people were willing to pay for a mediocre dinner in fine surroundings, but where were all the people who had been in Ruby's life? There was nobody here who loved her, unless you counted the three children, all of whom she had abandoned in one way or another. She had left everyone in the end.

'What about the money, Max?'

Max was tired. It had been a long night. 'I have to say goodbye to some people. You should come with me, enjoy being Kelly Valentine for a while.'

'Octavia's determined to have an investigation, did you know that?' she said.

'We're ready for her. A proper investigation would cost thousands of dollars, and she doesn't have that unless she has Ruby's money.'

'We?'

Max hesitated. 'CMG has a multi-million dollar turnover. Believe me, we've won bigger battles.'

'I'm selling this necklace.' Kelly's hand went to the ruby that nestled in her throat. 'Well, it's not really me, is it? And I'll sell the rest if I have to.'

She had a rare moment of courage against this man. Her latent fighting spirit surfaced. She was a bit surprised to find that she had one. How dare he? But more to the point, in a short while she would just be plain old Kelly Coltrane again; she could run away and shut the door, and she might not get a chance as good as this again.

'You can't sell anything until the estate is settled,' he said.

He presented this obstacle too quickly, as if he had already given the matter some thought. 'You've got it all figured out, haven't you?' she said.

'I don't know what you mean.' He fixed her with steady eyes that had survived many worse confrontations than this.

Kelly was tired of being intimidated. She was tired of feeling as though she was the only person in the room who didn't belong. Kelly thanked maids and chatted to waitresses, she liked her dresses to come in under fifty quid, seventy-five for a special occasion, she liked driving her own car and cooking her own meals. Most of all, Kelly was tired of trying to be something she was not. Her dad had raised her not to stand idly by and watch bad things happen.

'You should know,' she said, 'that Tomas suspects you did a lot worse than steal her money. And if Tomas and Octavia get their heads together you could be in a lot of trouble.'

Was it her imagination, or did Max skip a breath and struggle briefly to maintain his composure? 'I can handle trouble,' he said.

'Me too.'

The conversation, which minutes before had been so sweet and intimate, ground to a painful halt. Max downed the last of his brandy, then stood up and, in a corny gesture that made Kelly like him despite everything, he tipped an imaginary hat at her and went to say goodbye to his guests. That was the thing about Max, he seemed more like a charming grandfather than a merciless schemer. He truly seemed to care about Ruby too. Nothing made sense any more. Perhaps, as Max said, Ruby had just been careless with her money.

*

Kelly didn't want to see anybody. She didn't want to see Tomas and listen to false apologies, his version of their aborted kiss, which would just be an attempted side-route into her pants. She remembered the look on his face when he'd called her a prick tease. She didn't want to give him the chance to confuse her. She didn't want to see the photographers lined up outside the main entrance and put on a fake smile. She needed to find something real.

She left a message on Sofia's cellphone saying that she would make her own way home and slipped through the empty kitchens to the street. The distant flashes of light as famous faces left the tribute by the main entrance were like unseen explosions.

Beverly Hills at night was quiet. The traffic was lighter and the tourists were few and far between. Kelly had the wide, spotless pavements all to herself. The fancy store-fronts were shuttered in corrugated steel, allowing only the tiniest glimpse of the riches inside. Kelly ducked into a doorway and removed the ruby necklace. She wouldn't want to be an obvious target. She slipped it into her bag and doubted whether she would ever wear it again. She couldn't exactly see herself at the First Fiscal office party wearing more than her annual salary around her neck.

She wondered what Tomas had done after their dance on the rooftop. For just a moment then, with the fireworks all around them and the sound of his heart-beat next to her ear, she had thought that she could embark on a wild affair with a sophisticated older man and enjoy it. She had thought that she was someone else.

Tomas wasn't the right man for her; he wasn't even the right man for one night of passion. Because Kelly wasn't a one-night kind of girl and she couldn't pretend that a few weeks in LA would change who she was. She couldn't disconnect her heart from her head like that, and if she had kissed him back she would be involved. She just would be. Fact. And then she would have spent far too much of the next few days wondering if he was going to call, or if she should call him, or if she was good enough for him. It would end in tears. It was better to keep her distance. It wasn't her style to be caught up in a tormented relationship. She had friends like that, good luck to them, but Kelly didn't like rollercoaster rides, she liked solid ground beneath her feet. Did that make her boring? She had come out to Los Angeles to pursue adventure, to break away from the ordinary. Only problem was, she missed the ordinary.

She wasn't thinking about where she was going but when she saw an old-fashioned sign hanging in front of a building down the street, she felt as though her feet had brought her home. *Ye Olde Dragon's Head*. It was so cheesy that it made her laugh. It was futile to look for something real on these streets.

Inside the decor struggled to re-create a genuine British pub atmosphere. The air was too clean for one thing. Everything was spanking new and there were no cigarette burns in the upholstery. It was too brightly lit. There was no fruit machine, no tanked-up hen party in the corner, no darts. And where was the old guy nursing half a brown ale and checking the racing results? But the bar was a reassuring chunk of dark wood with beer pumps and a Guinness tap, and somewhere out the back she thought she could hear the voice of a BBC newsreader. It made her think fondly of the things she'd left behind. She ordered a lager shandy at the bar, although she had to explain what it was, and made her way to the back room where the artificial light was more forgiving and the reassuring tones of the Queen's English brought everything into sharp focus.

Her life didn't have to change just because she'd found out who she was; perhaps she had known all along. She wouldn't find happiness by running away from it. It was time to start liking who she was, instead of always thinking that she wasn't good enough. Ruby had her own reasons for leaving. Kelly wasn't to blame. And she realized then that for as long as she could remember she had thought she might be. She'd thought it was somehow her fault that her dad was all alone, that they were both alone with each other. While she'd been labouring under this false assumption she'd been blind to it; only now could she clearly see the effect it had had on her.

Ruby was the one with the issues, not me. She felt liberated. She felt ready to get on with the rest of her life.

And there in front of her, like an apparition, sitting with his feet up on a chair and a pint of orange squash, was Jez.

Jez. He'd found the nearest pub. It was like a homing instinct.

He saw her immediately and didn't flinch. She didn't have time to run and hide. She didn't want to. She hadn't the energy to do anything but smile.

'Come and have a look at this,' he said. 'It's amazing. You can watch breakfast television during last orders.' If he was shocked to see her, he didn't let on.

'That *is* amazing,' said Kelly. Sarcastic, but funny sarcastic, long-term couple sarcastic. Gently taking the piss and knowing that it wouldn't matter, because if it did, and walking together became like walking on thin ice, then the relationship was doomed.

He made room for her next to him and ripped open his bag of Walkers crisps so that she could share them. He raised an eyebrow. 'However did you find me?'

She didn't tell him she hadn't exactly been looking. Maybe she had.

They sat and watched the headlines: a Cabinet reshuffle, a new stadium in London, a missing girl. Then the weather; five grey clouds covered all of Wales.

She knew it was up to her to break the silence. 'I shouldn't have left you standing there,' she said. 'I freaked out.'

'I felt like a right twat.'

'I don't want you to feel like a twat. I was confused.'

'Why won't you let me love you, Kel? Is it because of your mum, do you think?'

How could she have forgotten how perceptive he was? She had only just figured these things out for herself. The thought of somebody knowing her so well no longer made her feel vulnerable. Instead it made her feel almost safe.

'I think she's a big part of it.'

'I won't hurt you,' he said. 'I can prove that to you, but you have to let me in.'

'It's hard for me. I really am sorry.'

'I believe you. You're forgiven.' He smiled. She had missed that smile. It always lifted her spirits. 'How did the party go?' he said.

Was that it? Apology accepted and they were back to being Kelly and Jez again. Could it really be that simple to forgive? With all the tantrums and grudges she had seen of late, it had been a while since she had spoken to someone as uncomplicated as Jez. Was uncomplicated the same thing as boring?

'Everyone seemed to be having a good time,' she said.

'And you?'

'It was okay,' said Kelly. She grabbed a handful of crisps. 'This is better.'

He laughed as if she was joking, and she was, a bit. But not altogether.

'I wanted to meet her friends and family. The family's kind of crazy, and the thing is, I don't think she had many friends, just this one guy, her agent, Max Parker.'

'What's he like?'

'Shifty.'

'Really?'

'Maybe I'm just being paranoid.'

'Paranoia is the worst,' said Jez. 'Try being me: my girl-friend is swanning around Los Angeles and all the newspapers keep banging on about how gorgeous she is.'

'Did they?'

'Oh yeah – *Welsh stunner Kelly, 25* – you know?'

'Seriously?'

'And I kept thinking, hey, that's the woman I love! I was dead proud of you, but still, it was weird.'

There he was again talking of love. Only this time it didn't make her want to run and hide, it made her feel optimistic. 'I can't believe you came all this way,' she said.

'Come off it. It was either that or sit at home feeling like a wanker, imagining you out on the town with tall, dark and handsome strangers.'

Which was a pretty good description of what he'd seen. 'That was Tomas,' she said. 'Tomas Valentine.'

'He fancied you, I could tell.'

She was able to think: well so what if he did? She didn't have to like him back just because he showed an interest. She didn't have to feel beholden because she was flattered. The guy was an arsehole. 'It's the dress,' she said.

'You look fantastic. How come you never get dressed up like that at home?'

'To do what? Go down to the chip shop and play on the arcade games? KFC and a video?'

'Yeah, why not?'

He was absolutely right. There was nothing stopping her going out for a newspaper dripping in jewels, wearing red satin to the chip shop or for a quiet dinner at home. She could always suggest a night out somewhere special, a break from the ordinary, an adventure, but she never did. And equally, if she was really as bored by her life as she'd claimed to be, there was nothing stopping her leaving Jez, moving to a city such as this to hunt out that elusive happiness. But she didn't want to. She felt as if she could be happy just to finish her drink and feel the safe softness of Jez's palm against hers. The question of what to do when her drink was finished could wait.

413

31

They took a drive. Jez had hired a car and Kelly was impressed. Not because it was a nifty little convertible, which screamed 'tourist', but because he had been sensible enough to get his own wheels. She'd been here weeks and had been relying on taxis, lifts and the occasional limo. Why hadn't she just strolled down to Hertz and picked something up? How come Jez, who usually struggled to find two matching socks in the morning, appeared to be more organized than she was? He had the car and a room in a funky-sounding hotel on the promenade at Venice Beach.

'You'll like it,' he said. 'There's surfers.' She hadn't seen a single surfer since she'd arrived in California. She'd been wondering where they'd been hiding. So many of her preconceptions had been proved wrong that she'd almost given up on the Beach Boys' image of California dreams.

The backdrop of the city unfurled before them like a road movie. She told him about Ruby's missing money. 'I get the strongest feeling that there's something Max isn't telling me,' she said.

'You should trust your instincts,' said Jez. 'You're a brilliant judge of character.'

She looked across at him in surprise – what a lovely compliment. Only trouble was that her instincts were being blurred by having Jez close to her once again. He'd caught the sun. There was a flush of red across his nose that she knew he would hate.

'Ask him to tell you the truth,' said Jez.

'I already have.'

'Ask him again. If something is important to you then you don't take no for an answer.' Jez grinned at her as he said this and she knew he was talking about her.

The companionable silence was as familiar to her as toast and jam. 'Is that it then?' said Kelly. 'Are we back together?' He hadn't tried to kiss her yet or anything. She wasn't sure what she would do when, if, he did.

'Don't sound so excited.'

Surely they were supposed to have some sort of big discussion about the obstacles in front of them? About the future? He had flown thousands of miles to see her, didn't he have a speech prepared? It was a grand gesture without the pay-off, the last scene in the movie but without the moral message. This was their cue to communicate, learn a little something and go forward with a clear understanding of what had gone wrong before. A passionate kiss and a big finish. Happy ever after as the credits rolled. If this was *it*, then was it enough? She loved him, just like she loved toast and jam, but what if what she really wanted to wake up to every morning was Eggs Benedict? Not that she was the biggest fan of hollandaise sauce, that wasn't the point, the point was – didn't she deserve something special?

'I should have known you'd make this complicated,' said Jez. 'Lighten up.'

'What's that supposed to mean?'

'Nothing, forget it.'

But she didn't want to forget it. 'No, tell me what you mean.'

'Let it go,' said Jez.

'You always have to let everything go. Why can't you get mad with me once in a while? I've never seen you angry.'

'You want me to be mad with you?'

'I want you to disagree with me occasionally. Otherwise, where's the spark? Where's the passion?'

Jez rubbed his nose. 'I thought you and me always had plenty of passion.'

'We do, I don't mean that, it's not about sex. I mean drama, excitement.'

'You know what I think?' said Jez. 'I think you're just afraid to be happy. You'd rather be in a bad relationship that's going to end than a good relationship that's for ever. You're safer that way.'

'That's just stupid,' said Kelly.

'You said it.'

'Why would anyone be scared of happiness?'

'Because you don't believe it can last. Maybe it's because of your mum. Or maybe because it means you'd have to choose someone, choose something to hold close, and live with your choice instead of running away whenever it gets hard.'

'Hey, I don't run away, okay? Not me.'

'You ran all the way here,' he pointed out. 'Just because we were getting serious.'

'Being here has got *nothing* to do with you!' She was amazed by his arrogance. She'd come out here for her mother's funeral; how much more of an excuse did she need?

'Then why didn't you want me to come with you?'

'Maybe I just don't like you any more,' she said.

'Now, we both know that's a lie. Admit it, you could stay with me for ever, and that scares the shit out of you.'

'You love yourself.'

'Nope, I love you. You just can't handle it.'

She was hurt. She stared out of the window in a bit of sulk for a while until Jez playfully punched her shoulder. 'How was that?' he said. 'Did I do okay?'

Their first row. She hadn't enjoyed it as much as she thought she would.

It was starting to get light and they stopped at an all-night diner for coffee and a slice of pie. Although Kelly was one hundred per cent certain she had never been in this diner before, there was something hauntingly familiar about the turquoise decor, the retro vibe and the view of Pico Boulevard. She sipped her coffee and tried to shake off the unsettling déjà vu.

'*True Romance*,' said Jez.

'What?'

'The Tarantino movie? And a bunch of others. They were filmed here.' He shovelled cherry pie into his mouth and spoke with his mouth full. 'That's the problem with this whole city, you feel like you've seen it all before.'

'You think you know it, but you don't,' she said.

'Like Ruby?'

'Exactly.'

Jez looked at her and saw that she was locked in thought. He wanted more than anything to help her. 'Let's go,' he said.

'Where to?'

'See this Max fella. Get some answers.'

'Now?'

'Yep, right now. Why not?'

'Oh, I don't know, maybe because it's five o'clock in the morning and he won't be at the office for hours?'

'So we'll go to his house.'

'I don't know where that is.' Her eyes flickered with a half-forgotten memory and Jez caught it.

'Liar.'

She felt deep in the bottom of her bag, past her priceless ruby, her new cellphone and her designer sunglasses, and pulled out the crumpled piece of paper that Sean had given her with Max's home address. It seemed like so long ago. 'Here. It's in Malibu.'

'Great, come on, finish your coffee.'

'You're serious about this, aren't you?'

'Deadly,' he said. 'I won't take no for an answer.'

A short while and a few wrong turns later they were parked up outside an imposing set of solid wooden gates. The sun was low in the sky behind them and the humid air was filled with the chattering sound of early birds. When they got out of the car, climbed up on to the hood and stood on tiptoe they could see a few tall treetops and some natty mock-Tudor panelling, a slate roof and a weathervane. The Old English style looked incongruous in the West Coast landscape, the morning traffic on the Pacific Coast Highway steadily building from a dribble to a flood

'This is silly,' said Kelly. 'Some housemaid will answer and she's just going to tell us to get lost.'

'There must be another way in, a back door.'

'I think the back garden of this place is the Pacific Ocean.'

'That's a start.' Jez turned the car around and drove off, looking for an access road to the beach, but there was nothing. The half-mile from here to the surfline was chock-a-block with valuable real estate, as if every last cent's worth of land had been snatched up and cemented over to keep out the riff-raff, a ghetto of privilege.

'What's that?' he said, stopping the car and backing up. 'There.' He pointed to the narrowest of stone staircases with a blink-and-you-miss-it signpost that said 'Beach'.

They parked the car, went down the dilapidated steps on to the wide flat sand and walked back the way they had come. Every few yards a sign reminded them not to come any closer to the houses than the high-tideline or they would face the risk of criminal prosecution for trespass. The damp sand shimmered silver beneath their feet. Now they could see that the houses were truly phenomenal. From the road they had only seen an endless succession of gates and bland concrete, but from their new vantage point these mansions with their million-dollar views were displayed in all their architectural splendour; steel and glass creations that reflected the prying rays of the sun like a mirror, white castles on the sand with turrets and trailing vines, sun-bleached stucco with wraparound decking on every floor.

A solitary jogger, i-pod firmly in place, gave them a curious look. Kelly took off her shoes and felt the exquisite pleasure of sand between her toes. Finally, she thought, I feel like I'm in California. In fact she was half-expecting David Hasselhoff to leap from the waves in his red swimsuit.

'This is great,' said Jez. 'Let's live here.'

'And work ourselves to death paying for it?'

'Good point. Maybe not, then.'

After a mile and a half they spotted a familiar weather-vane. One look at Jez told her that he fully intended to go through with this. He was sizing up the place like a petty criminal. For a second there she had thought that they were just enjoying a romantic walk on the beach.

'Do you remember when we met?' she said.

'On the beach, right? Early, just like this. You tasted like a cheeseburger.'

'Doesn't it worry you that's the most romantic moment we've ever had?'

'Nope.'

'How come?'

'Because whenever I think about that morning, seeing you sitting there like a mermaid staring at the waves, I know that I'm a lucky man. And I feel good, deep down inside.'

'Yeah?'

'Yeah. So don't spoil it for me with your needless madwoman worrying, all right, babe?'

She looked at him and fully understood how far he had come for her. He could have stayed at home moping, he could have gone out and got himself another girl-friend, but instead he had got on a plane and found her. What more could she possibly want? A man whose actions spoke louder than words, who wouldn't take no for an answer, who loved her and thought she was special.

That should be enough for anyone, more than enough, a gift. And she had almost pushed him away.

'I am special?' she said.

He looked up in surprise. He was staring at her so hard that she felt embarrassed under his gaze.

'What is it?' she asked.

'It's just that I don't think I've ever seen you be . . . well, needy.'

She closed up. Just like that. Jez could practically see the iron doors slam down. 'No, wait a second,' he said. 'I didn't say I didn't like it. People like to be needed.'

'Forget it.' She turned away from him and looked out at the endless blue, pretending that she didn't care.

'You're special to me,' he said behind her. 'You would be special to anyone that got to know you, but nobody gets the chance. And that's a shame, because they don't get to see just how amazing you really are. How sweet you are when you're not being defensive, how funny you are when you're not even trying, how smart you are about people . . .' She turned around. '. . . how beautiful you are when you look at me like that.'

'Stop,' she said. 'I believe you.' She threw herself at him and kissed him, long and hard. She could feel a smile stretching across both their lips as she did so. The sun warmed her face, the Pacific Ocean curled around her feet, and a wave of seagulls took flight around them, crying out like sirens. When they broke apart, Kelly could have sworn she saw a dolphin leap in a perfect arc out in the wide blue sea. Or perhaps she imagined it. Either way, she had her new romantic moment and knew that she'd be replaying this kiss for months to come.

'Ready?' he said.

'Let's do it.'

They walked up on to the dry sand towards Max's house. Kelly kept expecting big angry Rottweiler guard dogs to come out and stop them, or security guards with Rottweiler attitudes. But nobody did. A CCTV camera stared uselessly at the main back gate, several yards from where Jez gave her a leg-up over the wall.

She landed amid a bed of tree ferns feeling like a high-class assassin, like Bridget Fonda but without the gun. She was still wearing her red satin, not the best camouflage. Jez landed beside her with a dull thud.

'Okay,' she said. 'We are now officially trespassing.'

'I know, man, isn't it cool?'

32

It was six o'clock in the morning and Max Parker was swimming laps in his heated outdoor Olympic-sized pool. He churned the water thinking about Ruby and whether or not they would get the viewing figures they were looking for with tonight's new episode of *Next of Kin*. They needed to deliver three seasons before anyone got rich, they'd all known that from the start. The renewed interest in Ruby had practically guaranteed syndication, serious money, but the product had to be good. It had to be a hit. They had risked too much to fail.

He turned over and started swimming backstroke, looking up at the sky. He missed Ruby, he hadn't thought that he would, but he did. He had thought that her absence would give him a feeling of liberation, of closure, but he was working for her as hard ever, trying to organize her finances, dealing with her family. He had Octavia Valentine threatening to tie the process up for years, though he was sure he could dissuade her. And every other day he had Vincent Valentine, a small-time actor at best, clamouring for scripts and advice. Didn't Vincent realize that Max had only ever represented him as a favour to his mother? Now that she was gone, was he really expected to handle her second-rate offspring? But he had to keep Vincent happy for a while, he didn't need any more enemies, not right now. The threat that everything he had done would be exposed was a constant anxiety.

And then there was the other daughter, Kelly. So much brighter than the others, with a sense of perspective that only distance could give. She was the one who scared him the most. Her sense of morality was different to the rest of them. She had one.

Max saw a movement by the edge of the pool and looked up, his eyes stinging from the chemically treated water, and there stood a woman in red satin backlit by the early sun on his deck. She looked so much like Ruby that his heart leaped painfully in his chest and he momentarily feared death.

'Hi, Max,' said Kelly.

Max recovered his composure and climbed from the pool. 'Kelly, what a surprise!' He was terrified. What the hell was she doing here? He pretended to be pleased to see her. He saw a young man emerge from the bushes. Oh God, had she brought back-up? Why had he never hired a proper security guard?

'This is Jez,' said Kelly. 'My boyfriend.'

'All right?' said Jez. Max nodded, utterly bewildered. He pulled on his robe, feeling vulnerable.

It was the first time Kelly had seen Max without the power suit. He looked older, weaker and invertebrate. She wasn't afraid of him. 'I want you to know I'm going to the police,' she said, and braced herself for him to . . . what? Pull a gun? Flee? She had to keep trying to remember that she wasn't Bridget Fonda, this wasn't an action movie.

'You are?'

'Yes,' she said firmly. 'Ruby was worth millions. I think

some of her money has disappeared and I think you know where it's gone.'

'You're wrong. Ruby did movies before they were expensive and television when it was cheap.'

'Save the sound bites, Max. I don't believe you.'

They held each other's gaze for the longest time. Then Max softly shook his head and chuckled. 'I need some breakfast,' he said. 'Have you eaten?'

Kelly declined with a shake of her head. Breakfast? This was a showdown, didn't he realize?

Jez stepped forward eagerly – it felt like a long time since the cherry pie – but then stopped when he saw the look Kelly gave him.

Max walked into the house and they followed him. Kelly raised her eyebrows at Jez; he shrugged. She was starting to feel more apprehensive. She didn't like the idea of being contained in Max's house. What if he was dangerous?

In the kitchen Max opened his mammoth refrigerator and took out a jug of green sludge. He poured some into a glass. 'It's good for me,' he said, when he saw Jez's look of horror.

Kelly looked at her surroundings. Luxurious, masculine, lots of paperwork, just like Max's office but with more soft furnishings and twenty times as much space. The high walls at the back completely blocked out the view of the ocean.

'Sit down,' said Max. 'Both of you.' He pointed at the kitchen table. They sat down. Now what?

'Let me tell you what happened.'

33. Ruby Who? 2003

Ruby was miserable. Sometimes it seemed as if she had been miserable for all of her life. Or perhaps that was just being melodramatic, as she was often wont to be. She'd worked so hard over the years and for what? So that the new maître d' at Spago could question her credentials? She'd tried to book a table for lunch that day and he hadn't known who she was. What more proof did she need that her career was effectively over?

She paced the length of her bedroom, adjusting the drapes at the window to distract herself from her loneliness, and thinking that she might order some new ones, despite there being plenty of wear left in these. It wasn't as if she only changed things when they needed to be replaced. If that had been the case, then Ruby would still have her old browline and her original teeth.

The view of the Pacific Ocean from the pink beach house was the same as it had always been, but today it failed to inspire her. She preferred her home here to the one she'd had in Beverly Hills. She had offered that mansion to Octavia some years ago but Octavia had said she'd prefer Ruby to sell it and give her the money instead. Ruby ended up giving her half.

Welcome to the fabulous life of Ruby Valentine.

She picked up a script. Another lame Movie of the Week that she suspected Max had sent over just to keep her quiet. If she couldn't even be bothered to read it, what were the chances of her actually getting passionate about playing the part? When was the last time she had been passionate about anything?

She hadn't made a decent film since the Eighties. For two decades she had tried and failed to repeat her previous successes. Struggling to find parts had been bad in her thirties, worse in her forties, and now she had on her lap the first script that asked her to play a grand-mother.

Okay, so technically, no matter how infrequently she saw her children's children, she *was* a grandmother, but still, it was mortifying. She thought back to her carefree London days, painting the town red with Ella, poor, sweet Ella who had died a few years ago. Ruby never had the chance to tell her she was sorry. Ella was once her only friend. Now she had no one. Tears of self-pity threatened her expertly applied eyeliner. She needed to shift this grey mood otherwise she would drink the day down to the dregs.

A little buzz of excitement cut through her gloom. There was something she could do that always thrilled her. Something non-alcoholic that never failed to lift her spirits and give her a warm glow. Whenever she was feel-ing desolate she turned back to herself for comfort. Because if you can't rely on yourself, on number one, then it might as well be over.

Decided, she walked through to the guest bedroom with a spring in her step. Stashed behind a wall of false leather book jackets was her private video collection. There was a single copy of every film she had ever made.

There was a selection of family archives taken when the children were little and life was fun, transferred from super-eight film to videotape. There was some of the finest pornography, imported of course. There were also two deeply buried tapes of Ruby with Dante, intimate gifts she found the strength to watch on special occasions. But Ruby pushed them all aside; they would do nothing for her today.

She selected the tape she wanted and returned to her bedroom. This tape had been a birthday present from Max Parker for her fiftieth. Ruby had tried to hide her excitement when they first watched it together. But Max knew her too well, that was why he had known that this would be the perfect gift for Ruby Valentine. This was her favourite kind of porn.

Soon the drapes were drawn, the candles were lit and a bottle of champagne fizzed in the ice bucket. The bedroom was set for a seduction. Ruby let her hair fall to her shoulders and faced the mirror, letting her robe fall to the floor.

What she saw did not disappoint her, nor did it fill her with joy. For a woman of her age she knew that she looked incredible, but she was old. Ruby had fought valiantly against the signs of the times but nature's armoury was too robust. She'd had some surgery of course, mostly minor stuff, but it was only barely holding back the tide. She lifted her chin and watched her neck inevitably crêpe. The plastic surgeon who invented an effective procedure for a woman's neck would be a billionaire. The neck and the hands always give it away.

She lifted each plump breast in turn, mourning the loss of their original perfection. Her hair hung limp and lifeless across her shoulders, thin without its usual artificial assistance. A millimetre of grey roots, no more than a few days' worth, depressed her. But in the muted candlelight, without her contact lenses, it was possible to imagine she was a gorgeous young girl once more.

She pulled her robe back around her body and blew herself a kiss. She turned slowly in front of the mirror and then pushed the videotape into the machine.

The black screen slowly faded up to a face of such physical perfection it looked as if it had been crafted by artists. In a way it had. Her teeth were straight, her hair chopped and dyed, her eyebrows thinned and arched. The result was luminous. Of course, that was when Ruby had youth on her side. That was when she was the girl in the red bikini. The tape in the machine whirred like a lullaby.

The camera roamed luxuriously over her elegant cheekbones, her pale almond eyes emphasized with black kohl and fake eyelashes. A perfect bow mouth completed the face she knew so well. The face that had been her fortune. Strong artificial light washed out any imperfections, her skin looked as smooth as an eggshell. The dodgy soundtrack to *Viva Romance* had sensitively been replaced with a favourite Rachmaninov symphony. The broad vowels of her accent as a girl were still an embarrassment, buried within a couple of years by dedicated attention to the way she spoke.

Ruby gasped as if a lover had touched her when the scene changed to show her locked in a deep embrace with Earl . . . ? She couldn't remember his surname; her co-star on *Disturbance* had slipped into obscurity but she was still here, surviving. That film would always mean the most to her. It was the film that had bound her to Dante for ever.

Of all the many gifts Ruby had received in her life this tape of clips was her favourite. No jewel had the brilliance to compare to a journey through her life. No fur could keep her as warm as these happy memories. This was pure, unparalleled pleasure.

Her favourite section was coming up. With a self-indulgent tear in her eye she watched her twenty-something self glide up to the podium at the Dorothy Chandler Pavilion to take her first Academy Award for Best Actress. The camera cut to show Dante in the audience looking proud and head-over-heels in love. She hit the pause button.

Dante Valentine. What would her life have been like if they'd never met? She only ever wanted to be a star to make him happy. She only ever wanted to make him happy so that he would stay. So that she might continue to feel like a goddess in his bed. So much time had passed since his death that he had become almost mythical – a gifted director, victim of Hollywood excess, cut down in his prime. There had been too much written about his bad habits, the drugs and the women, but Ruby remembered the truth. She had loved him because he was the only man who lit the torch inside her, a torch which had died when he did. Call it chemistry, call it desire, call it masochism. He could inspire her.

Ruby poured herself a glass of chilled champagne and

walked over to the marble mantelpiece where Oscar stood with his twin. The golden figurine still gleamed with the same brilliance. Taking it with her free hand, she went back to the bed and watched the rest of the tape with the Oscar cradled close to her chest. All her greatest screen moments captured in one unique tape. Another Academy Award, the famous love scene from *Fell in Love with a Boy*, the best of the rest that she'd done. She adored herself.

By the time the clips ended Ruby was rapturous, drunk on her success rather than the champagne. Her robe fell open and the cool metal of the Academy Award was shocking against her hot, bare skin. Her nerve endings awoke and connected with the emotional intensity of her thoughts. Idly she rubbed the statuette across her nipples, watching them harden in response.

This award was absolute proof. Once, she had been the greatest of them all. She had been everybody's darling. She had been remarkable.

She felt the smooth shape of it, caressing the clean golden lines, and pushed it further down her body, quivering with anticipation. The Oscar was cold and thick between her legs and she rubbed herself slowly and deliberately with it, knowing exactly where this was heading but not wanting to rush the ultimate ego stroke.

As she pushed and it entered her Ruby gave a scream of unadulterated pleasure. Oscar was the best lover she'd had in years.

34

Later that week Max drove over to the beach with a script called *Next of Kin*.

'It's a television series,' he said, and continued before Ruby could speak, 'No, wait, hear me out. It's a CMG package. We'll build the show around you.'

'TV, Max? I don't mind doing the Movie of the Week stuff, but a series? Isn't that just a sexy way of saying soap opera?'

'Look what President Bartlett did for Martin Sheen.'

'President who?'

'*The West Wing*?'

Ruby continued to look blank.

'Never mind,' said Max. 'Just believe me, Ruby, all the best writers are working on television these days. This show is funny, smart and relevant. It'll give you job security, isn't that what you've always wanted?'

He had her there. She was too old to be running around town chasing down the few good parts going. Giving corny interviews to magazines just to keep herself in the public eye. Being inordinately grateful that Sofia was making a name for herself in case it reminded a casting director of her grandmother.

'I'd cut you a killer deal,' said Max. 'Unbreakable commitment, awards kickers, profit share.'

'So you think I should do it?'

Max took his time before answering her. CMG had a lot riding on the success of the show. Ruby was still newsworthy, her involvement would guarantee interest. He knew that if he phrased it right Ruby would take the job. 'It's steady and local and you'll make a hell of a lot of money.'

Money was always the dealmaker with Ruby. Promise her a few fat zeros and she'd do anything. She had millions stashed away that she'd made over the years. Max knew because he'd put it there for her.

Next of Kin was a television show about a dysfunctional family. Ruby was being asked to play Camille, the matriarchal head of the Burden clan.

She looked over the scripts and they perked her interest. Camille Burden was a class A bitch but deceptively wise. Maybe Max had a point. But television? Wasn't that as good as saying that she'd never be brilliant again? That she was a TV star and no longer a movie name? The line between the two might be blurring considerably but everybody still knew deep down which side had the most integrity. Or did they? She knew this decision was important. She read the scripts again, properly this time, and they were discerning.

That night she imagined how it would be to go to work at the same place every day and see the same colleagues. Didn't people say that working on a regular television show was like one big happy family? She might make some friends. It would be hard work but she liked that. One final push before she slowed down for good. Life was too short to worry that there were photographers

433

waiting outside your house first thing in the morning or reporters going through your trash. Lately the idea of a Garbo-like retirement had started to appeal. Then it wouldn't matter whether she was TV or film or goddam Broadway because she'd be sipping Pina Coladas by the beach and counting her money.

'Okay,' she said to Max the following day. 'I'll do it.'

'Great,' he said. 'I'll set up a meeting with the director and the exec producer.'

'I beg your pardon?'

'A meeting.'

'An audition?'

'Come on, Ruby. Of course they're going to want to meet you.'

'You said this was an offer. I never knew I'd have to test. What? Is the guy going to put me on tape with some reader and judge my improv? No way.'

'It won't be like that,' said Max.

'Damn right. I'm not auditioning for a television show. I don't think I'm quite down on that level yet, do you?'

Max was infuriated. Ruby could be so inflexible. The older she got, the more she dug her heels in and complained. He worried that it was symptomatic of her empty life. It had been an age since he saw her with a man.

'It's not about being down on any level. This is television; it's different.'

'You don't have to tell me that.'

'Won't you just meet them? They're both huge fans,' he lied. 'They're thrilled about it.'

'Fine. Whatever. When?'

*

Ruby was on time for her mid-afternoon meeting with *Next of Kin* and she looked incredible. She'd spent all morning at the Mondrian Spa and skipped lunch to make an emergency appointment with her hairdresser. She wanted to look her best. She hugged an oversized Louis Vuitton shoulder bag close to her side.

There were two men waiting for her in a room that smelt stale like dust. Not the glittering luxury she had hoped for, the high-budget event drama that Max had promised *Next of Kin* would be. But the younger of the two men was cute and his eyes lit up when she walked into the room. The director, she guessed, they always knew talent when they saw it. The other man was clearly a production executive, dazzling teeth and rigid hair slapped on top of a face that was fighting too many years in the sun.

Maybe the austere setting boded well. She had met many people with the mistaken impression that all you needed to make it in Hollywood was a really good decorator.

'It's a pleasure to meet you,' said the director. 'Seriously.'

'Good to see you, Ruby,' said the other guy. His eyes met hers with a judgemental stare and then ran over her body.

'Gentlemen,' she said. She sat down in the lonely chair on her side of the desk. 'So this is an audition, correct?' Ruby aimed her question at the director.

'Sorry about that,' he said. 'But this is an ensemble show, we need to make sure that everyone fits.'

Ruby took a deep breath. She reached down beside

her into the Louis Vuitton bag and she pulled out an Oscar. She planted it firmly on the table between them with a resounding thud.

Then she reached down again, pulled out a second Oscar and slammed it down next to the other one.

She met their curious gaze defiantly. 'That's my audition, guys. Hope it fits. I'll be waiting for your call.'

Then she picked up her Academy Awards, put them back in her bag and swept out of the room.

Six hours later she was cast, subject to contract, and her attitude had paid off. She wanted to make it very clear from the beginning that Ruby Valentine was still a star.

35

As far as Ruby was concerned *Next of Kin* was a disaster.
It wasn't just the outrageous storylines and unfamiliar
faces; it was the miserable weeks on location without a
single decent scene. It was having constantly to work at
a blistering pace, with people who thought that taking
time meant wasting money, not that taking time meant
getting things right. The seven-month shoot was the
hardest work of her life.

She watched the debut at home on her own with a
stiff drink.

The following morning she had breakfast with Max to
look over the reviews. She threw aside the newspapers
in disgust: a dozen flattering write-ups and not one of
them highlighted Ruby's performance.

'It's an ensemble show,' Max explained.

They were breakfasting at the Four Seasons. Max had
been fully prepared to cancel if the reviews were
unflattering, or at the very least change the venue to
somewhere more low-key. He didn't need self-satisfied
commiserations from all the other executives on the
shady terrace if things were bad.

The reviews had been solid. Not raves, not slaughters,
just solid. Slightly cautious, waiting for the next episode,
Max understood that. The overnight figures were good

and that was the main thing. It was true that Ruby hadn't received much individual praise but on the whole things were looking very positive.

'You should be pleased,' said Max. 'Don't spoil your moment. Everyone knows you're the star. They're interested in the new faces, but nothing more than that.'

'You're saying they're not interested in me?' said Ruby. 'Do you think they've had enough of me?'

Max sighed. Sometimes Ruby could be so steeped in self-pity that she was painful to watch. He didn't know if he could face it today.

The sad fact was that Ruby had looked slightly out of place in last night's show. Her clothes were all wrong – structured suits and flashy jewellery that didn't fit with the slick, fluid style of *Next of Kin*. Slightly dated. He made a mental note to speak to wardrobe. The character of Camille was an integral part of the storylines for the next season; after that maybe they could see.

'Is there anything about?' said Ruby.

'How do you mean?'

'I have ten weeks off. What do you expect me to do?'

'I'm not sure,' he said, taking his time, brain racing. He hadn't come prepared for this. 'I'll have to think, there might be something shooting in Canada. I didn't know you'd want to work.'

'Why the hell not?' asked Ruby. She had no intention of working, but she wanted to see Max squirm. He was earning his money too easily on this one. He was chipping off his steady 20 per cent at the end of every episode, when he hadn't had to make a single phone call on her behalf since she'd signed her contract. He was set up for years now, 20 per cent for doing sweet FA. She was the one out there risking her credibility, rising at dawn to shoot a twenty-second scene devoid of a good line for Camille. She was backdrop, a straight man, not the star, and she didn't know if she could do it all over again next season, and the season after that. Ruby was used to being the centre of attention. She had seen the way Max smiled when he read the early edition of the *New York Times* review, full of praise for some other cast members, also clients of his. Sometimes he seemed to forget that his entire career had been built around hers.

Max was still racking his mental casting sheets for a part for Ruby. If she wanted to make money then he wasn't about to talk himself out of a percentage. Ruby was obviously going through a high-maintenance period.

'Let's have dinner next week,' said Ruby. 'Just the two of us. Like old times.'

'That would be wonderful,' said Max, knowing that he wasn't free. He'd call her later and suggest a lunch instead. Right now he had to get back to the office; he had been able to feel his cellphone vibrating throughout the meal.

Ruby made her way home slowly. She stopped off at Bulgari on Rodeo Drive and considered buying a pearl choker that could be worn with the higher-necked gowns that were in her future. People would still say she was beautiful but would always add, 'for her age'.

Next of Kin made her feel archaic. There was a whole generation of adult actors below her and they got all the best storylines. All Camille seemed to do was ruin their fun. *Matriarch*. Such a horrible word. She stood out like a grandmother at a frat party against the backdrop of a hip television show like this.

The episode directors were cutting edge, experienced but innovative, with one or two features under their belts and loads of ideas. They treated her differently, they treated her the same as everyone else and she didn't like it. But what choice did she have? The money was excellent and her kickers over the next few seasons would ensure her financial comfort. She had points in the show and if the show was a success Ruby Valentine would be extremely rich, no matter what happened to Camille Burden.

By the time the second season of *Next of Kin* started shooting the producers were convinced that Ruby was completely wrong for the show. They had gambled, it hadn't worked. She was a name, and a name always ensured that the first season ratings were high, but they were beyond that now and could do without her.

36

Once upon a time Ruby had been Max's favourite client. These days he had to steel himself whenever they met. *Next of Kin* had brought out the very worst in her and sometimes the truth was that he hated her.

He visited the set and knocked on the door of her state-of-the-art trailer. 'What?' yelled Ruby from inside.

'Hey, Ruby, it's Max. Can I come in?'

'Just a second.' It was several minutes before Ruby opened the door. The air inside the trailer was warm and the light was poor. The narrow bed down one side was covered in grey chenille and littered with script pages. The fresh flowers that Ruby insisted were delivered every day were stuffed into the wastepaper bin. Max spotted an empty glass in the sink with a telltale glint of amber and he caught a whiff of Southern Comfort on Ruby's mouth when she offered her cheek for him to kiss. She'd always hidden it so well before.

'I'm glad you stopped by,' she said. 'I thought you might have forgotten me. I want this writer fired.'

'Which one?'

'Whoever wrote the piece of crap we're shooting this week.'

'Ruby, it's a great script.'

'For who? Certainly not for me. Three scenes, Max, and they're all useless.'

'Three's better than nothing.'

'Are you mocking me?' Ruby folded her arms and looked Max in the eye. She was acting like a spoilt teenager. 'Tell them I won't shoot it.'

The air was thick with Gucci perfume. The scent was so overpowering it smelt cheap.

'I can't fire the writer, Ruby. He's under contract.'

'So am I. Last time I checked I had script approval.'

A year ago he'd put a three-year contract under her nose and she hadn't even read it. 'I'll see what I can do,' he said. 'Anything else?'

'Yes. I think it's about time Jack and Camille made up.'

'Their rivalry is the core of the show.'

'I know, but he's the most popular character after me, and if I'm not talking to him by carrying on this ridiculous feud, then I can't have any scenes with him, can I? Think about it, surely there's a demand for it. The two most popular characters have a tearful reunion.'

Ruby was seriously deluded if she thought she was the most popular character on the show; she didn't even make the top five. Sometimes Max regretted setting her up with such a rock-solid deal in the first place, but to be honest he'd never thought that the show would be quite as successful as it was. He'd thought *Next of Kin* was the best way to keep Ruby in work and out of trouble. All he could do now was continue to pick up his commission on her salary and various bonuses. The problem was that her dated approach to acting stood out in the fluid, action-driven storylines which were helping to make *Next of Kin* a modern-day television phenomenon.

'I'll speak to the team, see if they think it's a good

idea,' said Max, knowing they would never go with it. More scenes with Ruby, the last thing anyone wanted.

When the dreaded call finally came it was cruelly terse.

'We're not picking up Valentine's option for the next series. She's fired.'

'Thanks for letting me know,' said Max.

He wasn't sure if Ruby would ever work again. The kind of parts he could get her now, after this, were not the kind of parts she would want. She'd had a long career, but it was as good as over; being fired from a hit TV show was the sort of thing from which people did not recover.

Sheridan walked into the office. 'What's wrong?' she asked. It was so unlike Max to be sitting at his desk doing nothing.

'They fired Ruby,' he said. 'Do you want to tell her?' Sheridan's face paled to the colour of raw pastry. 'I'm kidding,' said Max. 'Get her on the phone for me.'

Sheridan raced off to do as he asked. That was the nice thing about Max. He was always pretty philosophical when faced with a crisis.

Ruby, on the other hand, was horror-stricken. 'I don't understand how this could have happened. Really, Max, I don't think you've handled this at all well. I'm appalled. Is it time for me to find alternative representation?'

Max almost lost his temper. They both knew Ruby would never find anyone to do as much for her as he did. For a second he was tempted to tell her to go ahead and find someone else willing to be agent, lawyer, publicist and priest for a lousy 20 per cent. But he knew that he couldn't.

Finally Ruby realized she was in serious trouble. She started to cry. 'Max,' she said, 'what will I do?'

Everything she had worked hard for in her life was about to be destroyed. Her reputation had been on a downslide for a year or so, even she was aware of that in the recesses of her mind, but now it was in tatters. *Next of Kin* had seemed like such a big opportunity to get back on track; now it felt like a curse. Fired from a successful television show. Canned. Nobody would ever give her a movie. Her brilliant life was collapsing around her. There was only one way out. Only one way her star would shine for ever.

37

Kelly wasn't convinced. Max wanted her to believe that her mother, who had known such unhappiness in her life, killed herself over a broken contract? For vanity? It just didn't fit.

Could it be that she didn't want to believe it? She'd come all the way out here to try to find some memories of her mother. Who could blame her for wanting those memories to be of a better person than Ruby actually was? Maybe it wasn't all lies. Maybe her mother had been a selfish, lonely old woman, a bad mother. Perhaps the reason there were so few tears shed by friends and family was because those people who knew her personally knew what she was really like. She wasn't any of the strong, beautiful characters she portrayed. She was an insecure lush whose greatest achievement was a ten-year marriage to a man who had broken her spirit. The only reason Kelly didn't want to hear the truth was because she couldn't handle it.

She wanted the storybook version, the long-lost mother whose only crime was constantly being misunderstood. But she wasn't going to get her happy ending, because there would never be that tearful reunion and she would have to carry with her for ever the certain knowledge that her mother died alone because nobody loved her any more.

Jez, meanwhile, felt as though he was on the set of a soap opera. This was all great stuff. He was very comfortable listening to Max. He'd tried some of the green health shake and it wasn't too bad – appearances could be deceptive.

'You really want to do this?' asked Max. 'Get the police involved? What if I told you Ruby wouldn't want you to? Kelly, I'm begging you. You've got no idea what you're getting into.' There was no mistaking the tone of his voice. Max Parker was afraid of what she would do next.

She stared at him, thinking of all the pieces of the jigsaw. The massive ratings boost Ruby's death had engineered for *Next of Kin,* the missing millions. Max had just admitted that by the end he hated her. Ruby had trusted him. She had trusted him with her life.

Kelly froze, the most obvious answer to all of this becoming fully plausible in her mind. She asked him outright before she had time to think of her own safety, 'Max, did you kill my mother?'

He shook his head over and over, his hands trembling. 'You don't understand,' he pleaded, and his eyes were those of a guilty man.

'You killed her,' said Kelly. She backed away from the table, scraping her chair loudly across the floor, eager to get distance between them, as if he might shoot her dead there and then for working it out. She had to get to the police, right now.

'Wait!' he said. 'I'm going to tell you something, okay? The truth.'

'What?'

'It's a secret.'

'I'm good with secrets, I used to be one.'

'She's still alive.'

'You what?' said Kelly.

'Ruby. She's still alive.'

38

The audacious plan was all Ruby's own idea. She was going to kill off Ruby Valentine. When she explained what she meant Max was amused, but never in his wildest dreams did he think it was a serious option.

'We have to think outside the box,' she said.

'We'd never get away with it. We can't.'

'Don't say can't,' said Ruby. 'We won't know unless we try. What's the worst that can happen?'

'Both of us get tried by a high court for fraud?'

'No such thing as bad publicity, isn't that what you once said to me?'

Immediately Max knew she was right. It would be great for ratings.

Ruby chose to die because she could see her fame fading and she couldn't face the consequences. This way she would be spared the indignity of an old age in the public eye. It would be the ultimate retreat. She would out-Garbo Greta Garbo. She would have the chance to relax and spend the money she had worked so hard for, rather than giving it away as a replacement for the affection she could not muster. She'd laboured for most of her life. She deserved it.

Octavia and Vincent would not miss her. She would leave them the beach house to fight over. She would miss them, but not enough to make her stay. They stopped loving her the day that Dante died.

'Hypothetically, how would we do this?' she said.

And slowly they worked out the details.

At first the idea of suicide didn't appeal. Ruby screwed up her nose. Too messy, too pitiful. Ruby was a survivor, she would never quit. Then Max had said, 'Marilyn,' and suddenly it all made sense. To leave now would mean real immortality, not a lifetime of cameras trying to capture her decline.

'Where will you hide?' said Max.

'I know a place.'

'Where?'

'I'm not going to tell you. If I'm really going to do this then it has to be all or nothing.'

'I'll miss you,' he said.

'How long?'

'Ruby, it's for ever, you understand that, right?'

'I mean, until you can liquidize all my assets?'

'Everything?'

'Everything except the jewels and the beach house. They're for the children.'

'Are you absolutely sure about this?'

'How long, Max? How long do I have to live?' She was immersed in the self-created drama. It was the most spectacular production she had ever been a part of. It was the perfect ending. It didn't occur to her that she would never be able to take the credit.

It was impossible to break the news to the cast of *Next of Kin* gently. When Max Parker found Ruby's body in

449

her trailer on the empty *Next of Kin* lot, most of the cast were in cars on the way to work. They arrived to find an ambulance in the pick-up point and a makeshift barrier preventing them from entering the set. Simon Bull and Natasha Aldred, two second-string characters, exchanged pleasantries in the canteen and tried to guess what might have happened when they saw a body bag wheeled by on a gurney. It was enough to put Natasha off her probiotic oat bran.

Max came into the room shortly afterwards. He knew he had to nail this performance. His hands shook as he tried to dial a number on his cellphone.

'Who died?' Natasha was brutally succinct.

'Ruby.'

'Fuck.' Simon shared Natasha's way with words. 'Max, what happened? Sit down.'

'I can't. I have to call Octavia. She should hear this from a friend.' His hands were shaking so much that he dropped the phone.

'Let me do it,' said Natasha. She had recovered her composure and was simultaneously wondering if Ruby's death would enhance her career and if her lack of tact with Max would harm it. She took the phone from his hand and tried to make amends.

'What happened?' asked Simon.

'She was just lying there. I thought she was asleep and then I smelt . . . do you think I could get a glass of water?'

Simon looked around for a production runner and was momentarily at a loss without one. Realizing it was up to him, he walked over to the water cooler. Max sipped from a paper cone and some of the colour began to return to his milky-white face. He looked twenty years older. They waited for him to finish his sentence. 'And then I smelt her vomit.'

Natasha winced at the thought of such an unglamorous death. 'Octavia's machine is on at home. I'm dialling the cell. Um, Octavia? Hi, I have Max Parker for you.'

'Octavia, sweetheart, it's Max. Where are you?' Max sank on to one of the hard wooden chairs and Simon and Natasha left the canteen to give him privacy.

'Wow, pretty heavy, huh?' said Simon. 'You got a smoke? Gave up last week. If ever there was an excuse to start.'

Natasha pulled out a pack of Marlboro Lights. 'Do you think we'll work today?'

'I doubt it.' Simon pulled heavily on the cigarette and appraised Natasha with a critical eye. 'Wanna hang out in my trailer until they call us?' Hell, yeah, there were worse ways to spend an unexpected day off than banging a blonde with a shit-hot rack.

Natasha looked him straight in the eye. She knew exactly what he was suggesting. What was it that people said about coming together in a crisis? 'Sure.'

Simon and Natasha were just like the rest of Hollywood. They were stunned, but only for a short while, because this was a town where anything can happen and it takes a lot more than a drug-fuelled suicide to stop the clocks.

Right up until she died Max was convinced that it would never work. He had underestimated the influence of money and power. Ruby always got what she wanted. In Hollywood it would seem that even your death could be given the green light if you had the finance.

All you needed was a decommissioned ambulance off e-bay and a coroner willing to accept an enormous bribe. The media did the rest.

By ten o'clock that morning everybody knew a garbled version of the facts. By six, Ruby's death was knocked off the top of the news by a sharp fall in the Dow Jones. By Saturday night it was history. Then a long-lost daughter emerged and kept the story running, a tribute was arranged to coincide with the start of the new series, and Ruby Valentine was hotter than she'd been for years.

39

Kelly couldn't believe it. No way.

All her acquired knowledge about Ruby seemed to rearrange itself in her head with dizzying speed, like a magician's shuffle. It was preposterous, it was impossible. Max had to be lying. But her instincts were screaming at her to trust them. And they were telling her that what Max was saying was true.

'Why should I believe you?' she said. 'Do you have any proof?'

'Of course not,' replied Max. 'We covered our tracks very carefully. That was the whole point. Nobody will find anything, no matter how deep they dig.'

Kelly looked across at Jez, who was agog, bug-eyed and transfixed, looking first at Kelly then at Max. This was better than any soap opera. He was thrilled to be a part of it. He was happy for Kelly. Her mum was alive, that was good, right?

'Let's say I believe this crazy story,' said Kelly, 'Why would you tell me? Isn't that a big risk? I could go running off to the newspapers right now.'

'And tell them what? You said yourself, it's crazy. Besides, I don't think you're like that.'

'Like what?'

'A sell-out. Sheridan told me how many offers you got to tell your story, but apart from that one profile with

Sofia – which I know she kind of forced you into doing – you've kept your mouth shut. That's classy.'

'But being famous meant so much to her.'

'Not really,' said Max. 'Only when she was right on top. Success is elusive that way. Once you've tasted it, everything else is failure.'

Kelly felt tears swim in her eyes. Her vision misted. Ruby was alive? What kind of person pulled that sort of trick on their friends and family? Put them through all that grief? Except, when Kelly really thought about it, perhaps Ruby had known that their grief would only be superficial. She had known that Octavia's true concern would be money, Vincent's his career, Sofia's her profile.

But what about me? She didn't know how I would feel.

Then again, maybe Ruby would have expected her to be indifferent, not to care about a mother she had never known. Except that she *had* cared. And she wanted Ruby to know that somebody did.

'You don't know where she is?'

Max shook his head. 'I'll never see her again.'

'She doesn't call you or anything?'

'No.'

It was selfish and bold. Two things that she knew Ruby to be.

Jez pulled his chair closer to hers. 'Are you okay, babe?'

His sincere concern triggered her restrained tears and they rolled down her face. She could hardly speak. 'I want to go home.'

'Okay,' he said. 'Come on. We'll pick up your stuff from Octavia's and go to my hotel.'

'No,' she said. 'I want to go home.'

'Just like that?'

'Just like that.'

Max stood up to say goodbye and passed her a box of Kleenex. She wiped her messy face, all snot and tears, not very LA, and tried to decide whether or not she liked him. She did. She couldn't help it.

'Thank you,' she said. Her breath was coming in ragged bursts, juddering painfully into her lungs, not enough to calm her. She looked down and folded the tissue in her hands in half and then in half again, and again, trying to soothe herself. A moment passed before she could form a sentence. And it was important.

'Max, if she ever contacts you, will you tell her something from me?'

'Of course,' he said.

'Tell her . . . tell her that I miss her. I miss her all the time. I missed her before I knew who she was, before she died. But I think I understand why she left me. Tell her I'm happy.'

Max shook her hand formally. 'You're the best of her,' he said. 'She'd be so proud of you.'

Jez took Kelly's arm and led her outside. She could hardly see through her tears. Back on the beach, out of sight, she broke down and sobbed.

40

When their aeroplane burst through the thin layer of cloud and she first saw the lush green valleys of home Kelly felt a sense of peace wash over her. It didn't matter who her mother was. This was where she belonged. The journey to reach that conclusion had been an adventure, but it wasn't real.

Her dad picked them up from the airport. 'Are you going to tell him?' said Jez.

She shook her head. Ruby was dead. That's what she wanted everyone to believe and so Kelly would uphold her wishes. It was a mother/daughter confidence, the first secret they had ever shared. She intended to keep it. She made Jez promise never to break that trust. She made him swear on his collection of vintage movie posters, the thing dearest to his heart. Except perhaps for her. Why had she never before appreciated how good he was in a crisis? His laidback attitude was perfect for organizing a quick getaway. No fuss, no bother, just two tickets on the first plane home.

It had been easy to pack up and leave town, proof that her alter ego – Kelly Valentine, daughter to the stars – was flimsy and ephemeral. Sofia made her promise to keep in touch. 'Come out to Nikki Beach at Christmas,' she'd said. 'It's so, like, fabulous. It'd be good for your image.'

And maybe she would. Or maybe she'd sit and get pissed with her dad just as she had done every year since she was sixteen, mock the Queen, wear paper hats and play cards for big money. She could invite Jez. That would be, like, fabulous too. Your image didn't change who you were inside. Ruby Valentine had spent her whole life figuring that out.

Kelly ran into Sean's arms when she saw him at Arrivals, and he twirled her round as if she was a little girl again. 'How was it?' he said.

'Interesting.'

'Hiya, Jez. You found each other then?'

'We did,' said Jez. 'It wasn't too hard.'

'You staying at ours?'

Jez looked at Kelly and she nodded enthusiastically. 'Sure,' he said.

Kelly could hardly sleep that night. Jez had no such problem, snoring beside her, taking up too much of her narrow bed. She was looking forward to waking up to him, to getting closer to him, to letting him get close to her and no longer worrying that falling in love with him would be dangerous. If they made it in the long term, then it might be wonderful, and if they didn't, then it was better to try wholeheartedly and fail than never to try at all. She would just have to trust him. It would be the first time she had trusted anyone but her father. The truth was that she could let herself be loved by him, just like that. And she could love him back.

Kelly watched Jez sleeping until it started to get light and then she crept silently out of the bedroom and went downstairs. The kitchen was gloomy and every movement she made seemed to echo in the emptiness of this early hour. She fixed a mug of tea and stuffed her feet into a pair of Wellington boots stacked up by the back door. She grabbed her bag and walked out into the morning. There was the faintest suggestion of frost crunching beneath her feet but already the hills smelt fertile and alive, as if spring was on its way.

She climbed up to the wooden bench overlooking the valley and she drank down the air like a drug. No pollution, no air-con, just honest fresh air. She could practically feel the bloom of health rising to her cheeks.

She sat down and pulled two items from her bag. The ruby necklace she would never sell. The jewel glistened in her hand with an internal fire. Enduring, like its owner. She'd told Octavia she had reconsidered her offer to help pay for an investigation. After that Octavia couldn't get her out of the house fast enough.

Kelly looked next at the small photograph of a mother and her child. Taken not far from here, but a million miles away. Another lifetime. Ruby looked so happy.

Kelly looked up and saw the same view in the distance: the rolling hills, the isolated pond and the speck of white that was the remote old cottage. Some things had changed. The trees were a little taller, and so was the girl in the picture, but the landscape was as constant as the sky above her. Who could fail to find peace in a place like this?

The idea did not come to Kelly all of a sudden. She was on her feet and walking out into the fields before she understood where she was going. She was half-way there before she realized that the missing piece of the puzzle had just dropped into place. The cottage had been deserted for years. Sean had once tried to find out who owned it and reached a dead end, cordoned off with the red tape of bureaucracy. All the land between here and that cottage was privately owned. They never discovered who by. It was cold, she hadn't worn her coat, but she kept walking all the same. One foot in front of the other, searching for the truth, which she suspected could be happily exiled in her very own backyard.

The door of the cottage was unlocked. Kelly knocked and waited but there was no reply. Tentatively she pushed it open and walked inside.

She looked around. It was clearly no longer deserted. There were a few books on a big wooden table at the window, a computer and a phone that was unplugged at the wall. The kitchen smelt faintly of coffee and somebody had left a half-eaten apple on the side of the sink. Was she being unbelievably foolish? Was she walking around a stranger's humble home looking for a dead woman who was probably somewhere far more exotic? Perhaps she just wanted to believe that she'd come back. She climbed the stairs, expecting to be interrupted by a disgruntled neighbour at any moment. A big Hollywood star couldn't disappear in a small town like this.

In the bathroom, an Oscar was being used as a makeshift doorstop.

And Kelly heard the front door close.

*

She watched Ruby Valentine from the top of the stairs. Her hair was very short and almost entirely grey, and she had a pair of spectacles perched on her nose. Her arms were full of heather which she set down on the wooden table and started to arrange in an old instant coffee jar. She tinkered with the radio and found some classical music which soon gave way to a news report. She returned it immediately.

Kelly was gripped by every gesture. She could see the family resemblance more clearly than ever. Perhaps because without the makeup and styling Ruby looked as if she could be somebody's mother. Her mother.

So everything Max had said was true. She had thought about this so many times, coming face to face with the woman who gave birth to her, that she should have felt a little more prepared; instead she felt a sickening sense of curiosity tinged with absolute terror. Her stomach flipped and she thought she might throw up. What scared her most was the possibility of rejection. She wasn't sure that she could take it if Ruby turned her away and then disappeared again. Perhaps she really didn't want to be found. But, Kelly figured, if that were true then perhaps she shouldn't have set up camp so close to home.

It was as if she was desperate to be exposed.

When Ruby had finished with the flowers she picked up the jar and cast her eye around the room, looking for somewhere to put it. Kelly ducked into the shadows. She didn't know what to do next. A huge part of her wanted to escape without confronting Ruby, and never let anyone know what she had discovered. She could watch from a distance and enjoy the secret knowledge that she was close. She didn't have to do anything. She could just run. But for once in her life she didn't, she stayed where she was.

Ruby started to climb the stairs. Kelly instinctively looked for somewhere to hide but it was too late. She was standing in the middle of the bedroom when Ruby walked in.

Ruby saw a stranger in her house and let out a blood-curdling scream. She dropped the jar of heather and the glass shattered, skittering across the hard floor like crushed ice.

Kelly was startled and anxiously tried to fix this moment in time so that she would always remember it. 'Hello, Ruby,' she said. 'It's me. It's Kelly.'

Ruby stared. 'I saw your picture,' she said. 'At my funeral.' Her hands went to her cropped hair, as if she was embarrassed.

'Does Sean know you're here?' said Kelly. If he had known all along and kept this from her she would be devastated.

'No,' said Ruby. 'No one was supposed to know. Did Max tell you?'

'Sort of.'

They circled each other with interest, like toddlers in a playground, each thinking how they looked different yet the same. Kelly reached out to touch her mother. She needed assurance that this wasn't a dream, that she wasn't still in bed, wrapped up safe and warm with Jez.

Kelly recognized the smile that came over Ruby's

face. It was her Hollywood smile, the one she always wore in photographs. It didn't quite reach her eyes, but it showed off her jawline in its most flattering heart shape. She threw open her arms and Kelly realized that she was supposed to step into them and accept an embrace. She did, and it was stiff and unyielding, the lower half of their bodies not touching at all. A Hollywood hug to go with the smile. 'At last,' said Ruby. 'At last I get to meet you.'

'I've never been hard to find,' said Kelly. She folded her arms across her chest. This didn't feel right. The smile and the hug were the classic happy ending, the perfect fantasy of how this reunion should go, roll credits. But it couldn't be as easy as that. Ruby was acting strangely. She was looking directly into her eyes but not making eye contact, smiling but not looking happy, saying words but not really saying anything at all. Kelly felt defensive and confused. She didn't think Ruby was on drugs, she sensed that the glitter in her eyes was probably anxiety, but she had absolutely no connection with her whatsoever. The disappointment was crushing.

Ruby bent down and started to fuss with the heather and broken glass on the floor. Kelly crouched to help her. 'Watch your fingers,' said Ruby almost gaily.

'Is that it?' said Kelly. 'Is that all you have to say to me? "Watch your fingers"?'

Ruby looked up from the floor in surprise. For a split second the smile dropped from her face and Kelly could clearly see the panic in her eyes.

'What about "Let me explain" or "Please forgive me"?' said Kelly.

'For what?'

'For walking out.'

'It's complicated,' said Ruby. 'My contract for *Next of Kin* wasn't renewed, the press had turned on me, it would only have got worse. My situation became untenable.'

Kelly tried not to let the dismay show on her face. If Ruby could play it cool then so could she. She was determined not to let her see how much this coldness was clawing at her insides. She had thought about discovering her mother countless times since she was a little girl. Then spent weeks in Los Angeles trying to make sense of who she was. Now she had finally found her after all these years.

And the truth was that Kelly didn't like her.

'I didn't mean the faking-your-own-death spectacular,' she said grimly. 'I meant the first time. The time when you walked out on me and my dad.'

'Oh.' Ruby concentrated on separating stems of heather from the shards of broken glass. 'Sweetheart,' she said, 'that was years ago. Who can remember?'

It was as if Kelly had asked her who was playing at the UFO that night in the Sixties, or what song she'd danced to on the night of her wedding to Andrew Steele in Mexico, or the name of the director who'd slept with a model on her living-room floor at the beach. It was as if she'd asked nothing of consequence, just another footnote in Ruby's biography, details unknown.

This total lack of remorse was a brutal kind of rejection and it made angry tears rise in Kelly's eyes, threatening to spill out all over the floor amid the splinters of glass and the small purple flowers. 'I'm sorry I found

463

you,' she said, painfully squeezing out the words past the lump in her throat. She held up her head and walked down towards the front door, determined to walk out of Ruby's life and never look back.

'Wait,' said Ruby. 'Please.'

'Why should I?' said Kelly. 'I cried over you. When I was a little girl I sat in my bedroom and cried because my mother never loved me.'

'I'm sorry.'

'No,' said Kelly. 'I don't think you are.'

'What do you want from me?'

'Nothing,' said Kelly. 'Nothing at all.' She took the ruby necklace from her pocket and held it out. 'I think this belongs to you.' It was the perfect way to say good-bye.

'I wanted you to have it, to have all of my jewels. I wanted to remember you.'

'I know,' said Kelly. 'We got the suicide note, thanks. Do you have any idea how awful that was for my dad?'

She placed the necklace in Ruby's hand. 'Take it,' she said. 'I don't want it.' She turned her back and walked away.

Ruby looked down at the priceless rock and drew in a deep breath. She sank to the floor and began to wail.

Kelly paused on her way to the door. She stayed frozen for a few seconds, battling with her ego. Ruby's histrionics were completely stealing the thunder of her dramatic exit. She wanted to keep walking and take the high road but she couldn't leave someone crying like that. Not even Ruby.

'What is it?' she said. 'What's wrong?'

'I made the worst mistake of my life.'

For a fleeting moment Kelly honestly expected the apology she thought she deserved, but then she realized Ruby wasn't talking about that. She was talking about herself. And Kelly was supposed to listen.

Ruby had made a mistake. For the first few days exile had been blissful. She loved the silence most of all. No telephones ringing, no traffic, no demands on her time. As long as she continued to live in the moment she was fine. She felt gloriously, romantically free. It was when she started thinking about the future, of endless days like these until she died, and remembered that this was not a holiday, this was for ever, that she started to get scared.

Without anyone to tell her what to do she was lost. Without anyone to tell her she was fabulous she was miserable.

Within a week she was online finding out what the world thought about her suicide. She couldn't help seeking approval, even in death. There aren't many people who get to read their own obituaries from the comfort of an old armchair with a measure of single malt whisky warming them through. But it wasn't as funny as she thought it would be. She was unsettled by the people who were speaking out in remembrance of her. The very first seeds of doubt were planted. Look how many people had loved her all along. Not her family – their quotes were empty. Her true friends were few. But the fans, the contemporaries, the landscape of cinema: to them she was precious.

'The thing is, you want people to like you so badly,' said Ruby. 'You don't want people to write nasty things about you. Anybody who puts themselves out there basically wants to be adored. They might say they don't care what the public think but secretly they care beyond sense. And when you die, everything changes. You're a legend.'

'You always were,' said Kelly. She was frustrated. The mother/daughter roles were all mixed up. Wasn't Kelly entitled to some comfort? On top of that, this woman might be her mother but she was still a famous movie star, and right now she was messily spilling her heart all over the place. Like a car-crash talk-show spot when the subject is obviously unhinged. There was something gruesomely fascinating about it. Like road-kill.

'But I didn't *know* that I was,' said Ruby. 'You don't understand. I've lost everything. And the worst thing is that I didn't even know what I had.'

She started crying again. Weak little sobs that reminded Kelly of a puppy dog whining.

'Stop it,' said Kelly. She'd heard enough. 'Stop feeling sorry for yourself. So you made a mistake, so what? Everybody does.'

'Some mistakes are too awful to be forgiven.' Ruby looked up with sorrowful doe eyes which must have elicited a thousand pardons over her lifetime. 'Some people are too awful to forgive.' She had switched subjects and now it was obvious that Ruby was begging for Kelly's forgiveness.

Kelly bit her lip and mentally waved goodbye to the lonely moral high ground. To walk out on her mother now would be such a waste. She knew it was going to be almost impossible to forge a solid relationship with a woman like Ruby. But that didn't mean she couldn't try. 'That's not true,' she said.

Ruby smiled eagerly. 'I really am sorry,' she said. 'I could tell you that not a day went by when I didn't remember you and love you, but I don't think you'd believe me.'

She'd be right, Kelly didn't believe her, but at least she was trying. Slowly Ruby was starting to become more substantial, as if layers of gas were floating away from her concealed self. When Kelly looked in her eyes now there was something there, something authentic. She wasn't the nurturing storybook mother of her dreams, but seriously, what were the chances that those dreams would ever have come true? Some people might dream that their parents are really glamorous movie stars, but all Kelly had ever wanted was somebody who loved her, someone to fill the gaps.

'I was scared back then,' said Ruby. 'My life was so small that I thought I might disappear into nothing.'

'And now?'

'And now I have. I'm nothing. I have a fake passport and a couple of Oscars, that's it. I don't exist.'

'Why here?' said Kelly. 'Why so close to my dad and me? It's as if you wanted us to find you.'

'I bought the land with the house all those years ago. I kept the deeds separate. Maybe I knew that one day I'd need sanctuary again. This is the only place where I've ever had time to myself. Maybe it's the only place where

I've ever *been* myself. I was happy here, I think.'

'Are you happy now?'

Ruby pulled in a seriously deep breath and wailed anew, '*No-oo-oo!*' She shook her head from side to side to make it very clear how she felt about that point. 'What difference does it make? I can never go back.'

'But you can,' said Kelly. 'Of course you can.'

'I'm so ashamed. I deceived everyone,' said Ruby. 'It's all over.'

'It doesn't have to be.' Kelly was growing impatient. Ruby's problems, if you could call them that, were entirely of her own creation.

'People will think I'm crazy. They'll laugh at me. And I'll never work again. I look hideous,' said Ruby. 'The press will rip me apart.'

'Are you kidding? You're going to be the most famous woman on the planet. It's a second chance. Take it. Show up on Sunset Boulevard and what are they going to do? Tell you to go back to the grave?'

Ruby saw the light. It could be the ultimate comeback. This didn't have to be the end.

'Talk to Max,' said Kelly. He was paid to advise her. 'There must be something you can do.'

Max put down the telephone and contemplated the end of his illustrious career. If Ruby was determined to come back from the dead then there was only one way that her fans would ever forgive her. Her credibility depended on coming back against the odds. Somebody would have to take the fall.

Max would cast himself as the villain in this remarkable story – a ratings-hungry Machiavellian wrongdoer. Ruby would be the manipulated heroine – a tragic, broken figure. An angel (he liked that reference). A resurrection. He knew that this could mean the end for him. Actors didn't want agents who were ruthless schemers, chasing down the dollar no matter what. Or rather, they did, but only when it was on their behalf. What the hell, he couldn't go on for ever. He would walk away. He'd be able to spend more time at his villa in Boca Raton and chip away at his golf handicap. He had more money than he could ever spend and he might never have made it without her.

Ruby put down the phone and started thinking about the best way to return to the spotlight. Ideally she could wait for the perfect film, walk straight into a leading role in a massive movie and cap off this most sensational of comebacks with another Oscar. She could go on Oprah and tearfully admit to having had a nervous breakdown, play the sympathy card as if it was the last one in her hand, make America fall in love with her all over again.

Kelly saw renewed life dancing in Ruby's eyes and realized the sad reality of having Ruby Valentine for a mother. Finding her was bittersweet. Kelly would like to get to know her but she could tell that she would never be the most important person in Ruby's life. There simply wasn't room in the midst of the total self-obsession for anyone else to stand a chance. And maybe that was just the way it was meant to be. She was glad to have found her, glad to get some answers at last, but it wasn't up to Ruby to provide her happy ending. Kelly had to write it for herself. Her destiny was entirely in her own hands.

Anonova.com 14.32pm –
 REBORN! Full AMAZING story of Ruby's return . . .
 (click here for more details . . .)

ALISON BOND

HOW TO BE FAMOUS

Stars, secrets and celebrity obsession

Your invitation to the most glittering premiere of the year introducing ...

Lynsey Dixon
An employee at a top London talent agency that specializes in looking after neurotic actresses, like Melanie Chaplin. After keeping her cool in a crisis, Lynsey is offered a transfer to LA to help Melanie make the most of her big break in a new TV show. And Lynsey knows an opportunity for sunny days and serious star-spotting when she sees one ...

Melanie Chaplin
Star of a new hit TV series and the object of desire for LA's hottest players. She has everything – except Davy Black: the gorgeous director who is married in real life, but not in Melanie's dreams. And celebrity has a dangerous habit of occasionally making you forget which is which ...

Serena Simon
Serena didn't exactly choose Hollywood; when you're as beautiful as she is, it's the only place to go. Serena has a plan – and it's working; stardom is just a photoshoot away. But she also has a little secret. And in LA, secrets rarely stay that way for long ...

Three very different girls whose dreams all depend on one another – and who are all about to realize the true price of fame ...

'How dare Alison Bond write a debut novel this good? We defy you not to be glued to its pages from beginning to end' *Heat*